Release Me

A novel by Tim DeMarco

For information contact:
Unsolicited Press
Portland, Oregon
www.unsolicitedpress.com
orders@unsolicitedpress.com
619-354-8005

Editor: S.R. Stewart
Cover Design: Robert Scott Marshbank, Jr.

ISBN: 978-1-956692-69-3

Release Me

Book 1

Fall Back

"Wer stehen bleibt kann rosten
Und wer rennt kann sich verlaufen"
—muff potter

Chapter 1

My father's self-confident eyes judged me from above, his features exaggerated on the enormous billboard—the egotistic smirk, the dark eyes tinged with condescendence, the receding hairline that exuded experience and importance, the close-cropped beard outlining his strong jawline. "Peter Constantine Realtors—Helping You Cast Your Anchor Since 1979."

I squinted up through the brutal second summer sun and tried to figure out which was more oppressive—the heat or my father's ostentatious expression. Both were overwhelming, and I smirked at the acknowledgment that it was a particularly offensive "father-sun" combo.

From the driver's seat, I could feel my father's eyes burning through me like a magnifying glass in the sun. He must have noticed my smirk and mistaken it for pride or excitement. "Yep," he sighed contentedly, "soon I'll have to have them take that one down and replace it with a new one." He paused for dramatics. "'Peter Constantine *and Son* Realtors.' It's got a nice ring to it."

I glanced over to see him smiling. *And Son.* If my name was going to be spared on the billboard, would my face also be so lucky?

Despite the air conditioning pumping full force into my face, I was sweating. The exhaust from the gridlock on I-95 did not make matters much better. It was Thursday afternoon, the last day of September. Why was there so much traffic? Were all these people also headed to the airport?

"You hungry?"

I wasn't.

"Think of something you're not gonna be able to eat for the next year. What don't they have over there in Germany?"

I had to think. I hadn't really spent much time in Germany, besides one of those short, organized trips after sophomore year in high school, where your meals are taken care of and adjusted to meet US high schoolers' tastes—usually chicken fingers, or, if you're lucky and the tour company really wants to show you "authentic German culture," schnitzel, which is, after all, just a glorified chicken finger.

"I don't know. Maybe sush—"

"How 'bout a cheesesteak?" his voice barreled over mine. "They don't have them over there, I'm sure of it. Hell, you can't even find a good cheesesteak in *this* country anywheres outside of Philly." It was unclear whether he didn't hear me, or if he heard me and chose to ignore my suggestion.

In any case, I wasn't doing any better, actively ignoring my father's incessant ramblings about real estate, the "goddamn traffic," the unbearable weather, and my future.

Our future.

My focus was on the present. As the car slowly inched south, toward the airport, toward the plane that would take me away for the next nine months, my thoughts were anywhere but the future. Or the past, which had recently presented itself again…

I was on my way to a small town in southern Germany to work at a university's American Studies department. I had no real expectations or excitement regarding the job. I was just happy to have found something upon graduating. Something that wasn't working for my father. That would come.

I figured if my whole future was already sorted out for me, I might as well do something selfish and irrational. My own personal Grand Tour of sorts. A quick venture into independence, European-style. But instead of rubbing elbows with aristocrats and admiring fine art, I was on the search for something else. What exactly, I didn't know. Live in the present, I guess. Try new things. Remove the word "no" from my vocabulary.

The car had reached a walking pace by this point, the city slowly rising in the distance like a morning sun. The highway was shimmering with heat as if the asphalt were exhaling lethal vapors from a hidden subterranean realm. Sad, half-vacant strip malls lined the roadway, weeds overtaking the cracked parking lots. The only signs of life were the poor bastards sitting on tipped over shopping carts, waiting for the bus with t-shirts draped over their heads to protect them from the sun's merciless rays.

Above the landmark of despair we were inching by—a stretch of shops consisting of a dilapidated dollar store, a liquor store advertising checks cashed, and four empty storefronts—loomed a billboard, baby blue with neon pink cursive and sparkling silvery hearts. Through a cloud of blue diesel exhaust belched from the back end of a Greyhound bus I could make out the words: "Valentine's—Philadelphia's Newest Gentlemen's Club and More..." Beneath a nude woman, candy-apple-red-lacquered fingernails conveniently covering her nipples, was another suggestive slogan: "An erotic eXXXperience." I turned away as soon as I saw it, trying not to think about Deirdre.

The past.

The present.

The future?

My father must've caught my glance, but evidently could not read the look on my face suggesting the last thing that I wanted was to talk about that place.

"That place…" he said, reaching out his right hand to point at the building, ringed fingers inches from my face. "You know I sold that place? It used to be some huge garage. I got them one hell of a deal." He whistled between his teeth, a sound usually reserved for when the opposing team belted a home run off a Phillies reliever or when he read about a major tragedy in a country whose name he couldn't pronounce. "Man, the things they offered me when we closed the deal. Lifelong free admission. VIP-status. Private rooms. And stuff that would make a Vegas vice detective blush." He let out another raspy whistle, this time more air than melody, slowly shaking his head.

"Hm," I said, staring straight ahead, willing the traffic to clear up. Searching for a distraction, I reached over and—in a bold move in my father's car—flicked on the radio, quickly scanning past sports talk programs and HVAC commercials to the local college station. Debbie Harry was singing about a job in a garage, and I hurriedly clicked it off. I was not in the mood for Blondie or my father's snide comments about my taste in music.

My father looked at me, puzzled. "Anyway, alls I can say is there's a lot more than just dancing going on at that place…"

"I'm really looking forward to that cheesesteak right now," I said, hoping to change the subject.

***

Reading Terminal was equally crowded as I-95, but we were able to find a small plastic table. The market pulsed and throbbed, the crowd squirming and writhing like amoebas in a petri dish or some infectious disease at the end of a microscope. My father rambled on the whole time, mouth full of cheesesteak, fried onions dropping onto the paper plate beneath him like greasy worms slipping from a bird's beak. About real estate, about the million-dollar home he had just sold, about how as soon as I got back from "gallivanting" around Germany he'd set me up and have me poised to be making the same kind of sales as he was now. "You see," he said, wiping Cheez Whiz from his mustache, "the hardest part for me was getting myself established. You know how many people I had to schmooze just to make my first BIG sale? I mean, I've been selling since day one, don't get me wrong. I know what I'm doing. But to make those big sales? I needed to SCHMOOZE!" He finished his last bite and leaned back, the plastic chair creaking precariously beneath his weight. His eyes wandered contemplatively. I enjoyed the rare moment of silence and took another bite of my cheesesteak, wishing instead it were sushi.

Snapping out of his trance, my father leaned toward me, sliding his plate to the side for someone else to come pick up, his arms crossed and elbows resting on the table. "You see, I've got you covered. I've got you connected. And with your Ivy League smarts, you'll be making sales in no time. You'll practically start out on the top! Soon enough, *you'll* be the one buying a million-dollar house." He relaxed back into his seat, arms folded behind his head, a content smile spread across his face. "You'll be the first person ever to make money after graduating college with a philosophy degree!" he laughed.

I forced a quick obligatory laugh. I mean, he was setting me up for success, so I should be grateful. But quite frankly, my mind was elsewhere. I was about to get on a plane and cross the Atlantic for the first time in six years, to work in a country where I had barely spent any time. Though I was a little nervous, the excitement of being abroad, the time away, the freedom to come and go as I please, the space between me and everything that was to come, these feelings trumped the apprehension of the new job in the new country. That was all I had on my mind.

That and Deirdre.

***

We had met in high school through a mutual friend—who may or may not have been somehow related to her—and started dating as soon as I returned from my school trip to Europe. We remained a couple until the day I moved away to college, when Deirdre dumped me in the doorway to my dorm room.

Over the course of four years of college I stumbled through the stages of grief more than once. Many times I'd stop reading, holed up in the library or lying on my wafer-thin twin mattress, nose buried in Kierkegaard or Kant or Hobbes, and wonder what Deirdre was doing at that exact moment. Wonder where she was. It'd usually only take thirty seconds or so before I'd wind up in an uncomfortable scenario, shake my head, pick up my book, and get back to dissecting Existentialism or the Categorical Imperative.

I had ended up on the final stage of grief again, my hope redirected toward the future—whether it was the upcoming job in Germany or my career, which had already been established before I had fully entered puberty—when Deirdre had contacted me not much more than a week before my scheduled departure and invited me to come visit. She wasn't attending college but had moved onto campus with a friend who was studying in Philadelphia. I had begun sneaking over almost every night, borrowing my mother's Toyota—my mother never drove anymore, and I would never dare take my father's Mercedes—and returning in the wee hours of the morning, leaving myself enough time to shower and relax for an hour before heading off to my summer landscaping job with my friend Eric. Luckily, my late-night rendezvous had gone unnoticed to my father, especially considering his firm disapproval of Deirdre.

"You know you got a ticket from LaSalle last night," his comment dragged me out of my dreams. "Parking ticket. 2:16 AM. I found it on the windshield this morning when I went out to fill up the tank."

I looked away. Reading Terminal was still bustling, full of hungry city workers, school children on class trips, wayward tourists haphazardly wandering the stalls, being greeted with brotherly love, grumpy voices shouting, "Wake the hell up, yous guys're blocking up the path!"

"Oh, sorry about that," I responded, not offering any explanation. It was unnecessary. He knew. And I knew that it'd be the last time for at least several months I'd be making the twenty-five-minute trek out to visit her.

But how was I able to drive back home without noticing a parking ticket tucked under the windshield wiper? I must've been in a trance, dreaming of Deirdre, still trying to grasp the reality of us together again.

I dug into my pocket and pulled out the last bits of US currency I had on me. A twenty-dollar bill and two crumpled singles. I smoothed them out and handed them over to my father, unaware of the cost of the ticket.

He looked at me confused, almost irritated. "Don't worry about it. You think I'm really gonna pay it? The hell are they gonna do about it?" He eyed up the last few bites left on my plate. "Besides, the car will never be back on that campus anyway."

He wiped his mouth again, though he had already finished eating, slid his chair back, and stood up. "So, ready for Germany?"

***

The airplane was packed. I was lucky enough to be assigned an aisle seat in the middle row, the one neighbor to my right a young, pretty German girl. I stuffed my carry-on into the overhead compartment, tucked my iPod into the seat pocket in front of me, and fastened my seatbelt. Since airlines decided that portable electronic devices will cause the planes to burst into flames and crash for some reason, I decided to read until we reached cruising altitude. I had recently decided to revisit Goethe's classic *Die Leiden des jungen Werthers*, suddenly feeling its urgent relevance—a wealthy young man leaves home, travels about, and passionately describes his sensitivity when it comes to love. On the first page, I already felt myself agreeing with the delicate, whiny Werther. *"Ich will das Gegenwärtige genießen, und das Vergangene soll mir vergangen seyn."* Enjoy the present, let go of the past, I had kept telling myself. Though that was all easier said than done with Deirdre back in the picture.

After a few pages, Werther started weighing on my eyelids, so I pulled out my iPod. With my eyes closed and my seat leaned back, I took in the sounds of the newest Hot Water Music album. Ever since I had been talking to Deirdre again, the lyrics, the music, the whole sound of the album hit differently—as if it was speaking directly to me.

"It seems like we have the same dreams

It seems like we want the same things

A beginning

So right now, there's no doubt"

I hoped Deirdre would have the patience to wait for me. I'd be gone not even a full year. Plus, I had decided to come back during the break in March. Initially I was going to stick around, maybe backpack around Europe for a bit. But the day after Deirdre contacted me after four years of silence, I had second thoughts.

The engines started up for takeoff. I straightened my seat and paused the music, remembering the cardinal rule I was currently breaking. We ascended and I watched as the city curved away beneath me to the left. The cars on the highways morphed into scurrying insects, the skyscrapers and buildings bled into a child's playset, and the Delaware River turned into a trickle bisecting the landscape. Eventually, clouds enveloped the whole scene in some sort of reverse Polaroid action. I took a deep breath, leaned my head back, and relaxed. And thought of Deirdre.

***

My friend Tyler Brannan had introduced us when we were all sixteen. I had just returned home from my first trip abroad and was eager to tell him all about it. We had just started hanging out again after drifting apart. Inseparable as kids, we inexplicably grew apart about the time we hit puberty, bumping into each other throughout the years. Tyler was just as eager to tell me about Deirdre as I was to tell him about Europe. Apparently, she had just moved to town, the daughter of his mother's best friend from way back when, and also, according to Tyler's mom, related to him in some way. Maybe it wasn't a blood relative, but one of those "my-mom's-best-friend-is-my-aunt" relationships. Whatever the connection was, Deirdre was the new girl, and Tyler wanted me to meet her.

I was attracted to her at first sight. She was tiny with pale skin that made her sable hair appear darker than it really was, and the most intense, deep green eyes. Her eyes had something sad about them, or maybe just sincere. There was a mystery about her, and that was what sparked my immediate interest. She reminded me of a dark-haired Debbie Harry. Later on, after we had been dating for about two years, shortly before we broke up, she had taken to wearing tight shirts and

9

going braless, not unlike Debbie. This drove me crazy—because it turned me on like nothing else, and because it did the same for everyone else around, which sent extreme sparks of jealousy jolting through my veins. And the thrill of exhibitionism, of being the target of everyone's desire, was never lost on her. At first, I accepted it. She even allowed me to take a picture of her reenacting that one shot of Debbie Harry squatting in front of an old car, lifting up her white t-shirt and exposing her left breast, staring at the camera with a playful, open-mouthed grin. At the time, I found it sexy and risqué. In hindsight, the photo served as foreshadowing, if anything.

My father never liked Deirdre. He never expressed it vocally, but his silence spoke measures. He had plans for me and his mind had been set for years. And the only thing that could get in the way of these plans, my father thought, was Deirdre. When I was with her I let down my guard. She was the only one to help me step out of my comfort zone. Whether it was skinny dipping in a stranger's pool at night, going to a party full of college kids home on break, or sneaking out to her house at two in the morning, Deirdre was always tugging me out of the safety net I had become ensnared in. There was even a pregnancy scare our senior year that threatened to undo everything that had been laid out for me. At times, I even thought it was because she knew of my father's disapproval of her, and this was her way of rebelling against him—by making me inadvertently rebel.

Our rekindling came as an absolute shock to me and at the worst possible time. The last two weeks had been something like a dream, as if a thick sheet of fog had washed over reality. I was coasting through life on autopilot, guided by Deirdre's siren song, my body steered by impulses shot out of my spinal cord to the synapses of my brain. The night before my departure felt like I was in the music video to that Cursive song, "The Recluse," dreamlike and unsettling. I could almost hear Deirdre taunting me softly, "You're in my web now." All the while the lyrics spun through my head, about being too scared of leaving her bed in fear I'd never lie there again.

Was I really that desperate?

Before I could fall asleep, I was interrupted by the stewardess coming around with beverages. In English, she asked the pretty German girl next to me what she would like to drink. Then she turned to me and asked the same question in German.

"*Du kannst Deutsch?*" my neighbor half-asked, half-stated with genuine curiosity, after the stewardess handed us our beverages and pushed her cart farther down the aisle.

"*Uh, ja,*" was my best response.

She smiled and a conversation ensued. She told me her name was Anna and she was studying at the university in Frankfurt. She was in Philadelphia visiting friends she had made during some sort of exchange program in high school.

I told her I had just graduated from college with a degree in Philosophy and a minor in German. That I was on my way to the little town of Ankerich in southern Germany to work for the American Studies department at the university there. That it was a temporary job, and I would be there until June.

I told her I was excited.

What I didn't tell her was that, unlike many shiftless youths who go abroad because of murky horizons, my horizon was all too clear. I didn't tell her about my reluctance to approach that clear horizon, or how I had drifted through life spinelessly like a jellyfish following the tides and moon cycles. How my tides had consistently followed a September-to-June rhythm since kindergarten, and how my moon was my father, with me doing the orbiting. I didn't tell her about the dream I had been having recently, the one where I try to run, but my legs feel like they are made of concrete. I didn't tell her about the rest of my flawed family. About my mother's farewell to me, her beloved dachshund, Seymour, cradled in her arm and last night's—or this morning's—vodka tonic on her breath, the funky sweet stench whipping at my nostrils like a soggy flag in the wind, reminding me of Deirdre's breath when I'd sneak over late at night after she had been out partying with people I didn't know. Or my brother, who I hadn't seen in over a year. And poor Claudia, who deserved so much more than older siblings and parents who were consistently absent, either physically or emotionally.

And Deirdre. I also didn't tell her about Deirdre. That I was nervous about leaving behind my recently rekindled affair with her. And how I wasn't exactly sure whether we were back together or not, and that I was too afraid to ask. That although I was counting my blessings that she had decided to contact me recently—that it was her, for once, reaching out, and not me—that I was concerned about her new job at Valentine's. That I was disappointed. And worried.

All that I kept to myself, as I had grown accustomed to doing, and allowed our conversation to ease my racing mind. And Anna's choice to speak to me in German was a huge confidence boost.

However, after urgently excusing myself for the third time to head to the bathroom—I entirely regretted the cheesesteak that my father insisted on eating—the conversation ended. I returned to find her with her headphones on, nose buried in some fashion magazine, and understood she was done with me.

I settled back into my seat, scrolled through my iPod for a fitting soundtrack, and closed my eyes. Somewhere over the Atlantic Ocean, suspended in the evening 40,000 feet above ground, neither here nor there, neither past nor future, I relaxed as John K. Samson sang me to sleep.

"And I'm leaning on this broken fence

TIM DEMARCO

Between past and present tense…
But it almost feels okay"

Chapter 2

"Ladies and gentlemen, welcome to Frankfurt International Airport. The local time is 7:35 AM and the temperature is fifteen degrees Celsius."

Still rattled by the rough landing and explosion of applause that shook me from my sleep, I grabbed my bag from the overhead compartment, and, with a quick, embarrassed smile, bid Anna farewell. At least my stomach had settled by that point.

At passport control, I approached with confidence, placing my passport opened to the photo page on the counter, greeting the officer with a friendly "*Guten Morgen!*" His gaze shot quickly from my face to the photo in the passport and back. It seemed as if he himself was trying to imitate my biometric picture—no smiles, no facial expressions, no emotions allowed.

"What is the purpose of your stay in Germany?" he asked sternly, in German.

"To work," I replied in German, a sense of pride creeping up in me.

"To verk? Vere iss yor verking visa?" he demanded, switching to English and finally exhibiting a trace of emotion.

"Uh." I had no answer. My boss had told me that during one of the first days here she'd take me to get my papers. I could feel the crimson heat of embarrassment crawling up my back and into my face.

"If you verk in Tschermany, you mahst haff a verking visa."

Then I remembered my boss mentioned something about how I'd be able to take classes. How I'd technically be matriculated at the university. What had at first seemed a little odd now made sense to me, some sort of loophole to allow me to work there without necessitating a visa.

"Well, uh, actually," I stammered, "I'm actually a student."

The officer stared at me unconvinced.

"I just thought I'd get a side job while I was here," I added.

His partner leaned over and looked at my passport, then at me. The two chatted quietly for a few seconds.

Without taking his eyes off me, the officer stamped my passport with enough force to register as a small earthquake and handed it back to me.

"If you verk in Tschermany, you mahst haff a verking visa," he repeated.

Before I could come up with a response, he yelled over my head, "*DER NÄCHSTE, BITTE!*"

With a lump in my throat and armed with my belongings for the next nine months, I booked my train ticket to Ankerich, patting myself on the back for not selecting the English button on the automated ticket machine.

The train arrived punctually, and I was able to find an open seat to relax in. I stowed my luggage out of the way of the other passengers, and slid the ticket into my wallet, noticing the picture of Deirdre I had recently added. With my light jacket crumpled into a pillow, I leaned back into the seat and drifted off into a slumber that lasted until I was awoken by an announcement that the train had reached its final destination.

Groggy and disoriented, I stepped off the train and into the Stuttgart main station. The air was thick and slightly foul, like onions on the verge of rotting. Homeless men shuffled about, overly dressed for early autumn. Young, fuzzy-lipped teenagers loitered about, slapping hands and yelling at one another in a foreign tongue. Punks with face tattoos and infected piercings stared menacingly at passersby, riding out last night's bender or adding fuel to the embers of their waning inebriation. Out-of-place tourists wandered about confusedly, eyes fixated on the signs hanging above their heads or the awkwardly folded maps in their hands. Well-dressed businessmen hustled to work, sipping piping hot to-go coffee and talking determinedly into their cell phones. All the while a tinny, half-human voice incomprehensibly announced track changes, delays, arrivals, and departures.

When my train arrived, I grabbed a window seat and took a deep breath, immediately regretting it: the overheated train was peppered with the stench of stale sweat and soggy sandwiches. The automatic doors beeped and closed and the train started with a jolt.

With my face pressed against the window, I took in the scenery as it bled from an urban industrial landscape speckled with smokestacks to a picturesque rural countryside of rolling hills and a river which cut lazily through the fields. The tracks directly outside the city were surrounded by modest gardens, perfectly subdivided into individual plots, each complete with a tiny shack. Heavy-set grandmothers gardened and gossiped, shirtless men lounged lazily, and sleepy cats soaked in the early sun, all under the watchful eyes of the garden gnomes surreptitiously set in the grass.

As the train made its way into more rural areas, the gardens gave way to vineyards and farmlands, the hills shooting directly out of the ground. The colors filtering through the sweat-greased window reminded me of the flag of Rwanda—a patchwork of brownish-greens, with fields of breathtaking yellow flowers in the distance, the sky above a clear blue, with a bright golden sun, recently risen, doing its best to awaken the entire landscape.

The train chugged through the southern German countryside, occasionally sidling up against the river, stopping every five or ten minutes in a town whose name sounded exactly like the one before it, each consisting of reddish-brown-roofed houses protruding from the valley, the more fortunate ones containing a weathered stone castle perched upon a hill in the background.

At one point, the conductor shuffled down the narrow aisle of the train car, checking tickets and leaving in his wake the funk of dried sweat and mildewy clothes that were still damp when put away. I held my breath until he passed into the next car, then stood up and half-opened the thin, rectangular piece of glass that served as a vent above the main window. I sat back down, breathing in the early October air, still warm, but with a promise of coolness to come.

Not even a minute later, I was jolted by a loud bang. One of the grandmotherly women seated behind me had slammed my window shut. I stared at her in disbelief as she returned to her seat muttering something about "*der Zug.*" I knew we were on a train. It made no sense to me why she was so angry and why she kept repeating the word for "train." With my face red from embarrassment and discomfort, I settled back into my fabric-lined seat, closed my eyes, and thought of something more pleasant. A cold drink of water. Something warm to eat. Deirdre.

The conductor's voice on the train's PA pulled me from my daydream and announced our arrival in Ankerich. Heart racing, back aching, I walked purposefully through the shabby train station, slightly taken aback at the state of the building and people milling about. I hadn't done much research on Ankerich before accepting the job, but I seemed to remember the town being much more picturesque. Outside, the station opened into a large parking lot, full of idling buses. Behind the parking lot was a lush green park with a tiny lake, full of homeless-looking punks, or punk-looking homeless people, each of them with a bottle in their hands, tossing what I assumed to be bread to a dozen or so large, black crows. I checked the clock above my head. 11:03 AM. Trying my best to look like I knew what I was doing, I walked toward the buses, hoping I'd find one that would take me to the student housing area I had learned was up on a hill overlooking the town. What appeared to be several students were filing into the number two bus, so I followed suit. I bought a one-way ticket from the machine on the bus, praising myself for accepting the leftover euros my father had given to me upon his return from a conference in France the previous year.

The bus departed the station, passing a discount clothing shop and a Burger King. Just as the presence of a pawn shop or bail bondsmen usually spells trouble for whichever town you're in in the US, this didn't make a great first impression. At the corner, a huge house entirely covered in spray paint loomed over the bus. Something about not feeling your shackles if you don't move was all I could make out among the chaotic spattering of bright graffiti.

We eventually turned left and approached a bridge crossing the river and the whole scene changed. Bucolic homes with pastel facades and bay windows shouldered up to half-timbered houses, all mirrored in the calm water below. Bright maroon clay-tiled gables provided the foreground to the pale stone church towers poking up proudly in the background. Tall trees lined the river, their greens giving way to yellows, golds, and reds with the onset of autumn. On either side of the bridge, the railings were crowned with flowers, whose bright and lively colors lent a stunning contrast to the more muted solid shades of the town. The river itself was dotted with gondolas, steered effortlessly by young men. To the right, a restaurant with a cozy biergarten stretched out along the river, full of lunchtime customers sipping tall beers and laughing. To the left, a stone wall, speckled gray, white, and tan, provided a seat for several people perched casually on top, feet dangling above the river below.

The bus made its way across the bridge, down a narrow alley carved out between more ancient homes, and curved right at the top of a hill, passing unimpressive university buildings and hurrying students on their bikes. Leaving all this behind, we climbed yet another hill, one side thick with dark green trees and overgrown bushes spilling out onto the road, threatening to swallow the street, as if the town had completely dissolved into nature.

Toward what I thought must be the last stop on the route, a mechanical male voice announced *"Eichholzweg,"* the name of the bus stop my soon-to-be-boss, Heike, had emailed me a few weeks earlier. I pressed the stop button and alighted, taking note of my new surroundings.

I checked the mini-notebook I had in my pocket with the address of the student dorm I'd be staying in, internally grumbling about my foolish mistake at passport control earlier and made my way across the concrete pedestrian bridge leading to the student housing area, smirking at the immature graffiti scrawled in nearly illegible handwriting. Crudely drawn penises. Misspelled insults like "Fuck of Natalie." The word "Legalize" followed by what looked like a poor attempt at a maple leaf.

Three ugly buildings the color of uncooked liver, each one at least ten stories high and obviously built in the architecturally tasteless sixties or seventies, jutted into the sky at the middle of the hill, standing stoically as if they didn't realize they didn't belong in this town. Or realized and didn't care. I stood at the bottom of the building that matched the number in my notebook and craned my neck to look up at the top.

I wheeled my suitcase into the lobby. The room was sparsely decorated and devoid of human presence, short of an old, wiry-haired man and a pretty, blonde girl talking to him, both arms occupied with luggage.

The man turned his head toward me: "*Wolled Sie au heud dahana eizieha?*" I couldn't tell whether it was a question or statement.

"Uh," I stammered, feeling the sweat on my aching back cause my shirt to stick to it. "*Wie, bitte?*" I asked him to repeat himself.

"*Ob Sie au no dahana eizieha?*"

I had no idea what was going on. I had taken German in high school and earned a minor in German at college. But what I learned in high school was limited to ordering food at restaurants and describing clothing, and at college it was all about reading Goethe and identifying proper usage of the dative case. And not counting the few hours since landing, my only experience in the country itself was that "educational tour" after sophomore year, where the only Germans I came in contact with were the old women who served us food at the predetermined restaurants, unceremoniously dropping plates of warmed-up wurst in front of us with an emotionless "*Bitte schön.*"

The garbled nonsense coming out of this impatient man made no sense to me. If he were to only ask me something about Goethe or dative prepositions!

"*Uh, nein. Danke,*" I decided would be the best answer.

He looked at the pretty student in front of him, shook his head slowly, grabbed a ring full of keys, and disappeared into the tiny elevator in the next room.

I felt like I had made a mistake. Was he trying to check me in? Did he even mention that word?

What am I even doing here, anyway, I thought to myself. Why did I think it'd be such a great idea to take a job 4,000 miles away from home? Why am I surprised that I feel out of place—haven't I felt this way my whole life? With my friends, the non-drinker in a hard-partying crowd? At college, the punk-shirt-wearing public-school-product lost in a sea of popped-collar-preppies? With Deirdre, the poindexter with the pinup girlfriend?

And why did Deirdre decide she wanted me back just a few weeks before I had planned to go away, anyway?

Maybe my father was right, that what I was doing was foolish. Though he had never explicitly stated his opinion, it was always clear that he viewed my decision to study "dead-end" subjects like philosophy and German as valuable as my interest in punk music and Deirdre. To him, the words "desire" and "curiosity" belonged to a foreign language themselves. And the only time he ever used the word "interest" he followed it up with "rate."

The grumpy old man returned and interrupted my mini existential crisis. He looked me in the eyes, suddenly friendlier now, and asked, in clear-as-day German: "Are you here to move in?"

"*Ja*," I responded, relieved that I could finally understand him.

He smiled acknowledgingly, and continued, his German understandable now. "Well, why didn't you say something when I asked you before?" He turned his back to me to open the door he had just come through.

"I didn't hear you," I said.

He stopped and slowly turned around, hand still on the door. "You heard me. You didn't *understand* me," he corrected, a mischievous twinkle in his eyes.

Luckily he turned back around and didn't see my face redden in embarrassment and anger. If this asshole knew I didn't understand him, why didn't he speak clearly the first time, I thought to myself, fuming.

"In any case, my name is Herr Meindt. Like *nevermind*."

We stepped into the elevator, which felt more like a broom closet. As the tiny metallic death trap rattled upwards, I looked around at all the graffiti and etchings on the walls. Someone had added an "S" in front of the word for elevator, making a corny drinking joke. Someone else quoted Nietzsche. And directly beneath it someone insulted Nietzsche.

Herr Meindt must have seen my wandering eyes. He shook his head disapprovingly. "These students live like animals."

The doors parted on the sixth floor and we exited the claustrophobic chamber. The narrow hallway was lined with doors. Some had pictures or posters on them. Most were bare; a blank grayish-white. Herr Meindt droned on the whole time about bedrooms, bathrooms, and showers, but I wasn't listening. What was the point, anyway? His back was turned toward me, and he had slipped back into whatever nightmare of a dialect he had been speaking when we first met.

We stopped in front of room 624. Herr Meindt fumbled with the keys, finally opening the door to my room. It swung open and it took me all of five seconds to take in the entire room. A minuscule washroom area with a porcelain sink and mirror across from a small closet gave way to a bedroom, complete with a wooden desk and a bed so low it barely reached my knees. Across from the desk was a short bookshelf and two huge windows looking out over a parking garage, directly above the main entrance to the building.

In my head I could hear Deirdre, in her best Blondie impression, singing "Picture This," about how all she wants is a room with a view.

"Don't piss in the sink," Herr Meindt said to me sternly, eyes locked on mine.

"Uh, okay," I stammered, confused.

He walked me down the hallway to the common kitchen. The room was outfitted with a large table in the middle, a refrigerator in the corner, and cabinets above the sink and stove. There were also nine individual cabinets, symmetrical and identical in size. Some had locks on them.

"Each student gets his own cabinet," Herr Meindt said, reading my mind. "Don't steal from your neighbors," he warned me, again staring directly into my eyes.

There was also a mini-fridge with a lock on it, and a coffee maker on top.

I followed Herr Meindt to the large windows, which served as a sliding door to the balcony. Walking past a bowl of age-softened fruit with a cloud of tiny flies hovering over them like a thin web, I was happy to step outside. The room was a hodgepodge of odors: burnt eggs, assorted earthy teas, stale spilled beer, acrid cleaning products, vinegar, smoked meat.

As soon as I stepped past the grimy curtain caked with grease, the balcony gave way to a spectacular sight: fields patchworked in different shades of summer and autumn, and that bright yellow I had noticed through the window of the train. Behind the fields rose some impressive hills, gently lumbering off into the distance. I could feel the tension in my upper back easing as I stared off into the distance.

"Any questions?" Herr Meindt asked me, placing a set of keys in my hand. He was gone before I could even register his insincere inquiry.

I stood there, spellbound by the view. From somewhere nearby I thought I heard faint music, punk with German lyrics.

After a few moments, I pocketed my keys and returned to room 624. The room could definitely use some fresh air, so I walked to the two enormous windows and stared at them perplexed. The windows looked nothing like the ones at home. There was a handle that ran vertically from the frame, perpendicular to the windowsill. I grabbed it and turned it upwards, a full 180 degrees. If one position was closed, the opposite would be open, I foolishly assumed. Suddenly the entire pane came falling toward me from above. With both hands pressing hard against the glass and both ass cheeks pressing firmly against each other to keep the shit from escaping my bowels, I struggled to prevent myself from being minced to pieces by the massive pane. Eventually, I caught my breath, slowly and steadily pushed the window back into place, and returned the handle—and my asshole—to its original position. Fresh air would have to wait.

I turned, took two steps, and flopped down onto the tiny bed. There was a crack, then a rattling on the floor. I groaned and sat back up. Peering under the bed I noticed a wooden slat, which had apparently fallen loose from the frame. No box springs here.

I plopped back down onto the bed. I'll deal with that later, I thought to myself as I closed my eyes.

Chapter 3

The sound of the world ending woke me the next morning. Glass bottles smashed and popped, metal crunched and shrieked, all amplified by what sounded like a steel box of pure cacophony. I kicked off the thin sheets, pressed my bare feet to the cold floor, and scuttled over to the window. A recycling truck emptying the seemingly endless collection of metal recycling bins. I checked the time. 7:15 in the morning.

Immediately my swollen bladder announced its presence. I slid into a pair of shorts, tossed on a t-shirt, grabbed my keys, and hurried out into the hallway. I was greeted by the sterile row of off-white doors lining the endless hall. Reaching back into my mind, I could not remember which door Herr Meindt said led to the bathrooms. It didn't help that every door was closed. And I was not about to go trying every one of them until I found one that opened.

Gritting my teeth, I turned and went back to my room. I closed the door, turned on the faucet, stood on my tippy toes, and peed in the sink. *Nevermind, Herr Meindt.*

I decided to put together my room before showering—if I was able to find the shower—then head out to explore Ankerich. On my walls, I hung up a few posters I had brought from home along with some photos of bands cut out from magazines and two postcards, one depicting a night scene of Philadelphia and one of the Jersey Shore. My laptop and my German-English dictionary filled out my desk. Somehow, the room still looked naked. As I was dragging my empty suitcase into the closet, it hit me: the framed photo I had of Deirdre. I ran my hands through each of the pockets in the suitcase until I found it, sliding it out and cupping it softly in my hands like a stolen jewel.

She had given me the photo the day before I left for Ankerich. A photo of herself laughing, mouth open, head tilted slightly back and to the left, eyes half-closed. Her dark hair slightly lighter in the photo, and her face lit by the sun, so bright and alive. Caught mid-laugh, in a moment of pure bliss, the image radiated happiness. The type of photo displayed at a funeral or flashed on-screen during a news report about some tragedy.

I never asked who took the photo.

Taking a step back into the mini washroom area, I took it all in. Here I was, twenty-two-years old, recently graduated from college, and back in a dorm room. And excited about it.

Standing there, in that spot, I couldn't help but think of our end.

Deirdre had accompanied my father and me to help me move into college. My mother was probably too drunk or didn't know which day it was. My brother had already been gone for several months at that point, or maybe he was in rehab, I don't remember. My sister was too young, and with her issues it would've made no sense.

The few-hour drive felt like an eternity, despite my father's erratic driving. His incessant rambling battered our ears like an infinite summer storm, drumming out any chance of Deirdre and me talking. His mundane monologue was nothing new to me, and nothing Deirdre cared to know. His experience in college. The most recent homes he had sold. The traffic.

I kept stealing glances back at Deirdre in the mirror, but her attention was directed elsewhere.

After we had carried in my belongings and I had set up a picture of me and Deirdre on the boardwalk on my desk, my father picked a place for us to eat. Upon returning to the dorm, it was time to say goodbye.

I shook my father's hand, and he left, having at least enough decency to allow me and Deirdre to take leave of each other in privacy. She stood in my room, facing the hallway. I stood in the hallway, looking into my new room as if to block her from leaving. We embraced, and with her mouth inches from my ear, she said, quietly, "I think we should break up, Jake."

My heart stopped. I stared into my room, focused on the picture of us. Ocean City. The previous summer. July. I remembered the warmth resonating from the sand and the cool breeze blowing off the ocean.

"It's for the best," she continued. "I need space."

I was dumbfounded. My college wasn't exactly across the country, but a couple hundred miles surely provided enough space, right?

My numb limbs were finally able to loosen the embrace, my entire body suddenly feeling foreign.

"I don't get it, Didi." She hated being called Didi.

She broke the embrace, stepped back so that I'd maybe do the same. Once I had given her a few inches of space, she stepped past me into the hallway.

"Besides, Jake… I cheated on you." She looked down and brushed a stray strand of dark hair out of her face, tucking it behind her left ear. "Well, I've *been* cheating on you," she said, looking up.

I stood there, mouth agape, probably looking like a fucking idiot. I *was* a fucking idiot.

"I'm sorry. I mean," she paused and sighed. "I don't know. I love you, I really do. It's just… We need a break right now. Well, more than a break."

She took a step toward me, hugged me one last time. "Listen, you'll be fine. Focus on school. You'll do great. I know you'll crush it here. Maybe you'll even find a cute little brainiac girl to marry and have cute little brainiac kids with," she tried joking.
She kissed my cheek, patted my shoulder, and left.

I wondered how the drive back would be.

I forgot to ask who it was she had cheated on me with. Had been cheating on me with.

A toilet flushed, washing away that sour memory. A bathroom. Someone had just used a bathroom. I spun around and opened the door to look outside. Maybe I'd catch someone leaving and figure out which door would lead me to the secret room.

After thirty seconds of waiting, I gave up. But directly across from me was a door. It sounded like that's where the flushing had come from. Collecting all my courage, I cautiously opened the door and slowly peeked in. I was immediately overcome by an olfactory nightmare. With the collar of my t-shirt covering my nose, I took inventory of the room. Three stalls lined the right, two doors on the left. I opened one of the doors to the left. Showers. Holding my breath, I turned to leave. Out of the corner of my eye, I noticed something on the floor beneath the farthest stall. A small stack of neon pink papers. I tiptoed over and picked one up.

It was a flyer for a punk show. Thursday, November 11th. At a place called the *Schlachthof* in Ankerich. Only four euros.

Wondering to myself about what kind of person leaves flyers where they shit, I stuffed the piece of paper into my pocket and went back to my room to gather my showering supplies.

***

After showering, I felt like a new person. I decided to get dressed and go explore Ankerich. Maybe even find the *Schlachthof.*

The hallway reeked like vinegar. I couldn't tell whether it was the cleaning agent the *Putzfrau* was using or her sweat. Either way, I held my breath, excused myself by muttering an *"Entschuldigung,"* and squeezed past her toward the elevator.

Outside, the sun cut through the cool air, warming my face. I bought a ticket, nudged my way into the bus crowded with the children lugging around boxy backpacks, and headed into town. The clouds above the massive hill to the left reminded me of the opening credits to The Simpsons. Grayish-white puffs dotted the grassy slope, drifting lazily across the meadow. Sheep, I was able to determine as the bus slowly rattled toward the downtown.

Though it was only the second week of autumn, the season had loudly proclaimed its arrival in Ankerich. The sun falling through the cottony clouds washed the fifteenth-century homes in warm light, filtering the pale colors of the artistic architecture. Leaves, yellowed and reddened by the season, sparkled among the green in the trees lining the river. The ones dead enough to release themselves from their branches did so, spiraling graciously to the earth, landing with a muted tap.

I made my way from the bridge toward what appeared to be the old part of town. The tiny, cobblestoned roads were free of cars and lined with bakeries, ice cream cafés, bookstores, and antique shops. Almost every corner was occupied by a restaurant with tables outside and waiters wearing white shirts and black ties serving elderly couples coffee, cappuccinos, and cake.

I strolled aimlessly, the rubber soles of my sneakers producing a pleasant pattering in the crooked alleys. Though entranced by the ancient beauty of the town, my mind bounced back to Deirdre when I turned onto *Fuchsgasse*—fox alley—her favorite animal.

At the marketplace in the town center, I weaved between grandmothers haggling prices and children chewing on apples and apricots. I bought 200 grams of cherries—Deirdre's favorite fruit—from an old woman with soil-darkened hands.

In front of the town hall, built in the year 1435, I snacked on the cherries, greedily gnawing the candylike flesh from the pits, spitting the slippery stones onto the ground. I craned my neck and looked at the houses next to the impressive building, considering if they were also as old. How many families had lived in them in the past 570 years? How many times had they been sold? I wondered how much it costs now to buy a house like this.

The realization that I was thinking about real estate hit me like a slap on the back of the head. I spit out my last cherry pit and continued my stroll through town.

From one of the used bookstores, I bought the German version of *The Catcher in the Rye* for two euros, dogeared from previous use, the cover bleached by sunlight and the pages browned with age. Next to one of the 500-year-old homes was a tattoo and piercing shop. A pang of embarrassment and jealousy swept over me as I stood in front of the display window.

Deirdre had always wanted her belly button pierced. Her mother, never really a candidate for mother of the year, nonetheless put her foot down. Deirdre patiently waited until her eighteenth birthday to make that decision on her own. When I returned from work that day, she proudly lifted her shirt to show off her new hardware. Instead of this slightly erotic move leading into something more fulfilling, she continued to babble on dreamily about the piercer, Mikey, and how "cute" he was.

I couldn't help but think about what kind of twenty-something goes by the name Mikey, and what kind of failure decides to be a piercer, anyway? Was it even considered a career? Her compliments toward this loser left a sour taste in my mouth and I made some snide remarks. Deirdre fired back at me, "You're just scared. Scared of getting a piercing or tattoo. Scared because it might hurt. Or, worst of all, it might hurt your daddy."

I was silent. Because she was right. I was scared. Not of the pain, but of my father's strong disapproval of any body modification, hair dye included.

We were sitting around with her best friend Kelly, and Deirdre carried on, knowing that she was right.

"Anyway, I'm thinking about getting my nipples pierced next," she told Kelly, ignoring my presence, but knowing full well I was listening.

"As soon as I save up the money I'm doing it." Her eyes darted to the side, taking stock of my bitter face. "Mikey said he'd give me a discount."

"He just wants to see your tits," I blurted out, jealousy clouding my judgment. "And you want to show him," I added, half as loud.

Deirdre turned to face me. "Why don't you come with me?" she challenged, a cocky smile creeping across her face. "Get a tattoo or something. Prove you're not scared."

I thought about it for a second. As long as I didn't get something obvious, my father would never know, I rationalized.

"Get Deirdre's name tattooed on your dick," Kelly said, laughing at her own goofy suggestion.

"Yeah! Do it! Then it would belong to me forever!" Deirdre added.

The thought of my penis belonging to Deirdre forever excited me. But that excitement quickly gave way to the fear of the excruciating pain that would surely accompany the poor decision. "What about right above my dick? If it's on the actual thing it'll look all funny when it's hard, you know?" I offered my best excuse.

"Fine! Do it!"

And so it was decided.

By the time of the appointment three weeks later, I had decided to not get her name tattooed, but her nickname "Schatz." Though she hated when I called her Didi, she didn't mind the German term of endearment. She had also convinced me to shave my pubes. "A shaved dick is hot."

We walked into the parlor together, Deirdre determined to get her nipples pierced, me determined to make sure Mikey didn't let his fingers linger too long on Deirdre's breasts. The permanence of the tattoo took a backseat to my overprotective and possessive obsession.

Mikey was exactly what I expected: tall and muscular, completely covered in tattoos and facial piercings, with a sloppy haircut, perfectly disheveled—which I'm sure took at least a half-hour to achieve—and a cocky grin.

He shook my hand cordially, and I envisioned my hand smashing that shit-eating grin as soon as his hand slithered out of bounds.

"So," he said to Deirdre, "why don't you and I head back there to my piercing parlor and I'll put some rods in you." Deirdre blushed. He shot me a side-eyed glance and a little smirk. "And you, my man, will follow James back there to get your little pecker poked."

I looked over to my left. James, an overweight, leather-vested biker dude with a huge beard surely housing hundreds of food scraps, waved.

It had never crossed my mind that we'd be separated.

As I lay in the tiny room with some ogre needling Deirdre's nickname painfully into the skin above my penis, Deirdre was topless in another room with a guy she thought was "cute." Over the hum of the tattoo gun, I could hear her giggling.

I shook the memory from my mind and instinctively scratched at my crotch.

Above me, the church tower began clanging noisily. I looked up and realized it was noon. Besides the fifteen or so cherries, I hadn't had anything else to eat. With my stomach growling hollow and hungry, I made my way back toward the center of town.

The market was still going full force. Ducking down a side alley, I could hear a melody being carried through the narrow path, reverberating between the stone walls of the buildings on either side. An older man stood stooping to the side, a shabby violin tucked under his unshaven chin. Feeling wistful, I tossed him a coin and kept walking.

My nose led me to a tiny döner stand, where a mustached man sold me a kebab for two euros. With my warm pita bread stuffed with spiced meat held tightly in my hand, I strolled back to the bridge. I spotted some park benches on an island in the river, which seemed like a comfortable place to eat lunch. As I walked across the bridge, I noticed the rails were cluttered with hundreds of tiny locks, many of which had written or engraved initials and dates.

Plopping down on the bench my feet felt relieved. I tossed my book next to me and dug into my kebab. Pigeons slowly started expressing their interest in my lunch, zig-zagging their way back and forth in front of me. One particular pigeon stood relatively still, watching me eat, its purple and green collar of garage-floor filth shining iridescent in the early afternoon sun, its prehistoric claws padding the sandy soil below. "You'll get some," I assured it, feeling stupid for talking to an animal. Even if it could understand human language, it wouldn't be English. But it felt good to talk, considering I had barely spoken all day.

With the gorgeous view of the old town splayed out in front of me, framed by the bridge to my right and the lush, sunlit-speckled path leading down the length of the island to my left, my thoughts went back to Deirdre. I transferred my kebab to my left hand and fumbled with my right hand for my keys. Using the larger of the two keys, I leaned over and carved our initials into the weather-worn wood beneath my thighs. JC + DD. Just before I could sit upright and finish my lunch, I heard and felt a flurry of commotion in my hands. I looked up to see a greasy gray cluster of feathers fluttering on top of my kebab. I fell backward, flailing with one hand at the flying rat. The filthy vermin flopped back to the ground and resumed its clumsy pacing at my feet, picking up crumbs that were the result of my freakout.

"Fucking dickhead," I hissed at the oil-slicked asshole, not caring whether it understood words or English or insults.

I lifted the heavy trash can lid and tossed in my remaining bite. Wiping my hands on my pants, I began to stroll through the park located in the center of the island, stealing a quick glance at our initialed bench. Plane trees lined the paths, their bark peeling off, revealing different shades of browns and tans and grays, the camouflaged trunks lending an air of secrecy to the park. Dry bark, curled like cinnamon sticks, crunched under my Chucks, children on pedal-less wooden bikes wobbled past me, giggling and talking effortlessly in a language I was still trying to master. Elderly couples meandered about, the men with their hands clasped behind their backs in that universal old-man posture.

There was a clearing ahead, giving way to a huge weeping willow, a parasitic viny growth slithering up its side like a snake. A few pitch-black crows perched on the tree's limbs, which rose up majestically, then drooped back lazily around the trunk, one side even reaching into the river.

I thought of my older brother, Jamey. How as children, we'd play outdoors all summer. An older neighbor, Paul, used to torment us by telling us the weeping willow nearby was haunted, and that its bowed branches would swallow anyone near it at 8 o'clock. One night, while Jamey and I were playing near the tree, Paul walked by with his friends and said, casually, "Man, look at the time! 7:59!" Jamey, older and faster than me, grabbed his G.I. Joe and took off down the street. I did the same, forgetting to grab my favorite G.I. Joe. I can still remember watching the distance between us grow as the laughter of Paul and his teenage friends echoed in my ears, overpowering my own screams.

I never really forgave Jamey for that.

I shook the thought from my head and crossed the bridge leading back into town.

In a tiny café, I ordered a coffee.

"*Ein Americano?*" the friendly barista asked me.

Embarrassed, I muttered, "*Ja.*"

How the hell did she know I was American, I thought to myself as I sipped the coffee, which tasted richer than the ones at home. At the end of the block was that graffitied house I had noticed on the bus. Spray painted in headache-inducing incomprehensible font, I could just barely make out the name: *Schlachthof.* I instinctively touched my pocket and smiled, hearing the flyer crinkle beneath the fabric of my faded jeans.

By this point, my feet were killing me, not used to doing this much walking at home. And Chucks weren't exactly the best choice for this much wandering.

Feeling somewhat successful about the day, I decided to make my way back to the bus stop on the bridge. I turned around and almost bumped into a bald, homeless-looking man walking with a not-so-homeless-looking younger girl. He kept walking, full speed, his dark eyes focusing on me for a quick second. His lips parted, revealing a row of tiny, ground-down, blackened teeth. "*Deutsche Wut!*" he growled.

I put my head down and picked up my pace, his angry phrase echoing in my head. I could figure out the first word but had no idea what "*Wut*" meant.

I caught the first bus and began the ascent back to my dorm.

Back home, I grabbed a book and headed out to the balcony to sit and read in the late afternoon sun. My eyes were having a hard time focusing on Goethe with the spectacular beauty of the rolling hills in the distance. That and the jetlag was slowly starting to set in. My chin had just fallen to my chest when I was startled by a noise from behind me, and I turned to see someone in the kitchen for the first time since my arrival. A guy wearing a 311 shirt was bent over the mini-fridge, shaking it and messing around with the wires, all the while whistling to himself.

"Hello," I said cheerfully, after gathering my book and leaving the balcony.

"Hi," he responded, not looking up.

He continued to fumble with the mini-fridge. I pretended to put things into the cabinet designated for room 624, trying to block his view to keep him from noticing that my hands and the cabinet were actually empty.

I again noticed the coffee maker on his mini-fridge. Half out of actual interest, half out of just wanting a reason to talk, I asked him, in my best German, "Hey, is that coffee maker yours?"

"*Ja,*" his terse answer.

"Is it okay if I use it sometimes? I'll buy extra coffee as a contribu-"

"*Nein.*" He kept fumbling with his mini-fridge, never even looking up at me.

I stood there for a few seconds in pure disbelief. Eventually, I opened the door quietly and left.

Back in my room, I collapsed onto the uncomfortable wooden chair at the desk and flipped open my German-English dictionary.

Toward the back of the book, I found it: "*Wut,* (f.) - rage; anger."

Chapter 4

The uneventful first weekend allowed me to spend time wandering Ankerich, trying to accustom myself to the town and its people. Evenings I often spent either in my room or alone on the balcony, eating cereal for dinner and lamenting my own boredom.

More than once I could have sworn I heard faint punk music coming from somewhere, but I could never trace it back to the source.

On Sunday, when I realized I had nothing to eat and every shop was closed, I took the bus into town to get a döner for lunch. Standing ahead of me in line was a young punk, complete with leather jacket and mohawk, clunky maroon Doc Martens, and a wallet chain. I tried to muster up all of my courage and talk to him, maybe ask if he was going to the concert in November, but before I could form the words in my head, he had already gotten his food and was on his way with the cute girl accompanying him, laughing wide-mouthed and infectiously.

Monday morning my nerves were a mess getting ready for work. I was up early, ate breakfast on the balcony—more of the cereal ending up in the sink and trash than in my stomach—and left much earlier than necessary. The early-October morning wind cut straight through my shabby Dickies jacket, covered in buttons and with a huge Dillinger Four back patch. My father had always hated it.

"You look like one of those punks we used to beat up in college," he'd remark. He had always treated my interest in punk like he treated

Deirdre: with a mixture of disdain and squinted-eye disapproval. And maybe he was right to do so. Maybe my interest in both was a feeble attempt at living out my fantasy of freedom and rebellion.

Feeling self-conscious, I made my way toward the university for my first day. As far as I had understood it, my job would consist of working at the front desk of the American Studies department. I would answer basic questions for German and American students and whatever else an "administrative assistant" does.

Heike, my boss, was nice enough. She reminded me of a sober version of my mother—short and skinny, with reddish-brown hair that shined copper in the light, and a bright smile. She spent the morning walking me around the small office, chattering pleasantly about everything there was to know about the university, the department, the town, herself. Her stories bounced from German to English and back, but she was easy to understand. Nothing like Herr Meindt or half the people I had interacted with so far in Ankerich.

I was also introduced to my only colleague, Ursula. Ursula reminded me of the eponymous villain in *The Little Mermaid:* large and overly made up, she scowled at me, extending a damp, plump hand. "You can call me Uschi," she said, emotionless. She eyed my jacket draped across my left arm. "Oi! Oi! Oi!" she mocked me, before slithering off to steal someone's voice or whatever the hell she did in her office.

Who the hell names their kid Ursula, I thought to myself. And what person decides that the nickname "Uschi" is better than Ursula?

And what exactly about my jacket bothered her, anyway, I grumbled silently as I trailed Heike through the office, searching for traces of slime left by Uschi.

After the morning formalities concluded, I was given a spot at the front desk, tasked with entering information on incoming students into the computer. Within minutes, the sheer monotony of my new "job" had me questioning my decision to move halfway around the world, adding to the general discomfort of my first couple of days in my new home.

Shortly before noon I suddenly felt lightheaded. I stopped working and looked up from my desk into the cherubic face of a Disney princess. Her wavy, blonde hair swished gently across her shoulders as she looked around uncertainly. A navy blue and maroon scarf wrapped effortlessly, but stylishly, around her neck gave way to a fern-colored sleeveless knitted sweater, evoking images of springtime in my mind. For an instant, I swore I could smell fresh grass, buds, and blossoms, and feel the warmth of early spring sunshine emanating from her.

"*Guten Morgen,*" she greeted me, still cautiously looking around. "I'm looking for Frau Hoffmann." The statement came across as a question and her uncertainty was endearing.

Before I could point her in the direction of Heike's office, a door opened up behind me and Uschi lumbered over toward my desk.

"Are you the new intern?" she asked challengingly.

"Yes. I'm Julia, here to meet Frau Hoffmann. She wanted me to come in today before I start on Friday."

"Mm-hm," Uschi responded, eyeing the poor girl up as if deciding whether she'd be worthy enough fodder for her eels.

"Well then, I'm Uschi," she finally affirmed the intern's fate. "I'm the assistant director here," she added, never extending a hand. Uschi looked at me out of the corner of her eyes. "And this little punk rock wannabe ogling you is Jacob, our American administrative assistant."

Julia's emerald eyes lit up and she turned to face me. "Oh yeah! I totally forgot they told me I'd be working with an American," she blurted out excitedly as if I belonged to some exotic breed. She switched to English as she said this, ignoring the fact that the previous conversation had been conducted in German.

"I'm Julia," she pronounced her name in an almost American way this time, swapping the initial "y" sound for a soft and succinct "tsch."

"Hi," I fumbled with my hands beneath the desk. "I'm Jake."

"Where are you from, Tschake?" She asked excitedly, "I spent a year in the US just two years ago, I was living with a family in—"

"Okay, enough," Uschi interrupted. "Let's let Jacob get back to work, or whatever it is he's doing behind this computer. I'll bring you back to Heike."

She turned to leave, expecting Julia to follow her. Julia hesitated a moment, mouth still open mid-sentence, revealing two rows of perfectly aligned, pearl-white teeth behind coral lips.

She closed her mouth into a smile, her green eyes squinting, and, with a half-wave, followed Uschi into the back of the office. The room was once again silent and noticeably empty except for a lingering fragrance. Honeysuckle and fresh cotton.

I sat up straight, took a deep breath, and turned back to my computer to continue where I had left off, entering incoming exchange students' names into the program. "Applegate, Deirdre Anne…" I typed, feeling an awkward discomfort wash over me.

***

The rest of the workday flew by. My tasks were easy enough, and Uschi got dragged away by Heike to some surprise meeting or whatever, which left me in peace and quiet. And since the semester didn't officially start until Friday—an admittedly odd day to begin something—no students wandered into the department, so I wound up working alone all afternoon. I even put on some music I found online, choosing Dillinger

Four to spite that sea serpent Uschi, singing softly to myself, feeling the weight of every lyric about happiness just beyond your reach and the resignation of knowing it'll be that way forever.

I finished my work early, so I had plenty of time to kill before five. I wrote Deirdre a long email, letting her know that work was fine, that Heike was great and Uschi was an underwater atrocity, and that I missed her and that I couldn't wait to see her again, and how maybe she could come visit me sometime in the spring.

Knowing Deirdre, she'd probably have no money to spend on a plane ticket, even though she apparently was making great money at her new job. But I didn't want to think about that. I figured I could start setting aside money each paycheck, maybe fifty euros, so that by April or so, when I'd be returning for my second semester, I'd have enough money to pay for Deirdre to visit.

The final hour of the workday was spent conjuring up images of Deirdre and me strolling about town, walking hand in hand, sitting on our bench on the island in the river. At five o'clock, I turned off the computer, said goodbye to Uschi and Heike, and left the office.

On the bus, with my earbuds in and Bigwig's "The Girl in the Green Jacket" providing the soundtrack to the ride, I caught my reflection in the window and smiled. What a weird day, I thought, my mind bouncing between Heike's warm welcome, Uschi's obnoxious attitude, and Julia…

As I disembarked the bus, music still pounding in my ears, I felt a tap on my shoulder. I paused my iPod, popped one earbud out, and turned around.

Staring at me was the punk I had seen at the döner place.

"Hey," he said, his voice raspy. "There's a punk show coming up. At the *Schlachthof.* Only four euros." I was relieved to hear he spoke super clean German, clearly enunciated. Not like Herr Meindt's warbled bleating, the noise of a cat vomiting underwater.

"Cool. Thanks," I replied, quickly glancing at the flyer he extended to me. It was the same flyer I had found next to the reeking toilet.

He was about my size, probably my age. He had a pink mohawk and letters shaved into the almost bald sides of his head. A black hoodie poked out from beneath a black and white leather jacket emblazoned with buttons and names of bands I had never heard of. Intentionally distressed black jeans splotched with paint and bleach were tucked into maroon Doc Martens, a black and white checkered scarf was draped around his neck.

Upon closer look, I noticed his black hoodie had a cartoon depiction of George W. Bush with blood spurting out of the back of his head. "FUCK THE USA" framed his dying face. A tattered American flag served as the backdrop.

Despite his aggressive appearance, his face was warm and friendly. Deep wrinkles branched out from the sides of his eyes. Crow's feet, supposedly a bad thing, something for which older women buy expensive creams to get rid of. But these wrinkles were different, as if the crevasses and canyons were caused by excessive smiling and laughing.

As we walked together, I was conscious about how little I spoke in an effort to not give away too much info or to allow my accent to slip out and give me away. He introduced himself as Stinki, and I decided not to ask about the curious name. He asked me where I lived.

"Here," I answered.

Stinki laughed. "I understand that much, I mean which building?"

"Oh," I said, embarrassed at my own nervousness. "Building three."

"What?! Me, too!" he exclaimed, a childlike excitement coloring his voice. "*Krass!*"

I had no idea what that last word meant, but it seemed positive, so I let it go. We walked in together and boarded the tiny sardine can of an elevator. I pressed the button labeled six. Stinki rambled on excitedly about something I didn't quite understand.

When the bell dinged for the sixth floor, and I was desperately trying to come up with what would be the coolest way to say bye in German, Stinki stepped out with me.

"What?!" He exclaimed. "*Krass*! You live on the sixth floor, too! I live in room 615. I asked for room 666, but they said it didn't exist. Then I asked for room 669! Ha! Too bad that one doesn't exist either."

It turned out room 615 was on the opposite side of the shared toilets, which would explain the flyers in the stall and the faint punk music I swore I'd been hearing. Stinki explained to me that you could access either side of the floor by walking through the bathroom or the shared balcony.

We bid each other farewell, and I returned to my room, excited and exhausted from meeting so many new people in one day.

I fell back onto my bed, worn-out but content, thinking I might just actually find a way to enjoy myself here.

A few minutes later I heard heavy footsteps plod into the bathroom across the hall followed by an enormous, echoing fart.

Chapter 5

Despite the monotony of my work, the first week in the office flew by in a blur. Most of the days I was left alone, as Heike was almost always either in her office or at some meeting. Uschi, however, made herself visible daily. Always with something to say—about how I was or wasn't working, asking if I was on task, or if I had gotten around to the assignment given to me minutes before. Each time she passed I held my breath in fear she'd leave in her wake the stench of rotten sea sludge.

Friday morning I arrived at work in a sour mood. I had still not really heard from Deirdre, other than a quick email answering my first message to her, letting her know that I had gotten in safely, and a few one-word replies to the pictures I had sent her of the town. I was in no mood for Uschi's snide remarks and didn't even look up at her when she walked into work a half-hour after I did.

I was feeling sorry for myself in my own little world, music blaring in my ears, the Excel spreadsheet surprisingly cooperating with me for once, making a conscious effort to not look up, knowing that if anyone were to pass by my desk it'd be that sloppy serpent Uschi.

This determined ignorance backfired when around ten AM I felt someone's presence in front of my desk and continued working, adjusting the volume a bit to drown out any deriding comment that would be directed toward me.

The presence remained and eventually shifted into my eyesight. I gave in and looked up. In front of me was the furthest thing from a slimy sea monster. Emerald eyes looked at me warmly, inquisitively, framed by wavy blonde hair, the darker layers hidden beneath the lighter shades. "Hi! It's me, Julia," she said. "Do you remember me?" she added, cautiously, tilting her head ever so slightly, enough for me to notice a tiny blue earring dangling from her right ear.

I snapped to attention, fumbling to pause the music. I couldn't find the pause button or stop button or mute button or any fucking button, so I pulled the earbuds out of my ears, simultaneously ripping the cord out of the computer. Hot Water Music filled the front office, and I grabbed at the speakers, lucky enough to find the volume knob quickly. I turned down the music, smiled apologetically, my face by this time matching the shade of Julia's lipstick.

"Hi," I replied. "Yeah, I remember you. Hi."

She continued, in English, to tell me how she was sorry for showing up a few minutes late on her first day, that she had missed the bus and how she started walking in the wrong direction as soon as she got off, and…

"Oh, it's fine, don't worry about it," I tried to console her, as if I had the authority to excuse her tardiness.

"Can I leave my bag back here?" she asked me, pointing behind my desk.

"Sure," I told her, scooting to the side to make room for her. She bent over to place her Fjällräven Kånken backpack on the floor beside me, and the wide neck of her cream-colored blouse swung low, revealing two firm breasts cupped by a pale blue bra. I caught myself staring and whipped my head in the other direction.

"Thank you," she said, standing up. She reached her hands behind her head to pull her hair into a tiny ponytail, her shirt lifting up a bit to

reveal a thin strip of skin, punctuated by a shallow belly button.
"What was that terrible racket blaring out here?" Uschi asked, suddenly standing next to me. She gave me a dirty look, noticing my eyes focused on Julia's tight midsection, surely jealous, comparing it to her own jellied gut.

"You're late," she said to Julia, turning away from me. "Come with me."

Julia shot me a quick, wide-eyed, tight-lipped smile, and disappeared into the back with Uschi.

Around lunchtime, Julia came back to me and grabbed her backpack. "Whew," she whispered, "Uschi is a bit much, right?"

I laughed. "Tell me about it."

"I'm taking my lunch break. Care to join me?" she asked.

I looked at the time and agreed.

The weather was quite mild for October, so we decided to eat outside. "There's a great little spot on the wall overlooking the river, just a two-minute walk or so," Julia suggested. I had begun packing my own lunch to help cut costs so that it'd be easier for me to set aside money for Deirdre's potential visit. And so, with my money-saving cheese sandwich bobbing in a paper bag by my side, I followed Julia out of the building and headed downtown. Our little stroll led us to a wall along the river overlooking the island where I had been attacked by that kamikaze pigeon during my first week in Ankerich. Julia hopped up onto the ledge, signaling me to follow. I placed my paper bag up on the cool stone, speckled with pale green lichen and moss, and followed her lead. She opened her plastic sandwich box and pulled out a peanut butter and jelly sandwich.

"Are you serious?" I laughed. "I thought Germans hated those things!"

"It's something I learned to love when I was living in the US," she responded with a smile. "My host mother made the best peanut butter and jelly sandwiches!" She took a bite and reconsidered her statement. "I mean, I know they're not hard to make, but somehow she made them better than anyone else did."

I thought about her comment, and how my mother used to pour us the best cereal when we were kids. Nowadays, she only touches milk if it's in a White Russian.

"Man, you want to be American so badly," I teased her. I reached into my bag and pulled out a bottle of water. With a twist of the cap, I was instantly soaked by a torrent of lukewarm foam. I had forgotten that I had mistakenly picked up a bottle of carbonated water at the supermarket. The walk down to the river must have agitated it enough to result in an embarrassing explosion.

"Ha! Look at you! Drinking *Sprudel!*" Julia teased. "You want to be German so badly!"

We both laughed.

Julia pulled out a little pack of napkins that I had noticed most Germans carried. I thanked her and tried in vain to dry myself off.

"So, you said you lived in the US? Whereabouts?"

"Near Baltimore. A town called Havre de Grace."

"Oh yeah, I've heard of it."

"Yeah. It was nice." She took a bite of her sandwich. "You know who's from there?" she asked me after a short pause, her eyes lighting up.

"Cal Ripken, Jr., I'm pretty sure."

"Who?" Julia looked confused. "I mean, maybe, I don't know. I'm not sure who that is."

"What? You don't know Cal Ripken? The Iron Man? He's like the best shortstop ever."

"Oh. Hah! No. I'm talking about someone even more important." She closed her eyes and held up her bottle of still water to her mouth as if it was a microphone. "I've been looking for free-dom!" she sang out exaggeratedly.

I laughed and shook my head, "I have no idea what you're talking about."

Her eyes widened in shock. "David Hasselhoff! The best American singer ever!"

"He's a singer?" I asked in disbelief. "I always just thought he was just some shitty actor."

"No way! He was my childhood hero! I loved him!" Julia's microphone had turned back into a bottle of water. She took a sip. "I still love him!"

I watched her look out across the river, pondering her love for David Hasselhoff. She was pretty in a girl-next-door way. Her tawny-blonde hair illuminated in the October sun somehow reminded me of home. And those eyes! Clover, fern, forest…

"I was so excited to hear he was from Havre de Grace. Or at least lived there at some point." She looked out onto the island in the middle of the lazy river. I followed her gaze, scanning from the bench with Deirdre's and my initials carved into it and out toward the bridge with its thousands of locks.

"So, what did you do in Havre de Grace? Was there anything to do in town? Or did you just go to Baltimore all the time?"
Julia readjusted herself and turned slightly toward me, brushing crumbs off her lap. "Well, I was busy with schoolwork most of the time. But I did go to the Baltimore Aquarium a few times with my boyfriend."

I took a mouthful of water to wash away the odd taste in my mouth. I rolled a tiny piece of bread from my sandwich into a tight, soft ball and tossed it into the water below me. A colorful duck idly paddling in circles eyed the soggy clump of white and glided purposefully toward it, only to watch it disappear into the mouth of a fish that appeared from the dark depths. Disappointed, it spun around and drifted back to where it came from in search of something else to eat.

I leaned back on my arms. "I don't know. I find aquariums to be depressing. All those fish and creatures just spending all their time searching for a way to get out. Swimming in circles, hugging the glass, hoping for an opening that will set them free," I commented.

Julia stared straight ahead, thinking. "No… most of them don't even really have much of a memory. Certain fish can only remember like thirty seconds or something. So to them, whichever aquarium they're in must seem like the entire universe spreading out before them. I feel like they get to rediscover their world every day. They get to live with species they might not have ever seen in the wild. Plus, it's much safer for them. Safer than the real ocean, where it can get really brutal."

"I don't know. I just feel bad for them. People come to watch something trapped try to escape. And somehow that's entertaining?"
"I don't think they're trying to escape. They're exploring." She looked down into the river below as if searching for fish. "And even if they know they're trapped, they have the chance to learn how to find excitement in the same environment. I find it peaceful," Julia attempted to end the discussion. "You should go there sometime and see if you think differently."

"Maybe when I'm back in the States. Though I generally stay away from Baltimore." I turned to face Julia. "You know it's the STD capital of the US?"

"What's an STD?" she asked innocently.

"A *Tripper*," I blurted out before I had the chance to think how I even knew that word, and what Julia would think of my knowledge of it.

"Oh! Wow! I didn't know that." Julia paused. "Where'd you learn that word?" she asked with a smirk.

"You know, I was just asking myself the same thing," I admitted, blushing. "But don't worry, I don't have a *Tripper*," I added, immediately cringing at the comment.

"That's good to know," Julia nodded, eyes wide open, lips pursed. "I'll file that under 'Useless Information.'"

She dangled her legs happily.

"You know how many jokes I can make right now about Baltimore? And crabs?" I said, a dirty smile creeping across my face, a rare feeling of rebelliousness spreading through me.

"Actually," I continued before I could allow common sense to stop me, "do you know which seafood is even more popular than crabs in Baltimore?"

Julia looked at me unenthused, but I noted a hint of a smile behind the serious facade.

"Clam-mydia!" I laughed at my own terrible joke, and Julia bowed her head, shaking it in exaggerated disgust. Strands of her wavy blonde hair half-obscured her face, but I could tell she was smiling.

"Oh, Tschake! That was the worst dad joke I've ever heard." Her accented pronunciation of my name was endearing and the cuteness overpowered the crudeness of my poor joke.

We sat silently for a minute, digesting our homemade lunches and watching autumn settle on the town. The quiet afternoon was staccatoed by the sound of colorful leaves scraping across the sidewalk. Gondolas floated slowly down the tiny river, albeit noticeably fewer than just a week before. The autumn breeze swayed the long, droopy branches of the solitary weeping willow extending into the river, sending ripples cascading out into the water. Mahogany nuts fell from the chestnut trees, the familiar caw of crows sporadically filled the air.

I realized I hadn't seen any squirrels yet in Ankerich, though they ran rampant back home.

"What are you thinking about, Tschake," Julia interrupted my thoughts.

"Squirrels. *Eichhörnchen.*" I thought for a moment. "You ever realize that that word is hard to say in both English and German?"

Julia pondered the question for a second, then sounded out both words. First in English, then German. She smiled.

"Where I'm from, there are a ton of squirrels. They're literally everywhere. When I was a kid, we used to even get squirrels in our house sometimes."

"Oh really?" Julia asked. "So what did you do?"

"Well, my dad set up a trap. One of those non-fatal ones. We baited it with almonds. One morning my brother found the trap with a squirrel in it. We told my dad, and he took us to the park, the occupied trap in the back seat with me, my brother up front. I remember how mean the squirrel looked. Like ready to attack. When we got to the park, my dad set the trap down facing an oak tree. He let my brother open the lever to release the squirrel. My brother is older than me, but he seemed nervous. In any case, he pulled up the gate to release the squirrel, and it bolted so fast we could barely follow it with our eyes. Right up the huge oak tree. Or at least we thought it went up the tree. Maybe it just kept running!" I laughed.

Julia smiled politely.

I realized how boring the story was, and I shifted my position to face her. "Anyway, the next day I found a squirrel in the same trap. But it wasn't the same squirrel. This squirrel looked scared, not evil. Anyway, we took it to the same place and faced the trap toward the same big oak tree. I wasn't scared to set it free, because I had seen my older brother do it the day before, and also because this squirrel looked so timid. So I released it. But when I opened the gate, the squirrel did nothing. It just stood there, frozen with fear. As if it was scared to leave the cage surrounding it. I remember feeling at first sorry for the squirrel. Then I got angry. I shook the cage, but the squirrel wouldn't budge."

"So what did you do?" Julia asked.

"Eventually, my dad came over and picked up the cage. He walked over toward the oak tree and shook the trap. The squirrel fell out and ran away, but not very fast, as if it had no idea where to go."

"Well," Julia said, looking out over the town as if to see if she could spot any squirrels. "That's the kind of squirrel that would love to live in an aquarium," she said. "If it was a fish, of course," she added with a smile.

"Anyway, Tschake, speaking of aquariums, I think it's time we head back into *our* aquarium. I know of a certain sea creature who will be very angry if we are late." She smiled at me slyly. For a brief moment, I was confused.

She lowered her voice, "You know, Ursula, *The Little Mermaid?*"

I laughed, relieved I wasn't the only one who had made the association. I hopped off the ledge and followed her back to the office, watching her ponytail bounce with her gait.

***

On the bus ride home, I thought I spotted Stinki. But he completely ignored me. Figures, I thought. He's probably just like the border guard. And Herr Meindt. And Uschi.

But, being that it was Friday, I decided I was going to try to have a little fun. Maybe look for a bar or something. I still hadn't heard anything substantial from Deirdre, but I was determined not to dwell on that.

After relaxing and reading some more Goethe, I got changed and headed out. Werther was too much of a self-pitying sap, and I was afraid I'd turn into him if I kept lying around my room despairing about Deirdre and lamenting my loneliness.

I had seen people walk in and out of the building in the center of the circle of dorm buildings, oftentimes with beers in their hands, and decided to head there in hopes of finding something to do or some company.

Passing the rooms lining the hall of the dorm, I could hear the sounds of other people's lives escaping through the doors: voices, laughter, TVs, wooden chairs being slid across uncarpeted floors. Though I had been feeling lonely, these soft, domestic noises were comforting.

Approaching the building from the outside, I could already hear sounds of revelry. I opened the heavy wooden door beneath the hand-carved marquee with the inscription *Kleine Freiheit*—the letter "l" blackened with what appeared to be marker—and was immediately ambushed by the atmosphere. Sweaty bodies swayed seductively, ensconced by swirls of cigarette smoke. Shrill laughter, high-pitched giggles, and the sharp clinking of glass bottles punctuated the thick wall of bass thumping from the shitty speakers stacked along the wall. A few tables lined one side of the room; the bar hugged the other. The room was only half-filled, and I could only imagine what the place would be like at full capacity.

I nervously approached the bar and ordered a beer. I had never been much of a drinker and had never really cared for the taste of beer. But, being in Germany, and telling myself this was my year to try anything, to be open to everything, to live life unrestricted, I figured it was the right time and place to start.

Taking in my surroundings, I sipped the beer. It was nowhere near as cold as I remember beers in the US being, which exacerbated the effervescence, highlighting the bitter hop tones and tingling my tongue.

I spotted an empty table toward the back and made my way toward it. Suddenly a strong clap jolted me, sending a splash of beer sloshing out of the bottle.

"Ey! Punk rocker!"

I turned to see Stinki grinning at me.

"Oh, hey!" I said, surprised and secretly pleased that he wasn't ignoring me as he did earlier on the bus.

He was sitting at a table, a pretty girl standing above him, casually dangling an empty beer bottle in her hand, apparently on her way out.

"*Also, tschüss Stinki!*" she said, grabbing her scarf from the table. She shot me a quick smile and left.

Stinki waited a few seconds, watching her from behind, then turned to me with a mischievous smile. "I wouldn't mind seeing her with nothing but that scarf on, would you?"

"Ha!" I responded, a little caught off guard. "No, I... that'd be good," I agreed, immediately thinking of Deirdre.

"So," he took a sip of beer, pointing to the empty chair next to him.

"What's new? I haven't seen you on the bus, or in the dorm... or here," he waved his arms, gesticulating around the bar.

"Oh, well," I said, taking a seat, "I was on the bus today, actually. I saw you."

"Holy shit! That WAS you!" He laughed, mouth wide open, clapping his hand on the table in exaggerated enthusiasm. "I thought that was you. But then I saw the nerd clothes and figured it couldn't be."

"Yeah, they're my work clothes," I replied, relaxing a little.

He nodded. "So where do you work?"

"Oh, I work for the American Studies department."

"Nice." He suddenly turned toward me. "Oh yeah, I'm Stinki." He extended his hand.

"I'm Jake. Jake Constantine," I said, deciding not to remind him he had already introduced himself.

He must've mistaken the look on my face, and explained. "Well, my real name is Arwin." The bottle met his lips and he sipped. "It's some old German name my parents decided to torment me with. It means 'King of Flatulence,'" he added, assuming an air of exaggerated nobility. A moment passed then he laughed. "Not really. It means 'friend to all.' Even Americans!" His laugh boomed out of him like a thunderclap. Like a dad unleashing his best joke.

I was taken aback. I felt like I had been hiding my accent pretty well. "How'd you know I was American?" I asked in disbelief.

He paused and stared at me in the universal, "C'mon"-look, following it up with a toothy, sincere grin.

"So," I tried changing the subject. "What do you study?"

"Study?" he asked incredulously. "Who does that? I'm only here for the *BAFöG.*"

I had read somewhere that students in Germany received some sort of stipend for studying, meant to cover their housing and basic necessities. I assumed this is what BAFöG meant, but I had no idea, and quite frankly, was just happy to be involved in a conversation.

"I'm officially majoring in sociology," he continued, "but I like to think I'm majoring in punk rock, with a double minor in beer drinking and women's studies… if you know what I mean!" He reached across the table and smacked my shoulder, laughing wildly.

Thinking of how the Germans could essentially go to college for free, take as long as they want to finish, and get paid the whole time made me feel a bit uneasy. My father had paid an exorbitant amount of money to support me during my four years of college, where I spent my time deconstructing Kierkegaard and Kant, and now here I was, filling in spreadsheets on the other side of the ocean instead of working with him as he had always dreamed of. Or at least since it had become clear that my older brother wouldn't be the one to do it.

"I had no idea this bar was here. I've been living in this dorm for a month now and this is my first time here," I said, trying to keep the conversation alive and my mind from my family or my future.

"It's the student bar," Stinki said, looking around. "It's not the greatest. But beers for a euro fifty? Can't beat it!"

I nodded and looked around. Most of the crowd was students, with the exception of two older men sitting at the bar, silently sipping their drinks, not engaged, but still content. Sitting in the back corner, one older man with terrible skin chain-smoked, his jaundiced fingers rolling the next cigarette while the one he had just lit burned in his lips.

"Student bar?" I asked. "But who owns this bar?"

"Owns?" Stinki looked surprised. "No one. It's run by the students."

This made no sense to me. Clearly someone had to own the bar. I asked Stinki to explain to me what he meant.

"I mean, the *Studentenwerk* technically owns the building, but the students do everything: place orders, clean, organize events, tend bar. They just don't get paid. I don't really know too much except that they get me drunk!" Stinki took a big sip from his bottle.

"Too bad the music here sucks," he continued. I strained to listen to what was playing over the loud voices and shrieking laughter. That Killers song about watching the girl you love go home with another guy. Thoughts of Deirdre started creeping out from the shadows in the back of my mind.

"Who's Dillinger Four?" Stinki asked, pointing to my jacket and saving me from my bitter thoughts.

"Oh, it's an American punk band. They're awesome. You don't know them?"

"No, I only listen to *Deutschpunk*."

"Oh," I responded, not sure how to continue, hesitant to keep talking about American bands with Stinki's hoodie image still fresh in my memory. I stole a glance at his current attire, relieved to see a different black hoodie emblazoned with the letters APPD in Olde English font.

"I don't really know any *Deutschpunk* bands besides Wizo," I admitted. "Who are some good bands to check out?"

"Holy shit! There's so many. I can make you a mixtape! Actually, I've got a great one I can copy for you. You'll love it!" Stinki's eyes widened with excitement. He started spouting off the names of German punk bands, each one more crass than the next: *Knochenfabrik, Eisenpimmel, Blumen am Arsch der Hölle, Casanovas Schwule Seite...*

"What? There are really bands named Bone Factory, Iron Pecker, Flowers on the Ass of Hell, and Casanova's Gay Side?" I translated, laughing in delighted shock.

Stinki squealed with amusement. "They sound even funnier in English!"

We both laughed and sipped from our bottles.

"Oh," Stinki yelled abruptly, placing his bottle down on the table with a demonstrative slam. "And *Dackelblut*! You can't forget *Dackelblut*!"

"Dachshund's Blood?! That's awesome!" I laughed. "My mom has a dachshund. He sucks!"

Stinki laughed, then turned serious. "Are your parents divorced?" he asked.

"What? No, why?" I blurted out, taken aback by the question.

"Oh, sorry. It's just you said, 'my mom has a dachshund' and not 'my parents' or 'we.'"

"Oh, I mean, yeah, they're still married," I answered, thinking about what my parents were doing right now. I glanced at the clock. Almost 9:30. That meant 3:30 in the afternoon at home. My father was probably still working, on the phone making a sale or driving to the next McMansion to give a showing. My mother was probably on her sixth vodka tonic or passed out with Seymour on her lap.

"So where are you from?" I asked, changing the subject.

Stinki tipped his bottle all the way back, finishing off the last drops.

"The Black Forest, a little village called Bad Schamdorf—or as the Americans would call it, Bad Pubic Village!" He laughed and stood up.

"We've got some great names down there! To the south is Furtwangen, or as I like to say *Furzwangen*—Fart Cheeks! It's not too far from Titisee!" He laughed again, eyes bright and mouth agape. "I'm getting another beer. Want one?"

I looked down at my bottle. "Sure, why not?" I said, remembering my plan to not say no.

Stinki got us another round, and we sat, talking for what felt like hours. Mainly about music, but also about girls. I briefly mentioned Deirdre, leaving out as many details as possible. Though we were speaking German the whole time, the conversation flowed flawlessly, the words came easily and effortlessly, as if my tongue had been loosened by the alcohol. Stinki felt like an old friend, someone I had known forever and spent my formative years with.

"So what got you into German?" he asked at one point.

I had never really given it much thought before; it had just seemed to be something I had an interest in. But with this question, I was forced to dig a bit deeper.

"I don't know," I said, sipping from my barely chilled beer. "I guess it started in fifth grade. We had to do a partner report on some foreign country. My friend Tyler chose Germany since his grandfather had been there in the war and had some old coins and stuff. We did all this research on the country and had to make food from there. I think we made bratwurst and sauerkraut." I laughed. "But it was weird—the day the project was due, Tyler didn't come to school. The next day, either. So I had to present it all by myself. I guess that's kind of where it all started."

"That's kind of like me and punk rock," Stinki added. "There was this kid, everyone called him *Stange*. He just showed up one day in our school. We were all little village kids, cut off from the real world, no cities near us or anything, just pigs and potatoes and folk music and shit like that. Then *Stange* shows up with a pink mohawk and torn pants. He gave me a copy of a *Die Ärzte* cassette and it was all downhill from there! Ha!" Stinki grew quiet for a second. "Well, I mean the stories are similar cuz *Stange* was around for like three months then just disappeared. No idea whatever happened to him. Maybe he's dead. Or even worse—no longer a punk!"

"Weird," I pondered, "the guy who got me into music kind of disappeared, too. Teddy. We used to dig through his dad's records and choose albums based on their covers. The Kinks, The Stooges, Alice Cooper. They were our favorites. That turned me on to other stuff, then the whole '94 punk explosion on the radio and stuff. Last I heard, Teddy was in prison. I guess that's pretty punk rock!"

Stinki laughed, which felt like a success, to be able to bring this guy to laughter.

"Well, punk rocker, I gotta get going, I'm heading back to my parents' house tomorrow. Gotta do some laundry. Not very punk rock of me, but for some reason, the girls seem to prefer the smell of fresh clothes over my own personal musk." He pulled the cloth from his underarm to his nose and gave it a whiff. "Ahhh, Eau de Stinki," he laughed and pushed his chair back. I stood up to say bye and he stepped closer and embraced me, catching me off guard. "I'll drop off that tape tomorrow morning before I catch my train. You'll love it!"

I thanked him and he left, clapping my shoulder as he went.

I sat back down and took in my surroundings. Everyone appeared so content. The room was filled with laughter, faces were all smiles. At once I understood why people enjoyed bars so much. Maybe it had less to do with the actual drinks, and more to do with the company. I thought of my mom, who never went to bars, always just drank at home. And was she happy? I couldn't remember the last time I saw her smile.

Above the noise of the bustling bar, "This Must Be The Place" by the Talking Heads began playing, cheery and light. I ordered another beer and headed back toward where the old chain-smoker was seated. Even he looked content. I found a spot up against the wall, leaned back, and took a sip. I was content with being a wallflower. Content with *Kleine Freiheit*. Content with Ankerich. Content with myself.

Chapter 6

Autumn enveloped the town and the townsfolk swapped their skirts and shorts for stockings and scarves. As their outfits grew thicker, the trees changed their wardrobes as well, one last show, as if bursting into fire before shaking everything off for the winter months.

I fell into a pretty comfortable rhythm. Work was easy, Ushi had been busy enough to leave me alone, and I had Fridays to look forward to, when Julia and I would eat lunch together.

Even Deirdre had written to me. An actual letter, two whole pages, handwritten. I had already put aside close to 200 euros, which was a good start to the money I'd need for her plane ticket in the spring.

Stinki had kept his promise and dropped off the tape the morning after we had hung out at the student bar. The selection was great—full of trashy, obnoxious *Deutschpunk*, most of the songs with silly, perverse lyrics.

I had been impatiently looking forward to the punk show on the 11th and had been preparing myself by taking in as much of the *Deutschpunk* as I could. I even bought an overpriced Walkman and some crummy attachable speakers from an outdated electronics shop so I could play the mixtape on my way to work, while sitting behind my computer at the office, and while sitting around my room at night. I memorized a bunch of the lyrics, and, as a result, had learned quite a bit of German slang.

I wanted to make a mix CD for Stinki but wasn't sure how. Figuring I would probably have to do it on the work computer, I started to come up with a tracklist for him, choosing from more straightforward, aggressive punk, which I thought he would prefer, and peppering it with some poppier tunes from lesser-known bands that I thought he might also enjoy.

The night of the 11th, I was sitting at my desk in my closet-sized room, drafting an email to Deirdre, letting her know all that I had been up to the past few days, about how much I missed her, her eyes, her smile, her scent, her hair… Yet, the words weren't coming as easily as I had expected.

I pushed my chair back from my desk, took a sip from the plastic bottle of Schloss beer I had bought from the Penny-Markt in town, and leaned back with my face to the ceiling. Staring at the shitty light hanging above my head casting misshapen shadows across the ceiling, I became aware of what sounded like chanting. I leaned forward and turned down the music. Sure enough, there was a quiet chanting— children's voices—coming from somewhere outside.

Looking down from the sixth floor, peering into the darkness of a November evening, I could again make out the sounds of children's voices. I looked to the left, straining my eyes against the darkness, but couldn't see anything. Turning my head to the right, I saw at least thirty eyes glowing like flames in the night, piercing the darkness with solemn intent. The eyes crept slowly, steadily toward my building, bouncing ever so slightly, as if hovering, suspended by an invisible line. Fear crept up my spine, reaching the nape of my neck and sending a shiver down my body. The children's voices grew louder and louder until I realized the eyes were not in fact eyes, but flames. Flames illuminating lanterns held in the hands of slowly marching children, chanting. Instead of relief, I was even more terrified.

Suddenly, an electric drill-like buzzing cut through the room and I jumped, knocking over the beer on my desk. I grabbed my laptop just in time to save the slowly creeping liquid from enveloping it in a malty embrace and picked up the bottle. I tossed a few pocket tissues on the puddle and realized the buzzing was from my phone.

Trying to quell the fear, confusion, and clumsiness overpowering me, I answered.

"Tschake! Hi!" Julia's voice came through from the other side, sounding like sugary syrup over the creepy chanting of the children outside. "What's up?"

"Uh, nothing. You know, writing emails and stuff… to my family," I stammered, still trying to collect myself.

Julia laughed. "Well, I'm just calling about tomorrow."

Tomorrow? I asked myself, nervously running through the calendar in my brain.

Julia must have noticed my hesitance. "Lunch. Tomorrow's Friday." A short pause followed, then, in a quieter voice, "I mean, if you still want to eat lunch together."

"Oh yeah, yeah, no, Friday, duh! Ha! I'm an idiot. Friday," I exploded, sounding like a total fucking idiot.

Julia laughed again, sweet and sincere, from somewhere deep beneath those perfect breasts of hers. "Well, I'm bringing a special treat from my hometown—we'll have a little *Teetied.*"

She paused for effect, or for my reaction. I had no idea what the hell a *Teetied* was, but I trusted her judgment and was just excited to spend another afternoon with her.

She laughed into the phone, reading my mind. "*Teetied* is an east Frisian name for tea time." She paused for a few seconds. "I mean, I hope you like tea. And cookies. I would bring a *Snirtjebraten* or some *updrögt Bohnen*, but they don't really travel well." She laughed again, and I thought about how the Germans chose the least appetizing names for their foods.

"Oh, awesome! Great!" I said, having calmed myself to at least sound somewhat normal. "I'm looking forward to it."

"Okay, see you tomorrow!"

"Yeah, thanks. See you tomorrow!"

I exhaled as if I hadn't breathed the entire conversation, then turned up the volume on my cheap speakers as loud as it could get.

"*Ich will dich ficken*" by *Casanovas Schwule Seite* was playing, upbeat and unserious, and I started jumping around, air guitar in my hands, singing along obnoxiously.

I felt dirty, with the lyrics about fucking spouting out of my mouth while Julia's phone call was still so fresh in my mind, her sweet voice still echoing in my head.

A sharp banging on my door, followed by a gravelly voice yelling "Constantine!" quickly interrupted my singalong.

I turned off the music, grabbed my beer, and opened the door. Stinki stood on the other side, donning a freshly dyed neon green mohawk, leather jacket, and Doc Martens, with safety pins in his ears and a huge grin on his face. In each hand, he held a glass beer bottle, raised shoulder high, as if presenting an offering. His smile faded to a confused look of dismay, lips pursed and eyes squinting. "What the hell is that shit?" he asked, looking at the plastic bottle of Schloss beer in my hand, half of it still foam from the spill a few minutes before. "That stuff's worse than American beer."

He looked me in the eyes, and in a flash, his look of dismay was erased by his typical ear-to-ear grin.

"Ha! Just kidding!" He shoved one of the glass bottles into my chest. I cautiously accepted, and he slapped my shoulder with his newly freed hand. "But for real, you gotta drink this stuff. "*Hofratsbräu—Ein echtes*

Bier. Ein geschätztes Bier." I read along as Stinki recited the slogan on the label.

I grabbed my coat, placed the half-drunk Schloss into the sink, stuffed the new beer into my pants pockets, since my coat impractically had no front pockets, and closed my door behind me.

Stepping out into the cool November evening, I inhaled the autumn air and exhaled in a puff of gray steam. Stinki rattled on and on about punk bands, lamented the lack of punk girls on campus, and rambled on about upcoming parties and concerts. I shuffled along by his side, awkwardly trying to walk at a normal pace, encumbered by the bottle of beer contained in my front pocket.

Stinki paused to take a sip of his beer, held in his gloved hand. He looked over to me and asked, shocked: "Where's your beer?"
I pointed to my front pocket and he laughed. "What is it doing there? I know the bottle is pretty cold, but that's a weird way to warm it up. It'll get all shaken up that way. I just hold mine in my hands to warm it up a bit."

He demonstrated by wrapping both hands around his bottle. I was confused. Warm up a beer? Who would want to do that? And wasn't he afraid of the cops saying something about him drinking in public?

I reluctantly took the bottle out of my pants pocket and struggled with the cap. Stinki laughed and pulled out a lighter. He took my beer, and with one swift movement, popped the cap, a torrent of foam erupting from the neck. He quickly shoved the bottle in my hand and yelled "Drink!" I wrapped my lips around the glass neck and sucked the foam, slurping obnoxiously. Stinki laughed hysterically. "A Shakesbier!"

We both laughed at the awful dad joke. Even though I was nervous about the repercussions of drinking in public, I felt comfortable walking with Stinki. It had only been about six weeks since I had arrived in Ankerich, and I had already made a friend. Even though I spent a lot of time alone in my room missing Deirdre, having someone to go out with from time to time helped take my mind off her, and I was grateful for that.

We sipped our beers as the bus rumbled down the hill into the sleepy town, where, in a spray-painted and graffitied house somewhere near the train station, a punk show was to take place. At one point we drove past a group of children with lanterns, reminding me of my living nightmare earlier.

"Stinki," I asked, "what are all those kids doing?"
He looked at me confused. "It's *Martinstag*. You don't have that in the US?"

I shook my head.

"Oh. Well, the kids make those lanterns and walk around singing songs and getting treats from people. It's named after Saint Martin, whoever that was."

I nodded in agreement, still not certain what it was all about.

"Every Martin I've ever met is a weirdo," Stinki mused, sipping his beer.

When we arrived at the *Schlachthof*, there was already a decent amount of punks milling around outside. They were all in groups of three or four, laughing and yelling, the clouds in front of their faces reminiscent of word bubbles in comic strips. Their look was at the same time uniform and unique: leather jackets emblazoned with *Deutschpunk* band names scrawled in Wite-Out; neon mohawks, many of them multi-colored; red-laced Doc Martens; chains adorned with spikes and Mercedes hood ornaments. I looked down at myself—blue jeans, black Chuck Taylors, blue bomber jacket with a few patches and pins, all depicting American punk bands—and instantly felt out of place.

Luckily for me, Stinki seemed to know everyone there, and so the punks left me alone. At one point, a towering, mean-faced skinhead, vaguely familiar, loomed over me. "*Und wer ist das?*" he asked Stinki, all the while staring down at me, a mousy girl standing in his shadow.

Stinki laughed and said, "*Das ist der Ami—Jake!*"

The scary skinhead eyed me up and down. With an ever-so-slight nod, he responded in the deepest, most booming German I've ever heard: "Looks like one of the Cockney Rejects."

I couldn't tell whether this was a compliment or an insult, so I just nodded. Best not upset this guy, I thought to myself, as he turned and wandered off. "That's *Prügel*," Stinki whispered into my ear. "He's fine. A nice guy, actually. But kind of weird." He paused for a second. "Come to think of it, I think his real name is Martin. Didn't I say they were all weird?" He laughed and clapped me on my shoulder. Then it hit me. That penetrating stare. The tiny accomplice. That intimidating voice. "*Deutsche Wut!*" I shook my head and followed Stinki, as he wandered among the people standing outside the venue.

"And hey, we need a real punk rock nickname for you, too." He furrowed his brow in thought. "*Yankee* is too lame. *Ami* too unoriginal. Hm. We'll find something."

We finished our beers outside, Stinki excitedly talking to anyone who passed by, me silently sipping, trying not to stick out too much.

Stepping into the *Schlachthof* I was assaulted with neon lights, graffiti, and punk rock blaring at an oppressive volume. The walls were plastered with flyers and posters for events, both past and upcoming. There were no chairs or tables, but some of the younger punks were sitting directly on the filthy floor. One end of the room was occupied entirely by a professional stage, and the opposite end was lined with a bar. I immediately felt at home. The song playing over the speakers was familiar, yet foreign at the same time. I strained my ears to determine what it was. The music and voice were recognizable, but the lyrics were all in German.

Bad Religion, I finally identified the melody. "Punk Rock Song." But *auf Deutsch!* Everyone was singing along, pogo dancing and spilling beer everywhere. Even Stinki at my side was singing along to Greg Graffin's weathered voice. Within seconds I found myself singing along—albeit the English lyrics.

The bands who played weren't particularly great—three-chord street punk with growled, incoherent lyrics—but the crowd loved it. They danced—or slammed into each other—the entire night, more energetic and enthusiastic than any punk rock show I'd been to in the States. I asked Stinki how popular the one band was, and he looked at me confused. "I've never heard of them."

"Crazy," I replied, taking in the scenery—all reckless abandon and crooked smiles.

Stinki swilled his beer and smiled. "But punk rock is punk rock, right, Constantine!" he yelled, holding up his bottle for me to cheers with.

"And if you think this is crazy, wait 'til you see *Unser Haus!*"

I nodded in agreement, completely unaware of what he was talking about.

After the show, we stopped by the döner place for a late-night snack and last beer. As we waited in line, I pointed out the "fuck of Tanja" graffiti scrawled on the wall next to the ordering window. Stinki and I both laughed at the ignorance of whoever was trying to insult Tanja.

With our steaming kabobs in our hands, we continued on our way, deciding to walk back to the dorm rather than take the bus. Out of nowhere, with a mouth full of spiced meat, cabbage, and garlic sauce, Stinki asked me if I had any tattoos. I picked a piece of purple cabbage from my teeth and said yes, less embarrassed to admit my shitty tattoo to him than I had anticipated. Most people had no idea about it—even my friends at home—since it was such a stupid idea to begin with.

He acknowledged my response with a quick head nod and a burp. Before I could ask if he had any tattoos, or what made him think of the question in the first place, he held up his index finger in a "Wait-a-second" motion, handed me his döner, and placed his beer on a concrete ledge. He looked around quickly then unbuckled his belt, dropped his jeans and underwear, and presented his ass to me. Even though it was dark, I could make out some scribbling on his right cheek.

"Oh." I had no idea how to respond.

"*Geil, oder?*" Stinki asked.

"Yeah," I responded, still no idea what was written on his ass, and why he was showing it to me in the first place.

He pulled up his pants, buckled his belt, took a long pull from his beer, then reached out to take his döner back from me.

"*Ich hab mir 'Fuck Off' auf den Arsch tatöwiert,*" he sang out in his gravelly voice. It took me a second, but then it hit me—*Knochenfabrik*. The song "Fuck Off" he had put on my mixtape, about someone tattooing "fuck off" on their own ass, but backward since they used the mirror to do it. And how their boss has no idea what it says when the guy presents it to him.

I started singing along, Stinki surprised that I learned the lyrics so quickly.

"Sorry I was so confused at first. I couldn't figure out what it said," I apologized to Stinki. "I felt like the boss in the song."

"Ha! *Geil!* That's what we'll call you—*Chef!* The boss!"

We both laughed and clinked our beers. My own punk rock nickname, I thought to myself, feeling a sense of belonging surge through my body with an electric warmth.

We walked along, making our way up the steep hill. We could see some of the lights from the dorm lit up in the distance as if it were smiling at us with missing teeth.

"So what about your tattoo?" Stinki asked, much to my dismay.

I finished my beer and tossed the empty brown bottle into the bushes to my right.

"Well," I said. "It was kind of a dare. From my ex-girlfriend. Or girlfriend, I guess," I corrected myself. "It says *Schatz*, right above my penis. Luckily it's usually hidden by my pubes." Fortunately, the darkness concealed my embarrassment. Embarrassment for my own stupidity. Embarrassment for talking about dicks and pubes in front of someone I had known for barely a month. Yet somehow, I felt liberated talking about it after keeping it a secret for so long.

"Why *Schatz*?" Stinki asked. "Is that an English word, too?"

"Well, no. It was what I used to call my ex-girlfriend. Or girlfriend now, I guess. Again." For the life of me, I could never figure out which tense to use when talking about me and Deirdre.

"Cool," Stinki responded, and I was grateful he didn't press me any further. We walked quietly alongside each other for a while, the only sounds were the dried leaves crunching beneath his Doc Martens and my Chucks.

"The irony of the whole thing is that the reason we had originally broken up was that she cheated on me. With the piercer who set me up with the tattoo," I found myself talking before I even realized I had decided to continue.

Stinki stopped walking and looked at me. "So you got your girlfriend's nickname tattooed above your dick by a guy who wound up fucking her?" he asked.

"Well, not exactly. But I thought he was going to be the one doing it. I mean, I went into it thinking that. Not that he'd wind up fucking her," I added, "but that he'd be the one tattooing me."

I paused to catch my breath.

"Whatever. We're together now, so it's all good."
Stinki nodded and we kept trudging up the hill.

We're together now, so it's all good. But together how? There were 4,000 miles between us and we'd spent close to 1500 days apart before getting back together. After all that time, jumping right back into everything felt so… rushed. Forced, almost. I mean, it was comfortable, like sitting in your favorite chair. But even your favorite chair feels weird if you sit on it and it's been warmed by someone else's body heat. That warmth feels foreign. Off-putting. Gross, even.

I thought back to the first night Deirdre and I had spent together after our years of separation. Lying in her bed, going through the motions, trying to pretend there had been no distance between this time and the last time. I had begun peeling clothes off her slowly, wanting to cherish every moment. I started with the socks off her tiny feet, the toes as cute as I had remembered. Then her black jeans, a little snugger on her than four years before. She lay beneath me, just a white shirt—no bra—and pink panties. I peeled away the semitransparent white shirt and hesitated when I saw the tattoos, new and foreign. Two harps, black, already faded, poorly drawn and asymmetrical, resting right above the mini hills of her pelvis poking through her pale skin. I tried to ignore them but couldn't help think of Mikey. Or whoever had done them. I imagined her lying there, half-naked, while some guy drew on her, one hand operating the tattoo gun, the other hand… I shook the thought from my head and kept undressing her. The shirt gliding up her torso, revealing her belly button, still pierced, the fabric inching up toward her perfect breasts, the bubblegum-pink nipples ruined by the stainless-steel barbells bisecting them. My fingers found their way beneath the elastic of her panties, and I tugged gently, wanting this moment to last. Deirdre, eyes locked on mine, a calm expression of content on her face, lifted her hips ever so slightly. Effortless. Fluid. A practiced maneuver. She was completely nude beneath me, and I just hovered atop her, hesitant for a reason I could not explain. I stared at her pierced nipples, the black tattoos. I thought of the lyrics to Everclear's "Heroin Girl," not exactly the song you want to hear when you're about to have sex with the woman you love. When I had eventually stripped myself nude, unceremoniously, she pulled me on top of her and whispered in my ear, "I'm still on the pill."

I hesitated. It wasn't pregnancy I was scared of this time. I looked at the shitty harps, done by someone else's hands, most likely not paid for with money. A sock in the corner of the room caught my eye. Too big to be Deirdre's.

"Jake, I'm clean."

Sleeping with her for the first time in years felt like the old days, yet I couldn't clear my head entirely. The feeling of a chair warmed by someone else, a shared helmet in a batting cage, rental shoes at a bowling alley all circled my mind as I tried to show endurance and stamina after such a long time of celibacy, the only exception a few awkward nights with Olivia, my friend Aria's roommate. Afterward, we lay next to each other, nude and silent, the only sounds our breath and her heart beating in my ear. I didn't know what to say. I lay there, next to the love of my life, the person I spent my formative years with, the one to whom I lost my virginity, who I pictured my future with. The absent person who had occupied my mind for the past four years. The present, past, and future churned in my mind.

"I love you," was all I could muster. "I always have. And always will."

"I know."

And yet, here, in a different country, in the cold, walking next to someone I had met just weeks ago, everything felt just right. Stinki strode beside me in his confident, yet somewhat awkward, gait, his upper body leaning slightly forward, as if he couldn't wait to reach his destination, eager to greet everything ahead of him, a half-smile on his face, every few minutes casually taking a sip from his warming beer.

We passed houses with meticulously manicured gardens, our shadows growing and receding as we passed any house that still had a light on. The rhythmic shifting of shadows reminded me of the ocean. Of the time Deirdre and I had sex in the chest-deep water, allowing the waves to dictate the pace of our lusting. The same day the picture was taken of us, the one I couldn't stop looking at the day she broke up with me.

We stopped for a moment to catch our breath and to look out over the valley. An enormous hill rose up from the other side of the lazy river. Straight ahead, perched on top of the hill we were climbing, sat our grotesque, scab-colored student dorm, its ugliness masked by the night. Neither of us said a thing, but I was convinced we were both thinking identical thoughts: it's pretty nice here.

Stinki lifted a leg and ripped a fart that must've rattled the windows of the houses lining the sleepy street. He turned to me with his signature smile and said, "You still thirsty? I have something in mind."

It sounded cryptic, but I had grown to trust him. And this was my year to not say no. I had spent too much of my life wondering what the best thing to do was, the best decision to not let my father down. And for what? To be kept on his tracks, to follow in his footprints? Was that really what I wanted?

Besides, after the beer I drank in my room, the one we drank along the way to the show, the two I had at the show, and the one we took with us for the road—a *Fußpils*, Stinki had called it—I was feeling pretty good. One more drink couldn't hurt. And Julia was providing lunch the next day, so I didn't have to worry about that.

Back at the student village, we popped into *Kleine Freiheit* and each grabbed a beer before heading up to the sixth floor of the adjacent building. Stinki curiously had a lime in his hand, which I assumed he had smooth-talked the bartender into giving him.

We stepped off the elevator and turned left toward Stinki's hallway. In front of a door emblazoned with an obnoxious poster, ripped, folded at the edges and crookedly hung, Stinki fumbled with his keys and kicked open the door. What lay behind the door was a cleaning woman's nightmare: clothes strewn all over; ketchup-crusted plates piled up on the desk; empty beer bottles lined the walls; juice cartons, capless and on their sides, spilled sticky residue onto a floor caked in dust. Stinki had told me this was his first semester in Ankerich. Which means this mess had been made in less than six weeks. I couldn't decide whether I was appalled or impressed—and wasn't given the chance to since Stinki was already shoving things to the side to clear a path to the CD player. He pressed play, cranked the volume, then tipped the solitary chair forward, dumping its contents to the floor.

"Have a seat! Make yourself comfortable." He waved his hand in a welcoming gesture. "*Willkommen im Stinkreich!*" he said with a loud laugh.

I cautiously sat down and watched as Stinki got to work cutting the lime and pulling out two glasses, obviously not clean, but I decided not to say anything. From the stereo, a pounding bass sounded, followed by a distorted voice talking, not singing. It sounded familiar, but I couldn't place a name to the song. Stinki moved about the room with a purpose, knowing where everything was despite the mess. "Order through chaos," he called over his shoulder as if reading my mind, "kind of like punk rock!"

He turned to face me, brandishing two glasses filled with a cloudy, brownish-orange liquid. In perfect synchronization with the singer's voice booming from the speakers, he sang along. We clinked our glasses and I took a sip. Stinki knocked the entire thing back.

"Der letzte Drink," I said, recognizing the song at last. "That song by *Dackelblut* that you put on my tape." The singer—and Stinki—were yelling the ingredients.

Stinki banged his head to the music, and asked me, *"Geil, oder?"*

I took a bigger sip, hoping he hadn't noticed that I hadn't finished my drink in one gulp. "Yeah," I agreed, and I actually meant it. The drink wasn't bad—a sour concoction of rum, lime, and apple juice. And my mood was great. Despite sitting in a filthy room in a foreign country, I enjoyed the ambiance: loud punk music, a drink that wasn't half bad, and a friend who was all smiles.

I leaned back and listened to the music, as the singer repeated the recipe, each time adding more rum to the drink. *Der letzte Drink.* Somehow I felt this wouldn't be the last drink.

As I pondered the lyrics, Stinki stood up and grabbed the handle of the window. He turned it a complete 180 degrees like I had done the day of my arrival, nearly killing myself, and let the window fall a few inches toward him. Then he took a seat at his desk and started fiddling with something, his back hunched, obscuring what he was up to. I looked at the window, dumbfounded that there was apparently a special way to open it just a crack, where the pane leans inwards allowing the air to flow through the top, while preventing rain from getting in. I silently laughed at myself, at my fake near-death experience.

Stinki finished whatever he was doing, closed a drawer in his desk, turned to me, and held out his hand. In it was a sad cigarette, wrinkly and pointed at the tip. The smoke curling up from the pinched end smelled herbaceous and astringent.

"Haschisch?" he asked. From behind his extended arm I could see his brown eyes lit with excitement and his face twisted into a devilish grin.

What the hell, I thought to myself, reaching out to take the joint from Stinki's offering hand.

Chapter 7

My legs could work, but they were caught on something. I was sitting down, my hands gripping a rope that bound my feet and was tied to a black truck that was slowly driving away. The tension heated uncomfortably in my sweaty palms, stretching and pulling. My belly scraped the pavement as I fell back, twisting, and struggling. The microscopic fibers of the rope bored into the thick skin of my palms. Just as I was about to break free, the driver threw it into reverse, backup signals suddenly alerting its approach. I loosened my grip and took a deep breath to scream, the beeping coming closer, its warning growing louder.

7:15 flashed red on my alarm clock.

I slapped it off, rolled onto my back, and took a deep breath, noticing a tightness in my chest. The combo of *der letzte Drink* and the hash must've worked as a tag-team to wreak havoc on my dreams, I thought as I coughed phlegm onto the uncarpeted floor next to my bed.

A hazy cloud followed me throughout the day, a tom-tom hammered dully, monotonously in my brain, and I could barely choke down what Julia had brought for lunch. The butter cookies disintegrated into dusty crumbs in my mouth, fighting each other for any stray drop of saliva on my tongue. The tea was good but did nothing to replenish the liquids depleted from my body. And to make matters worse, Julia turned the whole process into an ordeal.

"So, Tschake, your first *Teetied*. I didn't bring the proper cups, and there's no *Stövchen*, but shh. Don't tell anyone." She smiled, digging around the wicker basket she had brought with her. "It's hard to do a proper *Teetied* out." She finished setting up the cups and took a deep breath. "So, first your *Kluntje*," she said, dropping an asymmetrical clump of crystalline sugar into my cup. "Then comes the tea," she continued, pouring a stream of steaming black tea from a thermos onto the chunk of sugar. "Listen to it *knistern*," she said, looking up at me, a smile squinting her eyes. For a brief moment, the warmth of her pride and excitement eased my hangover. "And, now for the *Wulkje Rohm*," she said, her voice taking on a Frisian twang as she carefully spooned a tiny dollop of cream around the side of the teacup.

"Don't stir!" she warned me, her eyes stern.

"Fair enough." I blew on the edge of the cup, sending swirls of steam off into the air in front of me, and took a sip. Each sip gave way to a different flavor, from the mild, milky smoothness of the cream to the earthy, herbal bitterness of the tea, followed by the thick, sugary sweet finish resting at the bottom of the cup.

"Are you sick, Tschake?" she asked me, showing genuine sympathy.

"No, no. I'm fine," I was able to mutter, struggling to chew with a dry mouth while simultaneously muffling my burps. Mini tornadoes of leaves whirled outside—we had opted for the atrium near the main entrance of our work building as a result of the cold.

"What are you thinking about? You're never this quiet."

I couldn't answer her. I didn't know what I was thinking about. I was hungover and, if I was being honest with myself, pissed that Deirdre had been ignoring me. Her continued lack of correspondence had begun to weigh on me and I was growing less optimistic about her visit and more pessimistic that we could ever build a future out of the embers we had stoked just before I left for Germany. How long had it even been? Six weeks? And she had only written one letter and a few brief emails.

Julia sighed. "I know. You're thinking about a girl."

I turned toward her, her attention focused on the leaf tornadoes. Her hair was wavy and goldenrod in the sunlight that filtered in through the dirty windows, her green eyes focused on something outside, sharp and clear. Her leg brushed up against mine for a short second and I readjusted, crossing my legs and pulling away a bit.

"No," I lied. I still hadn't made any mention of Deirdre to her. But why should I? It's not like I was going to date Julia anyway. And yet, I felt like I was hiding something.

"Yes you are. I can tell," she turned to me and laughed. "Do you have a girlfriend, actually?"

I didn't know how to answer her. *Actually,* I didn't know how to answer that question myself. What were Deirdre and I? She had said she wanted to be with me, but what did that even mean? I mean, physically speaking, we could not "be with" each other.

I popped another butter cookie into my mouth, washed it down with a sip from my tea, shifted my weight to face Julia, and said, "Tell me about your family." Though we had eaten lunch together almost every Friday for over a month now, we hadn't talked much about our families. Not that I wanted to talk about my sorry excuse for a family, but Deirdre was a topic I wanted to discuss even less.

"Well, they're normal, I guess." She considered this statement, looking back out across the walkway outside. "My brother Markus is two years older than me. He studies in Cologne. My parents are cool, we get along just fine." She tucked a stray strand of hair behind her ear. "My dad's a real jokester. He has the worst jokes. But the best, in a way." She flashed her Colgate smile, her eyes crinkling up at the corners. "He works for a tea company—the one who produces this stuff!" she said, extending the thermos toward me in an offering gesture. I held out my cup and allowed her to repeat the process of sugar clump, tea, and cream. "My parents are from a little town called Freihafen. But I was born near Bremen. Actually, we lived right near this little village called Völkersen. And you know whose family is from Völkersen?"

"Let me guess," I said, dryly. "David Hasselhoff's."

Julia smiled.

"For real, though! It's the truth!"

We both laughed, and I shook my head in exaggerated disgust at her Hasselhoff love.

"And your family. What about them?"

I should've known this was coming. It was my own fault for asking about her family. All so I wouldn't have to talk about Deirdre.

And what should I say? That my father was a workaholic who wasn't around much when I was a kid? That he had my life planned out for me ever since my older brother turned out to be an addict whom I hadn't seen or heard from in I don't even know how long anymore. How my sister, the sweetest little ten-year-old, had severe learning disabilities and various cognitive impairments. She required a lot of care, which neither my never-present father nor my always-inebriated mother were capable of. Who was taking care of her now since I wasn't around, I asked myself. I had felt that tug of guilt all four years I was away at college, but I did my best to make it back every chance I got to check up on Claudia. I pictured her now, probably sitting in front of the TV, basking in its blue glow.

"Well, my dad works a lot. My mom... kind of just does her own thing. I haven't seen my brother in a while." I was trying my best to come off as nonchalant and neutral, but it was tough trying to sum up my parents' mirage of a marriage and the sham of a family I was dealt. "But my sister's cool," I tried to salvage the sadness. "She's a sweet kid."

Julia smiled at me, then looked away. "That's nice," she said, sensing my disinterest in talking about my family. I wished I could tell her how grateful I was that she didn't make me open up the sores about my family or Deirdre.

I took another sip of tea and looked out the window. The old violin-playing beggar had made his way onto the campus and was playing his shabby tune near the bike stands, hoping to collect a few coins from the liberal college students.

> "'And so the conversation slips
>
> Among velleities and carefully caught regrets
>
> Through attenuated tones of violins…'"

Julia's voice interrupted the violin playing. I looked at her with a puzzled expression.

"'I shall sit here, serving tea to friends…'" I added, as soon as it came to me.

She turned, her eyes widening. "So the punk rocker also likes poetry?" she joked, her wide eyes crumbling into mirthful slits.

I returned the smile. "Kind of. I mean, I like T.S. Eliot. I love 'Portrait of a Lady.'"

She turned back to face the violinist. "Me too. I'm actually working on translating some of his works. Well, re-translating."

"Hm. I always thought translators were like the cover bands of literature."

Before I could realize how that came out, Julia had turned to me, an expression of exaggerated insult on her face. She stared at me, mouth agape. "*Fick dich!* Can you translate that?"

At first I felt bad, then I felt a sense of honor, hearing her actually use German with me.

Her playful smile returned. "So, the punk rock poet has jokes, too?" she asked.

"Sorry," I could taste the regret in my mouth. "I'm just kidding. I think it's cool you translate. And T.S. Eliot? Respect! That's no easy task."

We watched as the violinist packed up his case, either content with his earnings or too cold to keep playing outside.

Still looking out across the campus, she continued. "That's actually what brought me to Ankerich. There's a pretty good translation program here." She blew on her piping hot tea, her lips pursed into a soft circle of pink.

"I mean, why else would I leave the North Sea, the beaches, the breeze, even the seagulls? Leave and come here, to uptight, conservative Schwabenland?" She laughed exaggeratedly. "Surround myself with workaholic, penny-pinchers with their *Kehrwoche* and *Putzwut*. And that Schwäbisch dialect! They sound like little children with a mouthful of *Spätzle* trying to talk underwater!"

I laughed. I had heard Stinki slip into his dialect before and had no idea what the hell he was saying. And Herr Meindt? Nevermind!

"And speaking of food! The stuff they eat here? It's all heavy or just… I don't know. *Maultaschen, Linsen mit Spätzle, Saure Kutteln!* Blech!" She stuck her tongue out, feigning vomit. "And don't even get me started on the beer. You don't know how much I miss a crisp, clean Jever. Or even a Flensburger. They just don't have that soft, Frisian water down here."

I had no idea what those beers were about. My limited experience with German beer was with Hofratsbräu, or *Geschätztes,* as Stinki and I had nicknamed it after its slogan. I felt the warm, sludgy mass of tea and cookies in my belly rise to a cresting wave, and I realized thinking about drinking was not the greatest idea.

"Oh!" Julia blurted. "Did you hear? The *Weihnachtsmarkt* this year has been extended! I mean, that's at least ONE thing the Schwaben do right."

I didn't really know what she was talking about, and truth be told, I was never really a fan of Christmas. The faux-family happiness always bothered me. Forced smiles and false gratitude for presents I neither wanted nor needed, all accompanied by super corny carols and cheesy decorations. And, to make matters worse, right at the onset of the worst season of them all. Nevertheless, I was happy for the distraction from the discomfort in my belly brought on by the previous night's poor decisions.

"Oh," I feigned interest. "Cool. But what do you mean 'extended'?" I toned up the interest a bit.

"Well, the market's usually only two nights. The third week of Advent. But, since Christmas falls on a Saturday this year, they've decided to run it from Friday until Tuesday, the 21st."

She looked me in the eyes. "The first day of winter!"

I didn't have the heart to tell her how much I loathed Christmas and winter in general. Instead, I just forced a smile, which wasn't hard looking into such an excited and pretty face.

"Cool," I said. "I'll definitely have to check it out."

"Yeah," she mused. "Oh, and did you hear that Heike is giving us off early this year? Instead of the 23rd being the last workday, she's closing the office on the 22nd. So the 21st will be our last day of the year!"

"Nice!" I said, nodding. "I guess most of the American students or whatever are going home for the break anyway. Or I guess they finish early, right?"

"Yeah. They study according to the American schedule. That's why their summer semester ends in like June or something, instead of late July."

"Oh yeah, I forgot about that."

"Yeah," Julia looked down, almost sad. "The first day of winter," she repeated, "and also my last day in the office," she said, looking up.

I hadn't realized that Julia's internship was only for one semester. Or maybe I had but figured it would be based on the German semesters and that she would work through February. Even though I didn't really work with her, per se, it was nice having her around to balance the evilness of Uschi. I suddenly felt a pang of emptiness. And as a result, a flicker of foolishness. Here she was, sitting directly next to me, and I was lamenting the fact that in six weeks we wouldn't be working together anymore.

Julia began cleaning up, and I followed her lead. I thanked her for her thoughtfulness—and praised the deliciousness of the tea and cookies—and we slowly made our way back toward the office, each tossing one last glimpse out over the campus shedding its brightly-colored leaves for the brown and gray tones of winter, as if it were in a rush to be ready for the first day of the approaching season.

Chapter 8

Snow was forecasted for the night and the sky confirmed that prediction—a solid gray that extended from the colorless streets into the depths of the contourless clouds. The trees had shaken off most of their leaves, and those that were still left to blanket the ground were various shades of lifelessness—soggy, rusted reds, damp, decaying browns, sad, unhealthy ochres.

My mood matched these muted shades of misery. I had awoken feeling bright and cheery, excited for the last day of work before the holiday break, even excited about the Christmas market.

Then I read Deirdre's email and my mood curdled.

Jake,

Hows germany? Thanks for the pictures you sent me. The town looks really beautiful! Sorry I never wrote back Ive just been really busy and stuff with work and all.

Anyway Ive been thinking a lot. I think it might be best if we were to take some time apart from each other. I dont know I think I just need some space. I know what your thinking that Im just pushing you away again but thats not true. Its just that I need to spend some time figuring things out for myself. I still love you and all but I dont know. I guess what Im saying is its not you its me.

Also I feel like Im taking away from your time in Germany. I want you to have fun and not worry about me. Ill be fine I promise.

Be safe and have fun. We'll see each other when you come back in the spring.

Hearts and kisses,

Deirdre

Disgusted and angry, I powered off the laptop, the disappointing email disappearing into a plain black screen reflecting my own miserable face.

Her words echoed in my mind as I rode the bus to work. The first day of winter. How fitting, Deirdre. I guess it made sense: she made her attempt at rekindling whatever we had had on the first day of fall, why not shut it all down on the first day of winter?

We'd lasted one whole season.

I was particularly annoyed at the Dear John email. No greeting, just my name. The insincere question about Germany, as if I hadn't been trying for the past three months to tell her about it. Her mention of "work," which I told her I never wanted to discuss. The mention of time and space, as if four years and 4,000 miles weren't enough. I particularly appreciated the "and all" added to her half-assed proclamation of love. "It's not you, it's me," and "Hearts and kisses" were wonderful additions as well. And how kind of her to reassure me she'd be fine, without ever once thinking if I would be fine. And early March isn't the spring, I thought to myself, shaking my head in disgust.

Hearts and kisses.

And all.

I turned on my iPod, hoping to find some music to fit my bitter mood. Kill Creek's "Busted" felt seething and angsty enough. That is, until I heard the lyrics about the filthy things happening back in St. Valentine's Garage and instead felt buried beneath sour thoughts of Deirdre.

As I watched the town slide by through the foggy window, superimposed over my forlorn face, I couldn't help but think of our beginning. A group of us had met up at the high school football game and Deirdre and I wound up getting separated from the rest. At some point after half-time, she said she wanted to go home, and I offered to walk her back. My hands fluttered at my sides the whole walk. Deirdre was rambling on about her cat and I was using up all of my mental energy just to not say or do anything stupid.

When we had made it to the other side of town where she lived, Deirdre stopped mid-sentence and stood still in her tracks. I stopped a half-step ahead of her and followed her gaze to a backyard.

"Let's do it!" she said, an excited grin spreading across her face. My eyes bounced back and forth from her face to the backyard until I noticed it: in the center of the yard was a huge pile of leaves, close to five feet tall.

Before I could protest—after all, we were trespassing on someone's private property—Deirdre had grabbed my hand and was tugging me along behind her. In one swift motion, she hopped the fence, and I didn't even have time to think about what I was doing. I followed her— a sign of things to come—and we both jumped into the pile of leaves, disappearing into the depths of color. It was there, ensconced in a massive pile of dead leaves, that we kissed for the first time.

I should've read the signs. Deirdre and Jake, conceived in death.

The friendly female voice of the bus navigation system announced my stop. I had decided to get off one stop early to pick up a gift for Julia. At this point, I had already set aside close to 300 euros for Deirdre's plane ticket, and, after that email, I decided I could spare twenty or so to pick up a gift for the one person who I had spent the past ten Friday lunch breaks with. I decided on a bilingual collection of e. e. cummings poetry, *Like a perhaps hand,* translated by Lars Vollert. I figured it could provide some inspiration for her translation aspirations.

Since it was a Tuesday and not a Friday, Julia and I did not meet for lunch. I wanted to give her the present alone, mainly because it felt right that way, and also since I didn't want Uschi making any snide remarks. But I couldn't find the right moment.

Talk of the forecasted snow was nothing like it was at home. The excitement—that static anticipation lingering in the atmosphere—was entirely absent. Apparently in Germany they just talked about it factually, stating what is forecasted and content with expecting exactly that. Unlike the US, where each conversation adds an inch until it seems as if the apocalypse is approaching.

Luckily, work helped keep my mind off Deirdre. But as soon as the day started to slow, the disappointment returned. I wasn't even that sad, really. I was just annoyed. Pissed. At Deirdre for once again leading me on. At myself for believing her. And for living the past three months as if we were a couple again.

On the bus ride home, I mulled over whether I should even respond to the email and kicked myself for not having a chance—or enough courage—to give Julia her present.

I had decided against the Christmas market, choosing rather to sit around and read and feel sorry for myself. I had finished Goethe, that manifesto of self-pity, and had started reading the German translation of *The Catcher in the Rye.* But even that was too mopey for me, and I decided to take a break after reading enough of Holden whine about being alone and lost and breaking his own self-made rules.

With my anthology of Kierkegaard writings in my hand, I made my way out to the balcony, thinking about how in college, after Deirdre had just walked away from our relationship—literally just walked away—I had used all of my competing emotions as fuel to focus on my studies, partly to keep my mind off of her, but also to prove to myself and to her that I was better than her, that I could succeed and be something, and that maybe, somehow, this would help me win her back.

Despite the forecast of snow, the cold had not yet set in. I put my feet up on the rails and delved into the book, nodding in approval at the chronically morose philosopher's melancholic musings on human existence, and how its entire essence is uncertainty. But whereas Kierkegaard saw suffering as a beginning, an opening toward faith, I just felt defeated in my misery.

Not more than fifteen minutes of me being out on the balcony, I heard the door to the adjacent kitchen open and, ten seconds later, an earth-shattering fart. Heavy footsteps grew louder, then the sliding door to the other side opened and Stinki stepped out.

"Chef!" he saluted me, clumsily making his way over.

His ever-present smile was enough to slightly warm my miserable mood.

"Ah, Kierkegaard!" he acknowledged. I was shocked that he recognized the name. "Do you know that song by Pascow? *Kierkegaard und BWL?*" He immediately began singing text to a song I didn't recognize.

I faked a smile. Stinki picked up on it right away.

"What's wrong, Chef?" he asked, pulling up a plastic chair next to the couch.

"Nothing," I lied. "Just tired."

Stinki was preoccupied by the snow-laden clouds covering the sky and creeping over the mountains hugging the horizon.

He turned to me with an excited look in his eyes. "You know what?" he asked, not even waiting for me to answer. "I've got an idea. I'll come by your room in five minutes. It's too cold to be sitting out here anyway," he added, glancing again out over toward the horizon.

Though I wasn't really in the mood to do anything, I allowed myself to accept Stinki's positivity. If anyone could help me change my attitude, it was him. He was the type of guy who looked at a filthy pigeon and saw a rainbow on its neck. I was the type of person who looked for black in a rainbow. Why not go out and enjoy myself a bit? After all, there was nothing holding me back anymore. As if there ever really was.

Less than three minutes after leaving the kitchen balcony I heard a kicking at my door. I opened to find a grinning Stinki with two beers in his hands. "*Ein Geschätztes?*" he asked, extending one bottle toward me.

He walked in, looking around, fully taking in the room.

"Not bad," he reached his verdict, nodding approvingly. He stopped in front of my Hot Water Music poster. Before I could come up with a defense of the band, knowing that Stinki was more of the old-school punk type, he added, "I think I know them. I have a seven-inch with them on it. A split with Muff Potter." He turned toward me. "You know them?"

"Nah."

"Oh man, they're great! Just not as vulgar as some of my other recommendations."

I nodded, my unwillingness to talk still evident.

We sat down, me on my bed and Stinki on the chair.

He noticed the photo of Deirdre and picked it up. "Your girlfriend?"

"Yeah. Well, kind of. I don't know." I sighed. "No, actually."

He put the picture back. "No?"

"Na, she kind of broke up with me today. Or whatever. I don't know if we were ever really back together in the first place." I took a sip of beer to keep myself from talking.

"Shit." He said, sipping. "She's hot, man," he laughed. "Sorry, but she is!"

I forced a smile.

"So that's why you were all sad and philosophizing on the balcony. I figured it had to do with a girl."

I didn't respond and took another sip.

Stinki noticed my unwillingness to talk and leaned forward in the chair.

"Think of it this way: if you broke up, that means you're free."

"I guess."

"Not I guess! You're free! That calls for a celebration! We've got to celebrate your freedom tonight!" His voice rose and his face took on a look of genuine excitement. "And I've got the perfect way to celebrate! Hold on!" He finished his beer and jumped up, knocking the picture of Deirdre face down in the process. He lurched out the door, leaving it wide open. From across the hall and through the common bathrooms I could hear tinkling and banging coming from his room. Several minutes later he came lumbering back with two drinks in his hands.

"I've been looking for free-dom!" he sang as he handed me my glass.

We clinked glasses and I took a sip. I instantly recognized the taste: *der letzte Drink.*

Over our drinks, he convinced me to check out the Christmas market with him. He grabbed us each another *Geschätztes* and we headed into town, me doing everything I could to suppress a sigh.

The Christmas market had found a way to cram itself into every nook and cranny of the downtown. The marketplace housed the majority of the vendors—slender wooden booths occupied by elderly sellers, bundled up and donning heartfelt smiles. What couldn't fit into the marketplace spilled into the curvy streets and winding alleys, the booths misaligned like a crooked smile due to the cobblestones and five-hundred-plus-year-old streets.

Every couple of steps I was bombarded with a different scent. The earthy-sweet aroma of roasted chestnuts gave way to the spiciness of mulled wine. The smell of burning coals became enveloped by savory bratwurst. Sickly-sweet sugared almonds overpowered the rich and meaty fragrance of the mushrooms frying in huge pans. All of this was kept in check by the underlying evergreen essence emitted by the countless festive wreaths decorating the wooden stalls and the fresh, almost metallic scent of the impending snow.

Despite the cold and the crowds, jostling shoulder-to-shoulder at a crawling pace, I could feel myself smiling. This was like nothing I'd ever experienced before. And even after the disappointment of the morning's email, I felt ready to let go and embrace the evening.

Stinki and I finished our *Geschätztes* and each bought a bratwurst. I found it odd that the roll wasn't sliced, so I tore it open with my fingers and stuffed the sausage inside. Chewing, I watched as Stinki ate the meat separate from the bun and immediately felt out of place. He looked up, saw what I was doing, and laughed, his wide-open mouth displaying a half-masticated mess of bread, meat, and mustard.

"*Geil!*" he yelled.

We finished our food and Stinki told me to stay put. He mentioned something about *Glühwein*, which I imagined was the mulled wine everyone was sipping. He returned with two piping hot mugs, navy blue and emblazoned with a colorful depiction of downtown Ankerich decked out in mirthful festivity. We clinked mugs and sipped. The earthy spiciness of the cloves, cinnamon, and allspice was balanced by the sweetness provided by the oranges and sugar. The wine itself had a subtle kick to it, which tasted odd, though I had only ever sipped wine once or twice before.

Stinki watched me swallow the first sip with a mischievous smile. "Of course I opted for the extra shot of rum!" he laughed. "But be careful, this shit will DESTROY your skull tomorrow morning if you get too greedy."

We stood at the round wooden table, each with a foot up on the rail at the bottom, and sipped the mulled wine. I took in the sights: white Christmas lights, children holding their parents' hands, pointing with their free hands at everything that caught their eye, men with their arms around the waists of their girlfriends or wives, silently smiling and nodding. The air was charged with the electric anticipation of the snowfall. Moods were lubricated by Glühwein and urgency, knowing that the market would be over in a few hours, another 360-plus days until the next one.

I felt as if I should've felt something negative: jealousy, annoyance, frustration. Instead, I was content.

Before I could consider my situation any further, I felt a hand on my shoulder.

"Tschake? *Was machst du denn hier?*" Julia asked, using German with me for the first time since the day I met her. "I thought you weren't coming tonight. You had plans, right?"

I had totally forgotten that I had said that earlier in the day when my mood was still soured by Deirdre's email. I stood there, eyes fixated on her blonde hair creeping out from beneath a green wool hat, her eyes shining like emeralds, and couldn't say a word.

"He's celebrating his freedom!" Stinki yelled enthusiastically.

"Oh yeah?" Julia looked back and forth between Stinki and me. "Freedom from what, Tschake?"

I shook my head, cleared the cloudiness from my mind, and stammered, "Ha! Na, not really freedom, just that we don't have to work for a week!" Nice save, I thought to myself.

Julia looked vaguely convinced and smiled. "Anyway, we were just here to have a *Glühwein* or two. Mind if we join you?" She looked at both of us, then at her friend, a brunette with a tiny nose piercing and confident smile. "Oh yeah, sorry! This is Katja."

Stinki and I greeted Katja and told the girls they'd be more than welcome to join us. They agreed and sought out the closest *Glühwein* stand, shouldering their way through the crowd.

"That's Julia?" Stinki asked, eyebrows raised in question.

"Yeah." I could feel my face warming. I hadn't remembered mentioning her to Stinki but based on his question I apparently had. "My coworker," I added, and turned to watch Julia and Katja wait in line for their *Glühwein.*

"Well, shit!" Stinki commented. "She's even hotter than Deirdre!" He laughed, slapping me on the shoulder. I smiled back nervously and took another sip of the spiced wine.

Julia and Katja had their backs turned toward us, but their heads were leaning in together conspiringly. Despite the loudness of the market, I could hear them laughing. Katja was doing most of the talking. She put her arm around Julia's shoulder and whispered something in her ear. Julia pulled away from her grip, eyes wide open. Her surprise quickly turned toward what looked like embarrassment, and she turned back toward where Stinki and I were standing. Her eyes met mine, and I lifted my mug in acknowledgment. She forced an innocent smile and turned back to Katja, burying her face in her shoulder and laughing.

The girls returned, each holding their mugs in two hands, allowing the warmth to seep into their mittened palms and fingers.

"*Prost!*" they called out, as we clinked our mugs.

"You've got to look us in the eyes, Tschake!" Julia admonished me. "Otherwise you know what happens?"

Stinki interceded: "Seven years of bad sex!" He laughed, quickly adding, "But don't worry, Chef, you need to have sex first in order for it to be bad!" He bent over, clutching his stomach at his own joke, simultaneously pounding my back with his free hand. We all laughed, and I turned away to allow my face to return to its natural color.

The four of us stood at the table talking, laughing, and exchanging stories. I was more of an observer to Stinki's calm, casual, and confident storytelling, excited to be part of this, and happy to use my German with Julia for the first time since we'd been working together. Even though we had spent the past ten Fridays eating lunch together, it was nice to see her in a non-work environment. I thought about how lucky I was, despite all the negativity and pessimism involving Deirdre, that there was not only one person, but two people here in this foreign country, my ephemeral home, who accepted me for who I was and treated me as one of their own.

"What are you thinking about, Tschake?" Julia's sweet voice pulled me away from my thoughts.

"Uh, nothing, really. Just taking in the sights," I stammered an excuse. "This market really is nice, thanks for recommending it, Julia."

"And to think you were gonna spend the night sitting alone, drowning in *Weltschmerz*, reading philosophy and moping over some gi-"

"Look!" Katja interrupted Stinki. She held out her hand, catching the first snowflakes that were drifting gracefully from the sky.

Julia turned her face away from Stinki's, an expression of confusion slowly fading. We all looked at Katja's mittened hand, watched as the snowflake melted into a tiny droplet and was absorbed by the green wool.

"The first snowfall of the year," Julia mused, as if deep in thought. "My mother always told me you could make a wish on the first snowflake you catch." We all considered this for a second, then, as if on cue, all reached out our hands to catch a snowflake, silent for a brief moment in our wishes.

"You know what?" Stinki's eyes lit up. "I have an idea! What do you say we show these ladies our favorite little bar, *Kleine Freiheit?*"

Truth be told, I was perfectly content sticking around at the market. My aversion to Christmas had lessened significantly, not having to spend it with my barely functional family, and far removed from the capitalistic, commercial nightmare of the holiday season that dwelled in the shadow of Black Friday.

But I could tell Stinki had an ulterior motive. He and Katja had really hit it off, each of his jokes a home run with her, the two of them in what looked like an endless smiling competition.

The girls seemed to approve of the suggestion, so we finished our *Glühweins*, pocketed the souvenir mugs, and elbowed our way toward the bus stop. As we walked, I took in the sights one last time, knowing that in a few short hours this would all be gone—the booths dismantled and carted off by trucks, the decorations packed away for next year, the streets swept clean of pine needles and food wrappers, the pigeons having taken care of the dropped almonds and bread crumbs.

Along the way we stopped at the döner stand to grab a beer.

"*Prost,* Tschake!" This time I remembered to make eye contact. Julia's eyes held my gaze for a fraction of a second longer than usual.

Sitting on the bus surrounded by two friends and a new acquaintance, I felt ready to embrace the night. I could feel the warmth of the alcohol swimming through my veins, matching the heat coming through the vents next to me on the bus. Julia sat to my right with Stinki and Katja in front of us, giggling and tickling each other.

"Oh, by the way," I said, trying to mask my nervousness of sitting next to Julia, heading back to my dorm, "I have a little Christmas present for you. I didn't get the chance to give it to you today at work."

Julia looked at me, her green eyes bright as ever in the poorly lit bus, snowflakes melting on her wool hat, turning from individual, unique geometric shapes to tiny shining beads of water. "A present?" she asked with an ambiguous smile.

As we stepped off the bus, Julia took a quick glance at the departure times listed on the schedule. "The last bus here leaves at 1:35, Katja," she commented, her words falling on deaf ears. By this point, it was pretty obvious Katja wouldn't be taking the bus back with Julia. And the skies were predicting weather no bus would be able to drive in.

The four of us walked up the hill toward the bar. Music was already discernible from a distance, the heavy bass providing a background to shrill laughter and booming voices.

By the time we arrived at *Kleine Freiheit*, the party was raging full force. Bodies were packed together, gyrating rhythmically to the terrible music. The stench of sweat fought its way through shields of booze, cologne, and cigarette smoke. We had to shout to be heard over the deafening noise of jubilation heightened by the approaching holiday break.

I don't remember how long we stayed at the bar. Reality slowly began to fade and my body shifted to autopilot, my brain firing off directions and my body reacting. Images from my childhood resurfaced: Krang controlling his oafish body from a safe glass chamber. I felt as if each eye was operating separately, my vision two straight lines, fogged at the edges.

"So, didn't you say you have a present for me, Tschake?" Julia asked, her green eyes reflecting the lights from behind the bottles of booze lining the back of the bar.

Chapter 9

I opened my eyes and immediately regretted it. The sun reflecting off the fresh snow burnt a hole straight through the sludge surrounding my brain, bounced off the back of my skull, and pierced my eyelids from behind.

Rolling to my side I felt soft heat.

What the fuck! I thought, and quickly rolled back onto my shoulders. With my left eye half-open I stole a glimpse of the heat source next to me. Wavy dark blonde hair shielded a face. The duvet pulled down enough to reveal a melon-pink areola, the chest rising and falling slowly, rhythmically.

She stirred, yawned, and rolled over to face me. I quickly closed my eyes. Realizing how hard I was clamping the lids shut, I gently relaxed them, slowly, trying to set my breathing to mimic hers from moments before.

There was no way I could deal with this right now, I thought. Best just pretend I'm still asleep.

But what had happened? My mind raced. Pieces of the night fluttered back to me like the snow still drifting down slowly outside my window.

The Christmas market. *Glühwein. Kleine Freiheit.* The kitchen. My room.

Flashbacks of me lying on my back. Hands on my shoulders and in my hair. The awkwardness of new lovers, all teeth and pointy hips. The feeling of soft skin, punctuated with the sharpness of freshly shaven stubble.

I could tell she was awake next to me; her breathing had taken on a livelier rhythm. After what felt like an eternity, she sat up and scooted toward the foot of the bed. With her back to me, I dared to open my eyes a sliver. Her bare skin lit by the sun pouring through the window. Her wavy hair somehow only barely unkempt, falling in waves over her firm breasts as she bent over and picked up her bra and shirt, stuffing the former into her purse and slipping the latter over her head in one smooth movement. She stood up and I closed my eyes again, images in my head matching the sounds of her slipping on her panties and jeans.

She shuffled about, trying to keep as quiet as possible. An awkward silence filled the room, interrupted only by a slight scribbling.

One minute later she gently closed the door behind her.

A deep breath escaped my lips and I opened my eyes. I waited for the sound of the elevator doors closing before I got out of bed and checked to see if my door was completely shut. Then I walked over to the window and looked out. The whole landscape was blanketed in snow. The whiteness was blinding and Stinki's warning about the *Glühwein* screamed in my skull, chasing away fragmentary memories of the night.

Squinting, I watched as Julia exited the building and made her way to the bus stop, leaving fresh footprints and puffs of steam in her wake. Crouching beneath the window so only my eyes reached above the sill, I watched her disappear, not once looking back up at my window.

I took stock of my desk: two Ankerich *Weihnachtsmarkt* mugs, the rims sticky and stained with *Glühwein*. Two bottles of beer, mostly empty, the mouth of one greasy with lip gloss. A handful of euro coins.

A pack of cigarettes. A weathered book: *Prufrock and Other Observations,* by T.S. Eliot.

And a note.

Jake,

I had a great time last night! I hope you did, too. Thanks for giving me a place to stay after my dumb ass missed the bus.

Thanks, too, for the book! How thoughtful! Here's a little something for you as well. I hope you enjoy.

See you after the break! Merry Christmas!

xo Julia

I dropped the note back onto the desk and picked up the book. A bookmark protruded from page fourteen, *Portrait of a Lady.* "Thou hast committed—Fornication: but that was in another country…"

I clapped the book shut and tossed it onto the desk. Feeling the need to air out the room, despite the frigid temperature outside, I opened the window completely. I had no idea where the cigarettes had come from, but I took one out of the pack, counting fifteen remaining. With a green plastic lighter I found under the desk, I lit it. Freezing fresh air filled the room as I took the first drag, coughing instantly. I had never really smoked—neither did Julia, from what I remembered—but it seemed like the thing to do in this situation.

With lungs full of smoke, I turned and looked around the room: my clothes piled next to the bed. A condom wrapper next to the pile.

The framed picture of Deirdre, face down on the desk.

"Shit!" I thought. "Did Julia see that?" Then I remembered Stinki knocking it over, and exhaled with relief, silently thanking him for his clumsiness.

Then my thoughts soured: "Deirdre."

I could feel my mood shift, the hazy fog of confusion surrounding my head congealing into a caustic ether of regret. Was this cheating? Deirdre broke up with me, right?

Was this wrong?

I shook my head, which did nothing but send sparks of pain pinging through my brain.

I needed coffee. And water.

Groaning, I flicked the cigarette butt out the window, watching it disappear into the snow six floors below. Gingerly bending over to grab my jeans and rifling through the pockets to look for my phone, I noticed three wooden slats from the bed lying beneath the frame.

Luckily the kitchen was empty. That is, devoid of human presence. But evidence of the revelry that must have taken place the previous night was unavoidable. My shoes made a sickly suctioning sound as I walked across the *Glühwein*-stained linoleum, matching the sounds my brain made as it slowly peeled itself from the insides of my skull.

I took the last unused glass from the cabinets and filled it to the brim with tap water. In one gulp I finished it then refilled it, letting the water run the entire time.

Pushing aside bottle cap ashtrays and half-full mugs and glasses of beer, *Glühwein*, and other assorted beverages the color of the dipping water from a child's watercolor paint set, I took a seat at the table. A hookah was set up in the center and I remembered a comment from the previous night, when I naively asked what it was. "A hookah! A Middle Eastern water pipe. For tobacco. But then again, Bush probably has these things banned in your country!" followed by laughter.

Images of the party in the kitchen returned to me. Julia and I poking our heads into the room to see what the commotion was. The room packed with people, spilling out onto the balcony. Being asked if Julia was my girlfriend. Our awkward responses colliding clumsily like students at a middle school dance.

I had never let myself go like that before. I couldn't tell whether I was hungover or still half-asleep.

Maybe I was still drunk.

Of course I was all out of instant coffee when I checked. And the asshole who owned the coffee machine didn't have any coffee either.

I needed to get out.

***

The icy December air instantly awakened me. Despite the snow and ice blanketing the sidewalks and streets—apparently the Germans weren't as hell-bent on preventing lawsuits as the Americans were—I gingerly made my way by foot into town, the steady crunching of my feet on the ground muffled and muted by the cushion of snow.

Equally as surprising as the lack of salted streets and shoveled sidewalks was the lack of young children out and about. As a child, I had spent every snow day with either Tyler or Jamey, shoveling the neighborhood for money. Tyler and I would spend our earnings on cassettes, Jamey most likely on drugs. I could still vividly remember the eagerness with which I shoveled one January morning and afternoon, working til my back and shoulders throbbed, a fire burning beneath the skin and an ache set deep in my bones, all so I could buy a Catherine Wheel tape after seeing the video to "The Nude." The British band had served as my gateway into what I considered "underground" music, bridging the gap between my curiosity inspired by Teddy's dad's record collection and my contemporary taste in music.

Trudging down the snow-slicked streets of residential Ankerich, the song returned to me, the lyrics about doubt and naked lust, the texture of familiar skin all spinning around my clouded head. How a nude could break your heart.

I shook my head, trying not to think about the previous night. But the earworm would not go away that easily. Lines from the song were overlapping just as images of both Deirdre and Julia combated in my head.

Entering downtown, I stepped into the first café I could find and ordered a double espresso and an almond croissant. A flashback as the cashier placed the change in my palm. Neon lights reflecting off a filthy bathroom floor. The condom machine. Three euros a pack, only accepts 1-euro coins. Me asking for change at the bar, specifically requesting the change to be made differently. The bartender's pause, a devilish grin replacing his initial confusion.

Despite the temperature of the espresso, I finished it before I even left the café. I decided to check out the modest castle perched atop the hill in the center of town, hoping for a complete view of Ankerich in the snow. The croissant tasted spectacular. With the almonds crunching between my molars, I couldn't help but think of the squirrel story I told Julia. In an instant, I remembered another bit of the previous night, at *Kleine Freiheit*. Somewhere above the noise of the revelers and Stinki's powerful voice, Julia yelling "Squirrel!" breaking off midway into a choking fit of laughter.

Passing the church I remembered her question, *"Bist du jüdisch?"* I couldn't think of what could've provoked her to ask if I was Jewish.

The crunching and squeaking of the snow beneath my Chucks accompanied my thoughts as I made my way up the slippery hill. Half of me was struggling to recollect fragments of the previous night while the other half was attempting to build a wall around the events. Somehow I felt bad about what happened. Like I had cheated on Deirdre, though we were technically "taking a break." Still, I felt like I was deceiving her. I hadn't ever even mentioned Julia to her. Then again, she never really even gave me the chance to, even if I had wanted to. Similarly, I had never mentioned Deirdre to Julia, which in itself seemed deceitful. To both of them.

At the same time, it was almost exhilarating. I had never really had a one-night stand. Was it a one-night stand? Or did Julia expect more? Did she see it as a start to something? Or was she using me? The thought of being used for sex was new and exciting.

At the top of the hill, I leaned on the stone wall and took in the spectacular view. Ankerich spread out below me like a photo negative beneath a smeared newspaper-ink sky. The town was buried in soft snow, delicate and bright, and veiled in the thin, smoke-like fog of early winter. The red-brown clay roofs were dusted in a pure whiteness, naked trees dressed as if in clean linens, all of this reflected upside down in the frosty river, the non-frozen parts drifting lazily, viscously to the north.

An icy gust of wind blew up from below. I licked my lips to moisten them, looking down at the ledge Julia and I had eaten lunch on several times, and remembered the feeling of glossed lips, the slight taste of artificial strawberry.

I fumbled a cigarette out of the mystery pack I had pocketed from my desk. As my polluted breath mixed with the late December cold, the belltower rang, powerful and bold. Eleven solid clangs, resonating with thuds in my chest. Five AM on the east coast. Deirdre was probably still dancing. Or sleeping.

Where?

I thought of Julia at home, in bed, comfortable in pajamas or sweats. What did she normally wear to bed? Maybe she was sitting at her desk, a cup of piping hot tea warming her hands, sending up swirls of steam into the space between her face and the book I had given her.

Then I realized I hadn't gotten anything for Deirdre for Christmas. I took one last drag from my cigarette and flicked it over the wall. I exhaled a cloud of smoke and steam into the gray above and turned to make my way down the hill from the castle.

No point in looking for a Christmas present for her. With the holiday only three days away, there was no way it would even get there in time.

And would she even care?

***

A stampede resounded from the other kitchen. Glasses clinked, furniture was shoved, and heavy, clumsy footsteps stomped. I quietly stocked my cabinet with the instant coffee and canned soups I had picked up in town and tried to slink back to my room. From the other side of the wall erupted an earthquake-inducing fart.

Before I had the chance to react, the sliding glass door to the balcony slid open and Stinki appeared, clad in unfamiliar sweats and his all-too-familiar ear-to-ear grin.

"*Morgen, Chef!*" he yelled, then, looking at the grease- and dust-coated plastic clock, corrected himself. "*Eh, Tag, Chef!*"

He clomped over to me and clapped my back.

"Hey," I muttered.

"Pssh! Holy shit! Whew!" he jerked his head away. "Chef, your *Fahne! Geil!*" he laughed.

"My *Fahne?*" I questioned, scanning through my mental dictionary. Flag?

"Yeah, your *Fahne,*" he repeated, waving his hand in front of his nose, his face scrunched up in disgust. "Your *Alkoholfahne.*"

I realized I hadn't brushed my teeth that morning.

"Is it worse than what you just produced in that kitchen over there? Is that why you came over here, to escape the stench?" I countered, smiling.

His eyes widened.

"You heard that?"

"Of course I heard that! They heard that shit in Stuttgart, man!"

He laughed, bending over at the waist, eyes wrinkling shut.

"Man," he gasped, trying to catch his breath. "Speaking of shit, last night was a total shitshow, huh?"

A hoarse sound of agreement escaped my lips.

"Dude, that girl Katja just left." He scratched his head, then his ass. "Hopefully before I let that one rip!" He burst out laughing again. Though my headache had receded with the help of the espresso and the long walk in the cold air, I couldn't imagine laughing as hard as Stinki was. How was his head not splitting in half? Where did he get this never-ending wellspring of positive energy?

"Hey! Whatever happened to your Julia?"

I was trying to process his use of the phrase "your Julia" and didn't respond quickly enough.

"Wait!" His eyes lit up, and he took a step closer despite my *Fahne*. "Did she maybe... stay over last night?" He nudged my ribs conspiratorially. I stepped away from his playful prodding and took a few steps toward my cabinet to rearrange the items in an attempt to avoid facing him. He followed my lead, trailing at my heels like my mom's stupid dachshund. "So, Chef? Did you 'score,' as you Americans say?"

"No one says that anymore," I responded, hoping to derail his course of conversation.

He grinned. "I get it. A gentleman doesn't kiss and tell." He placed his hand on my shoulder. "I like that about you."

I closed the cabinet and turned toward him with a forced smile. "Alright, man. I'm gonna head back to my room. I'm beat from last night. I need some rest."

Stinki nodded and stepped aside to let me pass.

"Oh, Chef!" he called out from behind me. "What are you doing for Christmas?"

I had no plans. Lie around and read. Maybe Skype Deirdre, though that thought was growing more and more unlikely.

"I don't know, actually. Nothing, probably."

"Come to my parents' house. In Bad Schamdorf," Stinki said sincerely. "I'm planning on spending a little over a week there. You can come for as little or as long as you'd like. It'll be fun!"

I hesitated for a moment. Though I hated Christmas, it would beat sitting around feeling sorry for myself.

"Sure." I shrugged. "Why not?"

Chapter 10

The train chugged along through southern Germany, skirting dense forests darkened with coniferous growth and hugging quaint villages with pleasant names. Despite the frigid weather, the sun shone high in the winter sky, a ball of blinding gold set in the depths of a clean, cadet blue backdrop.

Stinki sang softly to himself. Through his tone-deaf rasp and heavily accented English I was able to make out something about a day in December and freezing cold weather.

I looked at him astonished. "You like Blondie?"

"Who?"

"Blondie. That song you were singing. 'Picture This.'"

"No, it's *Blumen am Arsch der Hölle*." Stinki looked genuinely confused. "Or maybe it's a cover." He paused to reflect. "I mean, it *is* their only song in English, so…"

We laughed and turned our gazes back to the beauty of the landscape flying by, so unlike the congested highways and potholed roads of southern New Jersey.

"Next stop's ours. My dad will pick us up there."

I nodded, my gaze still focused out the window.

"Another *Geschätztes*?" Stinki asked, not waiting for me to answer. He popped open two beers with his lighter and handed me one. With my right hand, I downed the warm dregs of my first beer, accepting with my left hand Stinki's offering of a not much cooler *Geschätztes.* After three months, I still was having a hard time getting used to drinking beers just a tick under body temperature.

"*Prostata!*" Stinki held up his beer.

"*Prost!*" I burped. Stinki laughed. He told me about the plans for the week: Christmas Eve dinner, presents, more Christmas festivities, maybe hiking in nearby Holdenach—*Hodenach*, Stinki called it—New Year's Eve with his friends. All of which seemed to me both foreign and exciting.

I couldn't remember the last time my family had spent Christmas together. The mornings usually consisted of a brief exchange of clearance-sticker presents, forced smiles, and fake wishes, followed by breakfast at the diner. Though the last diner breakfast we shared together was probably during my freshman year of college. No one talked. A few questions were asked about my classes, but as soon as I answered, my father just carried on about his newest sale and who he had just gotten one over on. Claudia played with her scrambled eggs, yet still managed to eat more than my mother, whose diner diet had devolved into taking advantage of the ten-dollar pitchers of Bloody Marys.

Even before leaving on this trip no one seemed to care that I wouldn't be around for Christmas, myself included. I doubt my mother would even remember I was away. Or that it was Christmas. But I felt bad for Claudia. The poor kid didn't deserve our sorry excuse for a family.

"*Nächster Halt, Huldendorf am Neckar,*" the conductor announced over the crackling intercom, indicating our stop. The train came to a sliding halt and we stepped out onto the mostly empty platform. A metallic blue BMW was waiting for us in the parking lot. An older man—thin gray beard, friendly eyes surrounded by a web of wrinkles—

popped energetically out of the driver's-side door and hurried over to grab our bags.

"*Morga Jungs, guad gfahra?*" he asked without waiting for an answer. He grabbed both of our bags and turned back toward the car, tossing them into the already opened trunk. "Wolfgang," he said to me, extending his large hand. A warm grin lit up his face and his eyes squinted playfully.

"Jacob," I said, returning the handshake and smile.

We stepped into the car, Stinki in the front and me in the back. As soon as we were buckled, Stinki turned to me and said, "My dad's a proud Swabian, but still drives a Bavarian car!"

He exploded into laughter as if it was the funniest thing he had ever said and slapped his father on the shoulder. "*Ned wahr, baba?*" His father mumbled something incoherent in the front seat: "*Da muadr isch Schuld dro, die alde Bayern.*"

The two of them babbled back and forth in an unintelligible bumble of gargled noises, even more exaggerated than I had heard Stinki speak before. I tried following along for a few sentences but gave up after less than a minute, too distracted by the beauty around me. Half-timbered houses dotted the snow-covered landscape peppered with spots of deep green and earthy brown poking through the frost blanket, aided by the clear golden sun shining above. Every minute or so we would slow down and turn onto a different street, each one growing narrower and shorter. Eventually, we coasted into a driveway which sat to the left of a two-story white house, its dark brown frame exposed like a skeleton.

"Welcome home!" Stinki said.

I had never really pictured where he had come from, though he had told me it was near the Black Forest. But standing in front of this beautiful home, after taking a drive in a spotless BMW, it was hard for me to picture my mohawked, ass-tattooed, fart-ripping, punk rock friend growing up here.

He pushed open a heavy oak door and we walked in. The house smelled of dark wood and domesticity, *Maultaschen* and memories. We walked through a narrow hallway lined with family portraits, opening up into a large living room. Next to the living room was a door to a bright, white-tiled room, where the sounds of cooking emanated—the staccato of a spoon being rapped against the rim of a pot, the faucet being turned on and off, oil sizzling in a pan. An aproned woman hurried out, wiping her hands with a dishtowel. She embraced Stinki and kissed his cheek. "*Mein lieber Arwin,*" she said, taking his face in both of her hands.

"*Muddi,* this is Jake, a friend of mine from Ankerich," Stinki introduced me, pulling away from her grip, his face slightly pink—from embarrassment, or his mother's violent squeezing and kissing I couldn't tell.

"*Guten Tag,*" I offered my hand.

"Martha," she said, taking my hand in hers. "*Freut mich.*"

"Actually, Jake's not from Ankerich. He's from George-Bush-Land!"

He laughed and his mother smacked him with her dishtowel. "Arwin, be nice."

I laughed and thought of his violent hoodie.

As if reading my mind, Stinki's mother asked, "Do you boys have any laundry you'd like me to wash?"

Stinki pointed to his bag. "It's chock-full of dirty laundry. Beer- and fart-infused," he laughed.

His mother shook her head with a half-smile, and, after I thanked her and told her I had no dirty laundry on hand, picked up his bag and disappeared into a different room.

Wolfgang sighed and said, "*Also Buaba, glei gibt's ebbas zom essa,*" and clapped us both on the back of our shoulders as he headed into the kitchen to inspect the meal.

***

After showing me my room for the next week—Stinki's sister's old room, turned into a guest room since she had moved out—we met up in the dining room for lunch. His mother had prepared for us *Zwiebelrostbraten* with *Spätzle* and red cabbage. The food was amazing—easily the best meal I'd had in years.

The conversation was primarily a three-person affair, with Stinki catching his parents up on his studies. I wondered what he was telling them, since, according to him, he had attended something like three classes all semester. But I had to just assume he was filling them with pleasant lies because it sounded like they were speaking underwater.

After a lull in the conversation, Wolfgang asked me, "*Schdudierschd au Soziologie mid moim Sohn?*" I looked at him confused.

"Dad! He's an *Ami!* You have to speak *Hochdeutsch* with him!"

His father finished his mouthful of *Zwiebelrostbraten*, wiped his lips with his linen napkin, and repeated, leaning closer to me and raising his voice several decibels: "*OB DU AU SOZIOLOGIE MID DÄM ARWIN SCHDUDIERSCHD.*" This sounded like the same exact question, delivered in the same exact underwater dialect, just louder and a bit slower. And followed up with a large forkful of red cabbage.

I was able to make out the words "sociology" and "Arwin" and put two and two together. I took a sip of room-temperature carbonated water and, in my best *Hochdeutsch*, answered: "Well, I'm at the university with him, but I don't actually study. I work for the American Studies department. I graduated college in May."

112

Stinki's parents seemed content with this answer. Martha lifted up the plate of *Zwiebelrostbraten* and asked, "Would you like another?" plopping another piece onto my plate before I could answer. Stinki burped, and his mother admonished him jovially.

"What will our American guest think of us if that's how you behave at the table?"

"This is my good behavior. You should see how I behave *away* from the table!" he laughed, open-mouthed, a mess of chewed beef and onions on display.

After lunch, a light dessert of cookies and coffee was served. The topic—from what I could understand—shifted to Wolfgang's impending retirement and his search for someone to take over the family business. He apparently owned a company that produced cardboard boxes. The company had belonged to Stinki's grandfather and he had planned on keeping it in the family. Stinki, however, had shown no interest in it, and his older sister, Anja, had already found a career and moved away. The biggest shock to me was Wolfgang's apparent complete understanding that his son had no interest in running the family business. It was less of a discussion and more so a question with a simple answer.

There was no argument, no sullen silence, no air of disappointment. No lecture on responsibility and expectation hidden in a frown. Just a question, an honest response, and a continuation of the conversation. It all seemed so simple.

Sitting there at that table with a real family—one who ate together, who talked to each other, who laughed and smiled and asked about each other, one who cooked homemade meals and offered seconds—I should have felt out of place. Instead, I felt at home.

***

The next few days were surprisingly pleasant. Surprising not in the sense that I was not expecting to enjoy myself with Stinki's family, but that I actually enjoyed myself over Christmas.

In Bad Schamdorf, the holiday felt like what I imagined it was supposed to feel like. Like a celebration of family, tradition, and generosity. Stinki's parents had even surprised me with a few thoughtful Christmas presents—a bottle-opener keychain with a scenic illustration of Bad Schamdorf, a handmade leather wallet with a coin pouch, three pairs of black socks, and a tiny glass jar full of homemade spiced almonds.

Floating along in my dreamlike trance of holiday mirth, I almost forgot to contact my real family.

On Christmas day, after we had eaten a wonderfully delicious late lunch—roasted goose, red cabbage, and dumplings, followed by an assortment of sweet and spiced cookies—I decided it was best to at least call. If anything to wish Claudia a Merry Christmas.

I politely excused myself and went to my temporary bedroom to make the call. Though I knew it would be expensive to call directly, Stinki's mother informed me that there was a phone in the room I was staying in and that I could use that one if I wished to have a bit of privacy. I thanked her and headed back to my room, feeling slightly guilty that I was not helping the family clean up after the magnificent meal.

Only after my father answered on the sixth ring did I realize I was holding my breath.

"Hi Dad."

"Hello? Jacob? Is that you?"

"Yeah. Merry Christmas."

"Oh yeah, Merry Christmas to you, too. Sorry, I was just going over some things. We've got this huge sale lined up… HUGE! Jake, things are looking up. I'm telling you, once you get back—whew!—we're gonna reinvent this whole goddamn market! I mean, just the other day…" He rambled on and I knew the schtick. I had become a pro in what I called filter listening, where I zoned out and instead thought of more pleasant situations, all the while making sure to pick up on keywords in case questions were asked, peppering the conversation with participatory tidbits like "yeah," "oh," or "gotcha," or, if I could tell by my father's voice that he was particularly animated, words like an unbelievable "really?" or an exclamatory "wow!" half-muttered in fake, astonished disbelief. This particular conversation featured the phrases "unheard of," "sitting pretty," and "a goddamn GOLDMINE!"

When I could tell he was nearing the end of his monologue, I dropped a few more participatory phrases and waited for his climax.

"I'm telling you, I've got you set up. I've already talked to Angelo, he's onboard. We just gotta get a few things squared away—you know, bullshit tests and stuff like that—but you'll be fine. I mean, you've got an Ivy League education, for Chrissake!"

"Yeah. Well, cool," I responded, eager to change the subject. "Is Claudia home? Or mom?"

"Oh. Yeah. Hold on a sec." I could hear as he cupped his hand over the mouthpiece of the phone and yelled for both of them, my mom's name first, then Claudia's, followed by my mom's name repeated again, this time louder and more annoyed.

"They're coming."

I thought he'd ask where I was, if I was spending the holiday alone, if I was enjoying my time in Germany. Something. Anything. Instead, in the ten or fifteen seconds it took for Claudia to grab the phone from my father, he remained quiet with the exception of, "Yep. Good stuff," which I could only assume was in reference to his—and soon to be my—work.

Claudia grabbed the phone from my father and yelled so loudly into the mouthpiece that I had to pull the receiver away from my ear.

"Jakey!"

"Hi Claudia, Merry Christm-"

"When are you coming home, Jakey?"

My heart slid into my throat.

"I'll be home before you know it, Claudia. In two months." I said this knowing damn well that in her young and tender mind, fogged by her ailment, that two months could have easily been two days or two years.

Before I could say anything else to convince my little sister that it wouldn't be too long until I returned, I could hear the unmistakable slight muffled click of another phone being picked up. A few sounds of clumsy fumbling followed, then a heavy breath.

"Jake, izzat you?"

"Merry Christmas, mom," I answered, my lack of enthusiasm echoing in my ear.

"Hi! Yeah! Merry Chrizzmas! Are you still over there in Djermany?" she asked.

"Yeah. I'm still here. But I was just telling Claudia that I'll be back for a bit in two months, right Claudia?"

I could hear Claudia crying. On the other line it sounded like my mother was trying to speak Schwäbisch through her nine AM buzz. Somewhere in the background, Seymour barked and my father cursed.

From the kitchen I heard Stinki's loud, boisterous laughter explode like a Roman candle.

"Well listen, I should probably get going. I don't want to run up the bill too much." Not like they even knew who was paying for it.

"Okay, Jake. Have fun."

"I don't want to say goodbye," Claudia said.

I took a deep breath.

"Claudia, don't worry. Before you know it, I'll be back. I promise. And I'll even bring you a present!"

The mention of a present seemed to console her a bit, though this was one of two days a year that presents were already part of the program. Then again, I had no idea how my family had spent the morning thus far.

"Claudia, do you know how they say goodbye in German?"

She sniffled.

"*Auf Wiedersehen!*" It means 'until we see each other again.' So just think of it that way—we'll see each other again. Soon!"

"Af vivizee, Jakey," she tried.

I said goodbye to my vacant mother and asked Claudia to send my regards to my father, who apparently had gotten back to his work.

Hanging up the phone I had a sudden overwhelming urge to call Julia. Or at least send her a text message. I pulled out my cell phone and started typing.

The green letters glowing on the black screen stared back at me. From the kitchen, I again heard Stinki's laughter pierce the silence. I paused, then pressed and held down the delete button.

***

The festive no man's land between Christmas and New Year's Eve was spent hiking in the Black Forest. The air was spiced with fresh pine and spruce and the cold felt crisp and clean, not heavy and oppressive as I remembered the winters of New Jersey to be, where the cold stole your breath and filled your lungs with an icy slush. Evenings were spent in the only bar in town. The smoke-filled, dark-paneled, and aptly-named tiny dive *Trinkbar* had more character than any of the shitholes in the suburbs where I grew up, so I didn't mind. We would sit around with three or four of Stinki's high school friends, swapping stories and swilling beers while old mustached men in short-sleeved plaid shirts sat silently slapping playing cards, soft with wear, on the table in front of them. The silence was periodically punctuated by the dull clunk of thick-bottomed beer mugs being set down heavy-handedly. There was never any music in the background, but the lone animated poker game tucked away in the corner near the bathroom provided a bubbling, tinkling soundtrack to the beery evenings.

"All they serve here is Ketterer beer. It's good, but be careful. If not, you'll find out why we call it *Katerer!*" Stinki joked to me. The punchline was over my head, still I laughed.

New Year's Eve was spent with the family, and even Stinki's sister and her five-year-old son Felix came to join us. The whole family sat around the dining room table and had a fondue dinner, basking in the warmth of the cozy fireplace, the logs periodically tumbling and emitting short bursts of sparks and ash. The conversation was light and casual, and laughter overpowered the sounds of hands dipping various cuts of meat into the simmering oil in the center of the table. Afterward, Stinki and I headed to *Trinkbar* to ring in the new year with his friends.

As the evening approached midnight and the previous year crept slowly, steadily toward its end, the drinks from dinner and the past two hours spent at the bar started sneaking up on me. Using my need to urinate as an excuse to step away from the table cluttered with beer mugs, ashtrays, and soiled napkins, I passed the babbling poker machine and stepped into the bathroom. Forcing out a few sprays of pee, I reached into my pocket to check the time. 11:54. An airy lightness brought on by the alcohol and my experience in Bad Schamdorf filled me, and for the first time I felt free. Like I could breathe. I inhaled deeply—a mistake given my location—and exhaled heavily. I suddenly had the urge to talk to someone. But before I could even decide who to text or call, my phone buzzed.

Guten Rutsch! xo Julia

I bit my lip and thought about how I could reply. Or if I should at all.

Just then I heard Stinki's thunderous voice, strained from excessive storytelling and laughter, yell, "Chef, it's almost time! Put your dick away and get out here!" Laughter followed. "Or keep it out, for all I care."

I dropped the phone back into my pocket, flushed, and stepped out past the lonely poker machine blinking away some Morse code message of solitude.

With the new year seconds away, and the past year, full of all of its milestones—college graduation, transatlantic move, Deirdre's return... and departure—I looked out across the town, fireworks already dotting the sky in premature celebration, and tried to feel something. From my left, a bottle was shoved into my hand.

***

Gravel crunched under our shoes in the patches of walkway that weren't covered in snow. The steady thudding of feet on ground matched the constant pounding in my head whenever we emerged from the tree cover and back into the winter-blanketed path.

Stinki had had the idea of walking off our hangovers in the forest that skirted the village. I grudgingly obliged.

The sun cut through the treetops and, though filtered through the dense cover above us, still assaulted my eyes, intensifying the headache I couldn't seem to shake. But the fresh forest air, icy cold and tinged with the sweet spice of fir, did what it could to wake me up.

All of the merrymaking from the night before—complete with my almost invincible feeling of freedom—had faded by the morning. The reality of a new year and everything that would come with it—the end of my time in Ankerich sometime in June, the classes and tests I'd have to take to get certified as a real estate agent, the future of sharing a workplace with my father until he retired, or, more likely, died on the job, the uncertainty of a future with Deirdre—had settled in heavily as soon as I awoke beneath the overstuffed comforter in the guest bed.

The change in attitude hadn't been lost on Stinki.

"*Alles klar, Chef?*" he asked. "You seem to be sad about something. Or maybe you're just really fucking hungover!" He let out a short, quick burst of laughter, scaring a large, black crow out from the thick foliage along the right side of the hiking path.

I smiled. The beauty of the surrounding area was astounding. Emerald hills rolled out in all directions, cresting and swelling into peaks dotted with tiny wooden cabins or blue-gray stone lookout towers. White snow, untouched by man or machine, dusted the faces of the hills where the sun hadn't had the chance to pull the green out from beneath it. Narrow, winding hiking paths snaked their way from village to village, delicately cutting across the hills, disappearing into the blackened forests before reappearing somewhere on the other side. Birds fluttered and tweeted, children laughed and screamed in pleasure, an occasional tractor sputtered by languidly.

"Could you ever see yourself living here again?" I asked.

Stinki spit out a shotgun-blast laugh. "Here?" he asked incredulously. "In Bad Pubic Village?"

Though he didn't say no, his answer was evident.

"I mean, it's beautiful, man!" I said, extending my arms as if presenting him this view for the very first time. "Just look at it!"

Stinki considered my comment. "Yeah, it's great to visit. Great to go for a little hike after a long night of drowning yourself in Ketterer—didn't I tell you that shit is dangerous?" He laughed. "But LIVE here? No way."

I looked around to see what could be so objectionable to living here.

"I mean, growing up here was great, don't get me wrong," Stinki continued, his voice a bit more subdued now, an unfamiliar tone of seriousness creeping into it. "As a kid, I was always outside. We played everywhere. Each day there was something new to discover." He smiled as if he were revisiting a secret favorite childhood memory. Then his face turned and the smile disappeared. "But as soon as I hit puberty it was like the blindfold was taken off. There was nothing to do here. NOTHING! The closest city was an hour and a half away. No bands ever came here. The closest place to buy CDs that weren't Herbert Grönemeyer or Roland Kaiser or fucking Heino was a half-hour away." He paused for effect. "It sucked, man. That's why I got out as soon as I was done my civil service. You think I really cared about going back to school? Yeah right! I just wanted an excuse to get out."

We walked side-by-side, flanked by the suffocating beauty. I could understand where Stinki was coming from—after all, I was asking to help sort out my own feelings about my hometown—but it was hard to hate on so much beauty.

"I mean..." I hesitated. "I ask because I feel like that's what I'm destined to do." I looked at Stinki. He looked back at me confused. "I mean, destined to spend the rest of my life back in my hometown."

I sighed. Stinki had been good to me. He had accepted me for who I was. He had never given me shit for any of my perceived shortcomings.

That I wasn't punk enough. That I couldn't drink as much as everyone else. That I had actually completed my studies and taken them seriously. That I was American. Come to think of it, I hadn't even seen that hoodie with Bush getting his brains blown out since the day we first spoke.

"So, I'm only here—in Germany—to buy some time. Like, I already graduated college. I already know how I'll spend the rest of my life. It's all figured out for me. I'm just here to delay the inevitable for one more year. Kind of like running away from home, but knowing all the while you're going to return to exactly what you were trying to escape in the first place."

I looked over at Stinki to see if he was following, to make sure he was able to understand my clumsy and accented German.

He was focused straight ahead but gave a slight nod to show he was listening.

"My dad runs a real estate business, and it's just expected that I'll work with him when I get back. Eventually take over the business."

Stinki nodded again, then looked over at me. "So, I mean, what's wrong with that?" he asked, genuinely interested.

"What's wrong with it is that I don't want to do that."

He nodded.

"And like, not only do I not give a shit about real estate—I mean, I studied philosophy and German, and I'm into punk rock and literature and stuff like that—it's also that I really don't want to work with my dad. FOR my dad, really. To have to live in the town I grew up in, to drive to the same office as him every day. To convince people to buy homes they can't afford so that we can make money off of them. It all just sounds so… depressing."

Stinki listened the whole time, taking it all in. "Well," he said, clearing his throat, which did nothing to relieve the raspiness of his voice, "then why are you moving back?" He looked at me.

I remained silent, thinking of the answer, which was non-existent. Or, existent, but repressed. I had the shackles of the past binding my ankles and the yoke of the future steering the way. I just wasn't yet ready to admit it.

"No chance there's a dark-haired girl waiting for you at home?" Stinki hinted in a hushed tone, one eye squinted, head slightly tilted.

I had no idea he was the perceptive type. As someone who expressed his feelings via eructation and flatulence, it seemed beyond him to be able to read another human's emotions.

"Well, I mean, there's Deirdre, too," I sighed. "There's always Deirdre. But," I continued, "that's another thing. She wants a break. I mean, we were together years ago, then she wanted a break—I mean, she broke up with me—then that was that. Years go by, I get my degree, I 'move on,'" this I emphasized with air quotations, "then out of nowhere she shows up again. Right when I'm about to move out of the country!"

We kept walking, snow crunching and squeaking beneath our feet.

"I feel anchored," I said. "Anchored to my future. To my dad. To the real estate business. I feel like I owe it to him, after my brother fucked up and all." I was letting it all out. The new year had breathed a new life into me. I was ready to own it all. "And anchored to the past, too. Deirdre. That's the past, but somehow coming back. It's still somehow there." I paused. "It might even be my future, who knows..."

I exhaled heavily, the cloud of steam momentarily obscuring my view.

"You know an anchor's only as strong as the rope bound to it," Stinki commented.

I stopped. Stinki kept walking but stopped as soon as he realized I had stopped walking. I waited for the fart. Or fart joke. But none came.

"Chef, an anchor can break. It WILL break, eventually. It'll corrode and crack. But before that happens, before the anchor itself withers away, the rope's gonna break. It's gotta. And even then, the anchor will still be an anchor. It'll still exist but serve a different purpose. A house for some crabs or mussels or something. It just won't anchor anything anymore because the ship it was anchoring has moved on. But before any of that can happen, the rope's gotta break. Or be cut." He paused and looked out over the scenic landscape. "That's where the real freedom comes from. When the rope to the anchor is cut."

I stared at him.

He looked back at me, his crow's feet spreading like cracks from the corners of his eyes.

"Or, better put, like that song," he added, changing his voice into a snotty snarl, quoting 30footFALL:

"When the past still runs your life

you're only living half the time.

Half dead or half alive."

"I don't know about you, but I want to live full alive," he added, delivering the last two words in English. Then he turned and continued walking.

I thought of the conversation the other day between Stinki and his father. How casually he had told his father he wouldn't be taking over the business. How free Stinki seemed. How the anchor of the future—and the past—didn't weigh him down.

Full alive, I thought to myself, slowly nodding in approval.

Cut the rope.

Then I hastened my pace to catch up.

Chapter 11

January and February crept by in a gray smear, the ash-colored morning skies bled seamlessly into drab and dreary evenings, the afternoons nothing but an uneventful afterthought. I no longer had Friday lunches with Julia to look forward to and I had not contacted her since the night of the Christmas market. Besides her quick message on New Year's Eve, she hadn't reached out to me, either.

Deirdre remained absent apart from one email I received from her in February. A quick spark of hope rose in my chest when I noticed the date—the fourteenth—but then settled into a sharp, acid-reflux-like burning when I realized it was just to tell me that she wasn't sure if she'd be able to pick me up from the airport. Valentine's only had one association to me ever since she'd started stripping.

Stinki had offered to accompany me to the airport, and, despite the early hour of the flight, he had come prepared, a backpack of clinking bottles in tow.

"It can go one of two ways," I said to Stinki about my impending reunion with Deirdre. "She'll either take me by the hand and whisper in my ear, 'Let's fuck,' or she'll look at me coldly and say, 'Fuck off,' then ignore me."

"Well, let's hope for the former!" he laughed, his crow's feet on full display.

I forced a tight-lipped smile. We hugged and said our goodbyes. I'd only be gone for a month, then I'd return and we'd pick up where we left off, we assured each other. I grabbed my bag lying on the floor between us and swung it over my shoulder, waving briefly as I headed toward the security gate.

The eight-hour flight awarded me plenty of time for reflecting on the past five months, and I found myself smiling and laughing out loud at times, thinking about Stinki's antics and fondly recalling my Friday lunches with Julia. I also had enough time to go over every possible scenario with Deirdre upon my arrival. The two scenarios I had given Stinki were the two extremes. The black and white. And there was an ocean of gray in between.

But it was March 1st. I was going to spend the entire month back home. March, the deceptively transitional month. Though it could be as cold and dismal as January, March signified the end of winter and the beginning of the slow, steady climb toward more pleasant weather and longer days, toward brighter mornings and later nights.

The cold season itself was a cruel joke, waving its despair in your face like a Polaroid developing a crime scene you never wanted to see. The silence of people trapped indoors searching for relief from the brutal cold and depressive, oppressive outside, every sound muffled by snow. The frigid, unbearable, and inescapable coldness. The colorless cities, not even white or black, but dressed in a drab monotony of muted misery. Dirty snow, exhaust-grayed skies, pale, somber faces smothered in depressing coats. Mornings that lead straight into nights. It even smelled of cold.

But March is the end of that. March is a beginning. March is a transition.

***

I landed at 7:15 PM, curious and apprehensive of how Deirdre would react.

Luggage circled in front of me at the baggage claim as I manually set the clock on my phone back six hours. I noticed Deirdre walk through the revolving glass doors, head down, preoccupied with a text message. She glanced up quickly, then turned her head back to her phone and continued typing without any change of expression. In no apparent rush, she made her way toward me.

"Hey Deirdre," I said with a smile as I embraced her, her body limp and nonreciprocal in my arms.

The car ride was short and the conversation was limited to quick bursts of questions and monosyllabic answers from Deirdre. She was driving a new car, an upgrade from her high school jalopy given to her by her estranged father. I figured she'd be making more money with the new job, but such a quick change of fortune seemed suspect to me. Squirming in my seat, I watched the mini-city of the airport bleed into the industrial surroundings as we made our way toward the bridge.

Back in New Jersey the suburbs sprawled and filthy snow melted in patches. I asked Deirdre if she wanted to go out for a drink to catch up after I dropped off my bags.

"Maybe. I gotta pick something up real quick. I'll see how I feel afterward." Her voice was quiet and flat. I sat there silently and listened to the music. A mixtape I had made for her years ago. Descendents' "Clean Sheets" was playing, and I leaned forward to turn it up a bit.

The lyrics made me uneasy, but I was happy to have a distraction. I knew she didn't care about my experience abroad, and as far as I was concerned with her, no news was good news.

"Want to come in?" I asked as we pulled up to my parents' house.

Deirdre looked straight ahead and shook her head absently, the pine tree air freshener mimicking her movements.

"So, wanna meet at Time Out in like a half hour?" I asked as I opened the car door.

Deirdre shrugged. "I guess."

I nodded and stepped out. As I slammed the trunk after grabbing my bag, Deirdre lifted her foot from the brake. The car was never in park.

***

The house was silent when I unlocked the door and walked in.

I wanted to call out to see if anyone was home, but stopped myself, knowing that Claudia probably had no recollection of my return.

Creeping on my toes toward the back room, I could see the glow of the TV flickering in the dark. There on the floor, sitting with her legs folded at an uncomfortable angle beneath her, was Claudia, eyes glued to the screen, a bowl of ice cream or cereal in front of her.

I watched her for a moment, gripping the door frame to hold myself still. Fearing I would terrify her if I snuck up behind her, I cleared my throat trying to get her attention.

She reached for the remote to turn down the volume, then turned her head slightly to the left to concentrate better.

"Special delivery for Miss Claudia," I bellowed.

She popped up and yelled, "Jakey!" Her bare feet slapped the hardwood and she projected herself into my arms.

"Hey princess, how've you been?" I asked her, squeezing her tight to my chest. Her fingers gripped my shirt at my side, and she buried her face into my belly. "I brought you a belated Christmas present," I said,

129

handing her a plush hedgehog holding a sign that said *Ich liebe dich* in pink lettering.

"What the hell," a groggy voice grumbled. "Jake, is that you?" A tired body rose and looked over the back of the couch. I hadn't noticed my father lying there; he must've been sleeping, hidden by the backrest.

"Hey dad," I said. He pulled himself upright and walked over to me.

"Welcome back," he said, his voice hoarse with exhaustion. He flicked on the light. "At least for the time being, right?" He forced a smile, and I noticed the salt outnumbering the pepper in his hair and beard.

Claudia started to say something but was interrupted by yapping and the sound of nails scampering across the uncarpeted floor. In no time, Seymour was at my feet, nipping my ankles and barking like I was there to murder the entire family. I glanced down at him and laughed, thinking of Stinki and his *letzter Drink* concoction, from the band whose name meant "dachshund's blood." Based on the amount of time he spent in my mother's presence his blood would probably get us just as drunk as that drink, I thought to myself.

"Wuthehell izzy yappin at now?" I heard from the other room, followed by the sound of a piece of furniture being banged into.

My mother appeared in the doorway, a glass in her hand. "Oh, hi Jake! I wasn't expecting you here!" She gave me a weak one-armed hug, careful not to spill her drink.

"I told you last week. And reminded you again today," my father said quietly, a look of exasperation on his face.

"Yeah, I just got in. I just wanted to swing by and say hi and give Claudia her gift."

Claudia had since resumed her position in front of the screen and was watching intently, volume back up, her new stuffed animal clutched tightly under her left arm and her thumb in her mouth.

My parents and I stood silently. Seymour had quit his yapping and was now cradled in my mother's free arm.

"Well, I'm gonna head out. I'm supposed to meet up with Deirdre at Time Out."

"Oh, okay." My father looked a little caught off guard at the mention of Deirdre.

I turned to leave.

"Oh, Jake? Let's talk tomorrow. Angelo's got some things for you to look over." He paused. "You know, to help speed up the process when you get back in June."

"Sure. Just let me know."

I grabbed the keys to the Toyota hanging from the hook next to the door and texted my friend Randy to tell him about Time Out, figuring a backup plan was a good idea since the promise of an enjoyable evening with Deirdre seemed farther from reality than originally anticipated.

"Oh, and Jake," my father's voice seemed closer, quieter. I turned to face him with the doorknob in my hand. "Be careful."

I smiled, genuinely. "Thanks. I'll be fine," I assured him, stepping outside and closing the door behind me.

***

The neon sign to Time Out cast a milky bluish-purple haze over the cars in the parking lot. The T and E of the first word were completely out, and some of the letters occasionally flickered like an insect struggling to free itself from a spiderweb. Deirdre's new car was noticeably absent.

Inside, I spotted Randy standing at a round table toward the back, laughing and acting something out exaggeratedly, trying hard to win over one of the girls there.

I approached the table and he turned to acknowledge me with a head nod. Without missing a beat, he handed me a full plastic cup of beer, the pale, piss-colored liquid lapping over the edges. "Welcome back, *Scheißkopf!*" he half-yelled into my ear.

I laughed and accepted the beer. Before I even had the chance to introduce myself to the others, I noticed Deirdre walking out of the bathroom, tucking something into her purse. I told Randy I'd catch up with him later and made my way toward Deirdre. I met her halfway at a high top with no chairs.

"Hey," I said.

"Hey."

The air was thick, the mood felt forced.

"So," I figured it would be a long night if I didn't even try, "what's new?"

"Nothing. Work. Same shit different day."

"What's wrong?" I asked, not really wanting to hear the answer. "Are you just not gonna talk?" I asked, growing weary of her emotional distance at the airport, in her car, here.

Deirdre finally stopped biting her nail and focused her attention on me.

"How many people have you slept with since me?"

The bar went silent. Or at least my ears stopped hearing.

"What?"

"Stop stalling. How many?"

I immediately thought of Julia. But Deirdre didn't know about her. And why should it matter anyway? I could think of at least five guys she had slept with in the year after we had broken up. Or was it seven? I could hear Stifler's voice buzzing through my brain, his lesson regarding the mathematics of male and female sex partners. "Didn't you fuckers learn anything in college?" and I winced at the thought of applying an American Pie quote to my life. But he was probably right about multiplying the number of sexual partners a girl tells you about by three.

In any case, I decided this moment wasn't the time to mention Julia. If ever. Then again, maybe the mention of Julia would ease the tension, douse her bitter mood with some jealousy. But would she even be jealous of me sleeping with someone else? Or just relieved? Whatever, I thought, not like there had been anyone else anyway.

Though there had been Olivia.

***

Olivia was my friend Aria's roommate, whose interest in me I always wound up shaking off, focused more on being available in the off-chance Deirdre would ever come back to me.

One night during a spring break I found myself at Aria's apartment. My friend Eric was dating her and was spending the night, so Olivia offered to let me crash in her room. We wound up fooling around for a minute or two before I stopped it. Things eventually progressed between us, but only ever when I spent the night there after a party. Olivia was usually drunk and I always felt guilty about it since I rarely had more than two drinks.

At one point I finally gave in to my friends' insistence of giving Olivia a chance and went on a date with her.

The ultimate kick in the dick was that Deirdre unknowingly ruined that date.

After a mostly pleasant dinner, we went to Eric's apartment to ease the awkward tension of the first date. As we were about to leave his apartment, Aria said, "Oh my God, I forgot to tell you guys! Remember Deirdre? You'll never guess where she's working now!"

No one guessed right. The news hit like a bomb. The fraction of a second between detonation and death when, despite the incredible noise, everything is silent and in slow motion. That's exactly how it felt.

The presence of the past had overshadowed the hope of a different future.

I left the house in a stupor, Olivia trailing me. I declined her offer to come inside when I dropped her off. I was tired, I told her.

In a way I was tired.

***

"So you're just not going to answer me?" Deirdre brought me back to the now.

"Why?" I asked, shirking the question.

"How many?" she persisted.

"One," I finally mumbled, hoping she wouldn't catch me in a lie.

"Who? That slut Olivia?" she asked, her voice showing premature signs of victory.

"She's not a slut!" I countered, louder than I had intended. I fiddled with the plastic cup. "This was before me and you were even talking again. You were with Mikey or Steven or Marco or Brian or whoever. We were drinking." I was making excuses and it was pathetic.

"You don't even really drink, so stop making excuses."

"Well, she's not a slut," I mumbled.

"Well, she is a slut, because I got an STD from you, which obviously came from her." Deirdre stopped spinning the plastic cup in her hand.

"Wait, what? What kind of STD? We always had protected sex," I stammered.

She broke her stare at her Michelob Ultra and looked at me with a smirk. "Always? How many times did you fuck her, Jake?"

I picked up my beer and drank slowly, changing my mind as soon as the beer registered on my tastebuds. The vinegary funk almost made me gag. Next beer better be a bottle, I thought to myself. "I dunno. Not a lot. But whatever, we were always smart about it," I said, wincing as I let out a burp. "What STD?" I repeated.

"Chlamydia. Does it really matter? That skank gave it to you and you gave it to me. So thanks."

My head was spinning.

"Deirdre, are you sure you didn't get it from someone else? Or from work?" I couldn't help but think that this was the first time I ever referred to her stripping as work.

"Fuck you."

In like a lion, out like a lamb? I thought to myself, wishfully.

"I have to take a piss," I said. I could feel Deirdre's eyes burning on my back as I walked from the table.

There were only three urinals in the bathroom and the middle one was occupied. Checkmate. The pisser was aptly dressed—stained white undershirt, black mesh basketball shorts, white socks slipped into black Adidas sandals, sunglasses on the back of his head, despite the dreary, miserable March evening. A visor. He was leaning forward, one hand propped on the wall above his head, spitting into the urinal. The urinal-spitters are a special breed, I thought to myself. The type of guy who buys body wash infused with pheromones and has a subscription to

Men's Health, though they only read the advice columns on "How to Last Longer" and "What She REALLY Wants In Bed But Is Too Afraid To Say Out Loud." UFC fans who wear Tapout and Punisher shirts, using the emblems to proclaim their own invincibility. The type of men who would name their boat *Master Baiter* if they could ever afford one. The ones who hang a set of rubber testicles from the hitch on their pickup truck. I never understood that anyway. If the balls were located there, would the driver then be sitting inside a urethra? Did the cab then take on the role of foreskin?

Shaking my head, I shuffled past the urinal-spitter and squeezed into a stall. Someone had left a nasty streak of shit along the side of the porcelain bowl and I concentrated my stream onto the smear, pissing the stain away. It felt good to pee standing up and not feel guilty as a result of the countless signs in Germany admonishing you to sit down to do your business.

Glancing to my left I caught some piss-room poetry. "All you talk-to-yourself-while-shitting-motherfuckers better hurry the fuck UP!" I mentally added these "talk-to-yourself-while-shitting-motherfuckers" to the same drawer as the "spit-in-the-urinal-slobs."

I used my right foot to stomp the handle, interrupting the silence left in the bathroom ever since spitboy shuffled out, obviously not washing his hands.

After splashing some cold water on my face I checked my reflection in the pale light seeping through the cracked plastic cover framing the glass, shining like a weak halo above my head. I looked defeated, but I just felt angry.

Back at the table, Deirdre stood absent-mindedly staring off into the distance. I approached her with an air of self-assurance, confident to not let her ruin my night and feel terrible for something I should not even have to explain to her.

"Hey," I said. "I didn't give you the STD."

She stared at me. "How do you know? I mean you've been fucking that slut Olivia for God knows how long."

"That's not true, Deirdre! And you know it. Besides—"

A shaggy-haired slob interrupted us.

"Deirdre! Hey!" He embraced her.

I recognized his outfit instantly: the urinal-spitter.

He turned to me, and his eyes widened. "Jake! Holy shit! Long time no see, buddy!"

"Hey Tyler," I said, extending my hand.

He looked terrible. His body didn't seem to quite fit into his urinal-spitter uniform. The collar of his slightly stained white t-shirt hung loosely around his neck, his pasty white skin stretched thinly across his protruding collarbones. His eyes were deep-set and dark, and his jawline was carpeted in a thin, patchy stubble. His dirty hands were capped by filthy fingernails, and his knees bore the faint marks of mud or scrapes. He looked like he had been landscaping, though it was winter.

"I didn't know you two were still together," he continued, looking back and forth between Deirdre and me.

"Well..." I said.

"We're not," she reported matter of factly, her words bulldozing my attempt at a response.

I rubbed at an orange stain on my shirt, probably from Claudia's Cheetos-fingers, trying to avoid eye contact with Tyler. Though we had spent so much of our childhood together, we had really gone our separate ways once he had introduced me to Deirdre. He had begun to retreat back into himself, growing more reserved and quiet, or spending his time with people I wanted nothing to do with. Rumors began to swirl about him—that he was doing drugs or selling drugs. I even heard someone refer to him as a pimp. I took another quick look at his clothes and chalked that rumor up to bullshit.

"So what are you guys up to? I heard you were in Germany or something," Tyler asked, eyeing me up.

"Yeah. Well, I was. I just got back a few hours ago."

He nodded, glancing over at Deirdre, who had her head down and was fiddling with something.

"So hey, I'm glad I ran into you guys," he said cheerily, propping his sock-and-sandaled foot up on the metal bar beneath the table. "I've been trying to organize this big get-together with a bunch of people from school. I figured we could all go to a Phillies game together. Pre-game in the parking lot beforehand, you know? Reminisce."

The idea sounded like a nightmare. But I wanted to keep Tyler talking. His interruption was a welcome break from the bickering between Deirdre and me.

"I figure like twenty-five bucks a person. I'll get us a group deal," he continued.

Not having any idea how this whole chlamydia situation would unfold, and under the naive impression that there was still something worth salvaging of us, I reached into the wallet Stinki's mom had given me and pulled out three twenty-dollar bills, their faded-tattoo green looking even duller behind the colorful euros.

"For both of us."

Tyler eyed the money.

"Keep the change," I added, figuring I'd just deduct it from the money I had been putting aside to save for Deirdre's visit to Ankerich. Which at this point seemed as likely as me being the one who gave her chlamydia.

"Well I'll let you two lovebirds catch up then," he flashed a quick smile, removing his foot from the bar, the wobbly table causing my still-full beer to splash over the plastic rim. Three steps from the table, he spun on his heels. "Oh, Jake, I forgot to tell you. I ran into Jamey the other day."

He flashed an ambiguous smile and turned back toward the bar.

An awkward silence shrouded us as Deirdre and I both frantically stockpiled arsenal for our next verbal assault. Before either of us could unleash, Randy appeared out of nowhere.

"Hey," he half-whispered, "I think I'm gonna take off with those two girls over there." He nodded ever so slightly toward the table he had been standing at all night.

Deirdre looked up, surprised. "Uh, hey. I was kinda hoping I could catch a ride with you," she said to Randy. Though they knew each other, I had never really seen them interact and was just as confused as Randy was by the proposition.

"Uh, sorry, Deirdre," Randy said, looking from her to me as if searching for an answer. "We're taking off right now, and I kinda, you know, just thought it would be me and them," he said quietly.

"It's fine," Deirdre mumbled softly.

"I'm sure Jake can give you a ride, right Jake?" He clapped me on the shoulder and left.

I didn't answer, unsure of how long I even felt like staying at the bar. The night seemed like a waste and showed no signs of changing course.

The two of us stood there uncomfortably.

"Where's your car?" I broke the silence.

"I got dropped off."

"By wh-" I decided not to ask.

Deirdre huffed and looked around.

I had to act quickly.

"Didi, it's not from me."

"Whatever, Jake."

I stared at a stain on the floor that looked like a lopsided smirk.

"I mean, just compare your history to mine. And your current situation to mine…" I took one more sip of sour beer and grabbed my keys from the table.

I didn't say bye. I didn't wait for a response. I just left.

Outside the air felt refreshing and cold. I filled my lungs with the icy March night and looked up at the broken bar sign before climbing into the Toyota.

"I'm out," I snickered to myself.

Chapter 12

Star Wars was playing in the waiting room of my pediatrician's office as I sat uncomfortably waiting to be seen. A twenty-two-year-old with a cryptic call requesting to be seen ASAP. I had scheduled a physical. "Just in case, you know?" I'd told my father to ease his suspicions when I'd asked for the insurance information.

My main motivation was to confirm my innocence and prove that Deirdre had contracted the disease from someone else. Though there was also a lingering suspicion in my mind that the disease was not new, the diagnosis was. Which meant there was a chance she had spread it to me when we had slept together before my departure to Ankerich.

I turned back to the TV. Luke Skywalker was maneuvering his X-Wing through the valleys of the Death Star, dodging attacks from TIE fighters, and battling his way toward the particle exhaust vent. Jamey and I would watch this movie every Christmas after our sad diner breakfast. Though I never cared for it, Jamey always insisted, and I began to regard it as some sort of consolation prize, the only real sense of family I felt on a day meant to be spent with families. As I watched Luke outsmart the Galactic Empire in a series of daring dogfights, I couldn't help but wonder where Jamey was.

"Jacob?" I jumped. Darleen, the receptionist, smiled sympathetically at my nervousness. "You can head back to the examination room." I glanced back at the screen just as the Death Star exploded in a sideways Saturn of stardust.

I headed down the tiny hallway to the last room, where I was instructed to strip down to my underwear and wait, while Mickey and Donald and Goofy judged me from their places on the wallpaper.

The door opened without a knock.

Dr. Schatz looked exactly the same. Old, but with a young man's haircut and youthful eyes. Neither of these matched his powerful, booming voice. A bass version of Ben Stein. The worst possible voice for a pediatrician.

"Back from Germany, huh?" he tried breaking the ice.

"Well, yeah. Just for a few weeks," I managed to stammer, my voice quaking.

"You know, I was there when I was just out of college." He paused, slapping on a pair of latex gloves. "Just me and five girls…" His eyes met mine, their icy blue piercing me, as if peering into my soul. "We traveled all over Europe. Spent a lot of time in Germany. Traveling with five girls can be taxing, but it can also be a lot of fun." He looked up again from his clipboard with a wink. My bare legs dangled from the paper-lined examination table.

"Yeah, I hear ya. Uh, that's kind of what I'm here for," I said, barely audible.

He looked up again. This time there was no wink.

"My ex-girlfriend says I gave her chlamydia. But I didn't. Well, at least I don't think I did. I mean, I think she got it from someone else, she—"

He waved his hand. "Let's have a look, shall we?"

I slid off the table and stood there, twenty-two years old with my pediatrician seated on a stool in front of me, rolling my penis back and forth like a salted slug between his cold gloved fingers.

"You know, I've got some German in me," Dr. Schatz attempted to alleviate the awkward situation. "I'm sure you could tell by my last name."

Then it hit me: the tattoo. I had gotten it shortly after my last visit to Dr. Schatz, my pre-college physical. So he had never seen it, and I stupidly—my judgment once again clouded by Deirdre—hadn't recognized the correlation between my nickname for my girlfriend and the actual name of my doctor. The same fucking word. And now my freshly-shaven dick—a hopeful-yet-futile gesture in anticipation of seeing Deirdre again—was proclaiming his own name, twelve inches from his face.

I could feel my face heating with the blood rushing toward it, and my few inches shriveled into a few centimeters.

"Are you sexually active, Jacob?"

As much as I wanted to respond to him with a snarky comment, I just muttered, "Kind of."

"You know, you should always use protection, regardless of who you are with. And you have to make sure you trust your partner. And if you are in a relationship, you should make sure to stay monogamous," he lectured, assuming a total opposite stance from the "I-traveled-Europe-with-five-girls" one he had taken less than four minutes earlier.

"I know. I am monogamous. Well, we're not together anymore, but I was."

He slid my shrunken penis back into my boxer briefs and looked me in the eyes.

"Do you trust her?"

"Well, I mean, yeah," I said. Lied.

He smirked. "Well, I can't see anything that looks off. But I'll refer you to a urologist. He'll be able to give you a better read." He scribbled on his clipboard for a moment, then turned to walk out. With the doorknob in his hand, he turned and looked at me. "Be careful who you have relations with. You might not actually know them as well as you think."

He almost looked fatherly. And I almost actually liked him at that moment. I wanted to hug him for not saying anything about the tattoo. "Get dressed and I'll meet you at the receptionist's desk." He left, closing the door behind him, leaving me alone with the slanted scrutiny of the Disney gang.

***

"Good morning, Jacob. Fill out this paperwork and then we'll need you to produce a urine sample in this cup here." The receptionist at the urologist's office was about my age and attractive. I awkwardly took the cup from her outstretched arm and leaned forward. "I, umm, I'm here for… well, um… I don't think you need the…"

Unfazed, she interrupted at regular volume, "Doesn't matter what you're here for. It's standard procedure. The bathroom is the first door on your left," she pointed down the hall, never looking up from her computer screen.

"Okay. Thanks," I muttered.

After I "produced a sample" and placed it in front of the receptionist, muttering something like "Here you go" or "Here" or whatever you say when you hand over a cup of piss, I took a seat in the waiting room.

I was by far the youngest person in the half-empty room, the rest consisting of old men and women, mostly men. They looked up at me with milky, glaucoma eyes and went back to staring at the walls, since they could no longer focus on magazines. The walls were covered with informational posters about prostate pills and incontinence relief. I joined them in their silence, the only noise in the room provided by Engelbert Humperdinck or one of those old crooners whining about old love or new love or some phony shit like that.

The urologist was a younger man, probably less than fifteen years older than me, and his tenor voice was pleasant and calming.

We made small talk about school and my time abroad. "So what brings you here?" he asked, cutting to the chase.

I kept my explanation short.

He had me drop my pants and examined my penis silently. What a shit job, I thought to myself.

"You said it was your girlfriend who told you you gave her chlamydia?" he asked, letting the elastic band of my boxer briefs snap back to my skin with an ugly smack.

"Ex," I corrected him.

"Well, I detect no evidence of chlamydia. The urine sample looks fine, you show no signs of any bacteria—"

"But I thought you couldn't tell without a blood test or—"

He shot me a slanted look as if I were really trying to challenge his expertise. "As far as I can see, the only thing out of the ordinary is that you've got some scribbling above your penis."

I blushed but was grateful for his humanity.

He tucked his clipboard under his arm. "We will be conducting a more thorough urinalysis to check for any discrepancies. You'll receive the results in the mail. It'll take about three to four weeks. But, like I said before, I am fairly certain it will come back negative." At the door, he paused and gave me a fatherly look.

"Want my advice?"

I nodded.

"Stay the hell away from that girl."

***

Two weeks before my return to Ankerich, on a particularly frigid Saturday afternoon, I was scheduled to meet my father for lunch and had asked Deirdre to give me a ride. After our encounter at Time Out I figured it'd be the only way to convince her to see me. She reluctantly agreed since the restaurant was on her way to work.

I stood outside admiring the enormous cumulus clouds deep in the icy blue sky, shivering, when her new car pulled up. She sat behind the wheel, staring straight-faced ahead. No honk, no turn of the head. As if she was expecting me to be waiting for her.

"Hey!" I called out cheerily as I slid in next to her. My words were lost in the air thick with latent conflict. The ride was silent, but I felt like what a smirk would feel like if it were a person.

In an effort to alleviate the awkward silence, I pressed play on the tape deck. Music from the mixtape I had made for her filled the car. I recognized the song, "Sunshine" by Samiam, and sang along, making sure Deirdre could understand the lyrics.

"They fall in love with the girl they perceive not you

They see what they want in you

They get what they need from you

They take advantage of you"

I knew I couldn't endure the whole ride without any conversation, so I started talking. Anything to establish my upper hand in the situation.

"Thanks for the ride, by the way. I'm not particularly amped to hang out with my dad, but I mean, after all, he has done a lot for me. And he's set up a lot of shit to have me join him as soon as I get back from Germany." I hoped my ersatz-excitement was strong enough to blanket my apprehension.

Deirdre grunted in acknowledgment.

I decided to go on the offensive. Since she hadn't asked me a thing about my time in Germany, I decided to go full force in questioning her about her recent life decisions.

"So, like, for your audition, did you like have to just take off your clothes in front of a bunch of creepy dudes or something?"

She stared straight ahead.

I kept at it.

"Or did you just sit across from some dude at a desk and show him your tits? Is that enough? Or do they want to see you completely nude? Do they even ask if you can dance?"

"Fuck you."

"No, I'm serious!" I persisted. "I don't know these things. Like, is it like in that movie *Showgirls* where that creepy dude from *The Goonies* tells the girl from *Saved By The Bell* that she has to give him a blowjob if she wants to last longer than a week?"

"You're an asshole."

"But for real, did you have to try out? Or did you just have to put out?"

I was on a roll. Like a sick dog vomiting uncontrollably, the hateful words just poured from my mouth.

"And what do you do when you're on your period? Do they let you call out sick? Or are some guys into that shit? Maybe the creeps tip you extra on those days?"

"It's actually hard work, Jake," she spit out my name razor-sharp. "It takes skill and athleticism. You DO need to know how to dance. And do you even KNOW what kind of workout I get doing it? It's a talent."

"Yeah, an ugly talent."

"Why does it even bother you so much? Why the fuck do MY decisions about how I earn MY money bother YOU?"

I could feel her gaining steam and I squirmed in my seat.

"Because I actually care about you, Deirdre!" These words came as a surprise to both of us. "Those guys just want to see your tits and ass and pussy! That's all you are to them. You're more than that to me!" I added, quieter.

"What am I to you?"

I had no answer. I felt like the tables had turned. Though I didn't want to add to my vulnerability, I couldn't help it. Maybe it was being back home. Maybe it was my own discomfort with myself.

"I know what you look like when you're dreaming, Deirdre. I know how you get goosebumps every time you sneeze. I know how you always sleep with socks on. I know YOU, Deirdre. All those other guys just know Vixen."

"Sometimes I don't feel like you know anything about me, Jake." Her voice was quiet, cryptic.

"I know a hell of a lot more about you than your 'clients' do. And all those other guys that came after me." A bitter taste filled my mouth. "You know, I just hate that you're living your life according to what other people want. I just think you should…"

"I'M NOT YOUR PROPERTY, JAKE!"

I sat in silence.

"Besides," she continued, "I'M in control of THEM. Don't you see that? When I'm on stage I look down at them and see them watching my every move like they're under a spell. MY spell. Like I've got them wrapped up in my web. I decide my routine, I decide which music to dance—"

"But they decide THAT you do it! If they had no money, you wouldn't be doing it! Think about it: if someone needs their toilet fixed, they can ask Randy to come over in his free time and offer to pay him to fix it. If someone needs help with math, they can call Aria and pay her to help them in her free time. If someone needs landscaping done, they can call Eric and pay him to do it during his free time. Same goes for Tommy and electrical work! What if I were to offer you money right now to get naked?"

She had no response and seemed flustered. "It's different, Jake."

We sat in silence, speeding by Taco Bells and Wawas and gas stations and dollar stores. The salt-sheened streets were lined with plowed snow that looked like burnt marshmallows, unceremoniously shoved to the curb like chewed-up gum.

"I don't get why you're so pissed at me all of a sudden," Deirdre broke the silence. "I mean, before you went away you seemed okay with my work. There were no complaints then when you were sneaking out every night to come over. Then you just leave me and all of a sudden come back pissed off, somehow better than me or something."

"I left YOU?" I asked, incredulous. "What about YOU leaving me standing in my dorm room, having to digest that breakup right as I'm trying to start college?"

"Jake, you just up and moved away to college! YOU left ME! For what?"

"For my future, Deirdre! Have you ever once thought about your future? You can't be doing this shit your whole life, you know."

"YOUR future?" she forced out a scathing fake laugh. "Yeah right! This is your dad's future and you know that. Talk about someone else making decisions for you. Take a look in the fucking mirror, Jake. You're just as bad as you say I am."

The suburbs continued to bleed by in silence.

"What would've become of us anyway?" she continued after a long pause. "Like, if we had decided to stay together?" She didn't give me a chance to answer. I had no answer anyway. "I would've waited around however many more months until you got back from Germany, then you'd be busy again with classes, then it'd be workworkworkworkwork. Just like your dad. You never saw him when you were growing up, what makes you think I would see you? Our schedules would be completely different, and anytime we would be together you'd either be too tired to do anything, or you would waste all of your energy on criticizing my decisions." Her eyes were focused on the road. I looked at her profile. Hair tucked behind her ear, a few freckles spattered across her button nose, dark eyeliner accented her eyes. Despite the makeup and attitude, a slight resemblance of youth was evident in her face. "We were doomed from the start and you can't always blame me for that."

She had established her position at the table, and I was desperate to turn it again.

"Whatever, Deirdre," I added, exasperated. "At least I never cheated on you." I knew it was a low blow, but I was grasping at straws.

"Why must you always pick scabs? Like, why relive that now? Can't you ever just let things go? Forgive and forget?"

"I can forgive and I can forget. But somewhere in between those two I lose respect."

Deirdre took an audible breath. "Well, I never cheated on you," she said.

"Oh yeah?" I laughed mockingly. "What about that fucking loser Mikey?"

"I never cheated on you, Jake," she continued. An uncomfortable silence filled the car. I teetered between disbelief and shock. "I just didn't want to be with you anymore. And just breaking up with you would've never worked. You know that. I needed something to make you agree to it. As if you need to agree to a breakup in the first place," she added half under her breath. "That's how it is with you."

I swallowed hard.

"What?" I forced a laugh. "So you're telling me you just made that shit up? I mean, you were dating him like a week after we broke up."

"Yeah. That was the first time we hooked up." Her eyes were focused on the road. Her face was expressionless. "I never cheated on you," she repeated.

I was pissed.

And I wasn't done yet.

I cleared my throat.

"So, I went to the doctor, by the way," I said. I sounded like a dickhead and I knew it. And I loved it.

No response.

"He says I'm clean."

Still no response. Deirdre stared out the windshield, focused on the road ahead of her.

I wasn't going to let her win.

I waited until we hit a red light.

"Which means I didn't give you chlamydia."

No response.

"You probably picked it up from one of the five—or is it seven?—more now, probably, I'm sure, guys you've slept with since we broke up. Er, since you broke up with me," I corrected myself. "Or actually, come to think of it, maybe you got it from work. Those poles are probably just dripping with diseases!"

I paused.

"In any case, if anything, you almost gave it to me. So thanks, I guess, for being so generous."

"Get out," she said, still looking straight ahead. She doesn't even have the guts to look at me, I thought.

"Or actually, maybe it came from one of your clients, I've heard there are some pretty special 'deals' they offer at Valen—"

"Get out," she repeated and pulled the car over to the shoulder of the road.

Salt and broken asphalt speckled the chunky, iced-over frozen snow. It had begun snowing again, softly swirling flakes were blanketing the black snow with a fresh, new coat, the ugly winter rearing its vengeful head again.

For the first time during the whole drive, she looked at me. I opened the car door, but before I got out I reached over and ejected the cassette from the tape deck.

Stepping out into the wintry wind with the cassette in my hand, I steadied myself on the slippery ice and faced Deirdre. "You know I'm right."

I closed the door. The light turned green and Deirdre left.

I tightened my light hoodie and crossed the highway toward the traffic circle. Somewhere on the other side, across the busy lanes of traffic, past all the heated cars speeding recklessly toward work or home or a lover or wherever, my father was waiting in a warm restaurant.

I hoped I wasn't late. He'd probably try to order for me, and there was no chance of changing that if I was late.

And I was determined to order my own food.

Chapter 13

Jagged blocks of ice floated lethargically down the Delaware, occasionally dipping below the surface and reemerging from the filthy depths of the dark river. Randy's pickup truck cruised across the Ben Franklin Bridge bringing us into the city for a party at Aria's apartment.

Lunch with my father had gone surprisingly well. He had chosen a Chinese restaurant he was fond of, and I was excited to eat something I hadn't had much of a chance to eat in Ankerich.

He'd only had to wait for me for a few minutes, so the mood wasn't soured by my tardiness. He immediately started talking to me about the food at the restaurant, casually ignoring my arrival in wet shoes and coated in a light layer of snow, despite telling him that Deirdre would be dropping me off.

"Jake, you gotta get the kung pao scallops here, they're phenomenal!"

I glanced over the menu, skipping past the seafood section.

"I'll take the dan dan noodles—extra spicy," I told the waiter when he came to take our order. My father's eyes peered over the edge of his menu, the rest of his expression hidden by the laminated card.

"Uh, I'll get the kung pao scallops, but make sure they're not super spicy like last time. Damn near had to cancel my three o'clock appointment..." he added under his breath after the waiter had stepped away.

The conversation consisted of the technicalities of me joining his firm. "I mean, I was kind of hoping you could get a head start on the seventy-five hours of mandatory schooling while you were home this month, but Angelo tells me he thinks it's best if you just knock it out all at once when you get back. When do you get back again? End of June?"

"June 22nd," I said, sipping from my water to clear the lump in my throat.

"Yeah," he continued, his mouth full of fried wonton strips. "Then you still gotta take that exam, but I know you'll be fine. I'll teach you all the tricks, what they ask, and all that stuff. I'm sure I can even get my hands on an old exam, I know some people."

He tossed another handful of greasy crisps into his mouth and resumed the one-sided conversation. "As far as sponsoring goes, we've obviously got that covered. And all the paperwork—applications, forms, registrations, all that shit—Angelo will help with that."

I fiddled with my chopsticks.

"In any case, by year's end, I'll have you on board. In no time you'll be helping people cast their anchor!" he concluded, smiling at the reference to his corny slogan.

I forced a reciprocal smile.

***

Olivia answered the door wearing a tight, thin, baby blue t-shirt.

"Jake," she said delicately, pressing herself into me with a welcoming hug. "How's Germany? I bet the ladies are just loving you over there!"

"Ha," I let out a half-hearted laugh. "It's been good. Looking forward to going back."

I slipped out of her embrace and squeezed past her into the living room. The apartment was already full, the majority of the people crammed into the kitchen. I made my way to the fridge, trying to avoid eye contact, not in the mood for small talk with secondary acquaintances.

I had consciously decided to drink more than I usually did at parties with my friends in the US. Randy had already finished three beers in the first hour, so it was pretty evident we would be spending the night. Besides, Katie—Aria and Olivia's elusive roommate—was at the party, and Randy had been trying for years to find a way to share a bed with her. Looking up from my beer, things looked promising, with Katie resting one hand on Randy's shoulder, the other one clutching her red Solo cup and folded across her belly, doubled over in laughter. He winked at me. I raised my can of PBR toward his direction and left the kitchen.

In the living room, I ran into Amy, an old classmate from elementary school. Surrounded by a sea of revelers, all bobbing knees and swaying arms, she latched onto me, eager to catch up or gossip or feel like she belonged.

"Holy shit! Jake!" she exclaimed. "I don't think I've seen you since like, I don't even know… middle school?" she slurred. We had also gone to high school together, but the alcohol had obviously erased that memory.

"Ha, yeah," I agreed, taking a big sip. The beer tasted overly carbonated and artificial. Like old apple juice from concentrate that was fermented in a rusty aluminum barrel.

"So, what have you been up to? What does an Ivy League graduate like yourself do now?" she asked, a snide tone hidden just beneath the surface of the question.

"Well, I've been working in Germany since October."

"Really?"

"Yeah. I'll be there until the end of June."

"That's cool…"

Before she could continue and inevitably ask me what comes after that, I shifted gears.

"How 'bout you? What's new?"

She took a tiny sip, combed a strand of her ashy blonde hair behind an ear, and answered, "Well, I actually just graduated in December. I had to complete another semester since the requirements for my program were all screwed up and my academic adviser…"

I switched over to filter listening and glanced around the room, occasionally nodding my head in agreement at her incessant rambling about her degree in anthropology or art history or geology or whatever. Partygoers reveled, the invited and the uninvited, the dressed up and dressed down, the hipsters waxing poetic and the wallflowers hopelessly hitting on the girls too shy or polite to reject them outright. The walls were sheened with sweat and abandoned cups and cans danced on the vibrating speakers tucked away in the corners. Outside the smokers and non-smokers convened, looking identical with clouds in front of their faces and half-moons of perspiration beneath their arms.

I noticed a silence and realized Amy had finished her disquisition on her difficulties obtaining her diploma and had asked me a question.

"What? Sorry, I got distracted for a second. What did you ask?"

"No, I was just saying, did you hear the latest on Teddy?"

Before I could figure out who Teddy was, and why she was asking me if I had heard the latest on him, she continued.

"Apparently he killed someone in prison!" She leaned in toward me, eyes agape in exaggerated astonishment, each word emphatically enunciated.

Then it hit me. Teddy Russell, my childhood friend.

"Oh shit," I said. "I mean, I heard he was in prison—for drugs or something, right?—but I had no idea he killed someone!" I was genuinely surprised. A weird feeling of intrigue and infinite sadness washed over me. Teddy was my closest friend, along with Tyler, but I could never hang out with the two of them together. They absolutely despised each other, for reasons I could never understand. Like two identical magnets, they seemed to repel each other. And I always had to be super careful not to mention one's name while spending time with the other.

"Yeah, apparently he was in jail for some drug offense—using, not selling, I think. Then he and two other inmates beat a child molester to death. I read about it in the paper."

"Jesus Christ. When did this happen?" I asked, looking around for someone to flag down to get me another drink.

"I don't know, like November or something."

For the life of me, I couldn't picture what Teddy would look like as an adult. The last time I had seen him was early in high school. He had gotten expelled for setting a fire in the boys' bathroom. Even at that time it had just felt like a cry for attention. We had by that point already drifted apart, the chasm opening seemingly out of nowhere in fifth grade. Still, standing here in this living room, overwhelmed by sights and sounds and smells, the only images of Teddy I could conjure up were of me and him sitting in his living room, a stack of records in front of us, taking turns playing them based on their cover artwork.

My thoughts were interrupted by Amy continuing the briefing on my childhood friendships.

"And your OTHER buddy..." she added, her head dipped and eyes glancing up at me in a secretive, almost scolding look. "Tyler?"

I felt like I couldn't escape Tyler. After not seeing him for years, all of a sudden he was back in my life. And I felt a pang of regret after giving him money for the Phillies tickets the other day.

"Apparently he's been up to no good lately either. Drugs," she whispered.

What was it about my two closest friends growing up that had drawn them to drugs? I had never had any interest whatsoever in anything harder than alcohol, and even that I had always treated with a latent curiosity at best. Until recently, at least.

Before Amy could continue, Randy appeared behind me, reaching a full can of PBR over my shoulder. I thanked him and told him I'd take another as soon as possible. Without even acknowledging the comment, he reached over my shoulder again with a red Solo cup.

"Drink that," he said in my ear. "It'll do the trick."

I placed the full can on the closest table, shoving a few wounded soldiers to the side to make room, and accepted the plastic cup. Inside swirled a melted-sherbet-colored concoction of artificial fruit juices spiked with something that smelled of turpentine. I took a sip, grimaced at the burn, and decided to finish it all in one quick chug.

Wiping my mouth with the back of my hand, I asked, "Wait, what's up with Tyler?"

"Well," she continued, "apparently he's been scamming people out of money. For pills."

I took a sip from my PBR, washing away the acrid burn of the putrid potion I had just downed, and nodded, urging her to continue.

"He keeps reaching out to people saying he's putting together some big event—Flyers game, or Phillies game or something. Then he takes the money and is MIA. He tried with me when I ran into him at a bar a few months ago, but I wasn't falling for it. I mean, why would I want to hang out with HIM?" She made a disgusted face. "Besides, I don't even like sports."

"So wait, who'd you hear this from? I mean, is this really true?"

"Well, like I said, he tried it on me. And Kimmy already lost money to him last summer. As far as the pills go, I don't really know, that's just what I've heard. But the fake game thing is definitely real."

She must've read the dumbfounded look on my face.

"Wait! Don't tell me he got you, too?" a schadenfreude smile spread across her face, then quickly disappeared. "Well, I guess not, though, if you've been in Germany. And besides, you probably know him well enough not to fall for that trick. You guys used to be so close back in the day. Whatever happened to that anyway?" she added, looking out into the living room pulsing with people.

I had no idea myself. Both he and Teddy started drifting away from me toward the end of elementary school. I always chalked it up to puberty and the changes in interest boys go through. Tyler and I did cross paths from time to time, his introducing me to Deirdre evidence of our casually maintained friendship. We never really had a falling out or anything, even after the whole incident with the Germany report. The friendship between Teddy and me had dissolved like a tissue in water, and he had really begun to get himself into a lot of trouble. Though Tyler had issues of his own, it never seemed like anything serious. Now it all started making sense. His shitty outfit. His mention of my brother the other day.

It was all too much. Thanking Amy for the update on my old friends, and feigning an urge to go to the bathroom, I excused myself from her presence and headed upstairs toward the roommates-only bathroom I was privy to.

The door to Olivia's bedroom was slightly ajar as I walked by, and I took a quick peek inside. The room looked recently straightened up.

The carpet had been vacuumed, the picture frames and candles on the dresser had been tastefully displayed, the bed freshly made. I noticed an extra pillow, the cream-colored pillowcase standing out on the navy blue bedspread.

Back downstairs, the night throbbed on, the crowd of people grew and receded, conversations popped up and dissipated after small talk topics had exhausted themselves. I continued drinking, but the energy of the night kept me feeling mostly sober. After some of the guests had started making their way home or to other parties elsewhere in the city, a group of us climbed out onto the roof. Though it was the end of March, the last day of winter, the night air had shed most of its chill and had turned mild and pleasant.

Three stories below us the city opened itself up as a sea of lights set on a black winter night canvas. Lights twinkled off and on as people turned in for the night or awoke for their early shifts. A bottle of some low percentage liquor was passed around and sipped from. Olivia pressed it into my hand and I thanked her with a silent smile, likely lost in the night's darkness. I tilted my head back to take a drink and peered into the depths of the night sky, trying to make out a constellation or two behind the city's pollution and the wispy cloud cover.

One by one people started heading back inside.

Olivia, sitting next to me, rested her head on my shoulder and said, quiet enough for only me to hear, "I think I'm gonna get ready for bed soon."

I nodded, without looking toward her. She waited a few seconds, then, using my shoulder as support, hoisted herself to her feet and headed toward the window to climb back in. Her fingers drifted across my back as she left.

At some point, I agreed with Randy to head back inside "for a nightcap," as he put it. The two of us stood in the kitchen. The remainder of the partygoers sober enough to keep their eyes open were congregated in the living room, engaged in a serious conversation. Katie was still with them; Aria and Eric had gone to bed.

Randy poured me a shot of whatever non-empty bottle he found lying around the kitchen. We raised our glasses, a clear liquid running stickily down my thumb and index finger pinching the glass, and drank. A warm, licorice spice lined my insides and heated my stomach.

"Yo, I think Katie's actually really into me," Randy said, flashing a genuine, but not overly confident smile.

"Nice," I said.

"I think I'm about to turn in soon. She said it's cool if I crash in her bed." His eyes were wide with anticipation.

I smiled and punched his shoulder lightly. "Good for you, man."

He stood silently for a second, his eyes unfocused in the distance. Then he snapped his head toward me and said, "So what's up with you? Are you going to crash in Olivia's room?"

"Ha, I don't know." I reached across the table between us and grabbed the bottle. Holding it up to the single burning bulb in the kitchen I mentally measured the contents, deciding that there was enough for the both of us to have one more drink. I filled both glasses and we drank again. "To be honest with you," I said, gulping, "I'm not tired at all." I glanced at the kitchen clock. Shortly after four in the morning.

"I'm not that tired, either," Randy agreed. "I'm going to bed, not to sleep," he smirked at me, and left, patting my back on his way to the living room. I putzed around the kitchen for a while, rummaging around the cupboards and fridge for something else to drink. Buried behind bottles of ranch dressing and browned guacamole I discovered a tallboy of PBR. On its side, wedged between the trash bin and the stove, I found a three-quarters-empty bottle of rum. With my plundered supply, I climbed the stairs and made my way to the window leading out to the rooftop.

On my toes, I crept past Olivia's room. The door was ajar as it had been earlier. I slowed my step and poked my head into the room. Olivia was under the covers, on her side with her back turned toward me. She was asleep, I could tell by her slow, rhythmic breathing. Her computer was on, and music played softly. I crept past the door and out the window as quietly as possible.

Outside the night air had warmed. I walked out toward the edge and took a seat with my back against the chimney. It was approaching morning, and lights were slowly being flicked on across the city like fireflies in the summer.

I sat back and took a drink from the rum, chasing it with the beer. "If only I could scrounge up a few lemons and limes and a splash of apple juice, hey Stinki?" I said quietly to myself, smiling.

Iron and Wine drifted up quietly from Olivia's room, a hushed voice singing about the sunrise bringing hope where it once was forgotten. Sons as birds, flying away.

The sun was still below the horizon, but its light had started to permeate the darkness. A slight, cool drizzle had begun. The earliest birds had appeared, seeking worms that would leave the earth to avoid drowning.

I took another sip. It was the first day of spring.

I lay back, feeling the cool rain on my face. It was starting to come down heavier, but it was still pleasant. The steady sound of the rain was soothing, like a breeze through the trees on a summer night. I pictured the rain washing away the vomit and spit and piss from the sidewalks below me. With my back against the hard roof and my face toward the early morning sky, I thought, "Out like a lamb..." and smiled, feeling the creases form at the sides of my eyes.

Book 2

Spring Forward

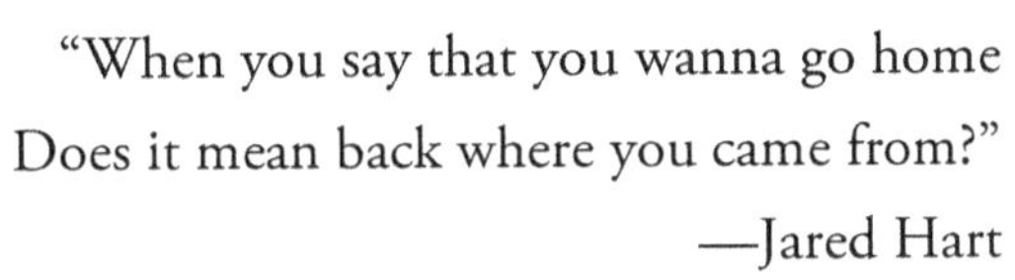

"When you say that you wanna go home
Does it mean back where you came from?"
—Jared Hart

Chapter 14

I pressed my feet eagerly to the floor beneath me as the plane gently touched down. Armed with experience and a new sense of belonging in southern Germany, I walked confidently past the smiling flight attendants and disembarked, effortlessly making my way through customs and to the train to start the ride to Ankerich. The morning was fresh and pleasant, the sky cloudless and bright, and the slightly cool air held the promise of a warm afternoon in its breeze.

Boarding the newly painted red train bound for Ankerich, I smiled at the conductor, who reciprocated with a minuscule head nod, his tightly-sealed lips hidden by a flimsy mustache. I grabbed a seat and daydreamed about my trip back home. Though not exactly how I expected it to be, it had served as a refresher of sorts. A chance to charge my batteries. Not necessarily a break, or a further example of the futility of holding on to hopes of a future with Deirdre, but more of a perspective gauge. It was the first day of April. Springtime in Germany. I had almost three more months to spend in Ankerich. Though this semester would be notably shorter than the previous semester, I was more excited and less nervous. There would be no time wasted trying to make friends.

The only thing that would be lacking was the lunches with Julia.

I sighed and focused my attention forward and on the fun times I would be having with Stinki. If last semester my approach had been to try anything, not say no, be open, have fun, this semester was going to be that magnified. I fished my iPod from my bag and scrolled down to Leatherface, "Springtime." Smiling, I leaned my head back against the ugly blue patterned headrest as Frankie's wine-weathered rasp narrated the upcoming semester:

> "And everything is new
>
> And everything is clean
>
> And everything is free
>
> And there were still so many things to see..."

The train hummed along the rails and sleepy towns and bucolic villages zipped by. Music filled my ears and each time I opened my eyes I was greeted with a more pleasant sight than before. The landscape had shaken off its October outfit of dark greens and rusty browns and replaced it with lighter shades of green, brighter and more lively, speckled with brilliant buds of blazing blues and dazzling yellows, hugging the earth like a comfortable sweater. The fields had been harvested and the new seeds sowed, the earth lined with rows of bumpy brown mounds, the soil bulging in anticipation of the first sprouts of spring.

As the train neared Ankerich, its pace slowed, displaying through the windows a flipbook depicting domesticity. With a hiss of brakes, the train came to a stop and I alighted, stepping into the beautiful late morning sun. Because the weather was so pleasant and I was wide awake despite the overnight flight, I decided to spend the day walking around town and exploring Ankerich in this new atmosphere of awakening and anticipation of better days.

I dropped my suitcase and bag in my room, slipped out of the light jacket I had been wearing, since the New Jersey spring had not yet reached its full potential, and headed straight back into town.

As I disembarked the bus on the bridge over the river and made a left into the curving alleyway that fed into the old part of town, I felt like I was stepping into a transformed world. The snow and ice were long melted, once again exposing the cobblestoned pedestrian paths and red clay roofs. The April sun, warm and welcoming, shined past the scattered clouds and reflected in the shop windows. The tall houses and stores lining the narrow streets no longer appeared as crooked teeth in a mouth in desperate need of braces, but as drunken comrades leaning into each other for support after an evening of raucous revelry.

The change in the people was evident as well. Gone were the grumpy grumblings of the likes of Herr Meindt and the passport control police officer, and in their place were smiling men smoking in doorways, shoulders propped lazily against the frames, slightly nodding in greeting as I walked by. Elderly men and women appeared in windows above, leaning to shake the dust from a cloth or curiously poke their heads out to take in the day's occurrences, their ears straining to pick up on the voices drifting from neighbors' windows.

The claustrophobia of the winter had been replaced by a gregarious communality. Cafés had traded their well-heated, wood-paneled interiors for clothed tables outside. Young couples sat on the lip of the fountain, passing bottles and swapping kisses, giggling, and bobbing in and out of carefree embraces.

I strolled down *Fuchsgasse*, looking up at the tall half-timbered homes above me and the stream that trickled through the alley, watching as tiny tadpoles whipped their tails to keep steady in the slowly moving shallow water. It seemed as if everything around me surged and buzzed with energy, teeming with life.

Making my way back toward the marketplace, I stopped at a bakery and bought an egg sandwich and a beer. I hoisted myself up onto the ledge of the fountain, careful to give the romancing couple their respected space, and ate my lunch. Pigeons strutted about at my feet, bobbing their heads rhythmically and pecking at crumbs on the ground, but, for the most part, left me alone. A butterfly fluttered by, landing briefly on my hand as I finished the last bite of my sandwich. Its dusted, parchment-like wings pulsed gently, as if flexing, before taking off, graciously dipping and diving through the air.

"'April is the cruelest month,' huh, Mr. Eliot?" I asked myself, out loud, noticing a couple sitting behind me. They were leaning into each other, the man's ear pressed into the woman's hair, his mouth moving incomprehensibly. She burst out into loving laughter, and in turn nestled her head into the space between his chin and chest. I thought of Julia and her ambitious translation efforts of great poets. "Mixing memory and desire..." I muttered.

I racked my memory to think of the e. e. cummings book I had given her. How did the eponymous poem go? "Spring is like a perhaps hand... changing everything carefully... without breaking anything..."

After I had finished my lunch and taken my last sip from the lukewarm bottle of *Geschätztes* in my hand, I hopped down from the ledge and headed back home on foot. The disappointment of forgetting my iPod back in my room was quickly dispelled by the pleasant sounds of nature. Birds tweeted cheerfully, the soft new leaves rustled delicately in the breeze. Coffee- and cake-time conversations drifted lazily from the open windows of homes with well-manicured lawns. Even the sound of the bus chugging its way past me up the steep hill contributed to the melody of the sweet and welcoming spring.

Back in my room, I kicked off my shoes, opened the window all the way, and plopped down on my bed, careful not to knock loose any of the wooden slats of the frame. Eric had given me a copy of his Fingers-Cut, Megamachine! CD shortly before I left, and I had not yet given it a spin. Like a lot of my friends, he had been showing signs of growing up and moving past our old love of punk rock. I had heard that Devon from Osker had a new project that was basically a folk band, and I had little interest in it. Nonetheless, I slid it into the portable CD player I had found tucked away in the common kitchen, covered in dust and a filthy film of stickiness.

Seconds into the first song, I was hooked.

"Sometimes I'd rather be a good memory,

But I, I won't be there to comfort you."

With the window open and the cool spring breeze drifting into my tiny room, I dozed off.

I awoke to the sound of my door being smashed down by what sounded like a rabid bear fighting off a t-rex.

"Chef!" Stinki's unmistakable energetic rasp cut through the door. He alternated between yelling and kicking, his Doc Martens shaking the frame of the door. The CD skipped and I rolled over, rubbing my eyes.

He greeted me at the door with a bear hug and a bottle of *Geschätztes* in each hand.

I took a step back to let him in. He squeezed past me and pulled out the chair at my desk, taking a seat and handing me one of the already opened beers. We clinked our bottles and a puzzled look crept across his face.

"I leave you unsupervised for one month and you come back a hippie?!" he accused.

I jumped up to turn off the music, fumbling for an excuse.

"Just kidding," he laughed. "I kinda liked it!"

Stinki continued. "Welcome back to Sauerkrautland. How was your visit back? Any of this?" he asked, rapidly inserting the index finger of his right hand into a circle made from the thumb and index finger of his left hand, grinning crudely.

I guess there was a lot I could have told him. The failed rekindling of the romance between Deirdre and me. The STD accusation. The news about Tyler and Teddy. The heavy reconsideration of my future with my father.

"Na," I answered, taking a sip. "None of that."

"Bummer," Stinki replied, sympathetically.

"It's fine," I said, waving it off with my free hand. "Better off that way anyway," I added, unconvincingly.

Stinki eyed me suspiciously and took another sip. "If you insist." He lifted a leg and farted.

"Hey, let's go to the park and drink some more beers! It's beautiful out and it's Friday! Plus, if we're lucky there might be some babes tanning!" He winked and heaved himself from the chair, tilting the nearly empty bottle to his lips in an overexaggerated motion. He belched and made his way toward the door, patting me on the back. "Let's meet in ten minutes at the supermarket downstairs. I gotta 'drop something off' real quick," he said, tilting his head toward the common bathroom.

"Sounds good to me," I agreed, happy to be able to speak German again after a month off.

He hovered in front of me for a moment. Then, extending his arm and placing his hand on my shoulder, said, "It's good to have you back!"

"It feels great to be home."

***

The supermarket was nearly empty as the semester wasn't supposed to start for another week or so. Stinki and I headed straight toward the back where the cheapest beers were kept. I took a bottle in each hand and watched as Stinki took two in each hand, then slid one more into each armpit. I quickly reached toward the case and nonchalantly added a few more to my grip.

We swapped stories and laughed as the bus jostled us and our beers along the cobblestone streets into town.

"You ever hang out back here?" Stinki asked as we got off the bus near the train station. "There's a park right behind the building with a lake and stuff. It's really cool!" He excitedly led the way and I followed, awkwardly trying to grip all the large, half-liter glass bottles in my hands. Our feet crushed the assorted colorful blossoms and petals blanketing the pavement, their fragrance lending a pleasant perfume to the beautiful afternoon.

We found a place near the edge of the lake in the middle of the park I had noticed on my first day. Gently slipping the beers into the water to keep them slightly cool, we plopped down and lay on our backs. The sky was a bright, light blue, deep and friendly. Cumulus clouds drifted by calmly, faint wisps of cirrus clouds streaked the background.

"So, how long until you head back to Bush-land this time?" Stinki's question interrupted my aimless wondering.

"Oh, um, June 22nd is my flight back."

"June 22nd? Shit! That's only what," he did some quick math in his head, "like ten weeks away?"

It hadn't hit me yet, but as I lay there double-checking his math, I realized Stinki was right. I had just over eleven weeks left in Ankerich. Suddenly, time took on a new dimension. After having spent close to twenty weeks in Ankerich during the winter semester, which flew by, having only about half that time this semester was an uneasy thought.

"But wait, don't you work for the university? I thought the semester ended in late July."

"Yeah, well, because I work for the American Studies department, our office follows the American university schedule, since a lot of those students are either planning on going to the US or returning from the US." I paused for a minute. "Sucks, actually."

"Ah, don't worry about it. We'll have plenty of time to have fun," Stinki reassured me. "Because guess what? I'm not going to class anymore. I'm dropping out." He paused. I turned my head to the left and looked over at him. He was still staring straight at the sky. His sunglasses covered his eyes, but I could still see the creases running in straight lines from the corner of his eyelids. "Well, I mean, I'm not necessarily dropping out. That'd cancel my *BAFöG*. I figure I'll just pretend I'm a student, collect my monthly stipend, and spend it all on beer and parties."

Between the realization that, although I had just arrived back, I only had eleven weeks left, and the knowledge that Stinki was essentially quitting school, I was dumbfounded.

"Cool," I said, trying to be supportive. "But what will you do after that? I mean, how long can you continue being a student?" I framed the last word with air quotations, unsure if Stinki saw me.

"I don't know. But who cares? I mean, I can probably milk the system for another five, six years. After that, I'll probably get tired of it and do something else. Probably just find odd jobs here and there to cover beer and food costs. What else do I need money for?" He turned to me.

"Well," I considered. "I mean, you've gotta find somewhere to live," I said, the intonation more like a question than a statement.

"Whatever. I'll move into a squat house or something. I'll figure it out."

Though we had gone to a few shows at a squat house in Degerloch the previous semester, the whole concept continued to perplex me. Not that I had done a ton of research on real estate, but from what I knew, every home belonged to someone. Or if not to a person, to a bank, or a town, or some organization. How all those punks basically just lived in that squat house in Degerloch for free was beyond me. And the fact they were able to put on shows, sell beer and food, and that the whole thing ran rather smoothly added to my perplexion.

"What if you found a job doing something you liked?" The question surprised me as it came from my mouth. To hide my own shock, I continued. "I mean, is there anything you like doing? Think of your interests, maybe there's something along those lines that can also make you money."

Stinki looked at me, a serious look on his face. The expression fit him like how my Dillinger Four jacket would fit my father.

"Well, last I checked, you can't get paid for drinking beer, listening to punk rock music, and fucking." He took a sip and contemplated. "Well, maybe for the last thing, but that's about it. And as much as I hate to admit it, I don't know how much people would be willing to pay for this," he lifted up his shirt, extending his belly, the skin stretching tight like a pregnant woman's.

I felt like a hypocrite. Who was I to tell someone how they should live their life? Who was I to tell someone to follow their heart, their interests, their dreams? In a sense, I felt justified, living in Germany after graduating from college instead of jumping at the first opportunity to work for a bank, or a law firm, or as a consultant, whatever the hell that was. But in eleven weeks' time, what would I be doing? Definitely nothing to do with my interests, that's for sure. Soon I'd be entering the world of selling rich people shit they don't need and convincing the wannabe rich to sign their lives away in an attempt to fit into a club that will never accept them. I'd be part of the sad world dominated by repulsive people and racist policies—the exclusionary practices of Levittowns and Frederick Trumps. A real estate agent is just a glorified used car salesperson after all.

And besides, I barely even knew what a mortgage or a home equity loan was, had no idea what those words and phrases my father tossed around even meant—APR, escrow, lien. I rarely ever thought that at some point I would own a house myself, and when I did, the idea of homeownership seemed as appealing to me as having a canker sore. "It's a work in progress, it never ends! As soon as one thing is finished the next thing pops up," everyone always says, as if repeating these lines makes their own misery more bearable. Owning a house was just another way of showing off, of proving you have your shit together. But everyone knows it's just a lie. A ball and chain. Another anchor.

"But for real, sociology?" Stinki went on. "I just did it for the *BAFöG*, and if I'm going to be honest with myself, I might as well just collect the *BAFöG* and not pretend to study anything." He took another sip, emptying his bottle and chucking it softly toward the weeds growing in front of the metal trash can.

"But hey," he said, turning toward me. "I'm only twenty-three. I'm still young. I've got time to figure this shit out. I might as well enjoy myself in the meantime, right? Why waste all my time focused on the future. This is here," he said, extending his arms in an all-encompassing motion, signaling to the park, the lake, the people, "and this is now."

"True," was all I could manage to reply. Stinki hopped up and headed to the lake to grab two more beers. Returning and plopping down next to me, he popped both bottles and handed me one.

"It's like that song you put on my CD. From Screeching Weasel. Awesome name, by the way," he contemplated for a second, trying to line up the English in his mind. "Something about being lazy bums and being stupid and having fun because we don't give a shit about tomorrow."

"Yeah, 'Hey Suburbia,' that's a good one."

"*Prost!*" he extended his arm toward me.

"*Prost!*"

I took a big sip. The first half of the sip was warm, as the beer in the neck of the bottle was not submerged in the cool water of the lake. Halfway through the gulp, the cooler beer followed, taking me by surprise. I coughed, spraying a bit of beer onto my lap, droplets landing on Stinki as well.

"Chef! What the hell, man?" He laughed, filling his mouth with beer and also showering the sky above us with foam. Warm droplets of *Geschätztes* showered down on us, the German sky raining down German beer. Had this happened back home I would've been pissed. But for some reason, lying here in the grass in this park in Ankerich, with Stinki grabbing his gut in tortured laughter, it felt just fine.

Chapter 15

Heike welcomed me back the following Monday with a smile and a hug, Uschi flashed a quick, half-hearted smile. "Work's gonna pick up a bit now, since the end of your semester is approaching," she snapped at me, a particular bite to the word "your." "Then again, maybe you'll work better with nobody to ogle all day long." She spun and disappeared into her office.

Her threat proved to be a lie since the days went by as slowly as they were boring. I continued entering information into spreadsheets—former students, current students, future students—and corresponded with students currently studying abroad, helping them with simple questions regarding the American university system. I still had no idea what Uschi did all day long behind the closed door of her office. And why did the Germans have such an obsession with closed doors anyway?

Uschi was, however, right about missing Julia every day. Her absence was exacerbated by the weather. In January and February, though she had already stopped working in the office, the weather was so bitter and cold that most days I either ate at my desk or walked a few steps down to the cafeteria. With the weather now unseasonably pleasant—at least by northeastern US standards—I had the urge to take a short walk every day at lunch. I avoided the stone wall overlooking the river, teeming with its memories, fearing I could accidentally run into Julia there. Though I had no reason to avoid her, I could not bring myself to face her after the night of the Christmas market. Had I allowed myself time to think it over, maybe I could have come up with a reason why. But, for whatever reason, every time I thought back to that night, an awkward and uncomfortable feeling of guilt, shame, and anxiety overtook me, and I would quickly shake my head as if to physically remove the memory from my brain.

I had taken to eating lunch on the island in the river, where, shrouded by trees, I felt hidden enough to not be seen, but able from my vantage point to see people sitting on the wall. Julia had not made an appearance, as far as I was able to tell, which I chalked up to her schedule since I knew she was taking more classes than in the previous semester.

One Friday during lunch, I received a text from Stinki. "Hey, Chef! Today's a special day—the most important day in German history! To celebrate, I figured we could go on a little adventure. Text me when you're done work!"

Back home I headed to the balcony to enjoy the pleasant weather. I had texted Stinki when I was on the bus but hadn't heard back from him. With a *Geschätztes* in my hand and Julia's dogeared gift of T.S. Eliot poetry on my lap, I sat with my feet up on the railing looking over the rolling hills in the distance. After a week of working, I was tired, and I dozed off gently, slipping into a dream where I was sitting on a chair in a dark and empty room. Next to me was a door, and I reached out with my left hand and opened it. I was curious what was in the new room, but when I tried to stand up and look into the open doorway, I was unable to move. I reached down with my hands and tried prying my legs from the chair, but they wouldn't move. I yanked and tugged, jerked and pulled, and suddenly they ripped free—

"Holy shit!" I yelled, eyes agape, as I awoke to Stinki hovering over me, both hands gripping my ankles, which he had managed to pull out from under me. I had slipped back on the chair, nearly knocking over my beer in the raucous commotion. He let go and doubled over in laughter, spinning around, using one hand to grip the metal rail of the balcony, the other hand clutching his gut.

"Chef!" he gasped between laughs, "you might want to go check yourself… in the bathroom. I think you might have… shit yourself!"

He calmed himself enough to plop down unceremoniously onto the filth-sheened couch next to me. Pointing to my beer he said, "Nice save, by the way. But I hope that's your first."

Surprised by Stinki's concern about how much I had been drinking, I assured him it was my first, and that I had only taken a sip or two before slipping off into my dream.

"Good," he said, reaching into his oversized black canvas backpack. "Because you need to drink this. All of it," he said, handing me a tall liter-and-a-half bottle of carbonated water.

I was confused about what was going on. Stinki never offered me anything to drink that didn't contain at least 4.9% alcohol, and even then, he scoffed at how weak it was. "Remember, export has 5.4%, pilsner only 4.9%," he would say, tapping his head in the universal "the-more-you-know" gesture.

"Before we go on our adventure—don't worry, it involves beer," he added as a side note, "we're going to earn the money for our adventure. Twenty-five euros," his eyes twinkled with secrecy.

I looked at him confused.

"It's easy. All you need is blood!"

He twisted off the cap of his water bottle and guzzled greedily, spilling water down his chin and *Chefdenker* t-shirt.

Still confused, I grabbed a sweatshirt from my room and met him downstairs as he had instructed. There he explained to me his plan. In Germany, he said, when you donate blood, you get paid twenty-five euros and are provided a free meal. "It doesn't even matter if you have shit blood!" Stinki explained. "That's another bonus—they screen it for you, too!"

I was able to finish off the bottle by the time the bus arrived at the university clinic, and squirmed anxiously, my bladder stretched like the skin on an alcoholic's beer belly. With my legs crossed as tightly as possible, I signed in, filling out a quick survey of medical history, sexual activity, and intravenous drug use.

After returning from the nearest restroom, a nurse led us to a back room and had us lie down in adjacent beds. Stinki cracked jokes and flirted with the nurse while she set us up, and I was silently grateful for the distraction as I watched the needle slide into a blue vein at the crook of my elbow. Despite starting the process at just about the same time, Stinki had filled his collection bag in the time it had taken me to fill just under half of my bag.

The nurse came over and removed the syringe from his arm and, with a smile, he told me he'd be waiting for me in the cafeteria. "I don't have time to sit around for you and your American syrup blood. There's food waiting for me!" Then he lowered his voice and leaned in a bit closer. "And beer!" he added, pointing to the large backpack slung over one shoulder. "And do you know what happens when you replace a half-liter of blood with a half-liter of beer?" he rolled his eyes in a goofy, cartoonish clown expression.

He patted my shoulder and turned toward the cantina, the sound of clinking bottles echoing in his wake.

I lay there for another five or six minutes, thinking about if it was morally right to donate blood for money. In the US, as far as I knew, people donated blood for the sole purpose of helping. That's why we called it "donating." The Germans apparently used the same word, though this felt a bit different from donating in the classic sense of the word.

Stinki shrugged off my concerns minutes later when I eventually met up with him in the sterile clinic cafeteria. With a mouthful of meat and bread, his hands already working to spread butter on the next roll in front of him, he mumbled, "I look at it this way: did we help someone? Did we potentially save someone's life? Multiple people, even? Were we willingly here? The answer to all those questions is: yes." He took a bite from his freshly prepared open-faced sandwich. "Did we demand money and food?" he asked, raising his bitten-into bread. "No. They offered. And when someone offers something, you should always say yes." He laughed, then caught himself. "I mean, almost always."

I nodded, awkwardly trying to spread the cold butter on a fresh roll, the soft insides of the bread tearing and balling up into wet crumbs. "It's the outcome that matters, not the intention," he philosophized. Though I had written my senior thesis arguing the exact opposite not even a year ago, I decided to silently agree.

As we stuffed our faces, Stinki explained to me his cryptic reference to the most important day in German history. "You know how on every bottle of *Geschätztes* there's a reference to 1516?"

A muffled sound of affirmation came from my bread-stuffed mouth.

"Well, that's because all beers in Germany are brewed in accordance with a law written that year. I don't really know what the law says, something like 'all German beers must taste delicious and get you wrecked' or something like that." He laughed at his own joke and I joined him. "But," he continued, "the law wasn't just written during that year. It was written on April 23rd of that year." He paused to allow me to draw the connection.

"So today's the anniversary of the law, right?" I asked, attempting to show him that I followed his thought.

"Exactly. Today is officially *Tag des deutschen Bieres*. In honor of the *Reinheitsgebot*."

"Nice," I commented. Then added, "So in 2016 the law will turn 500, right? We definitely should meet up again and throw a major party!"

Stinki laughed, puzzled. "Ah, Chef. You and your future thoughts. I don't even know what I'm gonna have for dinner tonight!"

I laughed, and he joined me when I pointed to the plate full of crumbs and waxed cheese rinds. "Holy shit, I totally forgot that I just ate!" His deafening laughter filled the room, causing the four or five other people, all older, all alone, to turn toward us with distrusting eyes.

We finished our free meal, collected our twenty-five euros cash from the cute, young receptionist, and walked out the automatic doors into the early evening.

"So," Stinki popped open two beers, handing one to me. "*Auf das deutsche Reinheitsgebot! Herzlichen Glückwunsch zum Geburtstag!*"

I repeated his birthday wishes, consonants colliding as we clinked bottles. Still unaware of how we would be celebrating the occasion—other than drinking plenty of beers—I followed in Stinki's footsteps as he made his way toward a gas station.

"First stop, fill up our tank," he said, patting his backpack.

With enough cold cans of beer to give Stinki scoliosis, and my contribution, a heavy-duty plastic bag cutting into the undersides of my fingers, we made our way via train and bus into a rural area in the middle of nowhere. The only signs of life around us were the constant airplanes flying overhead, low and thunderous.

The bus had nearly emptied, save for a businessman with a suitcase and an elderly woman, also with a suitcase clutched between her knees, when Stinki pulled the cord alerting the driver that we would be getting off at the next stop.

"Here we are," Stinki proclaimed, as we stood at the edge of a cabbage field, the pneumatic brakes of the bus disengaging, blanketing us in a caustic cloud of diesel exhaust. I looked at the manicured lines of vegetables, clusters of deep green running parallel into the horizon. I scratched my head in confusion.

"I mean, I like cabbage and all, but what is the plan? Are we—" my voice was drowned out by an approaching plane, less than one hundred feet above our heads. Stinki leaned his head all the way back, pivoting his neck to follow the trajectory of the jet. We both spun on our heels as it passed, watching the landing gears appear, slowly and mechanically from the underbelly of the machine. The jet glided noisily, yet gracefully above the field, clearing a fence before descending softly onto the tarmac in the distance. Three or four seconds passed then the sound of the landing reached our ears in a thunderous thud.

"If we walk toward that fence there's a clearing. We can sit there and watch as the planes land." He looked over at me with the eyes of a child presenting his artwork to his parents. "Cool, huh?"

I nodded and sipped my beer. "Definitely different," I acknowledged.

We trudged through the field, following dirt paths between the countless rows of cabbages. The lines of crops stretched out infinitely, their deep, dark greens not strong enough to cover the iridescent hint of a majestic purple hidden beneath. Eventually, we approached the tarmac, separated from us by a tall fence topped with curls of brand new razor wire glistening in the evening sun and a sign issuing a stern warning about trespassing. Despite the presence of a shabby wooden bench at the corner of one field, Stinki dropped his bag onto the asphalt, immediately cursing at the remembrance of beers in the bag. I laughed and offered him one of mine.

Within a minute of us taking a seat on the sun-warmed ground, a faint light appeared in the distance straight ahead.

"Here comes one!" Stinki yelled out, unable to conceal his excitement. The light grew brighter, followed by the outline of a jet, dimmer speckles of light extending out to the right and left of the center light. The sound increased from an ominous rumble and took on a loud roar, steady and booming. The metallic, whiny hum of mechanical gears engaging added to the deafening noise. Just as the jet appeared to cross above our heads, Stinki reached out and grabbed my shoulder, pulling me onto my back. In seconds, the jet had cleared our heads, its entire underbelly visible in detail—serial numbers legible, splattered mud noticeably crusted to the white exterior—and we rolled onto our bellies to watch as it landed on the tarmac, the ground beneath the plane shimmering in waves of heat.

"How cool is THAT?!" Stinki yelled.

We lost track of time as we watched planes land, one coming every five to ten minutes. Each one was just as exciting as the last. Though this was not Stinki's first time here, he seemed just as excited as I was, if not more. As soon as a jet would land, the eagerness and anticipation for the next one would set in, his eyes gleaming and scanning the evening sky for a sign of arrival.

"The only thing I wish I had was a way to tell where each of these planes is coming from. I mean, this airport's not that huge, but it's still an international airport. If there was some kind of database that shared that info with you, that would be so cool."

I drank from my can. "Yeah. Like, a computer thing, or what?"

Stinki's eyes remained focused on the distant sky. "Yeah, like imagine if you could get that information sent to your phone or something."

I laughed at the absurd idea. "So you're basically wishing for a pocket computer."

He turned to me. "Nothing wrong with wishing, right?" he said, sipping his freshly opened beer. "I bet sometime in the future we'll be able to do that. Like in 2016 when we celebrate the 500-year-anniversary of the *Reinheitsgebot.* Right here. With our pocket computers! Like that *Blumen am Arsch der Hölle* song, we'll get one and try to do what we used to do!"

A twinge of sadness twisted in my gut. 2016 was so far away. Would I make it back for that planned celebration?

And if I did, would it be different?

"Ahhh," Stinki groaned in relief as he lay back on the warm asphalt, stretching his legs. A squeaky, creaking fart escaped his ass. We both laughed.

"It's Blondie, by the way," I corrected him. "That song."

"Whatever," he dismissed my comment, waving his hand. "Speaking of hot women, whatever happened with your girlfriend back home?"

I looked over at him puzzled.

"Didn't you say you guys would either fuck on the spot or she would tell you to fuck off?"

The conversation with Stinki at the airport came back to me. "Yeah. Well…" I emptied the rest of the can in my mouth, underestimating how much I had left. Trickles of foamy beer ran in rivulets down my chin and onto my shirt. I shot a quick glance over at Stinki. He hadn't noticed. "The latter," I answered.

"Well," Stinki sighed, "it's like they sing in that Fifteen song, about how there's billions of people in the world, and if you keep trying you'll find the right one."

I was continually surprised and honored that he had been listening to the CD I had made him. Yet I couldn't help but think of Deirdre when I remembered the next lines, about only after sleeping with every one of those billions of people that you might realize the problem is on the inside.

I guzzled from a freshly-opened can.

"Speaking of 'the right one,'" he perked up, "what's up with that Julia girl?"

The name alone made me almost choke on my beer. I put down the can and fumbled with the bandage on the inside of my elbow, peeling it back to see if I was bleeding. A little blot of dry blood had soaked into the cloth like a miniature Rorschach test. I peeled off the entire bandage and crumpled it in my fingers, eying up the colors slowly forming at the wound, an ugly sunset of yellows, pinks, and blues.

"I don't know. I haven't seen her since the Christmas market." I drank again. "She doesn't work with me anymore."

"Doesn't mean you can't still see her. In fact, it's probably better that way."

A plane cruised above our heads, drowning out what Stinki had started to say.

We turned our necks to watch the jet touch down, gently, loudly.

"What did you say?" I asked Stinki.

"I said that I have a plan for you. That girl back at home was holding you down. Your anchor. Remember me telling you about breaking your anchor? Or cutting the rope that bound you to it?" He paused.

"You told me about your apprehension of taking over your dad's business and moving back to your hometown," he continued. "What about your old girlfriend?"

I listened and considered his thoughts.

"Do you really want your life to be a palindrome, the end matching the beginning?" he added.

I had no answer. I searched the slowly dimming evening sky for the next plane.

"Basically what I'm saying is that you've got to stop being such a *Schattenparker*, Chef. Your next step in breaking that anchor is getting laid by Julia. Or at least asking her out."

I looked at him, and, though I had no idea what a "shadow parker" was, I knew I didn't want to be one.

"And if all else fails…" a filthy grin spread across his face, his eyes squinted mischievously. I could read his mind.

"*Der letzte Drink,*" I finished his thought, leaning over to chuck my wadded bandage toward where all the empties were piled up.

Our laughter was overpowered by the jet passing above us. I followed its trajectory with my head, tilting it all the way back then allowing myself to fall onto the asphalt behind me. A light, comfortable tipsiness had settled in—that pleasant dizziness high in the forehead as if helium had filled up the space between brain and skull. The hard ground warmed my back, the earthy smell of the cabbage wafted over, filling my nostrils when the jet fuel fumes weren't too astringent. The sky had darkened from pale blue to melon-pink to indigo. The lights of the arriving planes were noticeable in rows, sometimes even as many as three were evident in the queue.

"Hey Stinki," I asked, "Do you think more of those people in the plane are landing here for a trip, or do you think more of them are coming home from vacation?"

He watched the next plane approach in the distance, its size growing exponentially as it neared. "I don't know," he finally answered. "But what does it matter? This is AWESOME!"

I turned my head and looked at him, an excited little boy in a twenty-three-year-old's body. I inhaled deeply, breathing in the cool spring breeze blowing across the fields, and watched as the next plane descended upon Stuttgart.

Chapter 16

Stinki's advice occupied my mind for the better part of the next two weeks. I had decided to wait until the first weekend of May to contact Julia. She had told me her birthday was the seventh, so I figured I'd write her a message, or, if I was feeling bold enough, call. I thought Friday would be a good time, since it would create the possibility of meeting up on Saturday. But Stinki damn near chewed my head off for the suggestion.

"Friday?! No way! You can't do that!" he almost screamed.

"I mean, it's the day before her birthday. I'll be the first to congratulate her, maybe that'll count for something."

He shook his head in disgust. "You can't wish someone a happy birthday before their actual birthday. It's bad luck."

I didn't get it and didn't try to. I just agreed and decided to push my plan back one more day. After four and a half months of not being in contact with Julia, what harm could an extra twenty-four hours do, I figured.

The week before her birthday crawled by at a soul-crushingly slow pace. I was half-tempted to stray from my original plan and just break down and call Julia early.

Luckily for me, however, another strange German holiday provided a pleasant distraction.

The Tuesday night before Julia's birthday Stinki and I met up for a beer at *Kleine Freiheit*. After pouring back half of his first beer in one gulp, he burped and asked, "So, what are your plans for tomorrow night?"

I sipped my beer and shrugged my shoulders. "I don't know. Nothing really."

"Come on! We've gotta do something!"

Though I cherished my time with Stinki, sometimes it was a bit much. He had stopped going to class altogether and constantly wanted to hang out, regardless of the day. For some reason, it wouldn't connect with him that I had a job and responsibilities and commitments and an alarm set every morning. The four-AM- and four-too-many-beer-nights were fine, but not on a weeknight.

I sighed. "I don't know, man. I gotta work the next morning. You know that." I took another sip. "I mean, '*Arbeit ist Scheiße*' and all that, I get it, work sucks. But still… it's that work that's allowing me to stay in this country."

Stinki finished his beer, placed the empty on the table between us, and leaned forward. "Chef, you don't have work on Thursday. Nobody does. The university's closed!" He stood up to head toward the bar and order another drink, pointing at my nearly empty bottle to ask if I wanted one. I placed the bottle to my lips, nodding to him. "Come to think of it, I doubt you'll have work Friday, either," he added, disappearing toward the bar.

I was confused. Neither Heike nor Uschi had informed me that the office would be closed, though I rarely ever saw Heike, and Uschi only spoke to me to reprimand or criticize me.

Stinki returned, clunking two bottles down on the table.

"So why would the office be closed? No one said anything to me about a holiday or anything."

Stinki greedily drank from his bottle. "*Himmelfahrt!*" he said, loudly, after quenching his thirst.

"What kind of fart?" I asked.

Beer exploded from Stinki's nose, and he doubled over, gripping the table with his free hand. "*Geil!*" He struggled to catch his breath. "*Himmelfahrt!* Heaven's fart!"

We both laughed, though I still had no idea why I wouldn't have to go to work on Thursday.

"*Himmelfahrt.* It's some religious holiday," Stinki explained. "I have no idea what it means or why it's celebrated. Or even IF anyone celebrates it. But, the point is, you don't have to go to work on Thursday or Friday. So we should definitely have some fun. Four-day weekend, Chef!" he yelled, leaning across the table and into my face.

The next day at work, I asked Heike about the holiday.

"Oh yeah! Sorry! Did I forget to tell you?" Heike was incessantly absent-minded, as evidenced by her constantly cluttered office. "Yeah, we're off tomorrow. I'm going to keep the office closed Friday, too. Enjoy yourself. Take a trip!" She smiled and disappeared into her office.

As soon as she stepped away, I noticed Uschi in the doorway.

With a scowl on her face, she asked me accusingly, "You didn't know about *Himmelfahrt?* What DO you know about this country, anyway?"

I had learned to not even try to answer her. I kept my head down, looking at the blank computer screen.

"I figured it'd be your favorite holiday here," she continued. "Getting drunk with a bunch of other sexist, empty-skulled assholes trying to prove their masculinity by upholding every negative stereotype possible."

I didn't understand and continued to ignore her. Eventually, she walked past me toward her office, shaking her head the whole time, her face plastered with that snarky scowl I had grown to know so well.

The following evening, after we had cooked dinner together—a practice that we had adopted, something like a replacement for the lack of lunches shared with Julia—Stinki and I sat on a train headed to Stuttgart. The train zipped past patches of neon yellow flowers, blindingly bright.

"So there's an anti-*Vatertag* concert tonight," Stinki explained to me. I nodded, my eyes still focused on the extraordinarily vivid colors outside the window. "It's four feminist bands playing, all punk."

I nodded in agreement, though I didn't really get the Father's Day reference. But it reminded me of how I had promised I'd keep my father updated on my progress with registering for classes and doing my own preliminary research into real estate. Which I had not yet done.

"Hey Stinki, what are those crazy yellow fields out there? They don't look like sunflowers."

Stinki glanced out the window, beer bottle to his lips. "*Raps*," he said, half into his bottle. Noticing my lack of understanding he said, "They use it for cooking oil and stuff."

"Ah-hah!"

Stinki nodded. "How do you say *Raps* in English?"

It took me a few seconds to think. Then a filthy grin crept across my face and I said: "Rapeseed."

Stinki almost spit his beer all over me. "Rape! Holy shit! That's hilarious."

We both laughed at the absurdity of the name. "When you get back home, you have to tell everyone, 'Germany was great! There was so much rape! It was EVERYWHERE! So beautiful! Everywhere you look, rape, rape, rape!'"

We both clutched our stomachs laughing, though I noticed an uncomfortable pull somewhere at the mention of home.

The beautiful surroundings released in me an urge to embrace the gorgeous weather, so I popped up out of my seat and cracked open the top of the window to let the warm air flow in. Stinki's eyes immediately narrowed, and he pointed to the window I had just opened.

"Chef," he said, shaking his head. "*Der Zug.*"

For the second time since arriving in Germany, someone had chastised me for opening a window on the train, all the while telling me the word for train. I didn't get it.

"Stinki, I can speak German. You know that. We're speaking German now. And I know we're on a train."

He shook his head again, heaved himself out of his seat, and slammed the window shut. "It's unhealthy," he said, chugging the remnants of his beer.

I shook my head and admitted defeat in this battle of cultural differences.

After a few minutes, the train pulled into Degerloch, the stop just before Stuttgart where the squat house was located. Though the town was small compared to Stuttgart, or even Ankerich, the train station was lively. Men of all ages shuffled and staggered around, many of them pulling wagons piled high with beer and bottles of booze, some even complete with portable coal grills, their flimsy aluminum legs wobbling unsteadily on the wagon, mimicking the men leading them. We stepped into the warm evening, where even more men milled about, hooting and hollering, obnoxious and intoxicated.

Stinki pressed on, avoiding eye contact with any of them.

"What's going on?" I asked.

Without looking over at me or slowing his pace, Stinki answered, "*Vatertag.*"

I shook my head in disbelief. "This is completely different from how we celebrate Father's Day in the US," I mumbled.

"Well it's *Vatertag,* but most of these idiots just consider it *Männertag.* An excuse to get drunk as shit and act sexist and stupid."

I thought of what Uschi said and shook my head. What a bitch, I thought to myself, immediately catching the irony of calling a woman a bitch while on the way to a feminist punk show.

Or making rape jokes.

The farther we distanced ourselves from the train station, the fewer drunk men exhibiting toxic masculinity we encountered, and slowly, but surely, more and more punks started popping up like weeds in a cracked sidewalk.

Though I had already been to this squat house—or *Unser Haus,* as Stinki called it—I still felt foreign. Not American-in-Germany foreign, but more socially out of place. This was not an outwardly projected judgment, but rather an inner self-doubt. The punks surrounding me— all with mohawks, dyed hair, men and women alike, clad in leather jackets studded with steel spikes and Doc Martens laced up to the mid-shins—accepted me for who I was, or who they thought I was. Yet I felt like an imposter. The music acted as a commentary to everything that was entirely contrary to my life. Standing on the threshold of the building, the cynical snarl of Johnny Rotten mixed with the snotty voices all around me screaming about no future, no future for me.

No future? For them, maybe. For me, it was too much future.

I couldn't help but think that this sense of not fitting in had always accompanied me throughout life. In school, at college, with Deirdre. Even with Stinki sometimes, when I thought about how he had abandoned his plan of attending college and getting a degree like me to just coast through life and live day by day.

Reaching all the way back to childhood these thoughts plagued me. I remembered driving down to Brigantine in Tyler's stepdad Sam's truck. They had invited me to join them at the house they had for a week, a perk for a job he had done in Atlantic City. "See that casino out there?" Sam asked, pointing with his hand, Marlboro Medium jammed between the index and middle finger, "I did the brickwork there," he said, switching the cigarette to his thumb and index finger for the last drag, before flicking the butt out the window. I sat quietly, remembering how the previous summer my father had pointed out the same building and said, "See that place? I sold it."

"You alright, Chef?" Stinki was behind me, trying to get into the house.

I nodded and stepped in. A few of the punks who Stinki knew must've also begun to recognize me, and they walked up, holding up beers for us to clink our bottles against.

"Chef!" they yelled out, their smiles exposing missing teeth and pierced gums.

"You remember Speichel and Eichel, right?" Stinki asked.

"Yeah," I said, shaking my head at their bizarre names.

Speichel and Eichel disappeared into the house and we followed. Raucous bodies clad in leather jackets and clunky boots bounced off the postered walls, their beer bottles held above their neon heads sloshing carelessly in the air like an alcoholic thunderstorm. From the depths of the house, Prügel paused to wave at me, the cigar-thick fingers of his other hand clasped tightly around a beer, his heavy boots stomping off-rhythm to the obnoxious music.

The first band had already begun. I checked the flyer hanging crooked and beer-stained on the wall. In intentionally poor handwriting it announced "*Anti-Vatertag / Anti-Männertag / Pro-Feminismus Punk Party*" featuring *Giftige Girls, Brutal Bitches, Scheißschlampen*, and *Die*

Verrückten Fotzen. I had no idea which band was on "stage," a stacked up pile of cracking, splintery pallets, but based on the flyer I assumed it was *Giftige Girls.*

The band consisted of four intimidating women. The singer had a half-shaved head, the stubble dyed into a leopard print, and the longer hair the color of antifreeze. I could barely make out a word she was screaming, but the crowd hopped and jumped, pushed and pulled, pulsing like one large organism. The pungent stench of sweat mixed with stale tobacco, malty spilled beer, and the acrid bite of cheap marijuana.

Over the course of the night, I weaved in and out of the crowd, splitting my time between the sweltering heat and chaos of the inside and the cool and welcoming night out back. I had made it a point to catch all four bands, each one more impressive than the last. The women performing exuded a cocky arrogance, their bold femininity on display, forcing everyone present to accept—and be awed—by their intense demonstration of women in power. They blended aggression and confrontation with musicianship and talent into an anarchic display of showmanship, at times sexy, at times scary. The whole time I couldn't help but think that it was such a better example of expressing feminism than standing on stage, exposing yourself and allowing men to toss filthy, crumpled up one-dollar bills at the organ that determined your sex.

At one point, after *Die Verrückten Fotzen* had finished their raucous set, culminating with a rousing rendition of "Girls Just Want to Have Fun," a noticeably non-punk song came on, and everyone started cheering and singing along, grabbing the closest person to them and linking arms. It wasn't until the chorus of the simple, drum-and-piano song that I recognized it as a song Stinki had added to my mixtape, remembering how it stuck out amid the fart-joke and alcohol-praising punk songs. Yet standing in the squat house, with Stinki gripping my one arm and another punk whose face I recognized, but whose nickname was lost on me, it all made sense. *"DAS IST UNSER HAUS!"* we screamed out in one messy medley of unique voices, united in our euphoria of togetherness. Or maybe it was all the booze and weed and other drugs being passed around.

It was then that I understood why Stinki included *Ton Steine Scherben* on the mixtape. Though the music wasn't punk, the message was more punk than anything else we listened to. It was about unity. Freedom. A sense of belonging. Places belonging to communities not individuals. Homes consisting of who is in them, not who owns them. *DAS IST UNSER HAUS.* This is OUR house. And I was part of that word *"UNSER."*

***

As the night blended into morning and the crowd thinned out, I found Stinki in the backyard, bobbing and weaving.

"Hey," I said, laughing at his drunken dance of trying to keep upright.

"Chef!" he slurred, raising his empty beer bottle.

We clinked our bottles together, and he sipped from the air-filled brown glass, not noticing the lack of liquid within.

"So," I lowered my voice, "doesn't the last train to Ankerich leave at like three?" I asked. I pulled out my phone. "It's 3:54."

His half-closed eyes met mine. He placed his hand on my shoulder to steady himself. "We'll just sleep here." He hiccupped. *"Das ist unser Haus!"*

We left the backyard to raised bottles and calls of *"Fick heil!"* Stinki and I stumbled our way through the nearly empty house, kicking aside empty beer bottles, packs of cigarettes, and crumpled Tetra Paks still seeping fruit juice that reeked of cheap booze. I walked behind Stinki as he climbed the stairs, struggling and gripping the sagging railing with all his might. He giggled and grunted as he made his way to the top.

I hadn't ever been upstairs before as I never had a reason to. The hallway led to three doors. Behind one was a tiny bathroom, filthy, but pristine in comparison to the bathroom downstairs, which was nothing short of a tiled room with a French drain-type gulley that you pissed into. I didn't even want to know what people did when they needed to shit. Behind the other two ajar doors were bedrooms. Or what could be called bedrooms.

We stepped into the first one where a collection of mattresses haphazardly covered the floor. Each one was occupied by someone, some of them occupied by two or even three people. Stinki snickered as he pointed a wobbling arm to a mattress where a woman lay, her sleeping bag peeled down to her waist against the heat of the uncharacteristically warm night. Her breasts were exposed, each one covered in cobweb tattoos, the nipple a patient pink spider. I grabbed him by the elbow and led him to the next room.

With my toe, I gently kicked open the door. Of the six or seven mattresses in this room, only two were occupied. Stinki staggered in, his unlaced boots making enough noise to cause one of the sleeping punks to roll over, grumbling and cursing in his half-sleep. As I followed Stinki to an adjacent mattress, I felt a buzz in my pocket. Taken aback by the sudden sensation on my thigh, I turned my back to the room and pulled out my phone.

Deirdre.

I stepped over an occupied mattress and quickly made my way to the bathroom.

"Hello?"

There was a rustling on the other end. Then a tentative "Hello." It sounded distant.

"Deirdre?"

"Happy birthday!" a voice called out, Deirdre's, yet different.

"What? Deirdre, it's not my birthday," I said into the phone, taking in my surroundings. A tiny sink, speckled with remnants of purple-and-pink-marbled vomit, definitely not from this party. A toilet filled with yellowish water and toilet paper. A tiny shower with no curtain, black flecks of mildew creeping up the walls. In the soap dish rested a small bottle containing a clear liquid.

"I just wanted to say happy birthday."

"What the hell are you talking about?"

I reached over to inspect the bottle. *Doppelkorn*. It was sealed. Clenching the phone between my ear and my shoulder, I twisted the cap, breaking the seal with a pleasant cracking sound. I sniffed the bottle. It smelled like the cabbage field near the airport, jet fuel and vegetation.

Deirdre made a sound on the other end, a slight sniffle or a clearing of the throat. In the background, I could hear shitty hip-hop.

I took a sip, wincing through the slight burn. "Where are you, anyway?" I realized I didn't want to know the answer.

In the silence of Deirdre trying to figure out what was going on, I took another sip.

"Whatever," I said into the static. "All I'm saying is it's not my birthday. My birthday isn't for another month." I realized it was in exactly one month. Or, one month from where Deirdre was calling. I polished off the bottle, already feeling the presence of my shower surprise in my head. I hadn't truly noticed the intoxication until we started climbing the stairs.

"I… hold on…" I heard muffled sounds on the other end as her hand cupped the phone and she said something to someone.

I was tired. And drunk. And I had had a great night. I wasn't in the mood for Deirdre's shit.

"Ah-ha! I know where you are!" I said triumphantly. "You're in yesterday." I pulled the phone away from my ear and checked the time. 4:13 AM. 10:13 PM on the East Coast. "I'm talking to yesterday."

"Sorry, Jake," Deirdre sounded off. "I guess I thought… I don't know. Wait…"

"Hello past tense. How is it back there?" I carried on, edging on obnoxiousness. "I can tell you one thing, the future is great. I love it here."

I knew what I was saying was stupid and I didn't care.

"Well, in any case, have fun back there," I continued. The music in the background on the phone blended with the punk music drifting up the stairs from below. There was no answer on the other end.

I pressed the red button and made my way back to the bedroom to collapse onto a stained mattress smelling of barnyard animals, not before returning the empty bottle to the soap dish in the shower.

Chapter 17

The next morning I awoke to a zoo of loud and foul noises, all emanating from various body orifices. Smokers' coughs, allergic sneezes, burps and farts brought on by broke-people food. I stirred on my flimsy mattress, trying not to think about the thin layer of scum and diseases that I was certain coated the fabric. Stinki rolled over on the mattress beside me, adding to the corporal cacophony with a window-rattling expulsion of gas.

"*Morgen!*" he greeted me cheerily, his eyes opened to skinny slits.

We rolled out of our respective resting places and walked downstairs, already dressed from the night before.

In the kitchen, a few punks were putting together breakfast. Above the permanent funk of spilled beer, cigarette smoke, and wet furniture wafted the scent of scrambled eggs, buttered toast, and the unmistakable, vaguely suspicious spice of vegetarian sausage. At the communal table sat a handful of punks, more disheveled than usual. Friendly morning greetings were mumbled, and plates of food were politely passed. Tetra Paks of assorted fruit juices were strewn across the table, as well as several bottles of beer. Following Stinki's lead, I poured half a glass of some juice called *Multivitamin-Saft* and topped it off with sparkling water.

"An exception, Chef," he said with a smirk, noticing my curious gaze. "Just to get the engine started. Then I'll switch over to the real shit." He nodded his head toward a bottle of beer positioned in front of him.

Conversations about an apparent upcoming eviction on June 22nd and the injustice of it all were lightened with the random perverted joke delivered by Stinki. Taking a bite of my buttered breakfast pretzel, I looked around, still baffled by the idea that nobody technically owned the property, but that it still functioned as a home. Given the size of it, even despite its shabby condition, the house could fetch a ton of money in the US. As soon as the thought crossed my mind I silently cursed myself for thinking that way. Searching for a way to cleanse my palate, I opened a beer and held up my bottle to the guy sitting across from me—Speichel? Eichel?—who was also drinking a beer, and quietly said, "*Prost!*" taking a warm sip to wash down the rich and buttery mush of coarse salt and dough in my mouth.

After breakfast, Stinki and I half-heartedly helped straighten up a bit, sweeping up cigarette butts and cautiously collecting broken beer bottles. I stumbled upon a half-full pack of cigarettes and slipped it into my back pocket. Stinki looked at me after about twenty minutes and nodded toward the door. We quietly snuck outside, stepping past two drunk punks cuddled up on the stairs, still asleep, and a group of three passing around a joint. I checked my phone. 10:13 AM. Then I remembered Deirde's mysterious call.

Weird, I thought to myself, as Stinki started chattering about the plans for the day.

"So, Chef," he said. "First thing's first, we've gotta clean ourselves up a bit. But there's no way in hell I'm using that shower in there. I'm not that punk!" he laughed. "I've got a better spot in mind."

I nodded in agreement, sipping from a bottle of beer I had taken with me, and offered it to Stinki. He obliged and took a long sip. Letting out a weak burp he continued, "Then... actually." A puzzled expression commandeered his face. "I have no idea what to do today!"

He laughed and I joined him. It was Friday morning. We had the entire weekend ahead of us. Other than Julia's birthday on Saturday, which I was impatiently awaiting, hoping to text her and end the awkward static between us, I had not really thought of anything I wanted to do.

Stinki and I hopped on the subway and headed toward Stuttgart, cheerfully chatting the entire way. The sun was bright, the air was pleasant. Though it was early May, the weather was unseasonably warm.

"How awesome is this?" Stinki half-asked, half-commented as we stepped off the escalator feeding us from the dark and dank subway station into the sun-filled plaza, his arms outstretched and his face tilted toward the sky.

We made our way through the crowds of people strolling the main shopping avenue that led into either side of the plaza. Families meandered aimlessly, mothers pushing strollers, men holding their children's ice-cream sticky hands, the other hand holding a cigarette. Bums loafed on the park benches not occupied by necking couples, awkward in their teenage hormonal overdrive. Little children giggled and chased each other in the patches of grass that shot out in a circular pattern from the tall, 100-foot granite column in the center of the plaza. Behind the column, an expansive, ornate palace spread out, majestic and sobering. To either side of the column were two large fountains, the pools an artificial-looking blue, arcs of water spraying from the concentric bowls above.

"So, take your pick," Stinki said, pointing to the fountains. "Bathtub one or bathtub two?" Despite my hesitation of bathing in a public park in front of an audience enjoying its Friday afternoon, I couldn't help but think how absolutely refreshing both looked. Thinking of the grody mattress I spent the night on—how many filthy punks had slept there, how many drunk and/or high couples performed scandalous sex acts on it, how many times someone lost control of their bladder or beer- and liquor-loaded stomach—I decided a bath repudiated any reservation.

We decided on bathtub one. Stinki gently placed his canvas backpack on the ground, letting out a muffled clinking sound from the bottles we had picked up at the subway station. Following his lead, I stripped down to my underwear and climbed in. The water was surprisingly tepid yet refreshing. Stinki and I were the only ones in the water, and I couldn't help but notice the jealous looks from children and glaring scowls of disapproval from their parents. We silently sloshed about, passing each other like ships in the night, periodically swimming over to the edge of the fountain to sip from our beers lined up on the concrete lip.

I hadn't totally slept off the drunk from the night before, and the breakfast beer had helped keep the pleasant buzz steady. After a beer during the ride to Stuttgart and two while floating about in the fountain, the buzz had progressed into a solid, but not overpowering intoxication. With my eyes closed, I rolled onto my back and allowed my body to slowly sink to the bottom of the shallow fountain. The water from the spouts rained down above me, lending a satisfying rhythmic background to my welcomed drunkenness. Lying on the bottom of the tiled fountain, I took in the steady, static vibrations, enjoying the refreshing resonance, more felt than heard. I thought of how much I used to love sinking to the bottom of the deep end of the in-ground pool at home and sitting cross-legged on the bottom for as long as I could, enjoying the rippling silence of the dark depths.

A series of loud bubbles accompanied by what sounded like an antique chainsaw being started in a tarpit ripped me from my underwater head trip, and I resurfaced to see Stinki doubled over in laughter.

"Holy shit! That was a BEAST of a fart!" He caught his breath and added: "A *Himmelfahrt*!"

We laughed obnoxiously, chasing away a couple who had taken a seat at the edge of the fountain. A woman grabbed her two children by the hand and tugged them away from us, leaning over to whisper into their ears as they hustled from the fountain.

With my hands I combed the bottom of the fountain, picking up coins and holding them up in the light. I thought of the scene in *The Goonies* where Mouth decides to take back some of the wish coins, because they were his wishes, his dreams, and they didn't come true. And how I'd watch that movie on repeat with Jamey when I was a kid. And where was he right now?

And my friends. What were they doing right now? Probably just waking up to go to work, to spend the day doing something for someone else. Or the ones still in college would be headed to class to listen to someone tell them everything they need to know to get one of those jobs. And here I was, putzing about half-nude in a fountain with a Baroque palace as the background, drinking beers and laughing at farts.

I dropped the handful of coins back into the fountain. None of them came from me, and I wasn't about to steal away anyone's wishes or dreams.

We finished our beers and climbed out, shaking ourselves as dry as we could get. Stinki grabbed his backpack and pointed to the huge column in the middle of the plaza. The sun was shining full force and there were a few punks idling about on the steps below. Climbing over the chain barrier, we took up a spot with the group and let the sun's warm rays slowly continue the drying process.

Though a few of the faces seemed familiar, it was hard to tell if I actually knew any one of the members of the motley crew. The nights at *Unser Haus* were a blur, and quite frankly, though the punks did everything they could to establish their individuality they all looked the same to me.

After two or three hours of loafing about, and after we had heard the one punk with at least minimal musical abilities play that one *Die Kassierer* song about a thousand times—the one about having no skills and no future and just spending the days drunk around the clock—we had dried off to the point of being able to put our clothes back on. We had depleted our cache of beer, so we decided to make a move and go find some more.

We stocked up at a supermarket, the cashier avoiding eye contact and forgetting to wish us a pleasant day. Once outside, we each popped a bottle and strolled toward a sprawling park along the winding river.

"Oh, so guess what?" Stinki asked, after plopping down onto a patch of sun-warmed grass. "I've been thinking. And instead of doing nothing I am going to do something."

I looked at him confused, and he continued.

"Remember how I told you I worked in a hospital for my civil service? Well, I didn't hate it. I kinda liked it, actually," he admitted in a guiltily proud voice.

It dawned on me that he was referencing his decision to drop out of college and coast through life aimlessly. "Uh-huh," I agreed, my lips wrapped around the bottle.

"So I think I'm going to apply to a nursing program. It's not like school, it's more hands-on. Practical. Plus, I think it only lasts like a year or two."

"That's awesome, man!" I exclaimed, genuinely excited for him.

"Plus," he continued, "if the girls in the program look anything like the nurses we saw when we donated blood…" He whistled through his teeth to finish his thought.

Following Stinki's lead, I dropped to my back and closed my eyes. The combination of the warm sun on my face, the soft grass beneath me, and how I hadn't slept too well or too long the night before joined forces with the half dozen or more beers I had drunk in the past four hours and an enjoyable and cheerful sleep embraced me.

We must have slept for much longer than expected since when I awoke, the sun was no longer shining in my face. Luckily for our pasty pale skin the sun had dipped behind the ancient oak tree behind us, casting a bit of shade over our dozing bodies. I sat up and took a sip of my warm beer, fighting the urge to spit out the hot fizz. I nudged Stinki awake with my foot.

"Huh? What? Where are we?" he asked, looking around. "Oh shit, how long did we sleep? What time is it?" He fumbled in his backpack for a bit, searching for his phone. "Holy shit, dude! It's past six already!"

We laughed and groggily collected our things to make our move. We had no plan, but I imagined it involved finding more beers, since we were down to our last two.

"So, what do you want to do?" Stinki asked me, as if reading my mind. "I'd say we either head back to Ankerich, get wild at *Kleine Freiheit*, or we look for some punks here and see what there is to do in the city."

The thought of sleeping in my own bed, of feeling fresh and clean, both mentally and physically, prepared to contact Julia had me leaning toward the former. But before I could even say a word to Stinki, he interrupted me.

"Hey! Isn't that your girl?" he asked, prodding me in the ribs and pointing with his bottle.

In slow-motion, I watched a beautiful blonde walk down the pathway from the river toward downtown. Her hair fell loose around her shoulders, shining golden in the setting sun. She had on a moss green dress which came down to her mid-thighs, her legs surprisingly tanned for early May. Brown sandals covered her feet, but even from a distance, I could see the sapphire toenail polish glinting in the evening sun.

Then I noticed him.

At her side was a dark-haired boy, smiling like a buffoon and jabbering like a clown. I could see his mouth moving rapid-fire, the words must've been stumbling over themselves on their way out of his shit-eating grin. He was wearing cheap blue jeans, the kind you get on clearance at European department stores, embroidered with bullshit phrases like "Freedom Highway" or "Sunset Park Drive." His black Chucks looked brand new, most likely knockoffs. Skinny arms stuck out of his black Ramones t-shirt like microwaved string beans. I squinted and noticed one limp arm awkwardly wrapped around her waist.

"*Scheiße,*" Stinki half-whispered, his eyes emanating sincere sympathy.

I stared silently, my envious eyes glued on the happy couple, feeling a scowl crawl hot and bitter across my face.

"Fuck that guy," I said out loud. "Where'd she find that loser? I bet his name is Torben or Dieter or some shit. Look at him, with his brand new outfit picked out for tonight. He probably bought that shit yesterday. After he looked up the Ramones online. Probably only knows 'Blitzkrieg Bop.' And I bet he calls it 'Hey Ho!' And fuck that band anyway. Why hasn't Joey written a song about sucking George Bush's dick yet? Republican punks," I spit. "'Bonzo Goes to Bitburg' is their only good song, anyway. And that fucking dipshit is a Bonzo himself."

I was on a roll. My mind had been set and I was gearing up for a grand reunion with Julia, the final cut on the rope tied to the anchor of Deirdre. And then this.

"I bet that guy jerks off with two fingers. He probably showers with goggles." Resentment-fueled vitriol spewed from my mouth. "I guarantee he still lives at home, commutes from mommy and daddy's house, still calls them mommy and daddy. They butter his bread in the morning. Not toast, that might be too hot. And no marmalade, too much sugar. Paprika is too spicy for that prick. Probably wipes the salt off his pretzels before eating them. Julia better hope she's not going to have a wild night like she had with us, because that fucking pube is gonna take her to a PG-rated movie then maybe get some ice cream afterward, vanilla I'm sure. Beer is out of the question. He's probably had two his whole life, and those were probably those corny fucking Beck's Lime or Mixery or whatever a virgin drinks. He's the kind of crybaby who complains to the waiter when someone is smoking a cigarette near him. Probably pulls his shirt up over his nose and waves his hand in front of his face like the little bitch he is. Fucking loser."

Stinki stared at me with wide eyes, a smile slowly spreading across his face.

"Holy shit, Chef! I think I like it when you're angry. That's the most English I've ever heard you speak. And it sounded AWESOME!!!"

He laughed, and it hit me that I delivered that incensed diatribe in English. A slight wave of embarrassment rose up in me but was kept at bay by the beer-fueled lightness in my head. Picturing Torben or Dieter with his shirt pulled over his nose, I almost laughed and remembered the pack of cigarettes I had found earlier. I dug into my back pocket and pulled one out.

Stinki handed me the lighter he kept as a bottle opener without question. I lit the cigarette, inhaling slightly and exhaling deeply to calm myself down.

"Well," Stinki exhaled with me. "Remember my original plan?"

It took a minute to remember what he was talking about, trying too hard to fight my way out of the landfill of emotions I felt trapped in. The prospect of a ruined night, day, weekend, future, whatever just lingered too hard.

"Sorry to say," he continued, understanding that my thoughts were clouded in a fog of anger, "plan A might not work. Or at least not right now," he added optimistically. "But plan B..." he looked at me with mischievously squinted eyes.

"*Der letzte Drink*," I finished his thought.

"There's always room for one of those," he said cheerily, patting my back. We grabbed our belongings and made our way in the opposite direction of the couple credited with corrupting my mood.

Stinki tried to cheer me up a bit by adding his own insults to my replacement at Julia's side. "But, man, talk about *fremdschämen*," he whistled through his teeth. "That kid had the definition of a *Backpfeifengesicht.*"

I nodded at the foreign phrases and tossed my half-smoked cigarette into the river as we crossed the pedestrian bridge. I was determined to not let someone else ruin my mood, as I had allowed that to happen all too often in my life.

As the evening sky snuffed out the last rays of sunlight, we scrambled to find a grocery store open where we could buy the ingredients for some *letzte Drinks*.

After several unsuccessful attempts, we wound up in front of a movie theatre. I was nervous we would run into Julia and her stupid boyfriend, so I encouraged Stinki to just pull the plug on the evening. No sense in forcing something that wasn't meant to be.

Stinki, however, eyeing up the crowd milling about in front of the neon-lit cinema, said, "Hold on, I have a different plan. Give me ten euros."

I fished into my pocket and pulled out a salmon-colored ten-euro bill—money I had pocketed from my Deirdre fund—and handed it to Stinki.

Without giving me a chance to ask questions, he walked up to a couple sitting on the wall surrounding a few plants in front of the cinema. After a few seconds of talking to them awfully close, it seemed, the dark-haired girl looked quickly in both directions, reached into her bra and pulled out a fist. Stinki shook hands with her boyfriend, or whoever the slick-dressed man next to her was, and, after he shot a hasty look into his closed fist, nodded back at his girlfriend. She dropped something into Stinki's hand and he scurried away without saying goodbye.

In less than five seconds he was standing in front of me and said, "Pop this in your mouth and take a sip. Hurry."

In one motion, he did exactly what he told me to do and I followed suit, remembering his sage advice from when we donated blood. Without saying a word, we started walking away from the cinema, toward the impending darkness of the city's edge.

After we had made our way past the throngs of revel-seekers taking advantage of an extended weekend, Stinki finally spoke.

"We don't want to be surrounded by all those people when it kicks in. Besides, we need more booze."

I had no idea what I had ingested, and no idea what to expect. Part of me was curious, part of me was nervous. I did my best to allow curiosity to win.

"So, what was that?" I asked, trying to sound as casual as possible.

"Ecstasy." Stinki kept walking at a fast pace, occasionally looking side to side as if searching for something. "Or at least that's what she told me."

We kept walking, slowly edging farther from the city center and into the quiet hills that surrounded Stuttgart like the sides of a bowl. I had a feeling we would not be coming across any gas stations anytime soon, which was a shame, considering I had finished my last beer minutes after swallowing the pill.

As the distance between us and the downtown increased, so did my anticipation of the effects of the pill. After walking for what seemed like miles, I slowed down a bit and said, "I don't know, Stinki. I think we might have been ripped off. I don't feel shit."

Stinki slowed to a stop. "Whoah," he said, after a moment of uncharacteristic silence. "Whoah."

I looked at him. A vacant look took over his face, his rum-colored eyes dark and dilated.

"It's kicking in," he said, looking around slowly at the sky and the street around us. To our left was a quiet road, dark with the exception of a few colored lights flickering from around the bend ahead of us. To our right was a steep woody incline, the tree coverage thick and black. "You don't feel it yet?" Stinki managed to ask.

No sooner were the words out of his mouth then I felt the ground below me quiver, like a conveyor belt gently jerking to life. My thighs weakened a bit and an airy feeling started climbing my spine. I concentrated on the sensation for a moment, feeling the gentle, pleasant tingle of nothingness slinking its way up my body, following the rounded contours of my cranium from the back to the forehead.

"Oh shit!" I stared at Stinki, who was already making his way up the steep incline. I followed without saying a word, focusing on trying to keep my footing on the embankment slicked with dead leaves, the intoxication growing heavier with each heartbeat.

Stinki slumped to the ground with a dull thud. He spread his arms out next to him as wide as the smile that cut his face in two.

I sat down next to him, slowly falling back onto the soft, damp earth.

We didn't speak, we just lay there, looking up at the sky through a gap in the treetops. Time disappeared as the leaves all around me slowly started pulsating, the rhythm originating with my heartbeat and emanating into the ground, traveling into the roots and up the trunks. The brown, muddy dead leaves surrounding me changed shape, sprouting legs and standing upright like little dancing bears, smiling and chattering like apes. Slowly they transformed into more recognizable figures. Mickey Mouse. Donald Duck. Goofy. They pranced and twirled, nearing and retreating, moving to the ever-speeding rhythm in my chest. I stared up into the darkness to slow their frenzied movements. The stars that cut through the night sky began falling down on me, slowly at first, then quickly picking up speed. I lay there, mouth agape, and went along for a ride. The lights sped at my face, spreading out concentrically and avoiding contact. It felt like I was on the Star Tours ride at Disney World, dodging meteors and enemy lasers, zipping through the crevices of the Death Star in an X-Wing. In a final fanfare, I watched as the Death Star exploded in front of me, the earth beneath me rumbling, and a thousand little pieces falling down onto my face.

I turned my head to Stinki to see if he was experiencing the same thing. He lay there with his hands cupped, full of dead leaves, and tossed them into the air, the gentle breeze sending them careening carefully onto our faces. I remembered my cigarettes and lit one, allowing the tobacco trance to enhance the high.

The leaves fluttered toward the ground, no longer stars, but tadpoles wiggling their tails and swimming down to the earth. I watched as one swam directly toward my face, its head swelling and pulsing, the mouth on its cartoon face singing, "My brain is hanging upside down!"

"Sucks about that girl, man," Stinki finally broke his silence.

I lay there, allowing the fantasy film in front of my eyes to continue. "Yeah. Oh well. What can you do," I sighed, resigned.

Part of me never really even expected anything to come of me and Julia anyway. Maybe she would've just ignored my call. Or answered and chewed me out for never contacting her, let alone responding to her, after the night of the Christmas market. And even if she did answer, what would've happened? In six weeks I'd be gone anyway.

"You know my ex-girlfriend? Deirdre?"

I had no idea where the question came from, it just fell out of my mouth.

Stinki looked over at me and nodded, a puzzled look on his face.

"What kind of name is that, anyway?" he asked.

"I don't know. Irish?"

I had lost my train of thought. There was something I wanted to say to him, but his question threw a wrench in the gears. My brain, drunk on an assorted collection of chemicals and intoxicants, was unable to follow a straight line. I watched his words form out of his lips, encircled in comic-strip bubbles, floating humorously into the night air above his face before bursting, the cursive font disappearing into nothing.

"You're talking in cursive, man!"

He laughed. "Deirdre," he said, and I watched as the word drifted out of his mouth and quickly disappeared.

I shook my head. "You know the first time I wrote her a note in school, I spelled her name D-I-E-R-D-R-E?" I looked over at him.

He looked confused.

"Not D-E-I-R-D-R-E."

Still no response.

"She yelled at me for beginning her name with the word 'die.'"

A smile formed on Stinki's face. More consolatory than understanding. "I mean, that's how it should be spelled in German at least."

I nodded and sighed. "But most people don't know her as Deirdre. They just know her by her stripper name."

Stinki turned quickly toward me. "She's a stripper?"

I nodded in the darkness, unsure if he was able to see me.

"*Geil!*" he said.

I formed an uncomfortable half-smile. "Not really. At least I don't think so," I added.

"Hm." Stinki agreed.

Silence enshrouded us. I felt the high slowly receding, though my vision was still choppy when I moved my eyes side to side.

"What's her stripper name?" Stinki asked.

"Vixen," I said quietly.

"What?! Vixen?" Stinki yelled. I looked over at his wide eyes.

"Yeah. Why?"

"Vixen like *wichsen*?" He made a gesture of masturbating, then burst out into laughter.

I felt my mouth slide into a filthy smile. Deirdre's stripper name meant "to jerk off" in German.

"*Wir wichsen zu* Vixen!" Stinki laughed. "*Wie geil!*"

I laughed, too. I had never told anyone about Deirdre's "profession." I had always felt that if I kept it a secret, maybe it wouldn't actually be true. Or maybe fewer people would know about it. The thought of people I knew paying money to see what I used to see when we were in love stung. But it felt good to share this with someone. To be able to laugh at her. To laugh at my own simplicity and possessive jealousy.

"Shit," Stinki sighed. "I wish we had found beer. I could've sworn we would've walked by a gas station along the way."

I nodded in agreement. The high was fading, leaving in its wake an exhaustion that I would've ideally kept at bay with a beer or two. Or at least use the drinks to replace the feeling long enough to get back home where I could sleep off the comedown.

"Do you still feel the shit?" Stinki asked.

"No. Not really." I answered.

We had watched the edges of the evening bleed into night, and now we lay there, watching the contours of the morning crawl out of the darkness of the night.

"No," I repeated. "I feel pretty sober."

Just then, a deafening, high-pitched clattering, a garbled singsong, filled the sky behind us. We both looked up at the sky and watched as a flock of a half-dozen or so brightly colored tropical birds flew overhead, leaving trails of yellows and greens and reds in their wake.

We looked at each other.

"Or not," Stinki said.

We slowly hoisted ourselves up and brushed the dead leaves from our pants.

Gingerly sliding and stumbling down the embankment toward the street, we stood and faced each other on the sidewalk.

Stinki raised his arms to the sky in a majestic stretch, bathed in the neon glow of a gas station sign less than thirty meters down the street from us.

Chapter 18

The morning after our evening of ecstasy I felt like I had the bends. As we slowly made our way back to Ankerich, I slowly made my way back into reality. Back home, we each grabbed a bottle of beer and headed out to the balcony to doze in the early May sun.

Hours later, when I was awake and feeling almost normal again, I called my mother to wish her a happy Mother's Day. The conversation went nowhere. I had the impression she wasn't even aware of the day. God knows my brother didn't call. Claudia never registered holidays without a reminder. And my father was probably working too hard to remember. Or care.

After a few minutes of listening to her mumble incoherently—it was past noon US-time when I called, I should've known better—my father took the phone.

"Hey, Jake. So listen, I was talking to Angelo. He says your name isn't showing up on the course registry. I assured him it was just a mistake."

A wave of guilt swelled up in my chest. I had intentionally been putting off registering for the real estate classes, despite the constant urging of my father.

"Oh, yeah. Sorry. I've just been really busy with work and stuff, you know?"

"Yeah, yeah. It's fine. You've got until the fifteenth. That's what, like…" he paused to check the date. "One week from today. You've got time."

I assured him I'd do it sometime in the upcoming week.

Before I could hang up and finally get to bed—a real bed, not a filthy, sun-bleached couch on the balcony or a stained mattress on a squat floor—my father again caught my attention.

"Oh, uh, Jake." He sounded concerned, a tone of voice that fit him like a glass of fine wine fit Stinki.

"I ran into your old friend Tyler the other day." He paused for a reaction. I said nothing. "The new guy was holding an open house and I dropped by to check up on him. Selling some old couple's house. And Tyler was there. I just thought it was odd. I mean, he didn't really look like he was in the shape to buy a house. He looked pretty awful, to be honest with you."

"Oh." I didn't get why this information should interest me. I wanted nothing to do with him, especially after hearing about his conniving ways and how he most likely scammed me out of sixty dollars. Sixty dollars of Deirdre's money.

"He was with Deirdre."

I was silent for a moment. Questions swirled in my mind, but I was able to let ignorance overtake curiosity.

"Oh," was all I could mutter. "Weird."

"Yeah," my father breathed heavily. "Anyway, I just figured I'd let you know."

"Yeah. Thanks."

"Don't forget. The fifteenth."

"Got it."

***

The next week at work Uschi seemed a little less bitter toward me and began spending more and more time in Heike's office. Toward the end of the week, Heike informed me that the following Monday the office would be closed. She explained why, but the foreign word was lost on me and I decided not to pursue it further.

Stinki later told me it was because of *Pfingsten*, which, when pressed, he could not explain.

"Who cares," he exclaimed, throwing his hands up in the air. "An extra day to party!"

Sure enough, Saturday afternoon I heard the unmistakable sounds of Stinki opening the far door of the communal bathrooms that separated our halls, stomping through the tiled room, opening the door on my side of the hall, and then two seconds later attacking my door with a barrage of kicks, accompanied by his raspy call of "Chef!"

He greeted me with two *Geschätztes* and stumbled into my room.

"*Prost!*"

"*Prost!*"

"So, there's a show tonight at *Unser Haus*. I figured we could go check it out. If it's lame we could just head into the city. Or come back here. Whatever." He burped. "You don't have to work on Monday, and I don't have shit to do anyway, so why the hell not?"

Though I was excited for what was certain to be an entertaining couple of days, I was a little bummed when we arrived at *Unser Haus*, realizing that we would be spending most of our time inside the musty building, choked with smoke and sweat and deafening punk rock instead of enjoying the unbelievably beautiful weather.

Unlike previous times, this time I walked right into the house, owing the confidence to a mixture of the increasingly noticeable drunkenness after the many road beers we put away and my recognition of a lot of the tattooed and pierced faces. And they were beginning to recognize my clean-cut face. And accept it.

The house was stiflingly hot, the air was heavy and thick, and the bands playing were terrible. I had grown accustomed to the German punk popular among the squatters—gravelly, barked vocals over abrasive, three-chord songs pounded out on untuned instruments turned up to eleven. But the particular bands this night were either way too inexperienced, drunk, or cared absolutely nothing about their sound. Or all three.

I had decided the best way to tolerate the headache-inducing noise was to drink as much as possible. As soon as I had finished a beer I'd return to the impromptu bar—a splintery slab of wood attached to traffic cones with rusty, bent nails—and order another. Stinki and I had been taking turns buying rounds until at one point he disappeared.

Halfway through a song called *"Kackbullen"*—a cacophony of clobbered guitars and damaging drumbeats behind the obnoxious screaming of a shirtless overweight teenager in combat boots—Stinki grabbed my shoulder and pulled me away. He yelled something into my ear, but I couldn't understand him over the awful clamor.

He led me toward where the bathrooms were located but turned left before we could reach the French drain nightmare that was the men's room. Outside the door to the women's room stood a skinny girl, no older than seventeen, with a safety-vest orange mohawk and a nose ring. The hair on the sides of her head was shaved to a peachy fuzz and dyed in leopard print. She smirked at Stinki and winked at me. Without saying a word, she turned and pushed her way through the door into the bathroom. Stinki followed, pulling me behind him.

The women's bathroom was much nicer than the catastrophe that was considered a men's room. Across from the dual sinks and graffitied mirrors was a row of three stalls. The girl disappeared into the last stall and I followed Stinki's lead as he joined her.

The three of us crowded into the tiny space. As the last one in, I was told to shut the door behind me. She waited until I slid the latch closed, ensuring our privacy, though the sight of six feet under a bathroom stall would probably arouse suspicion to anyone entering the bathroom. She reached into her purse and pulled out a little bottle of hand sanitizer and a plastic baggie. She handed Stinki the tiny bottle and a wad of toilet paper and asked him to wipe down the top of the toilet paper dispenser. As Stinki was doing so, she shook the baggie vigorously, her eyes concentrated on the powdery substance inside.

"Do you have a ten-euro bill? Or a twenty? Or anything higher?" she asked me, then looked at Stinki, as if to ask him the same.

The sliding price scale was odd to me, nevertheless, I pulled out my wallet and noticed a crisp, orange fifty-euro bill inside. One of the deposits I had made for the delusionally optimistic Deirdre visit. I handed it to the girl who proceeded to roll it into a tight straw before giving it back to me.

"Your money, you go first."

My gaze followed her pointing finger. On top of the freshly wiped down toilet paper dispenser were three short, skinny lines of white powder. I had never snorted anything in my life and really only knew about it from movies. Figuring it was best to just do and not ask, I bent over, put the tip of the fifty-euro straw to one nostril, pressed the other nostril shut with a finger, and inhaled through my nose, theatrically craning my neck afterwards. I felt nothing in my nose and immediately heard muffled laughter. I looked first at Stinki and then the punk girl, who were laughing at me and pointing to the toilet paper dispenser, mouths hidden by cupped hands. Confused, I looked down. Three lines were still there.

I had missed the row entirely.

As quickly as I could before it became too embarrassing, I bent over and repeated the process, this time carefully focusing on the line with my eyes open as I snorted. A slightly uncomfortable sensation entered my nasal cavity, not unlike when I would forget to hold my nose as a kid when jumping off the diving board into our pool. Shortly thereafter I felt a tingling in my throat and suppressed a cough. A bitter taste trickled down my throat and crept into the back of my mouth. I handed the rolled-up bill to the girl, who quickly snorted her line, then traded off with Stinki. After they were both finished, Stinki handed me the fifty euros and we stepped out from the stall.

I checked my face in the filthy mirror. Reflected across my forehead, written in lipstick, was the question: *"Wer bist du?"* My pupils had already dilated drastically, and I could feel my heartbeat pounding in my chest.

We stepped back out into the overpowering onslaught of terrible punk music. After the initial, slightly uncomfortable feeling in my throat and bitter taste in my mouth dissipated, an unadulterated energy enveloped me, like an espresso enema.

Dismissing the terribleness of the untalented raw performance on stage, I forced my way up front and started jumping up and down, pushing and pulling people with me, laughing and screaming, banging my head to the rhythm of my heart beating in my chest. I became one with the sweaty, sloppy crowd, falling down and standing up, bending down to pick up others who toppled to the sticky, grimy floor. In my flickering vision, I saw Stinki stomping and clomping his booted feet, banging into everyone around him, a blank smile painted across his face.

After three or four songs that all blended together, Stinki squirmed his way toward me and motioned to the door. We pushed our way through the crowd and stepped out into the pleasant spring night.

"Whew! I need a breather!" he exhaled. He handed me a bottle of beer and I drank greedily.

"I don't know about you, but I think these bands are awful!" he said, rolling his eyes. "No amount of girls' room visits can fix that," he added, with a slight wink.

"Yeah," I agreed, still oblivious to what it was that I had put into my nose. The feeling was dissipating, definitely much faster than the ecstasy, but I could still feel my heart pounding steadily in my chest. I drank some more.

"Let's get out of here, I'm sure we can find something better."

We slipped into the night and hopped on the first S-Bahn headed toward the city. The huge, seventies-era clock hanging above the platform read 3:14. Beneath the clock was a framed public safety announcement depicting a cartoon woman wearing a blue dress, her hands pressed firmly into her crotch, her eyes wide as dinner plates. Behind her on a dresser was a cracked picture frame of a man. The quote was something to the effect of if your ex is still an itch to you, you should see a doctor.

I thought of my visit back home in March and took a sip of beer. Unlike last time, Stinki and I had been prepared for the comedown by stocking up on more beer at the kiosk.

After the first stop, before the city's subterranean tunnels could swallow the train, something caught Stinki's eye, and he jumped up. Stumbling and bobbing between the two rows of seats on the rocking train, he grabbed my shoulder and pulled me with him toward the door. With a hydraulic hiss, the doors split open, and we stepped out into the early morning.

Stinki pulled two more bottles from his bag and handed me one. I followed him down the winding pathway toward the sultry glow of pink and red neon lights.

As we approached, I could see the source of the light: the words "Pink Kitten Club" written in seductive cursive lettering on the wall of a tall building at the end of a deep and narrow alley. Men of all ages milled about, none of them talking to each other. Some stood silently smoking, others approached the entrance hesitatingly, glancing the whole time over their shoulders.

Stinki and I walked straight into the building, which was pitch black with the exception of a few dimly lit red lights hanging above the doors lining the halls. Just inside the entrance stood two huge men with arms the size of tree trunks crossed across their equally bulging chests, their collared shirts looking about to burst at any slight movement. Stinki started walking up the flight of stairs and I followed, periodically stepping aside to let someone pass from above, intentionally avoiding eye contact with me.

We walked the halls, floor after floor, peeking into room after room of women of all shapes and sizes cooing us in.

"Hey Chef, all this poking around has gotten me pretty horny," Stinki said after a while. "I think I'm gonna spend a few minutes with that silicone blonde in room 102."

He laughed, patted me on my back, and headed down the hall. After four or five steps he turned back to me and said, "Go find one for yourself. We'll meet outside afterward." With his back turned toward me he yelled over his shoulder, "Full alive!"

I stood there for a moment, thinking. Before I could allow my thoughts to wander too far, I popped open another beer and made my way toward the stairs.

In room 222 I remembered seeing a cute, petite brunette. Nervously I crept down the hallway, which to my relief was empty. No eyes to avoid, though we were all here for the same thing. The door was open and I poked my head in. She was seated on the bed, her back toward the door, head down as if reading or looking at her hands. I knocked gently on the doorframe.

She spun around, placing whatever it was in her hands into a drawer of the nightstand next to the ruby red bed covered in thick, velvety sheets.

"*Guten Abend, Herr. Kommense,*" she said, smiling, her dull eyes hiding something that didn't match her forced expression.

I timidly stepped into the room, closing the door behind me, making eye contact with the woman to make sure this was okay. She gave me a slight nod and pulled off her thin dress, revealing a lacy, pink slip that hung gently on her delicate frame. Her shoulders poked edges into the silk fabric, her small breasts barely noticeable beneath the loose cloth. Her dark eyes matched her mocha hair, almost black in the dimly lit room and cropped short, barely reaching her chin.

I had no idea what the protocol was in such a situation but didn't want to come off as a complete amateur. Noticing a wicker chair in the corner of the room, I took a seat and placed my beer on the floor next to me. As soon as I sat back upright, she was straddling my lap. I startled at the surprise, causing her to jump, and her stilettoed shoe kicked over my beer. Almost knocking her off my lap, I reached down and picked up the bottle.

"Is okay," she said in accented German, pointing to several rolls of paper towels next to the bed. "My name is Dimana—"

"I'm… uh… Sweeney," I responded, awkwardly offering her my hand, which was made all the more difficult by her proximity on my lap. I felt the temperature in the room climb uncomfortably. Who introduces themself to a prostitute, and why such an asinine name? Luckily she couldn't see my face in the room's poor lighting.

Dimana flashed her cryptic smile. "Sucky-sucky or fucky-fucky?" she asked, her hands sliding up her pink slip to reveal sheer stockings beneath.

I couldn't. Mentally, at least, I couldn't. I could feel the physical response mounting below and shifted my weight, embarrassed by my excitement pressing into Dimana's thin thigh. Thoughts of all of my studies whirled in my head—Kierkegaard and Kant, and the justification and morality of my actions. I had always been so upset about Deirdre's job, even if she always swore it was "just dancing." The thought of men reducing her to an item, a vehicle for their satisfaction, had tormented me for years. And here I was, saturated in my own hypocrisy, trying to shove all of my previously held beliefs to the side.

But I couldn't.

And then there was Dimana's off-putting smile. She was hiding something and I knew I would never get it out of her. What was her story? Where was she from? The accent gave away that she wasn't from Germany. Could she tell from mine that I was also foreign? Should I share that with her? Maybe we could just talk. I looked at the neatly made bed, the shabby sheets, and tacky decorations: a candle casting dancing shadows on the walls, a neon sign, lips that flashed from closed to open to closed again, a plush, stuffed fox. Did Dimana pick these things out? And that green dress slung across the edge of the bed, did she buy that with her own money? What did the cashier think? The color made me think of Julia, and I winced with discomfort.

"Fucky-fucky and sucky-sucky both thirty euro," Dimana saved me from my self-inflicted uneasiness.

It wasn't going to happen. I actually would've liked to talk, but both of us were speaking a foreign tongue. And she wasn't Dimana and I wasn't Sweeney, so what was the point anyway?

A single sock, too large to fit Dimana's foot, caught my eye and I felt a slight surge of nausea.

"Um, actually…" I stammered. "I kinda don't feel that great. I think I might just leave. Sorry."

"Fifteen minutes, thirty euros. Also one minute, thirty euros." Dimana's smile had faded, and she had stopped fidgeting with my belt.

"Okay," I said, eager to end the situation. I reached for my wallet and pulled out the fifty-euro bill. I handed it to her, noticing how it curled in her palm. Do you tip hookers? How much? And what if they performed no service?

Dimana hopped off my lap and walked toward the opposite side of the bed, a little unsteady in her stilettos. She bent over revealing her bare ass, pale in the flickering neon light.

Open. Closed. Open. Closed.

"Only ten," she said, holding up a single melon ten-euro bill. I assumed she was telling me that's all she had as change. I didn't believe her for a second, but I wanted out. I guess she'd get a ten-euro tip. Whatever. It was money I wanted spent, it had been saved for a pipe dream anyway. And besides, Dimana probably needed the money more than Sweeney did.

I accepted the change and stuffed it into my pocket. With a weak forced smile, I grabbed my mostly-empty beer and headed for the door.

"*Verboten,*" Dimana said, pointing to the bottle. "But I don't tell. Finish here."

I appreciated her advice, chugged the warm and flat dregs, and left the empty by the door. I turned to say goodbye, but Dimana was bent over, cleaning up the remnants of my mess with the paper towels.

I hurriedly made my way from the room and scampered down the stairs, cursing the absence of an elevator. Then again, how awkward would it have been to share an elevator with a bunch of strangers with fading boners and damp underwear?

Outside I leaned up against a pole and smoked. I wasn't really in the mood for a cigarette, but it felt like the thing to do after having sex. Even though I had failed at that. The sun had begun sending its rays out from the horizon, casting various shades of light blues and pinks and oranges into the waning night. Birds chirped. A nightingale's song took the lead.

A few minutes later, Stinki emerged, stumbling and smiling. He patted me on the back and we made our way toward the train station in silence.

***

The silence continued on the way home, our bodies doing their best to metabolize the stimulants in our systems, my mind a mixed bag of emotions. As we approached Ankerich, Stinki had yet another idea.

"Forget going straight home, I'm still awake. What do you say we go for a quick dip? Wash ourselves off a bit?" His eyes darted away from mine as soon as my gaze met his, the only acknowledgment of our early-morning escapade. "*Schnapsidee...*" he added quietly, shaking his head in disapproval.

I agreed and we rode the bus to the stop on the bridge, walking down the steep stairs onto the empty island. Though the sun had just risen and people had begun stirring about town, nobody had made it down to the island yet. We walked down the tree-lined pathway toward the clearing and found a spot beneath the giant weeping willow.

Before I could even consider my lack of bathing suit on hand, I watched as Stinki stripped nude and climbed down the slippery bank into the water.

"Whooh! Wow!" he called out after ducking his head under the water. "Come on in! The water's great! It's gotta be at least shrivel degrees in here!" He laughed.

With my head full of unspecified substances and the words "full alive," I followed suit. The water was jarringly cold and I almost knocked the wind out of me when I plunged beneath the surface.

Above our heads, the weeping willow cascaded down into the water, its branches tinged with the delicate and beautiful light purple of the wisteria growing on it. Tiny insects skimmed across the surface like miniature balls of mercury.

We bobbed about silently, feeling the water invigorate us in the early morning. I leaned back and floated, suspended in the murky water with the bright and friendly sky shining down on my face.

"Are you Jewish?" Stinki's question pierced the morning tranquility.

"Huh?" I responded, confused, dropping my feet back into the water and finding the slimy mud beneath me. I stood waist-deep, hands in the water, swishing the icy river back and forth around my hips. "No, why?" I asked, watching as dark black streaks of sludge drifted up from beneath my feet, marbling the water around me.

He pointed down. "You're circumcised."

I looked at my shriveled penis shimmering slightly beneath the brown river, pale peach refracting through the milky ripples. A vague recollection of Julia's similar question shot through my head.

"Hey, what do you call that tree in German?" I asked, changing the subject and pointing to the weeping willow.

"*Trauerweide*," Stinki answered, splashing water onto his face.

"Hm," I acknowledged his answer. "It's 'weeping willow' in English. So a similar name."

Stinki nodded. "But I think it's stupid. That tree doesn't look sad. I think it looks happy. Or whatever. A tree can't look happy. It just looks like a tree with a bad haircut."

I stared at the tree considering his thoughts.

"It's just a matter of perspective, you know?" he said, disappearing beneath the water. He resurfaced with a commotion, wiping his face with one hand while the other hand clutched something in a tight fist.

"Check it out!" he said, wading over toward me and opening his hand. In his palm lay a tiny key, slightly rusted, a few drops of mud or algae clinging to it.

"What is it?" I asked. "I mean, I know it's a key, but for what?"

Without looking up from his new discovery, he nodded quickly toward the bridge and said, "See those locks up there on the rails? Couples buy them and write their names on 'em. They attach them to the bridge and throw the key into the water. The idea is that as long as the key can't be found to unlock their symbol of love, their love will last."

"Hm," I said, looking up at the hundreds of locks shimmering like a rainbow in the early morning sun. More and more people were starting to make their way across the bridge, and despite the intoxicants coursing through my body, I was starting to feel embarrassed about being naked in the middle of town.

I thought back to when I carved my and Deirdre's initials into the bench on the island behind me on my first day in Ankerich. Instinctively, I looked toward the bench, a mere ten meters away. I couldn't make out the carving from where I was standing, but I was sure it was still there, my futile attempt at permanence, like the optimistic couples buying locks for the bridge. Looking up at the bridge, I couldn't help but notice the stone wall to my left, where Julia and I had spent so many lunches sitting with our feet dangling over the side, the delicate Easter basket of colors from the houses now reflected upside-down around me, rippled in the water, like images from a fading memory. Luckily it was the weekend so she didn't have to worry about her lunch being spoiled by the sight of me, naked with another man.

Stinki turned the key over in his hand as if contemplating which lock on the bridge it would fit. Then he wound up and threw the key as far as he could, farther down the river, away from the bridge. We heard a faint splash as it made contact with the water.

"There. I did the couple a favor. Made it even harder to find the key."

I nodded and slipped under the water, allowing my exhausted body to sink to the silt-lined bottom of the river. There I sat, cross-legged, holding my breath and listening to the murky nothingness. I dug my hands into the soft muck below me, digging up fistfuls of mud. Exhaling a cloud of bubbles, I allowed myself to float back up to the surface. I opened my right hand and saw a solitary clam, surprised at my discovery. I thought of how I used to spend a week each summer with Tyler and his family at their rented apartment at the beach. How the two of us would rake up handfuls of baby clams along the wash where the waves transformed to foam then disappeared into the sand.

I rinsed the clamshell and examined it closely. It was rounder and more brownish than the pastel purple, coral, and sky blue of the ones found in the Atlantic. And larger. I dipped my hand beneath the surface and allowed the clam to drift back to its home in the mud, where it would wait for the current or someone else to move it.

"Yo, Chef!" Stinki interrupted my thoughts. "You ever hear the legend of the White Whale of Ankerich?"

He noticed my confused look, smiled suspiciously, then disappeared beneath the water. Not five seconds later, a pale, round mound of flesh surfaced from the water and bobbed in place before disappearing, bringing with it a flash of black tattoo ink. Stinki erupted from the water, gasping and laughing. "Did you see it?"

"Yeah." I grinned. "I'm just glad it didn't open its blowhole."

"Ha! Next time maybe the White Eel will make an appearance!"

Laughing, we slowly climbed back out onto solid ground. Using our boxer shorts as towels, we dried ourselves off, tossing the underwear afterwards into the garbage. We dressed and made our way back home, eliciting some stares as our dripping hair made puddles on the bus floor at eight AM.

After bidding farewell in the hallway, I opened my door and plopped down on the desk chair, my legs feeling like Jell-O from the countless flights of stairs we had climbed. I flicked open my laptop and waited for it to power up, checking my reflection in the unlit screen. With one hand straightening out the tangles in my shaggy hair, I checked my emails, noticing one from my friend Tommy back home.

The email was titled "yo check this out" and contained no body, just a link to an article from the Tri-State Tribune.

State Police Raid Strip Club - Owner Arrested

Philadelphia, PA - The Pennsylvania State Police conducted a raid late Saturday night on a strip club that they allege was offering much more than just provocative dancing.

Valentine's, a popular gentlemen's club located in Port Richmond, had been under surveillance for close to a year, says police spokesperson Matthew Ehrlich.

"Through our investigation we were able to determine that there were a number of women engaging in acts of prostitution on and off-premises. Furthermore, after interviewing two former employees, who agreed to work with us under condition of anonymity, we have determined that the owner, Michael Fies, actually coerced the employees into these acts, threatening them with termination if they did not meet a certain monthly quota. These informants also allege that several dancers offered extra services on the side, enabling them to keep the whole profit without having to give a cut to Mr. Fies."

Shortly after 10 PM on Saturday, police entered the building after being contacted by undercover officers inside the establishment. Fies was arrested as well as four dancers for offences varying from solicitation of prostitution to possession of controlled substances. Throughout the course of the investigation, undercover police documented instances of being offered sexual acts in exchange for money, have observed sexual acts being performed in the club, and have been sold narcotics on the club's premises, says Ehrlich.

"Quite frankly, it is the most brazen case of organized prostitution I have come across in my thirteen years on the force."

Calls to Valentine's from the Tri-State Tribune have gone unanswered, and a visit to the club yielded no response, short of the handwritten "Closed" sign taped to the door of the 24/7 establishment.

I checked the date. The article was published at two AM on Sunday, May 15th. Ten PM US time was four AM German time. Just about the time Dimana was straddling my lap while my brain was trying to rid itself of some unknown substance.

I clapped the laptop shut and stared blankly at my wall.

Chapter 19

The tangle of emotions in my gut grew more and more into a knot, and I approached my departure from Ankerich like a convict awaiting sentencing. Reality was setting in and the false reality I had dreamed up—one that included Deirdre as the buffer for my sad existence as a real estate agent—was quickly fading into fantasy.

One Friday afternoon I sat in my room, slowly sipping a *Geschätztes*, eyes blankly staring at my computer screen, unfocused and unmotivated to do anything. Eighteen inches from my face was a poorly designed website loaded with sample questions for my real estate license exam. I looked at the bottom right-hand corner of my laptop and did the math. Nineteen days until my departure. Gazing back at the screen with the bottle pressed to my lips, I groaned. I had completed one whole question.

A pounding on my door shook me from my self-loathing and damn near caused me to chip a tooth on the bottle.

"Come in!" I yelled, completely understanding by this point what to expect.

Stinki kicked open the unlocked door, hands extended above his head, one containing an open beer, the other holding a six-pack.

"*Herzlichen Glückwunsch zum Geburtstag, Chef!*" he yelled, standing frozen in the doorframe like a starfish on display in a tacky shorehouse.

I could feel the warmth of appreciation chase away the disappointment of my impending departure. I had forgotten my own birthday, yet Stinki in his absentmindedness, his brain soggy from the millions of *Geschätztes* he had drunk in his short time on earth, had remembered.

"Thanks, man," I said through an affectionate smile, gratefully accepting the six-pack. Smaller brown bottles with a rubber-lined ceramic top poked up from the navy blue cardboard carrier, a drastic change from the usual *Geschätztes*.

"*Flensburger!*" Stinki smiled. "It might not be as cheap, or punk rock, but it's good. Even if it does come from the north."

I thanked him again and set the beer down on my desk, sliding my laptop back and out of the way.

"So what's the plan? How are we going to celebrate?" Stinki asked, sipping from his beer.

"I don't know, man. Maybe hang out downstairs? Or buy a bunch of beers and sit out on the balcony with some music?"

Stinki nodded in agreement, finishing off his bottle. "By the way, I do have a plan, but it'll only take an hour or so." He pointed to my beer. "First one?"

"Yeah."

"Good. Also your last one for a bit." A mischievous smile spread across his face, a look I had grown to know so well. And love. A look I knew I would soon be missing.

He checked his watch. "So, have you eaten?'

I hadn't, and Stinki decided we needed to eat before we embarked on his hour-long surprise. Given the time restraint, I had mentally crossed off plane-watching, giving blood, and taking some unknown drugs from the list. Nonetheless, I was confused. A little nervous. Mostly excited.

We made our way into the town, grabbing a döner along the way. What seemed to be an aimless and pleasant evening stroll through the gorgeous old downtown of Ankerich revealed its intention when we rounded a corner and Stinki came to a stop in front of a storefront with neon lights flashing in the window. I recognized the building as the tattoo shop I had seen during my stroll through town back in October.

"So," Stinki said, grinning, "here's your *real* gift from me. Forget the beer." He patted my back in a fatherly fashion. "Well, don't forget the beer, drink it, but, whatever, you know what I mean."

He pushed open the door and I followed him in. The room was tiny and silent except for the faint sound of punk rock in the background, a poor attempt at drowning out the incessant droning of a tattoo gun. I took in the various samples of flash tattoos displayed on the wall and was relieved to see very few tribal designs.

As I was examining the artwork, not really allowing myself to think too much about what would inevitably come next, a burly man with arms sleeved with tattoos walked through the bead curtain separating the display room from what I assumed were the tattooing rooms.

With a huge, friendly smile he hugged Stinki, then offered me his enormous paw. "Nadel," he introduced himself.

"Chef," I said with a smile.

He and Stinki chatted for a minute, most of which was lost on me, since Stinki had slipped back into his gurgling dialect. After a short pause, Nadel looked at me and said, "Shall we?"

Stinki placed his hand on my shoulder and looked at me earnestly. "Hey, would you mind if I came back with you?"

Accepting fate as it was, I shrugged and smiled. "Sure, man, whatever you want."

Curiosity got the best of me once we arrived in the room and I finally broke down and asked Stinki what he had up his sleeve.

"Well," he said, taking a seat on a chair against the wall, "remember how you told me about that tattoo you have? The word *Schatz* above your dick? And how you were embarrassed by it?"

I nodded.

"Well, I had the idea to have it fixed for you. So I talked to Nadel over here," he pointed with his head toward the tattoo artist, who had his back turned, preparing the needles and the tattoo gun, "and we came up with a plan."

Having no idea what you could do to fix a six-lettered word written in cursive, I just shook my head in willing defeat. I was amazed that Stinki had remembered my birthday, but even more amazed that he had the foresight to come up with a gift that would apparently rid me of the shame of a tattoo I had agreed to as a result of Deirdre. This ink that had been part of me for almost five years was a constant reminder of her every time I took a piss or a shower. Even when I wanted to jerk off I was forced to think of Deirdre. And every time I thought of her I just felt defeated.

Nadel turned toward me with a cheap, plastic razor held in his massive hands, bulging in their pale blue prison of latex. "So, my friend, time to shave your little pecker."

I should have been embarrassed. I should have felt like standing up and saying, "No, thanks, I'm good." I should have allowed the absurdity of the moment to act as a flashbulb, awakening me and calling me to my senses. My face should have reddened at the idea of dropping my pants in front of two men. Instead, I unbuckled my pants and slid them, along with my boxer shorts, down to my thighs, and grinned. "Full alive!"

Nadel got to work preparing for his handiwork, surprisingly professional in his demeanor. I looked over at Stinki. He had reached into his trusty black backpack and pulled out a tiny tape deck. He pressed play and the song *"Es gibt Millionen"* by Angeschissen filled the room, drowning out the sound of a plastic razor sliding across pubic hair. Then he reached back into his bag and produced a single bottle of beer.

"After you're done, I'll reward you with *ein Geschätztes*," he said, smiling as he slowly ran his finger beneath the slogan emblazoned on the label.

When it hit me I couldn't do anything but drop my head back onto the leather-wrapped seat and laugh.

***

Less than an hour later we were walking back toward our dorm, my steps taken a bit more gingerly than Stinki's, a result of the eight letters and one umlaut added to my old, embarrassing tattoo. A permanent reminder of Deirdre now a tribute to my drunken escapades with Stinki.

"You know," Stinki mused as we boarded the bus back home, "I think once I save up a bit more I'm gonna get a matching tattoo. To commemorate our time together. And this magnificent brew, of course!"

We clinked bottles and drank, the bus chugging its way up the winding hill toward the dorms. The sun was cutting through the trees nearly full with leaves, the refractions of light almost blinding. In the distance, the massive hill that mirrored the town appeared to be crawling with ants. Picnickers, dog-walkers, lovers, horseback riders. People enjoying the evening, eagerly anticipating the arrival of summer.

Kleine Freiheit was packed by the time we arrived. The sheer amount of people coupled with the absolutely beautiful June night led to the bar overflowing out into the area where the student mailboxes were located and even spilling out the door of the building. Stinki bought me a beer as a birthday present, as if the six-pack and the tattoo weren't enough. Other friends of ours—people we had met drinking in the bar or from

Stinki's short-lived time attending classes—also joined us, coming and going like the tide, many of them offering me shots and beers. Stinki and I also ebbed and flowed, moving from the bar to the mailroom to the outside and back.

"How's it feel?" Stinki asked me, as we stood in front of the entrance to the bar beneath the night sky speckled with shimmering stars.

"I dunno," I said, sipping. "Like twenty-two, but with a different number at the end, I guess."

Stinki laughed into his beer, dropping his head and shaking it, trying to keep the foam from squirting out his mouth. "No, you dope, I mean the tattoo?"

"Oh!" I laughed with him. "Well, it feels like a new tattoo. Like the old one, but with more letters." It felt pretty much like I remember the original feeling—itchy, a slight burning every once in a while. But unlike last time, there were no nagging second thoughts about whether I had made a poor decision.

I raised my beer and toasted Stinki. "Thanks, man. That was really thoughtful of you."

He nodded. "Well, I was going to give you an *Irokese,* but I figured that would've been harder to get you to agree to," he said, lifting the tufts of chartreuse hair lining the center of his mostly-shaven skull.

"Wait, you call that an *Irokese*? Like the Iroquois?" I asked.

Stinki looked confused. "Don't ask me where it comes from. It's just called an *Irokese.* Don't you guys call it a mohawk?'

"Yeah, but I also heard the Brits call it a Mohican. Are they all the same people? Or are they different tribes?"

"Again," Stinki said, emptying his bottle of beer, "don't ask me. You're the American. Whether they're the same tribe or different ones, it doesn't matter. You're the ones who wiped them out, not us!" He slapped my back in good nature.

"Do I really need to talk to you about genocide?" I asked.

"*Ach*! Tribes, religions, nationalities. It's all shit. Nonsense. Made up. You're American, I'm German. And sixty years ago our grandfathers were forced to kill each other. But really," his voice dropped, "my grandfather fought on the eastern front, so unless your grandfather was a Russki, mine didn't shoot at yours." He sipped from his beer and resumed his jovial philosophical rant. "I mean, your ancestors killed the Indians. And my ancestors—or relatives—killed the Jews. And here we are now, me and you, killing our brain cells *together*." He emphasized this last word by throwing his arm around my shoulders. "Apropos, killing brain cells…" he pointed to his empty beer. I looked at mine, finished it, and handed him the empty. He turned and headed back in to grab another round.

I took a few steps away from the building, away from the crowd of students laughing and talking and smoking and flirting and stepped out into the night. With my neck tilted all the way back I took in the black sky. Far above, Libra shined, that universal symbol of balance, dangling from the hands of Astrea.

With my gaze toward the stars I felt a buzzing in my pocket. The black screen lit up green with the number of my house line back in the US. I took a few steps farther seeking silence.

"Hello?"

"Jacob! There you are! Happy birthday!" my father's voice was distant.

"Oh, thanks." I pulled the phone away from my ear and checked the time. Just past two AM.

"So listen, I was talking to Angelo, he said he still hasn't seen your name on the registry. They closed the course three weeks ago. Did you forget to sign up?"

I looked up toward the black sky and pictured my father's words being transmitted from his mouth to the piece of plastic held at his ear and into the wires running out of the house and into the street being converted into magic dust and shot up into the darkness above my head, bouncing off a satellite somewhere, maybe even that tiny blinking dot next to Libra, and falling, rocketing down toward me, the millions of pieces of magic dust being reassembled and put back into English, funneling themselves through the piece of plastic held to my ear.

"Jacob, are you there?"

"Yeah." I cleared my throat. "Um, yeah, I didn't register. I don't know. I guess it just kind of slipped my mind." I thought back to the fifteenth, how I spent the day sleeping off the effects of whatever the hell that powder was that we had snorted. And how, upon waking, I spent the rest of the day in bed with my laptop, trying to digest the news about Valentine's, doing research on who was arrested or cited, scared to learn the truth.

"Shit, Jacob." There was no animosity in his voice. He just sounded tired.

"Sorry, dad."

"Ah, whatever." He sighed. "It's no big deal. I'm sure Angelo can figure it out."

"Yeah."

I waited for him to ask what I was doing. Where I was. Why I was up at two AM. If I was having a good time. If I was staring up at the night sky. If I had fallen in love. Or out of love.

"Well listen, I just wanted to see what was going on about those classes. It's late here, I just got back from the goddamn office, there's some shit going on with some of the properties. One we recently sold might need to be resold and it's turning into a whole mess. And these goddamn squatters shit up an entire property we were fixing to sell up in Fishtown. That place is the next hot spot, by the way. We really need to make a move on it. But man, Jake, I'll tell you, this whole heroin mess is getting out of hand over here. These junkies ruin everything. They steal all the copper or they just move in wherever they see fit, it's just a mess." He whistled through his teeth.

"Yeah."

"Alright, well I'll see you in what, like two weeks or so?"

"Eighteen days." I wondered if he noticed anything in my voice. The way I said that number.

"Yeah. Listen, we'll sit down then and talk it out, okay?"

"Yeah."

"Oh, Jake, I've been meaning to tell you. You got some piece of mail addressed to you. From a urologist. Should I open it for you? I just kept forgetting to tell you about it, it kept slipping my mind with work and all, and I-"

"Uh, nah," I interrupted him. "I mean. I'm sure it's nothing. But just toss it in my room. I'll open it when I get back."

"Hm. Okay."

Before I could say anything else he continued, eager to end the call. "Listen, I've gotta get going. We'll talk soon."

"Okay."

"Bye."

"Bye."

I slid the phone back into my pocket and went to find Stinki. Heading toward the bar, I made a quick stop at the mailboxes in the common area. I laughed at my own foolish optimism back in October, how I had made daily trips—sometimes twice a day—to this room in nervous anticipation and how I had left in bitter disappointment almost every time. Since December I had checked the mailbox maybe once a month. I spun in the five-digit code and the thin metal door popped open with a comforting click. Inside was an off-white envelope emblazoned with the words *Universitätsklinikum Ankerich.* I tucked the envelope into my pocket and walked back into the bar in search of Stinki.

I found him standing with a crowd of people, talking animatedly with beers in both hands.

"There he is!"

"Yeah, sorry." I took the beer he offered me. "My dad called."

"To wish you happy birthday?"

"Kind of."

The bar had been slowly emptying as it was well past midnight, but out of nowhere I felt the sudden urge to keep going.

"Hey Stinki, what do you say we head upstairs and sit out on the balcony. I've got that six-pack still, and I'm sure I could dig up something else. Maybe you still have enough stuff in your room to whip up a few *letzte Drinks?*"

"Sounds like a plan to me," he agreed. We said our goodbyes to the remaining people still milling about outside the door and headed back to our dorm.

As the cramped elevator climbed its way up toward the sixth floor, I read the motley assortment of graffiti scrawled or etched into the walls around us. Without thinking, I reached into my pocket, pulled out the thick key to the building door, and in crooked lettering added my own contribution.

When the elevator stopped on our floor, we stepped out and I cast a quick glance back into the tiny cage. Amid the black marker drawings and key-scraped sayings were the words "Full Alive."

Stinki disappeared to his room to see if he could scrounge up the ingredients for some *letzte Drinks*, and I went to my room to grab the six-pack he had given me hours before. The beer was sitting next to my laptop, still open from earlier. I ran my finger across the mousepad to check the time. The site with the practice questions popped up, a message in the center of the screen: "Sorry, but your session has been timed out." I exited the site and opened up my email. Among the spam, one caught my attention. An email from julia.gruenwald@gmx.de. I sat down and opened the message.

Hi Jake,

Long time, no talk. I just wanted to see if you were going to the American Studies Department's office closing party. Apparently they do it every year on the first day of summer. It's supposed to be a lot of fun. Heike told me I could invite my friends, so I think Katja's going to join us. She asked me if your friend is coming (is his name really Stinki?)

Anyway, I just wanted to ask you that.

Oh, and Happy Birthday :)

Hugs,

Julia

I clapped the laptop shut and walked over to the window, opening it all the way. I leaned out and breathed in the cool spring air. Standing at the window, looking up at the night sky, I felt for a moment a strong sense of the present. Not the past. Not the future. This moment. And I wanted to celebrate. Celebrate this exact moment. That I was here, in this town at this moment, beneath these stars, whose light was emitted a thousand years ago, yet on this night, in this moment, the light shining was still bright and alive. Their past was our present. And they'd continue to burn on long after we were all dead. Me. Stinki. Julia. All of us. Even Deirdre.

It fell heavy on my shoulders as soon as I realized that in a matter of weeks, this exact moment would be the past, a memory. A distraction from the future present—me making sales, pushing homes on people in an attempt to pad my wallet. Or my father's.

I closed the window and left the room, stopping first to pee in the sink.

Stinki was already on the balcony when I burst through the sticky plastic curtain dividing the inside from outside.

"There you are!" he exclaimed. "I was just about to come break down your door! Look at me!" he held up his empty hands. "I'm dying of thirst here."

I handed him one of the warm beers he had given me for my birthday. He accepted with an uncomfortable smile. "I feel bad, this is your present."

"Believe me," I said, "it's the least I can do."

Not needing much convincing, he gripped the bottle in both hands and used his thumbs to press up on the metal clasp holding down the ceramic stopper.

PLOP!

A muffled noise exploded out over the bar below us and careened toward the rolling hills in the distance.

PLOP!

I followed his lead. We raised our bottles and drank. The beer was definitely different from what I had grown accustomed to in southern Germany. Crisp, sharp, slightly bitter.

"This is great, man!" I thanked Stinki.

He nodded and sipped. We sat for a while, not talking, just sipping and looking out into the night. Most lights in the adjacent dorms were out. The ones that were on flickered with muted colors of tv screens behind curtains or played out puppet shows with the shadows of the inhabitants moving about. Most houses had turned out the lights for the night. It was approaching three AM.

We sat together in a comfortable silence, the kind that can only exist between two people who understand each other. The silence of friendship. After about an hour, we had finished the six-pack, each bottle a third-of-a-liter and not the half-liters we were accustomed to.

"What now?" Stinki asked, after sipping the foam from the bottom of his last bottle.

I had no idea. I was not in the mood to go to bed yet. I was loving the night and the sky and the stars and the company, watching the lights in the dorms turn off or on, feeling the rhythm of this quiet hilltop.

"I have an idea," I said to Stinki, as I climbed up from my chair and walked back into the kitchen. Crouching in front of the mini-fridge that belonged to my hallmate with the private coffee maker, I examined the lock. A three-digit code was needed. I remembered his t-shirt when I met him and he informed me that I was most certainly not allowed to share his coffee maker.

The lock popped open. Inside the mostly-empty fridge was an unopened bottle of white wine. It would do.

I helped myself to the cold bottle and locked up the fridge. I found a corkscrew in one of the communal drawers full of leftover kitchenware from the hundreds of students who had shuffled in and out of this dorm throughout the years.

Outside I presented Stinki the bottle.

"Whoa! White wine! Elegant!" He drank straight from the bottle and passed it back to me. I did the same.

Stinki sat quietly for a while, enveloped in an improbable calmness.

"You know what, Chef?" he asked, his eyes fixed on the darkness in the distance, beyond his untied boots resting on the railing in front of us. "I'm in a really good mood."

He turned and looked at me. He wasn't smiling, but he didn't need to. I believed him.

"Stinki," I said, taking a sip and passing the bottle back to him, "you're always in a good mood."

He accepted the bottle and sipped, looking back out into the darkness. "True," he said, "Good point."

I smiled and followed his gaze. Out in the distance, on the horizon where the hills of the modest mountain range rolled, their backs evident even in the darkness, a light slowly appeared. Growing brighter, yet awash in a milky light, I was able to make it out. The moon. I had never seen the moon rise. Stinki and I sat in silence and watched the awesome spectacle, periodically passing the sweat-beaded bottle back and forth.

"*Geil!* He said. "*Wahnsinn!*"

"Yeah, man, this is awesome."

We watched as the moon rose, silently, gently, determined.

"So where'd you get that bottle, anyway?" Stinki eventually broke the silence.

"Well, I know this guy who listens to 311. I figured he needed to be taught a lesson."

I reached out to accept the stolen bottle being handed to me. Stinki's face was bathed in moonlight. He wasn't looking at me, but I could tell he was smiling.

"Birthday card?" he asked, nodding toward my front left pocket, where the envelope was poking out.

"Oh," I laughed, sliding the letter out from my pocket. "No, it's from the clinic."

I ran my finger along the seal, the paper ripping neatly along the crease. Inside was a tri-folded letter, the results of my blood test. My eyes glided down the list of horrible diseases, looking for one specific result. I read from top to bottom then from bottom to top. On my second run I found it, fifth from the top.

Chlamydia : NEGATIV.

Chapter 20

I hadn't heard from my father since our talk on my birthday. I had called him on Sunday to wish him a happy Father's Day, but he never answered. And with my departure from Ankerich less than twenty-four hours away, I was riding a roller coaster of emotions.

Heike and, surprisingly, Uschi had told me about the little celebration the Monday after I had read Julia's email, and, though I was nervous about seeing her again, I figured there was no way I could miss the party.

In the midst of wrapping up work and packing my room, I had forgotten to respond to Julia. I had, however, mentioned the event to Stinki, who showed immediate interest in an excuse to hang out—and a potential chance to see Katja again.

The evening of the event, after spending most of the day packing my room, I had managed to stow most of my conflicting emotions away and focus on the excitement of one last night in Ankerich. My last day of work had been the Friday before, and, though I had had plenty of time to get things done, I had spent most of the time with Stinki, drinking and farting around on the balcony.

We stepped off the bus at the stop on the bridge. Already I could see the celebration in full swing on the island below us. Squeezing between two flower beds hanging on the railings, we leaned over and checked out the site. About thirty people stood or sat conversing and sipping drinks from bottles and glasses. There were several long beer benches set up along the river and a bar cart behind them. From above I could make out Julia, her hair shining butter golden in the sun, a pale yellow summer dress gently waving in the breeze. She had her back to us and was talking to Katja. No signs of a Ramones t-shirt anywhere.

With a knot in my stomach, we made our way down the metal staircase onto the island.

"Tschake!" Julia greeted me, friendly and warm. Her embrace was firm and lingering. She pulled away, leaving her non-drink hand on my shoulder. "It's so nice to see you again," she said to me, in German.

"Same," I heard myself respond.

For a brief moment, we stood there, looking at each other, her smile never fading. I tried to make out a hint of anger, disappointment, contempt—anything. But there was nothing. Just a genuine delight to see me.

"Want a drink?" she asked, breaking the silence.

"Yes," I managed to spit out.

We turned and walked toward the drink cart, leaving Stinki and Katja behind, the two of them already engaged in a lively conversation. I struggled to find something to say, but could only hear the rhythm of the gravel crunching under our feet. Where should I start? Do I just pick up where we left off? Where did we even leave off? Her politely and quietly leaving my room while I pretended to sleep and then me ignoring her for the next six months?

How could I explain to her why I never wrote or called or even answered text messages or emails? After a while, I stopped thinking about how to explain this all to Julia and realized I had no explanation for myself. Was it because of Deirdre? Or my fear of commitment, in case she ever came back? Or a misguided sense of fidelity toward someone who was no longer part of my life? That was how I had spent my college years, I was supposed to be over that by this point. For the past nine months I felt like I had been desparately blowing on cold ashes in hopes of stoking smoldering embers. And it was pathetic.

"So, Jake, how does it feel? Your last night in Ankerich?" Heike stood next to Julia, smiling at me with a glass of white wine in her hand.

"Well, I mean… God, I don't know!" I told her the truth.

Heike laughed. Julia smiled and turned to order some drinks.

"Well, I can understand. I felt the same way after coming back from St. Louis. I had been there three years, so you could imagine how tough it was for me." She sipped from her glass and looked out over the island toward the bridge, lost in her own thoughts.

"Yeah."

Julia returned with our drinks.

"To Tschake!" she said, after handing me my beer. We all raised our drinks and drank to me.

Uschi appeared out of nowhere, her slithering silenced by the surrounding revelry. "Food is ready," she announced unceremoniously.

We took a seat on the beer benches and helped ourselves to ceramic bowls and plates full of assorted grilled sausages and marinated steaks, warm, vinegary potato salad, crusty rolls with herb butter, and a simple salad of lettuce and sliced tomatoes.

Stories were swapped and jokes were cracked. Stinki fit in as if he had been working in the department his entire life. Students recently returned from studying in the US talked about their experiences, the good and the bad, the ups and downs. I enjoyed not being the focal point of the evening, allowing me to not spend all my time on the dwindling hours I had left in Ankerich.

After dinner, the benches cleared significantly, with guests standing up to feed the ducks or smoke and take in the splendor of the approaching evening.

Stinki and I sat on one side of the bench, Katja and Julia on the other. To my right sat another couple of students, across from them three others. During a lull in the conversation, Julia sighed and leaned back, hands gripping her belly.

"Whew! I think I need an after dinner drink. And maybe to go for a short stroll. Anyone care to join me?"

"I'll come with you," I offered.

The couple next to me had disappeared, but the group of three across from them remained. Julia stood up and told Katja she'd be back in a bit. I followed her lead and stood up. With the complete lack of counterweight on our side of the bench, the entire thing lifted to the right, dipping Stinki on my left to the ground. He tumbled to the grass and dirt and the bench came crashing back down. He lay there on his back, laughing, his bottle of beer held triumphantly above his head.

"Don't worry, I saved the beer!" he yelled to everyone who had turned to see what had happened, their conversations interrupted by the commotion.

Julia and Katja laughed, I shook my head, all too familiar with Stinki's antics. Leaving Katja to help Stinki up from the ground, Julia and I strolled toward the drink cart.

"So, did you hear Uschi is leaving?" she asked me, after we had each ordered a new drink.

"What? No, I hadn't heard. She doesn't talk to me much, you know?"

Julia laughed. "Well, apparently she's going on to get her master's or something. Somewhere else. So she's leaving." She took a tiny sip, delicate and soft. Her eyes looked out over the rim of her glass, not focused on anything in particular. "So," she continued, "Heike's going to have to replace her." She turned to me, her eyes glinting with excitement. "Oh, and I'm going to take over your job! I get to be the new Tschake!"

She laughed and we started walking slowly toward the bridge.

"Ah, you don't want that," I said. "Who would ever want to be me? I'm not a great person."

"Oh, come on," she said, exaggeratedly. "You're not *that* bad."

We took a seat on the bench. Looking up at the wall where Julia and I used to eat lunch, filtered by the wispy branches of the weeping willow, I ran my hand down along the lip of the seat, feeling for the initials I had carved in October.

"So where's Torben?" I asked.

Julia turned to me, her eyes squinted in confusion. My hand kept feeling for the letters beneath me.

"Who's Torben?"

"Or is his name Dieter?"

Julie shook her head in confusion.

"Your boyfriend?"

"What boyfriend? I don't have a boyfriend!" she said, her voice raised, incredulous.

I felt what might have been a letter D beneath my right thigh. I began picking at the paint and splintered wood around it.

"I saw you like five or six weeks ago walking with a guy in Stuttgart. He was wearing a Ramones shirt."

From the corner of my eye, I caught a flash of red wash over Julia's face. "Oh my god! That guy!" She put her palm to her forehead, then lowered her head to face her lap. I kept picking at the first D, feeling for the next D.

"God, Tschake, he was such a loser! He was in that translation class with me and we had to do a project together. He kept trying to get me to go on a date with him. It was so embarrassing."

"Looks like he succeeded," I said dryly.

I slid my hand back from the lip of the bench, afraid she'd see me and ask what I was doing.

"Not really. I agreed to go to a movie with him. He claimed that the movie had like 'the best dubbing ever.'" She used air quotes to emphasize, dropping the pitch of her voice to sound like a moron. "All the while he kept trying to hold my hand and stuff. It was awful."

I laughed.

"No, I'm serious, Tschake, it sucked. I wish you would've said something to me, it would've given me an excuse to ditch him."

I thought back to Stinki and me lying in the park, reeking of beer and sweat and chlorine from the fountain.

Julia sighed and leaned back, folding her arms behind her wavy locks, and looked out toward the gray stone wall. I stole a glance to my right. Her sundress had slipped above her knees, halfway up her thighs. The soft, fair hairs on her tanned skin were visible in the evening's gentle glow, sparkling like diamonds, like the snowflakes melting on her wool hat in December.

I leaned back, having decided that erasing Deirdre's name from the bench was good enough. My initials could stay for now.

"So does Heike know who's going to take over Uschi's position?" I asked, my eyes focused on the pastel facades changing shades in the setting sun.

"Well, she wants to hire someone who knows what they're doing. Someone with experience, you know. Ideally someone who's worked in the office before." I caught her looking at me.

I returned the gaze. For a second or two, I stared into her eyes. The green of her irises reflected everything around her. The magnificant hues of the evening sky. The bright colors of the surrounding architecture. My regretful face.

"Hey listen," I started, and immediately didn't know how to finish.

"Tschake," she said calmly, "don't worry about it," closing her eyes and waving it off with her hand.

But I couldn't let myself get away without saying anything.

"No, Julia, hear me out. I feel terrible. I mean, I obviously care about you, you've been so great to me, ever since that first lunch we had. And I just, I don't know… I wasn't expecting that whole thing with the Christmas market. Truth be told, my girlfriend, or who I thought was my girlfriend, or whatever, she kind of broke up with me that day. So my head was a mess, and I just wasn't thinking." I shook my head. "I'm still not thinking."

Julia faced the river, her thumb running smoothly up and down the stem of her wine glass. "You never told me you had a girlfriend," she said quietly.

I sighed. "Yeah, well, I don't know. I mean, it was my ex who wanted to get back with me. But then decided against it the day of the market. But in hindsight the whole idea was doomed from the start."

My fingers slid across the lip of the bench again, feeling for evidence of Deirdre's initials. Where I imagined them to be was just smooth wood, an occasional soft splinter sticking out.

I cleared my throat. "Remember how I told you I saw you in Stuttgart—"

"Tschake!" Julia yelled, sitting up abruptly. "Look! It's your squirrel!"

My gaze followed her extended arm and pointing finger. A solitary fox-red squirrel ran in a corkscrew around the trunk of the weeping willow in front of us.

I smiled, thinking of the story I had told her back in the fall.

Before I could work up the guts to continue what I had started to tell her, she spoke. "But really, Tschake. I understand. I figured you were just living your time here to the fullest. And wanted nothing to hold you back. I get it." She paused and took a tiny sip from her glass. "I kind of wish I had done that when I was in Maryland." She looked at me, her face open and honest. A smile appeared and she turned to look out over the river again. "And for what it's worth, that night was fun," she added quietly, bowing her head and allowing her honey golden locks to curtain her face. We sat silently, taking in the beauty of the old town, enjoying the idyllic pleasantness of a warm June evening. She breathed in deep and arched her back, her thin dress stretching across her chest. "But let's just forget about it. Or, maybe don't forget about it, but you know what I mean," she said, looking at me, her eyes half-squinted.

I thought about speaking but couldn't find the words.

Julia saved me from my tongue-tied silence by continuing her monologue. "So cheers! Let's celebrate tonight!" She held out her glass, holding my gaze in exaggerated focus as I touched my bottle of beer to her wine. "Of course I'm not exactly celebrating that you're leaving, but, hey, you'll be back, right?" she said, nudging me.

"There are the two lovers!" Stinki's distinct rasp called out as he and Katja walked up the dirt path toward us.

"I think your boss wants to do some balloon ceremony or something. She was looking for you," Katja told us. Stinki stood under the weeping willow, tugging at the wisteria growing up the trunk and creeping out into the branches, freeing the tree of the suffocating vine. Suddenly he jumped back and yelled something, though neither Julia nor I could understand his garbled dialect. She looked at me with an acknowledging smile.

"Underwater *Spätzle*," she whispered, and I broke out in laughter.

Stinki approached us, his outstretched hand offering up a selection of fresh green nuts topped with leafy caps. "Hazelnuts!" he exclaimed, looking like a child who just found a bag of candy on the street. He dropped the cluster onto the ground and gently stomped it with his filthy Doc Martens. Bending over to retrieve the mashed mess of shells and pulp he let out a tiny fart.

"Oops!" He smiled and popped a piece of the whitish flesh into his mouth. With the concentrated look of a sommelier, he mumbled, "Not ripe," and spit the half-masticated mush onto the dusty gravel. He looked me in the eyes. "You'll just have to come back in September!"

Katja shook her head. "You can take the boy out of the Black Forest, but you can't take the Black Forest out of the boy."

Laughing, we made our way back to the party. Around a tiny fire pit, some people stood roasting marshmallows, the students who had just returned from the US giving tips to those yet to spend time in America.

Heike had apparently planned a symbolic balloon release. For the students who had just returned from studying abroad it was meant to symbolize their newfound open minds. For those about to leave and study in the US, it was meant to symbolize their new journey. All I could think about as we released the balloons was which turtle would mistake it for a jellyfish and choke to death on the latex leaving my hand.

After doing our part in polluting the environment, we decided to make a move.

"Let's take one last stroll through the town. For Jake," Katja suggested.

"Last stroll for *now*," Stinki added, looking at me with a smile.

Julia and I headed over to part ways with Heike, who embraced me with a heartfelt hug. After thanking me profusely for the little work I did, she held onto my shoulders and looked me in the eyes. "You talked to Julia, right?"

I nodded with a puzzled look on my face.

"Well, let me know what you think."

I nodded in agreement, not entirely sure what she was talking about.

Uschi appeared out of nowhere and offered me a plump hand. "Well," she said, "it was kind of nice working with a New Jerseyan."

Again I just nodded, confused by this comment as well.

"I guess I never told you, but when I spent my year abroad it was in New Jersey. In a town called Neptune."

I almost laughed aloud at the irony. Luckily Julia's eyes met mine, making it clear that the humor needed no explanation.

"I had no idea," I said.

"Yeah, well, that's not a surprise. There's a lot you don't know. But you still have time to learn. Who knows, maybe someday you'll even be as smart as me. Well, maybe not that, but at least smart enough to do my job."

She smiled for the first time. It wasn't a bad look on her.

We broke away from Heike and Uschi and the rest of the revelers and headed toward the stairs. As we passed by the bench I took a quick peek at the lip. The letters JC were visible, preceded by a blank, paintless patch of chipped wood.

We made our way slowly to the marketplace with the remarkable, almost 600-year-old town hall, and stood still taking in the sight. The square was washed in the navy twilight of the darkening sky. The stone fountain with its baroque sculpture rising majestically out of the center sprayed water from its pipes, gently splashing the backs of the couples and groups of friends sitting along the edge, chatting, passing bottles, and smoking, the glow of their cigarettes flickering like fireflies.

Stinki disappeared around the corner to buy a bottle of wine, Katja agreeing to accompany him. Julia and I took a seat along the edge of the fountain.

"Ah, I love it so much. The blue hour," Julia said, her words nearly drowned out by the trickling of the fountain.

"The what?" I asked, following her gaze up into the sky.

"The blue hour," she repeated. "After the sun goes down, but before darkness takes over. The sky just takes on this amazing shade of blue. And every minute it looks different. Sometimes it can last for over an hour."

I had to admit, the sky was incredibly impressive. Nothing like I had ever seen at home. The full moon had illuminated much of the sky, causing it to appear deeper, fuller. Dark clouds drifted quickly across the clearer patches, casting shadows down on the square.

"'And so you are going abroad; and when do you return?

But that is a useless question.

You hardly know when you are coming back,

You will find so much to learn'"

I looked over at Julia and felt my smile fall heavily.

"Thanks for that T.S. Eliot book, by the way."

She smiled. "No problem. I guess I never thanked you for your present either."

"I never gave you the chance to."

Stinki and Katja came walking across the moonlit square, Katja glancing up toward the sky as they approached.

"So, a nice little treat to toast the special evening," Stinki said, placing a bottle of wine on the stone ledge of the fountain. "It's no *letzter Drink*, but that's okay. No need for a 'last drink' anyway, right?" He smiled at me.

"It looks like it's gonna pour," Katja said, once again looking up at the sky.

All four of us craned our necks to peer into the night sky. The royal blue had darkened noticeably into shades of violet and black. Clouds floated hurriedly from one side to the other as if being pulled on a line.

"*Ach*, plenty of time for a few drinks here with Jake!" Stinki said, immediately freezing. "Shit, I forgot glasses. And a corkscrew!"

He erupted into laughter. "I mean, I can get the bottle open, but we're all just gonna have to drink straight from the bottle. It's not like most of us haven't already swapped spit," he glanced at Katja, then shot me and Julia a grin.

We watched as Stinki used his key to jam the cork straight into the bottle. He handed the bottle to the girls and we took turns passing it around. I thought about how many thousands of people had sat on this same stone fountain. How many couples. Friends. And were they still couples? Friends? What were their stories? Their futures? Our present right now.

Julia sighed deeply, content. "Ah, isn't it just so beautiful?" she asked, quietly, as if to herself. "It's like that movie 'Before Sunset,' you know? The one that just came out?"

I didn't know what she was talking about and felt suddenly overwhelmed by everything. This perfect night, the heat of the day being swallowed by the damp coolness of the evening, sliding into it like a glove. The sky, which had shed its beautiful bruise-colored hues for a solemn darkness like ink spilling slowly into water, offered a confident promise of tomorrow. The company, these two girls who had every reason to despise me yet were content to spend their evening with me and my friend. The shared bottle of wine itself tasted as ancient as the buildings surrounding me, weathered but welcoming, mysterious yet familiar. I glanced over at Julia, her hands beneath her thighs, her sandals lying on the ground below her bare feet swinging carefree like a child's. I looked over at Stinki and Katja, flirting and poking each other, Katja's giggles occasionally bursting into shrieks of pleasure. And Stinki, happy as ever, that perpetual smile a source of constant energy, vibrant and warm.

I had the sudden urge to explode.

I excused myself to find a bathroom. Hurrying across the cobblestoned marketplace, I remembered seeing a public bathroom in the alley below the church.

The sounds of nightlife and early-summer merrymaking disappeared as I stepped into the tiled room. Standing at the urinal my eyes caught a white ceramic tile among the rest of the solid pale yellow ones. A simplistic painting of a man hiking with a satchel slung across his shoulder stood above the saying "*Abschied ist mir nicht so schwer, bald komme ich ja wieder her.*" I took a moment to translate in my head, trying to match the rhyme. "Saying goodbye is not so tough, I'll be back soon enough."

Immediately I was ambushed by the sudden urge to just leave. Make an Irish exit. No goodbyes. Walk out of the bathroom and head straight home. Grab my bags and take the first train to the airport. If you never say goodbye it's like you never even left, right?

Or does that in return also mean you were never even there in the first place?

I took a deep breath, splashed some cold water on my face, and left the bathroom.

The air outside had already dropped a few degrees and the wind had picked up. I hustled back to the square, stopping once to take in the view. An empty marketplace lined with half-timbered homes and shops, each one's roof pitched differently, unique. A towering, old town hall, leaning slightly forward in its age. Three figures sitting on a fountain, passing a bottle back and forth, heads tilting back with sips or laughter.

"Tschake, we should probably make a move, it really looks like it's about to open up any second now," Julia said as I approached. She passed me the bottle to finish, and I placed it down against the base of the fountain.

Just then a gust of wind came, eliciting shrieks of surprise from the few people still scattered about the square. A beer bottle rolled noisily across the cobblestones, the loud rattling echoing across the suddenly empty marketplace, hollow and rhythmic, like an unfollowable jazz tune. The first drops of rain came tumbling down from the sky, thick, heavy, and cold, crashing clumsily onto the hard ground, bursting like gunfire. Couples ducked their heads, hands held futilely above their hair, and ran for cover.

The four of us sprinted toward the closest awning, the girls shrieking and giggling with each assault from above. We stood shoulder-to-shoulder watching the storm roll over our heads, the thunder announcing its arrival.

Stinki launched into his favorite Blondie cover, singing about a sky full of thunder and telephone numbers.

"Oh yeah! Tschake, you've got to give me your American number. Or your address, too, I guess." Julia had already fished out a pen from her purse and was scribbling her information down in a mini notebook. She finished writing and handed the pen and notebook to me. After writing my address and phone number I handed the notebook back to her and folded up the sheet with her info.

Stinki continued his off-tune singing, botching the lyrics about photos in wallets, the song completely out of order.

I quickly slid Julia's information in front of the mini picture of Deirdre I had forgotten was in my wallet.

Just then, a shrill and obnoxious cawing filled the sky. We turned our heads upwards to see what appeared to be five or six parrots flying above us, clamoring in the quickly clearing sky.

"How cute!" Julia said, smiling. "That must be the offspring of the birds that broke out of the Wilhelma Zoo in Stuttgart a few years ago. I guess they've made their way down to Ankerich."

My eyes met Stinki's in slow motion, the night of our ecstasy trip in the woods rushing back in a flood of communal memory.

"I guess some animals do sometimes try to break out of their confinements," Julia added, a soft smile directed toward me, acknowledging my aquarium comment.

We stood for a few minutes admiring the rain-free sky, watching as the last storm clouds floated east, before deciding to go our separate ways. I knew that if I spent the night hanging out and partying, I'd likely miss my flight the next day. And even worse, the farewell would hit even harder. The idea of pulling an all-nighter was floated by Stinki, but I nixed it, and was surprised when he put up no fight.

We made our way toward the bus stop, walking quietly, the only sounds were our shoes squeaking on the wet stone. From the bus stop on the bridge we could see that the party had died down. The benches were all neatly stacked, the drink cart locked up, and the fire pit was smoldering, a thin trickle of smoke writhing above the gray coals.

When our bus approached, Katja first gave me a quick hug, then turned to Stinki. I turned to Julia.

"Well, then," she said, still speaking to me in German. "Tschake, it was a pleasure working with you. Too bad we didn't get a chance to spend more time together."

My stomach clenched into a tight fist. A fist I wished would just smash me in the face. Knock out a few teeth for being such a goddamned stupid idiot.

Her face turned blurry. I hugged her, not knowing what to say, and not wanting her to keep looking into my eyes.

"Julia, thanks for being a friend," was all I could manage to get out.

The doors of the bus opened. I let Julia's hug linger and breathed in that unforgettable scent—honeysuckle and fresh cotton—then pulled away, flashed her a quick smile, and boarded the number four for my last ride up the hill.

Chapter 21

The regional train rolled slowly, steadily north, rocking us back and forth in our seats, both of us clutching a *Geschätztes* in our hands despite the early hour. My face was glued to the window, watching everything that had become so familiar to me pass me by. Vibrant yellow fields of rapeseed. An equally yellow highway sign pointing toward Degerloch. Dark green fields of cabbage forming perfect geometric lines. The airport in the distance.

Stinki was peculiarly silent. His head pivoted from left to right, taking in the landscape around him. Familiar, but not to be missed. He'd be watching these same sights play out in front of him in reverse in less than an hour. If he made it back early enough, he'd still have time to protest the eviction of *Unser Haus.* How fitting, I thought. That on the day of my departure the place that had come to be a second home to me was being raided and turned over to a real estate developer. Someone like my father. Someone like who I was supposed to soon be.

I sighed, forcing myself to accept the inevitable truth. Then yawned. I had spent most of the night awake, putzing around my room, fingering everything left unpacked, weighing each item in my hands as if to determine its value, whether it passed the test to accompany me back to the US. I smiled to myself as I wrapped the Christmas market mug in a pair of boxer shorts and stuffed it into my suitcase. The collection of T.S. Eliot poems fit nicely along the edge, snuggled between my t-shirts and the thin plastic wall. Stinki's mixtape tucked easily into an inside pocket.

The framed photo of Deirdre felt light in my hands as I gently placed it in the wastebasket beneath my desk.

Herr Meindt visited me at six AM, impatiently rapping his weathered knuckles against my door. He walked around the room slowly, hands folded behind his back, deliberately inspecting every nook and cranny, searching for a chip or crack or stain. I had painstakingly replaced any thin wooden slat that had fallen loose from the bedframe, filled every thumbtack hole in the wall with toothpaste, and even washed the sink with some cheap disinfectant I found in the kitchen.

Herr Meindt seemed satisfied, unable to find any major flaws. We stood at the door, sandwiched between the sink and the closet, and I placed my keys in his massive hands.

"You didn't piss in the sink?"

I smirked and shook my head no. His eyes locked on mine for a few seconds longer, then he abruptly turned to leave the room. I followed, stopping in the doorway to take one last look into the room I had called home since October. How many other people had lived within these four walls before me? Who would be here next? Were they moving in today? What would they bring with them? What would they leave behind?

What was I leaving behind?

Silence accompanied the stale air of the elevator on the ride down. I noticed Herr Meindt's eyes drift to the newest graffiti, then to me. I shrugged.

He shook his head and muttered something under his breath.

My smile reflected in the train window, and I turned to Stinki, just as he lifted his leg and farted. He poured the last of his beer into his mouth and said, "Nothing like a breakfast beer, right?"

Despite the cheerful comment coming from an earnest smile, I could detect a slight catch in his voice.

"Next stop - Stuttgart airport. This train terminates here. Please exit," the mechanical voice of the woman on the train's PA announced.

"Well," Stinki said, standing up. I followed his lead, and we silently left the train and made our way into the nearly empty airport. The thudding of our feet on the sterile floors echoed lonely against the walls. I wanted to talk but couldn't. I was desperate to break the unbearable silence, to say anything, just something, but I felt frozen. My brain wasn't working, and even if it could form words, they wouldn't have been able to find their way out of my mouth. I gave up. Nothing I could've said would've made any sense, anyway. Words weren't strong enough for the situation.

In a daze, I checked in, exchanging my suitcase for a boarding pass. Stinki and I walked to security in silence.

"Well," Stinki said, repeating the only word that had been spoken between us in the last fifteen minutes. We stood looking at each other, neither of us knowing what to do with our empty hands, used to having them occupied with a beer, the awkward silence an uncomfortable replacement of the laughter and stories that we had grown so accustomed to.

My hands fluttered at my sides and I grabbed the straps of my backpack to steady them.

Stinki took a step toward me and embraced me in a powerful bearhug. "Take care, Chef."

I tried to find something to say and failed.

Stinki released me from his brotherly grip and held me by the shoulders at arms' length. "Well, it's been fun."

"Yeah," I finally managed. "Thank you."

"No problem. We'll do it again next year." It wasn't a question. And though there had been no plans made on my part for the future, and Stinki's future was even less certain, his eyes radiated sincerity.

He clapped me on my shoulder and smiled.

I turned my head and my body followed.

Through blurry eyes, I watched as the security woman took my boarding pass and passport. "You look different," she said, glancing back and forth from the photo to my face.

I forced a smile. "I've changed."

She handed me back my documents and I passed her, heading toward the security gates. I turned to wave at Stinki. One hand waved back at me enthusiastically while the other held a *Geschätztes*, miraculously conjured from somewhere. His grin widened as he lifted his leg in an inaudible farewell fart.

A beer seemed to be the only thing to help slow my racing mind, so I sought out the airport bar. Though I realized they wouldn't have *Geschätztes* on tap, and I didn't feel like explaining to the bartender how to make a *letzter Drink*, I figured anything would do. I grabbed a seat, ordered a beer, and pulled out my leather-bound notebook in an attempt to collect my thoughts.

Sipping the foam from a bitter and grassy Jever, my attention was torn away from my notebook. From the speakers, an unfamiliar voice was singing familiar lyrics. My brain fought through the waves of déjà vu to identify the source. Something about a rich man's son in his twenties. Born in June. Having no freedom.

With the next line, my memory instantly flashed back to me and Julia sitting on the ledge overlooking the river, her with a bottle of still water gripped in her hand like a microphone, belting out the chorus: "I've been looking for free-dom!"

I sat frozen, pen clutched in one hand, the other gently grasping my slightly-chilled beer, listening to the lyrics and feeling as if David Hasselhoff was singing my life story. As much as I had held it together while saying goodbye to Julia on the bridge and saying farewell to Stinki at the airport gate, this was too much. I felt the tears forming hot and salty behind my eyes, then brimming over and running down my cheeks in thick rivulets, tickling my face.

Despite the tears, I couldn't help but laugh imagining what everyone else at the bar thought of the sight: a twenty-something American sitting at a bar at ten AM, singing along to David Hasselhoff into his beer-bottle microphone, with tears streaming down his smiling face.

***

"Ladies and gentlemen, welcome to Philadelphia International Airport." I opened my eyes and stretched my legs. "Please be careful when opening the overhead bins as luggage may have shifted in flight. We wish you a pleasant stay in Philadelphia."

A grumpy, muscular man in a military uniform grilled me at customs, never allowing a smile to cross his smug face or a sense of ease slip into his air of false importance. "Do you have anything to declare? Are you bringing anything back with you?" I answered with a simple, cryptic no, and flashed him a condescending smirk.

On the other side of the customs gate, my father was waiting for me, a tired smile on his face. With a solid embrace he welcomed me back and we headed to the parking garage. After squeezing my suitcase into the trunk of his Mercedes, I slid into the passenger seat and we made our way back toward the suburbs.

The car crawled from the airport onto highways, past oil refineries and industrial parks, landfills and junkyards, and toward the massive steel bridge painted sky blue in a futile attempt to help it blend in with nature.

Awkward silence filled the car. There was no question about how I had enjoyed my time abroad. No talk about his real estate empire. No mention of how my mother or Claudia were doing. Definitely no mention of my brother.

The airport faded into the background, my connection to Ankerich dissipating with each mile. On the left side, I could see the billboard for Valentine's, the same one I tried avoiding in September. "What a shitshow," my father muttered as we passed, once again noticing my eyes glancing up at the huge sign. "We're gonna have to sell that one again," he shook his head. "I don't know if you heard, but they shut it down," he said, glancing over at me.

"Nah, I didn't hear that," I lied, not bothering to ask any questions.

"Not even three years they had that place," he shook his head again disapprovingly. "I should've known it from the start. That owner was a sleazebag."

"Mh," I acknowledged his comment, not willing for him to divulge any more information on the shutdown strip club. I hadn't talked to Deirdre since the raid and had no idea what she had been up to, or if she had found a replacement job. But as far as I could tell, no news was good news.

We drove in silence, past convenience stores where people leaned against walls, smoking or eating sandwiches, using the trash cans as tables. Stooped senior citizens and twenty-somethings in pajama pants and baggy sweatshirts clawed viciously at lottery tickets, hopelessly searching for a hint of happiness hidden beneath the dull silver shine of a scratch-off. We passed stagnating strip malls resembling a hockey player's smile, the majority of stores darkened and decrepit, devoid of any commerce or life. Signs for businesses that had closed since I had last been home were turned backward or upside down to signify their departure. "WE DELIVER" now read "REVILED EW." The tanning salon where Deirdre used to work in high school, SUNALIVE, now read EVILANUS. I silently snickered at the thought of how much Stinki would have appreciated the play on words.

My father cleared his throat.

"So, I talked to Angelo again…"

It had only been minutes since my arrival, and already the topic was being broached. I knew I had to keep the conversation short, like the conversation between Stinki and his father. My father wouldn't like it, but he had to accept it. It was a one-person decision, and I had finally come to realize that. But how could I keep it short? Tell him that I had a new perspective on life? How could I even articulate that? I knew I should feel grateful, for the offer itself, and for the life he had given me to this point. Growing up wealthier than my peers had been a source of discomfort for me now and again over the years. But how could I fault my father for trying to provide for his family? Maybe it was a bit self-motivated, but we all still reaped the benefits. My mother and Jamey took advantage of those benefits, but I shouldn't fault my father for that. All I wanted to tell him was that I wasn't ready to trade a life looking forward for a life looking backward. Not now, and not ever.

"Dad," I said, after also clearing my throat. "I just don't think it's for me." I paused. "I'm sorry."

He was silent for a moment or two. Then he inhaled deeply. "I know."

The car continued past even more closed businesses and all sorts of signs—for sale, clearance sale, going out of business sale. It seemed only the funeral homes had remained.

"You know, I had always hoped your brother would take over. Nothing against you, Jacob," he added, tossing a glance my way. "It's just, I never really saw you as a salesman, you know? And to do this job, you need to make deals. Push. Never take no for an answer. It just didn't seem like your build."

I nodded in agreement.

"I think I might just sell it. Angelo can take over, he's been with me since pretty much the beginning. And I can tell he's getting ready for bigger things. If I don't make a move now I might lose him. Plus, it'll be a pretty lucrative deal on my part, I'm sure of it."

"Yeah, Angelo will do a good job," I agreed, meaning it sincerely. My father was right, he was much more cut out for the business than I was.

"It's a shame, though. You could've made a ton of money, you know? But that sort of thing never seemed to really interest you, anyway, did it?"

I shook my head.

In the distance, a massive billboard atop the abandoned cardboard factory mirrored his face next to me.

"So, I guess I won't be needing to replace that sign." He looked at me. "It was gonna cost me an arm and a leg anyway," he turned back to the road, his smile slowly fading.

"You know I heard from your brother the other week."

I turned to him sharply. It had been years since I had heard from my brother, and the topic had been taboo to the point of avoidance.

"He got locked up. Breaking and entering." He paused. "Apparently, he was trying to steal stuff to scrap for drug money." He paused. "One of my buildings actually," he laughed a weary laugh. After a moment, he took a deep breath. "In any case, he's off to rehab," he said, exhaling. "He called me to bail him out. But I'm tired of that shit.

They want me to press charges, but I won't. We're gonna send him to rehab, one of those long-term ones. It's gonna cost a goddamn fortune, but why the hell do I make all this money anyway, right? It's not like I ever spend it on myself."

"Yeah," I muttered. "How's Claudia?" I wanted to change the subject. To talk about something more positive. About my sibling who hadn't abandoned me. The one I had abandoned instead.

"She's fine. Doing well, actually. She's been accepted to some special school for students like her." He hesitated, flipping his hand as if to acknowledge her issue with a vague gesture. "It's an all-day school, runs through the summer, too. She loves it," he added, a note higher than the rest. "We tried it out with her a few weeks ago, she started going for half days and it was a hit. She was even asking about it on Saturdays. I think she's got some friends there." He paused. "Your mother can't take care of her anymore, and I'm not around enough to be of much use."

"I think it'll be good for her. And for you, too," I added.

"You two! Ha! As if your mother and I were something of a pair," he added, obviously misunderstanding me.

"That's not what I meant, dad. I mean, it'd be good for you to not have to worry about Claudia as much. Especially if you wind up selling your agency. You'd finally have time to relax. Travel a bit, go gallivanting about." We shared a smile.

I looked out the window at the suburbs as we neared our home. Tree-lined streets, picket fences, long driveways. Not an ugly sight. But brutishly boring.

"Ah, I don't know about that," he said, resigned.

I turned to look at him. "What do you mean?"

He flicked the turn signal and maneuvered the car right, passing the welcome sign to our town. "You can leave, Jake. I can't."

Though what he was saying wasn't true, I understood him. Even if he sold the agency, he couldn't leave. There would still be Claudia, even if she was in a special school. And the ever-present thought of Jamey.

"So," he said, looking at me. "What are you going to do?"

I wasn't expecting the question. Not from him. Not even from myself. I had no idea. The talk I had with Julia just the night before reverberated in my head. I had a place to go. Yet I still felt anchored to this place, though I had just cut the line to my future with my father.

"I don't know," was all I could muster, and I felt pathetic. My father, who had worked his whole life to give me everything I could ever ask for, had asked for one thing in return. And I said no. With no reason other than I just did not want to.

Over my shoulder I felt his gaze, a slight smile on his face. "Did you meet someone over there?" he asked, his words steeped in a fatherly warmth lost since childhood.

I thought about Stinki. Julia. Katja and Heike. Eichel and Speichel and the squatter punks. Even Uschi and Herr Meindt.

"Yeah. A few people."

He nodded acknowledgingly.

We drove the final two minutes in silence. I could feel the memories from Ankerich already beginning to shape-shift, like clouds, there still, but already in a different form.

We pulled into the driveway behind the Toyota. The front door swung open and Claudia, adorned in a stained pink summer dress came bounding out toward me, her bare feet slapping on the concrete walkway.

"Jakey!" she shrieked, wrapping her arms around me, her melted-Popsicle sticky hands squeezing the back of my neck. "Are you back for good now, Jakey?"

I squeezed her back. "Well I'm here now."

Claudia loosened her grip and dropped her clammy hands to mine, tugging me toward the house. "One minute, Claudia, let me just get my things real quick."

My father grunted as he pulled my suitcase from the trunk. "Oh, one more thing." He watched as Claudia ran back toward the house, her long, uncombed hair flapping in the summer breeze behind her.

He waited until she disappeared inside, before lowering his voice. "Your friend Tyler showed up here a few days ago." His eyes met mine. "He took some money from her," he added, nodding toward the door.

"What? Claudia?" I asked, dumbfounded. "Tyler?"

"Yeah. Apparently he came asking if you or your mother were around or something. Obviously you were away and your mother…" he trailed off. "In any case, he said he needed money for some sort of emergency or something and eventually convinced Claudia to give him some. I mean, she's only a little kid, so all she had was like forty bucks in her piggy bank, but still, it was all she had. Probably her birthday money she had been saving."

I was speechless. I could get over Tyler ripping me off. But my sister…

My father cleared his throat. "Remember how I told you I ran into him at one of the open houses? Well," he continued, not allowing me any time to answer, "turns out he was there to check out the medicine cabinets. Looking for pills. It's an old pillhead trick. I only learned about it after they locked up your brother. Apparently he had been known to do the same."

I remembered Tyler mentioning seeing Jamey when I ran into him in March. And I was grateful my father didn't again mention who he saw with Tyler during the aforementioned sighting.

"I'll take care of it," I assured my father, as we made our way into the dark, overly air-conditioned house.

From upstairs I heard Seymour bark, followed by my mother's weary, hoarse voice yelling, "Shut up!" Ice clinked in a glass.

I lugged my things up to my room and was about to plop down onto my bed when I remembered the last bit of money I had left over from my savings for Deirdre's doomed visit. After my Hasselhoff-induced pity party, I'd had enough common sense to exchange it for dollars. I kicked my shoes off and crept as quietly as I could into Claudia's room and slipped two folded twenties into her piggy bank, leaving myself just enough to buy some booze for the next day's welcome back party.

Chapter 22

Waking in my childhood bed the next morning I felt rested, yet uneasy. Like I had awakened in a hotel.

My father had told me he'd run into some of my friends at the convenience store and suggested they come over for a welcome home party of sorts. I used this as a motivation to get through my first day back Stateside.

Wafting up from downstairs was the sickly smell of a hospital cafeteria. I scrunched my nose and heard my mother's voice call from the kitchen. "Jake, I made lunch!" I headed into the kitchen and looked at the stove toward the source of the hospital food smell. Memories of being a hungry twelve-year-old visiting Claudia in the NICU crept into my mind. Though always hungry at that age, I could never bring myself to eat the food there.

I took a seat at the mahogany dining room table. My father walked in from the back room and joined me, his knees matching the creaking of the ancient table.

"No Claudia today?" I asked, skeptically scrutinizing the scorched sandwiches and steaming soup.

"She's at school today," my father answered.

"She goes to school now, Jake," my mother added, the sweetness of her alcohol breath wafting over like the smell of scented trash bags. "Isn't that something?"

"Yeah. Dad told me," I muttered.

We ate in silence, my father and I doing our best to force down the awful food, my mother giving most of her attention to the dog and her drink. My stomach was tight, and the unappetizing food was not entirely to blame. I felt lightyears away from Christmas and my warm and welcome dinner with Stinki's family and longed to be elsewhere. Anywhere but the dimly lit room I found myself in. After my father and I had finished, and my mother had eaten almost half of both her soup and sandwich—a large amount for her—I cleared the table and thought of excuses to get out of the house.

"I think I'm gonna run out to the store," I said. "Pick up a few things for tonight."

"Jake," my father called to me, as I reached for the keys to the Toyota. I turned toward him. With a gentle underhand toss he flung me the keys to the Mercedes and smiled.

I thanked him, looking at my hand in disbelief. After six years of having my license, this privilege had never been bestowed upon me.

I shot him a sincere smile and stepped out into the satisfying summer air. With my head down examining the shiny, oddly shaped Mercedes keys, I headed toward the driveway with a bounce in my step.

A sudden sweet scent caught my attention and I stood stock still on the walkway. My gaze fell upon the honeysuckle bush dividing our house from the neighbors, its creamsicle blossoms emitting their saccharine-sweet perfume. From behind the bush, a cloud of fragrant steam arose from the dryer exhaust vent poking out from the neighbor's wall.

I stood for a moment savoring the scent, before allowing the here and now to chase away images of Julia from my mind. I turned toward the car and the here and now barreled over me like a freight train.

Deirdre stood at the end of the driveway, alone, dressed in a baggy black hoodie despite the late June warmth. Her dark hair was lighter, the dye faded. Her skin looked paler, her eyes defeated. Despite the difference in appearance, it was unmistakably her.

We stood facing each other, neither of us moving. I felt anchored to the ground, my legs couldn't move even if I wanted them to.

"Jake," she said softly, as if calling from a dream.

She took a cautious step forward. Her sleeves were pulled down over her hands, only the tips of her fingers were visible, the dark maroon nail polish cracked and chipping. Her hands were slender and veiny, her cheeks were sunken.

I swallowed hard and managed to also take a step forward. "Deirdre."

"Jake, can you help me?"

I couldn't bear to look her in the eyes. Her skin looked so thin her skull seemed to be transposed on top of her face. My gaze drifted instead toward her hands and I noticed what appeared to be a new tattoo in the web between her thumb and index finger. Some lettering or initials. Stick-and-poke, even worse than the harp tattoos above her hips.
She noticed me looking at her hands and tugged the sleeves down farther, gripping them more tightly.

"Can you give me a ride?" she asked, her voice foreign.

"Deirdre, what are you doing here?" I asked.

"I need a ride, Jake," she said, looking at the keys in my hand.

"Call a cab."

She looked at me shocked. Then her expression faded to shame.

"I don't have any money." She waited for an answer and continued when I offered none. "I just want to go home."

I could have asked where home was. I could have given her the leftover money I had been saving for her. But I had already decided to spend it on beer for myself and my friends.

"Call Tyler. I'm sure he'll give you a ride." Before I could wait for a reaction, I added: "I know he's got money. At least $100 from me and my sister. That should be enough to get you home."

Tears collected in her eyes.

"What?" I asked, taking another step forward, the question coming out more aggressively than I had anticipated. "Just ask him. If you want, I'll call him. I've been meaning to talk to him anyway."

"Jake, you don't understand," she started.

"I don't understand?" My raised voice startled me. "You're right I don't understand. There's so much I don't understand. You disappear from my life, then show up at the worst possible time, suck me back into your trap, spin me in your web, then leave again, this time for my ex-best friend!"

"Jake…" she hung her head. Her jean shorts were cut high, revealing her pale legs. The baggy black hoodie, emblazoned with a Corona logo, swam on her thin frame like a trash bag over an out-of-order urinal.

"What, Deirdre?"

She stood slumped, eyes focused on the pavement between us.

"What, Deirdre? What don't I understand? Enlighten me. I'm tired of being the fool."

"Tyler and I have a lot more in common than you think," she finally managed to mumble, her voice a barely audible whisper.

"Yeah, like DNA. Aren't you guys related?" I asked, taking pleasure in this nasty dig, the schadenfreude slowly boosting my confidence. She stood silently, her hands wrapped tightly around her belly, hugging herself, her head down.

"Listen," I resumed a normal tone. "You wanted space back when I went to college, and I gave you space. You had four years of independence. Then *you* came back to *me*, right before I was going away. I had lost you once, and I wasn't ready to lose you again. So I jumped at the opportunity. Then, out of nowhere, you want your space again. Well, guess what?" I tried taming the vitriol creeping back into my voice. "I tasted that independence that you've always craved so much. That you always demanded from me. And I'm not giving it up." I shook my head. "Find someone else for your web."

I stepped past her and toward the Toyota. Leaning in the front door, I ejected the cassette. She was frozen in her place when I glanced back and unlocked the Mercedes, sliding onto the leather seats. I started the engine and popped the cassette into the tape deck, smiling at the unintentional benefit of my father's preference for older vehicles. The final notes of a song rang out as I watched Deirdre slowly start walking in the direction she had come from, gripping the oversized hoodie tightly to her thin body, head down in defeat. I watched her for a few seconds, her posture a small victory for me.

Feedback bled into a cymbal count as I reversed out of the driveway and Mike Ness' snarl snaked out of the speakers, the snotty self-righteous Social Distortion version of "Under My Thumb" fitting my mood perfectly as I drove in the opposite direction of Deirdre. I turned up the volume and sang along.

I rolled down the windows and let the smell of the suburbs waft in: cut grass, chlorinated pools, the scent of hot asphalt activated by the misty spray from lawn sprinklers.

But the blaring music and the wind blowing through my hair couldn't stop my mind from reeling. The visit from Deirdre had come so unexpectedly, and I couldn't process it all. How she looked, how she was dressed. How she wouldn't look me in the eye. And what was with her hiding her hands? And a sweatshirt in June? Fucking Corona?

I turned the volume down as I pulled into the liquor store parking lot. After rolling up the windows and taking special care to lock up my father's car, I stood for a minute in admiration. The Mercedes looked like a piece of artwork next to the only other car in the parking lot, a shitty, souped-up Honda Civic. Though I never cared too much for cars, I did have to admit that it was an impressive vehicle. I almost even felt a pang of remorse for all of the Mercedes owners in Germany who had lost their hood ornaments to punks who wore them as belt buckles or chain decorations.

A satisfying peep confirmed the doors were locked, and I turned to head into the store to buy beer for the night.

And saw Tyler.

"Jesus fucking Christ," I said aloud. "First her, now you?"

He looked up at me, surprised.

"Oh shit! Jake! What's up, man?" He sounded genuinely pleased to see me. He had apparently forgotten about scamming me and my sister. Or was too fucked up to realize.

I walked toward him with determination.

"Nice car, man," he said, looking over at my father's Mercedes. I clicked the lock button again.

"Seen a lot of ten-year-olds here today?" I asked. "Liquor stores aren't really the hottest spot for them, maybe try a Chuck E. Cheese."

He laughed, confused. Then his look switched quickly to one of fake puzzlement. "Na, man. I was just chilling. 'Bout to go grab some beer after this," he said, holding up a half-smoked cigarette burning between his fingers.

"So," I said, cutting to the chase, "what were you doing at my house the other day?"

He was facing me, but his eyes searched for something else to look at. I half expected him to take the sunglasses off the back of his head and wear them properly in order to obscure his guilty face.

"What? I don't know what you're talking about, dude." He took a deep breath. "Look, if it's about the Phillies tickets, I'm working on it. The dude I buy the tickets from fuckin' ripped me off, man! I gave him the money like six months ago and…"

"I don't care about the money I gave you," I did the math in my head, "like four months ago. I'm asking you about the money you stole from my sister four DAYS ago!" I could feel my heart pounding in my chest.

"What? Na, man. It's not like that," he tried justifying his thievery.

"Tyler, it is like that. Even if you ask a ten-year-old for money and she says yes, it's still theft. And you know my sister. You know she doesn't think like your average ten-year-old. It's like ripping off a fucking kindergartner, which is pathetic even for your standards," I added with acerbic contempt.

His eyes searched the distance. Then he took another deep breath and looked me in the eyes.

"Listen, man, it's like this. I fucked up." He paused and dropped the butt to the ground, crushing it beneath his filthy sneaker. "I'm still fucking up."

I let him talk. He looked like shit. He had lost weight, his slender frame didn't match the slightly pudgy build he had always had, the result of a diet consisting of microwaved TV dinners and snack food. His hair, usually gelled, was greasy, as if it hadn't been washed in a while. The shine was there, but different.

He shifted his position and drew in a deep breath. "Remember that pervert substitute teacher we had back in fifth grade? Mr. Heimlich?"

The name came back to me in a deluge of repressed memories, sharp still-shots in a swamp of awkward confusion.

"Well, remember how he wound up going to jail, and the principal came and talked to us and explained it in kid talk. And told us that nothing happened in our school, that it was all somewhere else? That he got caught planning to do sick shit with kids and had bad pictures and shit but he never actually did anything?"

I stood silently, mouth slightly agape, hands dangling at my sides, waiting for the bomb.

"Well, he did do something. To me and someone else."

My ears rang and I had no idea what to do with my hands. Tyler was obviously not comfortable enough to look me in the eyes, so he kept looking at my helpless, fluttering hands, as my eyes searched for something, any image that would provide a sense of relief.

Tyler continued, his voice quiet and steady. I had known him long enough to tell he was being sincere. This was the painful truth he was unleashing on me. A thirteen-year dam of damning truths burst, unleashing a torrent of tormenting thoughts.

***

Mr. Heimlich. The name rang in my head, spinning along with it the image of his face. Early twenties. Awkward. Uncomfortable in his own skin. Our sub for two days in the winter. Already on the first day we could tell something was off with him. I was too quiet and reserved to join in, but Tyler, Teddy, and some others secretly lambasted the man. Scribbled messages with questions like "R U Gay?" and "Do U like boys?" and tossed them to the front of the classroom when his back was turned.

Then on the second day there was a fight. Tyler and Teddy had always hated each other, and I was the only bridge between the two. Or more like a wall. As much as they disliked each other, I always had the feeling that maybe they stayed away from each other because of me. As if each one was trying to win me over, and that if it ever came to blows between them I'd be out of the picture entirely.

But on that day I stirred the pot. I tore down the firewall.

We had gone on a bathroom break as a class. Three students were allowed in the bathroom at a time, and I was in line between Teddy and Tyler. They had been getting along well enough those two days, both wanting in on the harassment of the weird substitute teacher. But the cracks in the wall that separated the two were still visible.

And I provided the hammer that brought the whole thing down.

"I just don't get it, man," Tyler had said to me from behind me in line. "These people are brought in to watch over us. Like, they're in charge of our welfare, and they send us that creep?"

I snickered. "Welfare," I whispered, a shitty grin on my face, and nodded my head toward Teddy standing in front of me. Though it was understood Teddy's family wasn't exactly wealthy, they weren't on welfare. But in the vicious zoo of elementary school, that rumor had spread like wildfire. And though it would never be extinguished, there was no need for me to fan the flames with a comment like that.

Tyler snickered. Mr. Heimlich approached us and counted, "One. Two. Three. You boys go in together. But hurry up," he said in his timid, nasal voice.

We shuffled into the bathroom and Tyler snickered again.

"What's so funny?" Teddy asked.

"Nothing," Tyler said, shaking his head with an ugly, malicious grin.

"Seems like something has got you all giggly. Maybe it's the crush you've got on your boyfriend outside?" Teddy added.

Tyler smirked. "It's just weird. Like, how you get that fat... how you turn into such a fucking *slob*, when you're a welfare warrior, you know?" He said this to me, though loud enough that Teddy couldn't not hear it. It was clear that Tyler was referring to Teddy's overweight father.

Teddy zipped his pants and turned toward Tyler. "Yeah. Well, at least I know my real dad."

The wall between them came crumbling down with a flood of fists.

Tyler grabbed Teddy's Lenny Dykstra t-shirt and pulled it over his face like in a hockey fight. With all of his might he delivered a fierce blow right in between the upside-down K and S of the jersey. A dark red stain immediately spread across the white fabric.

Teddy yelled out and righted himself, pulling the shirt completely off and using his pudgy body to slam Tyler into the stall.

With a loud bang, the door swung open and Mr. Heimlich stood there, looking more scared than angry.

"What are you boys doing in here?!" he shrieked.

Tyler broke free from Teddy and darted past me, toward the door.

"Out! Out! All three of you! Now!"

Teddy wiped his red face with a damp paper towel, not wanting anyone to see the blood and assume he had lost the fight, and slipped back into his shirt.

Outside, Mr. Heimlich sent the rest of the class back to the classroom and told the three of us that we would have to stay after school.

The remainder of the school day dragged on at a torturous pace, my terrified heart counting each and every second until the bell would ring with its beat. We were supposed to be working on our country reports, but after the fight in the bathroom, the three of us were separated, so Tyler and I were forced to work on our joint project alone. But I couldn't think straight. I had never been in trouble before, and I was terrified of what would happen when my father found out. Even though I wasn't the one who had fought.

After I couldn't stand it anymore, with about twenty minutes left in the day, I left my seat in the first row and walked up to where Mr. Heimlich was sitting at our teacher's desk.

"Um, excuse me," I whispered, not wanting either Teddy or Tyler to hear me. He looked up from the book he was reading. "Um, do I have to stay after, too? I didn't fight. It was Teddy and Tyler."

He looked at me with an expressionless face. "I just tried to stop them," I added, feeling my face burn red with the guilt and shame of the lie.

Mr. Heimlich looked as if he were solving a math equation as his eyes darted back and forth between Teddy and Tyler sitting in the back on opposite sides of the classroom.

He cleared his voice. "No," he said, his eyes still focused on the two boys. "Just those two are fine."

I shuffled back to my seat, careful to make sure neither Teddy nor Tyler had seen me.

As soon as the bell rang, I sprang out of my seat, grabbed my coat from the closet, and headed toward the door.

With the doorknob in my hand, I heard Tyler's voice. "Wait, Jake. Aren't you gonna stay after with me?" An unfamiliar fear blemished his face.

I left.

***

Tyler stood in front of me, his head hung in shame.

"That shit fucked with me for years. And I just hid it. Then it all came back a few years ago, out of nowhere. So I started taking pills to deal with the pain. They helped me avoid thinking about it all." He paused for a moment. "I developed a bit of a problem." His voice had grown even quieter. "My dealer fronted me a bunch of shit, and now I'm in debt pretty bad. That's why I asked for that money from you. I swear I'm gonna get it back to you, man. I've actually been making a decent amount of money recently."

I was lost. And I wanted nothing more than to be anywhere other than in front of a decrepit liquor store with Tyler, where the heavy summer heat felt trapped between the blacktop and the power lines overhead.

"Jake, I promise, I'll get you the money back."

I couldn't respond. It was evident that after those days with Mr. Heimlich things had changed between Teddy and Tyler and me. I had always chalked it up to them being pissed that I instigated a fight. Rightfully so. Or that puberty was to blame. Or going to middle school shortly after, where our classes were split and we rarely saw each other. But there was more to it. Teddy turned quickly to drugs and got expelled. And from what Amy had told me he was in prison. The ground trembled beneath my feet when I remembered her comment about him beating a molester to death. For one quick moment I leaned a hand against the wall for support, before gathering myself and looking back at Tyler.

I stood there stupidly, feeling the waves of shame, guilt, and remorse wash over me in succession.

Then I remembered Claudia. And how shitty Deirdre looked moments before.

I cleared my throat with an awkward rasp.

"So this is your punishment to me? For leaving you?" I asked, shoving my hands into my pockets so he would stop looking at them. "Ripping off my sister? Fucking the girl I love? Loved," I corrected myself.

Tyler just looked at me, his face an expressionless stare.

"I had no idea what happened that day! How could I?" my voice cracked.

A short laugh shot from his nose. "Yeah, I mean, how could you? You left me."

I stared back blankly. "You said nothing happened. And I believed you," I said quietly.

"Well," he forced a weak smile. "I lied. And I'm sorry. Really. I'll get you the money."

"Listen," I managed to say, taking a step closer to him. "I don't care about the money." I turned to walk back to my father's car, deciding to do my beer shopping elsewhere. Before I reached the car, I turned back to him. "Just stay the fuck—the absolute FUCK—away from my sister."

I slammed the car door and pulled out without checking the mirrors, forgetting to breathe until I was a block away.

***

The small party that night was just what I needed to take my mind off the whirlwind of news and events that had barreled over me within the twenty-four hours since returning from Ankerich. Jamey's arrest. My father's plans to sell his business. Deirdre. Tyler. And the constant tug of the jet- and culture-lag pulling hard at my insides.

The first guests started arriving around eight.

"Eric might come later, he's finishing up a job," Aria greeted me with a hug. "Oh, and before you ask why I'm not drinking," she smiled, pointing at her belly. "But shhh," she said, placing her extended index finger to her lips and leaning in to whisper, "it's not really public knowledge yet."

Tommy showed up with a girl by his side. Understandably, he took it easy on the celebrating, as it was one of their first dates.

Randy showed up late as usual, ready to party, and I was eager to pick up where we had left off. After months of practice in Germany, I felt like I'd be able to keep up with my notoriously hard-drinking friends, even if the field was thinned to pretty much just Randy.

"Those beers and brats treated you well over there, huh?" he asked, slapping my noticeably chubbier gut. I laughed as I sucked it in and left to grab us both a beer.

At the liquor store I had bought a case of Jever, remembering Julia's praise of north German beer. I had also picked up some rum, apple juice, lemons, and limes.

After determining that I was going to need something stronger to help me forget about the past twenty-four hours and bridge the gap from Ankerich to home, I headed over to the deck to mix a *letzter Drink*.

I grabbed Randy and took him with me to share with him my newfound favorite drink.

"So this is that drink I was telling you about," I explained to him as I started pouring the ingredients into red Solo cups. "The recipe comes from this song by a really awesome German punk band, with a really awesome name. Their name means Dachshund Blood in German," I could tell the Jevers had left their mark on me, noticing my own verbal diarrhea and simultaneously not caring.

"I'll have one of those, whatever that is," a woman's voice reached me from the doorway.

I looked up. Basking in the warm glow of the porch light was my mother, actually dressed in something other than her nightgown, Seymour clutched in her left arm, her right hand noticeably empty.

I stared at her. I had never shared a drink with my mother.

Without responding, I grabbed a third cup and went back to pouring, smirking to myself at the irony of my mother drinking a *letzter Drink* with her pesky dachshund clutched in the other arm. I finished making the drinks, handed one to Randy, and reached one up to my mother. Our eyes met for a second and she smiled. I raised my cup and we drank together.

The night crept on and a few more people arrived, my loneliness growing with their number. Things were different. The conversations felt strained. No one cared for the drink selections I had made. At one point somebody turned down the music I had chosen for the night.

Feeling the alcohol running hot through my veins, I poured myself another heavy-handed *letzter Drink*, drunkenly singing the ingredients to myself. I staggered toward the side of the house to find a quiet place to piss in the bushes.

As I stood listening to my stream rustle the rhododendron, an owl perched in a tree above called out "Hoo? Hoo?"

I smirked, shaking the last drops of piss into the bush, and said out loud, "Good question."

Realizing I was talking to myself, I said, "You're talking to yourself." And laughed at the absurdity of the situation, realizing that a sure-fire sign that you're drunk is when you talk to yourself about talking to yourself.

I staggered back to the party and made my way toward the empty pool. An inflatable pretzel raft—a gift from Aria—floated lazily back and forth, bouncing off the edges like a DVD screensaver.

My mother was talking to Randy near the table with the booze. Seymour was asleep in her arms, Randy was listening politely.

Music drifted across the dark evening, periodically interrupted by a cicada crescendo. The smell of honeysuckle wafted over from the bush in the back of the yard, poisoned by the chlorine stench of the pool. I fumbled in my pockets, dropping my phone and wallet to the ground next to me, and slipped out of my shoes. With my drink still in my hands and fully clothed, I turned, and let my body fall backward into the pool, feeling my shirt and pants drink in the warm water, the fabric floating from my body like clouds of smoke. I sank, appreciating the absolute silence, my eyes closed, embracing the darkness of the depths, and rested on the bottom of the pool, thoughtless and numb.

Chapter 23

I awoke with a start, wondering where I was. Looking around at the vaguely familiar setting—a poster of the mulleted 1993 Phillies on the wall, concert and baseball game ticket stubs pinned to a corkboard, a framed diploma hanging above the dresser—it sunk in.

Groaning, I rubbed my head. I had had that dream again, where I couldn't move my legs no matter how hard I tried, struggling and straining as if they were concrete pilings driven deep into wet sand. Like everything was in slow motion.

Rolling out of bed, I noticed an empty red Solo cup sitting on my nightstand, a ring of sticky brown liquid lining the bottom. *Ein Absacker,* Stinki used to call that last bad-idea beer—the goodnight drink that never wished you good morning. I got up, ran a hand through my chlorine-dried hair, kicked my still-unpacked suitcase and backpack to the side, and made my way to the bathroom, where I noticed my damp clothes from the previous night draped across the edge of the bathtub. From the bathroom window the sky looked dark and menacing.

Maybe the saltwater air will help me come to my senses, I thought to myself, remembering Aria's offer to spend the weekend at her family's shorehouse. A weekend away—from this town, from my family, from my past, from my decisions—was just what I needed.

Trying for a moment to straighten my slow and hazy thoughts, I heard a car horn honk outside.

"Shit." I grabbed my backpack and ran downstairs. I leaned out the front door and shot Tommy a quick "one minute" hand gesture, then walked to the back room.

Though it was Friday, my father was sitting in front of the TV, his reading glasses on and his laptop open on his lap. Claudia sat cross-legged, a bowl of soggy cereal cradled in her hands. She didn't turn to acknowledge me, immersed in her morning cartoons.

"Dad, I'm headed down the shore for the weekend. I totally forgot to tell you yesterday."

He looked up at me and slowly removed his glasses, revealing his exhausted eyes resting in a sea of wrinkles. "Have fun," he said, smiling.

I looked out the large glass sliding doors toward the pool. Dark clouds reflected in the still water. Red cups littered the grass and a few chairs had been knocked over. The table of booze was littered with empty cans and bottles. The rum was nowhere to be found.

"Actually, let me go get Tommy and see if he can help me straighten up the backyard real quick. Sorry for the mess," I added, embarrassed by the disorder.

My father raised his hand slowly. "Leave it," he said. "The maid will take care of it."

"Maid?"

"Jake, when was the last time your mother did something around the house?" he asked, grinning at me like an old friend, a hint of defeat hidden behind the smile. "Besides that sorry excuse for a lunch yesterday." He laughed, a pleasant sound to drown out the dull buzzing in my head.

I smiled, tussled Claudia's hair, and left.

Tommy was waiting, left arm hanging out the window. Soft, acoustic indie music drifted lazily from the speakers.

"Have you gone soft on me, man?" I asked.

Tommy smiled, ignoring the question.

I hopped in, glancing up at the quickly moving clouds overhead.

Once on the highway, I rolled up my window to prevent the wind from blasting me in the face. I reached over and turned on the AC, but nothing happened. Without looking over at me, Tommy commented, "It's broken." Then, turning toward me with a smile, added, *"Kaputt."*

I cracked the window a bit and settled into the passenger seat. Though I was still in a daze from the night before, I embraced the drive down the shore. Ever since I was a little kid I had enjoyed the journey, pressing my face to the window, watching the scenery change. Once we would reach the marshes, my father would roll down the windows—a rare practice, much rather preferring the AC—and allow me and my brother to breathe in the murky, salty smells that welcomed the family to the ocean town. This was when Jamey was still young and before Claudia. Before my mother's drinking. When we were still a family.

My favorite memory was sitting backward in the family car so that I could see the scenery after it had passed, not as it passed. Everyone else would see the trees, signs, toll booths, and houses approach steadily, then whiz by too quickly to comprehend, before focusing on the next object ahead. I, however, would see everything as it passed, then slowly watch as it disappeared in the distance, watching each object until it faded into nothingness.

Sitting in the car with Tommy, I still enjoyed the ride, but more for the smell than the sites, all jughandles, retention ponds, and roadside memorials. In the suburbs, on the way out, there was the smell of car exhaust and congestion, a humid and filthy stench. After about fifteen minutes on the highway, the smell developed into the mild, earthy aroma of the farms. After we passed the farms and entered the forest, the clean, gin scent of the pines greeted us, followed by the familiar salty smell of the marshes, funky yet fertile in a way that instantly brought me back to my youth.

Tommy interrupted my thoughts with something unintelligible.

"Wait, what?" I said, rolling up the window to stop the noise of the wind whipping through the opening.

"I said what are you thinking about? You're so quiet today."

I looked out the window, debating on whether I should open up to him or not. We were friends, after all, but after the past nine months in Ankerich, I felt different. Distant. Or just not as present. "I don't know, man, I just got a lot on my mind." Tommy nodded. "Like, my future and stuff," I elaborated, vaguely. We had just passed Mohawk Farms. Thirty-five more minutes, I calculated, thinking about whether it should be called Iroquois Farms.

"Yeah man, I hear you," was Tommy's reply. Yeah, you *hear* me, I thought. But do you *understand*? Along the side of the road, a crow was ripping the rotting flesh away from a dead fox with its black beak. We passed a moving truck from Maryland. "We Bring You Home" its slogan proclaimed.

After a few minutes of silence, we both rolled down our windows and Tommy turned up the music, though it remained drowned out by the wind. I kept my head turned to the right and stared at the passing landscapes and slowly dozed off.

I awoke to the sound of crunching seashells under the tires of the car and opened my eyes to see Aria jogging down the wooden steps of the shorehouse to greet us.

She met us as we grabbed our bags and fishing gear from the trunk.

"Forget the fishing, guys, you'll have enough time to do that tomorrow. Besides, the weather's kind of shitty," she said, taking the rod from my hands and replacing it with a beer. "Let's day drink! It's five o'clock somewhere, right?"

I accepted the cold can of beer and did some time-zone math in my head. We made our way inside, sipping carefully while walking, glancing up at the overcast sky above our heads. Colorless clouds bled contourlessly into the equally bleak background. A wind had developed, gradually growing stronger, tossing the waves roughly along the shoreline, white foam being whipped up from the dark green-blue water. Seagulls swooped and dove in the salty spray, searching for small fish tossed up by the violent hands of nature.

Aria's family's shorehouse sat directly on the beach, the mid-century, two-storied home separated from the ocean by only a dune topped with sparse, reedy seagrass. The cozy interior made up for the unassuming exterior—the authentic old-school furniture that gave off a retro vibe was complemented by the tasteful beachy decorations adorning the walls and halls, working together to create a comfortable, shabby-chic atmosphere that felt welcoming, yet mysterious. The house shared that distinct shorehouse scent—spicy cedar, salted seaweed, and a mothball must.

We pulled up the tall bar stools surrounding the kitchen island and Aria brought us a new round. After handing me, Tommy, and Eric each a can from the fridge, she poured herself a glass of seltzer and sat down with us. "What the hell is…" I started, pointing to her drink. I immediately remembered her comment to me the previous night, and changed course, "taking Randy so long? I thought he was coming?"

Aria's look of confusion quickly transformed into a wry smile. "Oh, you know Randy. He'll be here at some point. He texted me and told me he had shit to do first, but he's probably just still nursing his hangover."

"Or trying to pick up a nineteen-year-old somewhere," Eric added, sipping from his can.

"Oh," Aria said over the laughter, "Tommy knows, by the way," pointing to her drink. "But thanks for the foresight."

I shot her a forced smile, hoping she wouldn't pick up on my disapproval.

I put my can down on the counter and extended a hand to Eric. "Congrats, dude!" I offered, trying to inject as much enthusiasm and conviction into the words as possible, without coming off as disingenuous. The thought of having children had never really crossed my mind—aside from the pregnancy scare I had with Deirdre—but now all I could think about is whether the kid would wind up an addict like Jamey or Tyler. Or a felon like Teddy. Or a stripper like Deirdre. Or spineless, like me.

"At least now you'll have the room for the little one to romp around," Tommy added.

I looked at Tommy confused. Then turned to Aria and Eric. They traded glances and Eric shifted in his seat, turning to face me.

"Yeah, man. Aria and I bought a house." He forced a smile. "We're moving back to the suburbs!"

Again I was forced to do my best to hide my initial reaction. For the past several years, Aria and Eric were the ones who hosted pretty much everything since they each had an apartment in the city. Now we'd all be back living in the suburbs, living a life of competitive boredom.

Before I could react, Aria added, "We didn't go through your dad's agency. Or yours, too, I guess I should say. Sorry. It's just…" she waved her hand in a gesture of futile exasperation. "I just don't think he really sells the type of home we were looking for."

"Yeah, no, it's fine," I stammered. "I wouldn't expect you to go through him. I mean, unless you were buying one of those shitty McMansions or something."

They laughed. "No, no. That's not us. We just needed a bigger place for the little one," Eric said, running his hand across Aria's still-flat belly.

"I just figured, I graduate soon and it wouldn't make sense for me to keep living in a cramped apartment in the city with two roommates. Though, I guess I'll have two different roommates," she said, looking over at Eric, placing her hand on top of his.

He took a small sip from his can, then shook it, and finished the last drops. "Yep. Time to say goodbye to city life." He sighed, standing up and turning toward the fridge. "It was fun while it lasted. But, hey, life goes on," he added, before following up with "Need one?" his voice muffled coming from the depths of the ancient fridge.

We spent the rest of the dark afternoon drinking and catching up. A few questions were asked about my time in Ankerich—superficial questions about the food, the weather, my job—but anytime I tried to share a funny story or moment in time that seemed significant to me, I could tell I was losing my audience. And that was fine. In a way, I appreciated the friendly gesture of even asking, and how it was left at that—a gesture. There was no need to relive it all, to analyze the entire experience, to try to put it into words. Or, even worse, to be forced to draw comparisons to my life in the US. Each was its own entity, and it was probably best to keep it as such. And, besides, compared to new homes and first pregnancies, nine months of living in Europe was nothing.

Randy showed up in the late afternoon and brought a bit of fresh breath into what was slowly turning into a boring day. Without the option of having the beach and ocean to provide a distraction from each other, we were running out of things to entertain ourselves with. But even Randy was subdued. He blamed it on his hangover, but something felt off.

The dark, smoke-gray day quickly bled into evening, yellow and rose. The foreboding clouds lifted and dissolved and the winds died down, taming the waves. There was no blue hour here, the night quickly overtook the day, bathing the beach in a shadowy stain.

After dinner, we moved outside, setting up folding chairs to look out over the night ocean. The almost full moon cast its light across the water doing its best to calm down after a rough day, like a child resting in bed after a temper tantrum. The conversation ebbed and flowed, periodically interrupted by laughter or the sound of a can being popped open.

After a while, Aria informed us we had finished off all the cans of beer. "Damn, dude," Eric laughed, "you're turning into one of us!"

We all laughed. "If I had known Germany had turned you into a seasoned drinker I would've picked up some more beers on the way," Randy added, heading down the wooden stairs to grab the case of beer he had in his trunk, the next day's reserve.

He returned a few minutes later, huffing and puffing with the labor of carrying the case up the stairs. "I'll put these in the cooler for tomorrow, and some in the freezer for now. Might take a half hour or so 'til we can drink 'em, though."

"I'll take one now," I said, extending my arm.

"Dude, they're warm," Randy replied. Through the darkness I could still see the look of astonishment on his face.

I grabbed a bottle from the case, fished out the bottle-opener I had been given by Stinki's parents, and opened it with a satisfying hiss. Foam spilled out of the neck and I quickly placed my lips to the bottle, sucking in the warm, creamy overflow.

"Fuck it, give me one, too," Eric said.

I tossed him my opener and he cracked his beer, sipping and admiring the opener, tilting it in the moonlight to read the lettering. "Bad Schamdorf," he said, stumbling over the foreign pronunciation. "Nice."

After an hour or so, Randy made his way to bed, departing with some lazy excuse about working around the house all day or something. Minutes later, Tommy followed.

"I'm catching tomorrow's dinner," he proclaimed as he headed toward the door.

We laughed, knowing damn well he wouldn't catch anything.

"Hey Tommy," I called over my shoulder. "You got a cigarette?"

He looked at me, confused. "Na. I quit." He turned back toward the door. "When did you start?" he asked, walking into the house before waiting for an answer.

I rolled the question around in my head for a moment, unaware of the answer myself.

Eric and I sat in silence, listening to the hushed crashing of the waves onto the sand. For a while we said nothing, just sat and took in the sights and sounds.

"Want another drink?" I finally interrupted the silence.

"Sure," he responded. Though he was right next to me, his voice sounded distant in the darkness. "But maybe save Randy's beers for tomorrow. I don't know if you're into it or not, but there's some wine inside. Aria bought it a while back, before the pregnancy. It'll be a while before she drinks again, so no one will miss it if we get into it tonight."

I stood up and headed inside to where he told me I'd find the bottle. Framed photographs of fish on the walls and dehydrated starfish and seahorses on the mantle watched me as I tried my best to make as little noise as possible opening the bottle. I decided against glasses—it'd probably make too much noise—and stepped back out into the cool night.

Taking a seat in my folding chair, I offered the bottle to Eric. He looked at me for a moment, confused, silent. "What, no glasses?" he asked.

"I figured we'd just drink from the bottle."

He nodded and accepted the wine, drinking slowly and deliberately, before returning it to me.

The flavor of the wine surprised me—deep, velvety, earthy, with a slight bite at the end. I tilted the bottle in the moonlight trying to read the label. Something French—*Peu de Liberté*. Since when did Aria and Eric develop such refined tastes? This was worlds away from what Stinki and I had drunk with Katja and Julia in the marketplace.

I sunk back into my chair and looked out over the ocean, allowing my mind to wander. The night sky had cleared up entirely and the moon was accompanied by countless stars poking holes in the darkness like cigarette burns in a heavy wool blanket. Unlike the suburbs, down the shore there was such little light pollution that the stars were really able to pierce the cobalt black screen of night. Looking east I could make out the constellation Lyra. I thought of Deirdre's terrible tattoos, those faded black harps on her hips. Not now, I told myself.

Memories from Latin class flickered in my mind as I tried to remember the story of Lyra. Something to do with Orpheus' harp, how he used it as a distraction from the Sirens on some journey. And how his wife was sent to Hades. Somehow he was granted permission to go save her, under the condition that he not look back at her on his way out. How he blew it all by looking back. Imagine getting that far just to lose it all by looking back. Then he was killed by a bunch of partiers. Followers of Bacchus or Dionysus. Oh yeah, that was it! He was a pedophile or something like that. And the wine drunks killed him. The jumbled story confused me, much like the events of the past three days, and I took a sip from the bottle and handed it silently to Eric.

Dropping my gaze from the sky to the sea, I thought of what was on the other side.

It was about eleven PM here. Five AM in Germany. Saturday already. Stinki was probably asleep. Or just heading to bed after partying all night. I wondered what Julia was doing.

"What are you thinking about?"

Eric's voice cut through the night, interrupting my thoughts. "Huh? Oh, nothing." How could I tell him that I was thinking about being with other people when it was just the two of us together at the moment. That, although I was physically present, my mind—and heart?—were elsewhere.

I looked out over the ocean, black as ink, a streak of midnight blue shimmering beneath the moon, the horizon invisible between the water and the sky. "I was just thinking about the ancient explorers. How they set out into that with no real knowledge of what to expect," I lied, pointing out over the water.

"Yeah, man, it's crazy," he agreed. He sipped and handed the bottle back. "Like," he said, settling deeper into his chair, "imagine just getting on some rickety-ass wooden boat, kissing your wife goodbye, and saying, 'Well, I'm off then. I'll be back at some point,' and not even believing it yourself."

"Yeah," I agreed and sat in silence for a minute. "Like, I wonder how many shipwrecks are out there? How many skeletons of old sailors. How many anchors at the bottom of the sea, just being eaten away by nature."

"Hm." Eric pondered the thought. "What's on the other side, actually?" he asked after a while.

I was confused. "What do you mean?"

"Like, if you were to swim straight across the ocean, where would you land?"

I thought for a second. "Portugal, I think." And if you kept on going you'd end up right back here, I added to myself.

He nodded.

I took another sip and held the wine in my mouth, feeling the cool temperature of the liquid yield to the heat of the alcohol seeping into the soft membrane of my mouth, being absorbed into my bloodstream. That pleasant numbness, the static warmth.

I repeated his question to myself.

Eric looked over at me for a minute, then reached for the bottle.

"So," he said, sipping, "what else is on the other side?"

I stared out across the ocean. How do I put the past nine months into words? How do my feelings translate into words? And which words could convey the experiences I'd had? Would it do any of them justice? Would it hurt the people I care about here?

"Man…" I said, sighing. "I don't know. A lot."

"Well," he said, swallowing audibly. He looked at me. "Then I guess the other question is what's on this side?"

Before I could answer, he smiled and leaned forward, pressing play on the portable tape deck at his feet. He turned the volume low and kicked his feet back up on the railing. "Rainy Day" by American Steel played softly from the speakers. I got up to use the bathroom, singing along quietly to myself:

> "I'm your cold sweat epiphanies
>
> You're my red wine soliloquies."

When I stepped back out onto the deck, Eric's head was leaned back and he was snoring quietly. I tiptoed over to the tape deck, turned it down even more, picked up the empty wine bottle to see if there was another sip left, then headed to bed, allowing the steady rhythm and static rumble of the rolling surf rock me to sleep.

Chapter 24

The hushed whispers of the ocean tiptoed gently through the open window waking me the next morning. With a grunt I rolled over to my side and spread open the blinds. Outside, the June sun had already risen over the sea and had baked away any trace of the previous day's storm. The sky was clear and cerulean, the ocean blue-green and serene.

I kicked the sheets from my feet and grabbed a t-shirt from my bag, dressing myself as I made my way into the kitchen. Aria was sitting on one of the tall stools at the counter, a mug of coffee cupped in her hands.

"Morning!" she greeted me cheerily.

"Morning," I responded, my voice sounding choked and hoarse. I poured myself a coffee, joining her at the counter.

"How late were you guys up last night?" she asked, tying her hair into a loose ponytail.

"I don't know. Not too late, I don't think."

"Hm," she said, sipping slowly from her steaming cup. "Well Eric's still asleep. I'll give him another hour or so, then I'm waking his ass up. It's too nice out today to spend the whole day in bed."

I agreed as I followed her onto the deck.

Outside the day felt promising. Not a cloud in the sky, and though there was no filter for the sun, the heat didn't come off as oppressive, but rather welcoming.

We stood side-by-side for a minute or two, taking in the spectacular view. Seagulls glided gracefully above the shoreline, periodically bobbing and diving. To the right, a man and a child were flying a kite, its movements mimicking those of the seagulls. In the opposite direction a man was walking, dangling a leash in his hand. I squinted and could see a dog running far ahead of him, romping its way across the beach, chasing birds and splashing in the surf.

The waves crested and swelled, surging to the shoreline in gentle washes, and I thought about the staggering perpetuity of the ocean. All-knowing and never-ending, its rhythm almost as old as the stars I had admired the previous night.

It had been too long since I had been here. After Deirdre and I had initially broken up, I almost avoided the shore, subconsciously or intentionally, since I had spent so much time with her at the beach.

"Have you heard from Deirdre recently?" Aria asked, her voice quiet and tentative.

I was caught off guard. My friends had essentially stopped asking about her by the time we had broken up. I knew that they never really liked her, that they just put up with her for my sake. I hadn't even told them that she and I had started seeing each other again just before I left for Ankerich.

And how should I respond? Was it even worth mentioning the short-lived rekindling of our relationship? That brief, doomed second summer of love? And how I had, in fact, heard from Deirdre recently, that I actually saw her unexpectedly in front of my parents' house two days ago. I felt embarrassed by the encounter. How she looked. How she pleaded with me for help. How I essentially left her, threw her to the wolves. And was my behavior justified? I hadn't even allowed myself to process the encounter entirely, too preoccupied with my friends and drinking and trying to figure out where the fuck I would even be in two months. My life seemed at this moment just as unanchored as Deirdre's. So who was I to judge?

"Um, na, not really." Aria nodded, I acknowledged from the corner of my eye.

"Yeah," she said, the word charged with hidden meaning. "Well, I've heard some nasty rumors about her." She looked at me. I didn't want to take my eyes off the ocean, didn't want to look Aria in the eyes. I could tell she was going to repeat the suspicions I had been suppressing. And if she thought what she heard was true it would show in her eyes. And I didn't know if I was ready for it.

Aria took another sip of coffee and turned back to face the ocean. She placed her mug on the soft, splintery railing and continued. "I ran into Kelly the other day. She was telling me how concerned she was for Deirdre. She said she's been spending a lot of time with Tyler. And how after the club shut down and all, she was out of work. Then Deirdre just kind of stopped talking to her, she said."

I nodded. If this was really coming from Kelly, Deirdre's oldest and closest friend, the only one who had been able to tolerate her mercurial mood swings and questionable life decisions, it was most likely true. And here, on the porch of this shorehouse, on this gorgeous, calm, and warm Saturday morning, I had no choice but to listen.

"She said she thinks Tyler might be pimping her out."

I wanted to put my fingers in my ears. To run to the beach and bury my head in the sand. Turn to Aria and yell "STOP!"

But she continued. "Like, she somehow started hanging out with him in the springtime. And then as soon as the club shut down, the two of them started this thing where he'd set her up with guys and then she'd give him a cut of the money and he'd supply her with pills or whatever."

You left me Deirdre said when she explained the truth about breaking up with me.

You left me was Tyler's smug reaction to my feeble attempt at justifying my cowardly actions in fifth grade, leaving him with a predator while I saved myself.

I left Deirdre with Tyler in March.

Victim turned predator.

Find someone else for your web I had told her two days ago.

Predator turned victim.

"Morning!" Randy called from behind us, simultaneously scratching the back of his head and his shirtless belly with both hands.

Using the interruption as an excuse, I told Aria I was going to head back inside for a refill of coffee.

She flashed me a sympathetic smile and sighed. "Well, I think it's about time I wake up Eric."

***

On the beach, we set up our chairs and Tommy and I started tending to our fishing gear. We argued for a minute about which bait would be best.

"Whatever, dude. We're not catching shit anyway," he laughed.

"You better catch something," Aria added, "or else it's Chef Boyardee for dinner."

I cast my line and rested my pole in the sand spike. Sipping a beer, I dropped into the beach chair and dug my feet into the warm, dry sand and dozed off.

In a shimmering bright and warm landscape, full of flowers and chattering birds, I strolled lightly, my feet barely touching the ground, as if I were floating. Passing between two azalea bushes ablaze with pink blossoms I felt as my face was ensnared by a cobweb. My fingers clawed at the sticky threads, my mouth spitting the fibers from the corners of my lips. Still, even after I had removed every last bit of the web from my face, the uncertainty of the whereabouts of the spider left me in a frenzied state of panic.

"You're in my web now," a soft female voice sang. Suddenly, I felt a clap on my back and a raspy voice called out, "Got it!" As I turned to see who had killed the spider on my back I felt my legs start rumbling as if something far away was jerking them from a distance.

"Yo! I think you got one!" Tommy's voice pulled the plug on my unsettling dream and I felt the jerking rod doing its best to free itself from the clasp of my legs. I put my half-empty beer down in the sand and hopped out of my seat to see if I could land the fish. With one finger on the line, I felt life on the other side and set the hook with a quick jerk. Immediately I felt a burst of resistance. Steadying the rod with both hands, the right hand holding the pole steady while the left hand worked the reel, I began nearing the shore as I reeled in. Eric and Randy had also noticed the excitement of the rod and came up to watch. After a rather weak fight, the fish began fighting harder as it neared the beach, splashing in the crashing surf. I had made my way into the water at this point, ankle-deep, and had a clear view of the fish as it approached my feet.

"A flounder," I said.

"You mean fluke," Tommy corrected.

"Whatever. An unflattering name either way," I resigned, as I carried the fish to my tackle box.

Bending down to take the hook out of its mouth, I couldn't help but notice the fish's pleading eyes, sad and somehow familiar.

Tommy laid the measuring tape over its body and measured sixteen and three-quarter inches.

"Dinner!" he remarked, clapping me on the back.

I stood up and placed the fish in the beer bucket next to my chair. Its two eyes looked up at me through melted ice and empty beer bottles floating on the surface.

I washed my hands in the surf and returned to my chair, only to find that I had knocked my beer over in my excitement. Most of the beer had spilled into the sand, and the rest was undrinkable due to the sand all over the mouth of the bottle. I dumped the rest out and asked if anyone needed another beer. I was met with three affirmative answers.

"Actually, I might take a quick ride to the liquor store to pick up another case. Any special requests?"

"Maybe get some of that German shit," Eric called out, smiling.

I nodded and headed back to the house, stopping at the dunes to dump the water out of the bucket. The fish would just suffocate soon enough anyway in the stale water. It was better to just place it on ice and no water.

Mounting the dune, I took a quick glance back at the others. They were still standing at the shore, Randy had grabbed my rod and had joined Tommy fishing, Eric stood watching with a beer in his hand. Side-by-side they stood looking out at the horizon, none of them speaking.

I continued on my way, staggering down the steep dune that served as a sound threshold, the tremendous thundering of the surf pounding the beach all but disappearing into the domestic silence of the shorehouse as soon as I had the mountain of sand behind me.

After burying the fish beneath a bag of ice, I went upstairs to grab my wallet and Tommy's keys.

Deciding that, even though the drive to the liquor store wouldn't even take ten minutes each way, I didn't want to be forced to listen to Tommy's toned-down whisper music, so I stopped in my room to grab a tape from my bag.

Picking up my phone to check the time, I saw I had a missed call from Kelly. The display screen stared back at my puzzled face before I pocketed Tommy's keys and left.

The car creaked with age and use as I climbed into it and started the ignition. I slid the mixtape Stinki had made into the tape deck. A simple drum beat started up, followed by some guitar chord picking and spoken-word German. I racked my memory, trying to identify the song, before realizing I must've taken a different tape. Whatever it was it was great, but entirely unfamiliar. At a stop light, I grabbed the jewel case and opened it. Inside, stuck to the clear plastic was a Post-it with a note scribbled in barely legible handwriting:

Chef! Check this out, a Muff Potter song from their upcoming album. The ending reminded me of you. But I felt gay handing it to you at the airport. Hopefully you find this. See you soon! -Stinki

I read the note twice in disbelief and turned the music up as the light turned green.

As much as I enjoyed the song, I was surprised that Stinki also liked it, as it was much more subdued than the typical three-chord grumble punk he usually listened to. After pulling up to the liquor store, I stayed in the car to finish out the song, waiting for what Stinki said made him think of me. After a quiet, slower decrescendo, with a melodica carrying the melody, the drums kicked back in with sudden urgency and the music came together in full force. The lyrics filled out the sound and immediately I understood what Stinki meant:

"Sicherheit wird zu Langeweile

Und Langeweile wird zu Zorn,

Und für den Heimatlosen

Ist Heimweh der Motor für die Flucht nach vorn.

Und der Schmerz macht lebendig, Schmerz macht frei…"

The song died out and I sat in the car for a minute digesting the lyrics, nodding in agreement. Security leads to boredom. Boredom leads to rage. But was I *heimatlos?* How do you even translate that German word *Heimat,* that concept of home that encompasses so much more than just a place?

With the melody of the song reverberating through my head, I bought a thirty-pack of beer and two bottles of wine to make up for the one Eric and I drank the previous night.

On the way back, I listened to the song twice more, feeling a way I couldn't describe. A smorgasbord of emotions. It was solemn and beautiful, melancholic and defiant. And in a way, painful. And in a way, I liked that pain.

Pain makes you alive, the lyrics said. Pain sets you free.

Upon returning, I put the beers in the fridge, taking out four to bring down to the beach. Then I remembered the missed call and checked my phone again.

A sudden cloud of uneasiness enveloped me and I took a seat on the couch. I stared at my phone, and the message stared back at me like a transmission from a distant place, a far-off world. *One missed call—Kelly cell.* I acknowledged the message by pressing a button and another notification displayed on the screen: *New Voicemail.*

I stood up and grabbed one of the bottles of wine, taking a corkscrew with me as I made my way to my room. It made no sense to ignore the call. It was about Deirdre, that much was obvious. But I couldn't bring myself to expect good news.

Without even listening to the voicemail first, I nestled the phone between my ear and my shoulder and maneuvered the corkscrew into the bottle, listening to the phone ring.

"Jake," Kelly answered the phone quietly, my name replacing a greeting.

"Hi," I said, slightly out of breath from struggling with the cork.

"Hey." Her voice was soft. She was silent for a moment. The cork came dislodged from the bottle with a muted *"thunk,"* and I thought of the beginning of that one Dinosaur Jr. song.

"Jake, Deirdre died."

For a brief moment, I felt the pain of everyone.

Then I felt nothing.

I brought the bottle to my lips and drank. The wine filled my mouth faster than I could swallow. Tiny rivulets dripped from the corners of my cheeks. I kept drinking, savoring the burn of the alcohol, prolonging the silence, not wanting to have to speak, to have to acknowledge what I had known, had felt in my gut when I saw the missed call. If I didn't offer any affirmation it wouldn't be true.

Kelly sniffled. "Jake, are you there?"

I pulled the bottle from my lips and exhaled loudly.

With my bare arm I wiped my mouth.

"Yes."

"Jake, I'm so sorry. I just… I don't know. I knew I had to tell you. You deserve to know."

I sat silently, listening to the ocean, thinking of the picture of Deirdre that I had left behind in Ankerich, stuffed into the wastebasket.

"You were the only one who ever really cared about her."

I fumbled for my wallet. "No, you did, too." I said, stumbling over the unfamiliarity of the past tense.

"Her mom called me today," Kelly continued. "She seemed perfectly normal on the phone. Not even distraught. As if she knew it was coming."

I nodded, though I realized afterwards that Kelly couldn't see my reactions. I opened my wallet and thumbed past Julia's address to get to the last remaining photo I had of Deirdre. I ran my thumb across her face in a meaningless gesture as Kelly explained what had happened.

"She told me that the hospital had called her last night. Someone dropped Deirdre off outside the ER and left. They said that she was already dead when they got to her."

She breathed in heavily and shared with me the foggy details of the night that she had been able to piece together, a bundle of bad news built out of hearsay and assumptions, held together with previous knowledge of past mistakes. Deirdre had been "performing" at a bachelor party somewhere in the suburbs. She had gone to use the bathroom, and after a half hour of being in there, the horny frat boys broke open the locked door and found her unresponsive. They called Tyler, who had apparently been working as her agent or bouncer or pimp or whatever.

I pictured popped-collared preppies pounding on the door, accusing the piece of meat they hired of wasting their time. I pictured Tyler driving Deirdre to the hospital, his forehead beaded with perspiration. Deirdre sprawled out unresponsive in the back seat. Saw the car idling in front of the hospital. Saw him dragging her out. One last glance before leaving her, then speeding off into the night.

You left me.

"Did you know she was using?" Kelly asked.

I didn't. Or I did. Whatever. I assumed. And assuming never got anyone anywhere. Deirdre assumed I gave her chlamydia.

"I don't know. She just kind of dropped off at some point. We were almost together, or we were back together, I still don't know. Then she got cold feet or whatever. Then we had an argument in March, then Tyler came back into the picture and that was it, I guess."

I left out the accusation. I left out me leaving her at the bar in March. I left out the interaction with her two days ago. I left out my run-in with Tyler that same day.

I left Tyler.

I left Deirdre.

"She had such a hard life, Jake."

"Yeah," I said, the insincerity so thick I could hear it myself.

"I mean it. With all that shit that happened with her pervert stepfather, to the constant moving, to her fucked-up mom. It was just a matter of time before something happened. I tried so hard, I really tried to keep her safe. But there's only so much one person can do. I mean, I thought she was doing better when she was with you, but even then, she would say things or do things when we would hang out, things I never told you, that maybe I should've told you, but I just... I don't know."

I let Kelly rattle on, it was probably good for her to get it all out. I had stopped listening at the mention of her ex-stepfather. She had always had an aversion to him, and I never got it. *We have a lot more in common than you think*," she had told me on Thursday, talking about Tyler. Minutes before he told me about what had really happened with Mr. Heimlich.

How could I have been so blind? So naive? So self-absorbed to not see the signs? In both Deirdre and Tyler.

The bottle was at my feet. I looked at it and felt sick.

"They're going to have her cremated. No word yet on a ceremony or anything. But I'll keep you updated."

I thanked Kelly.

"I'm really sorry, Jake," she said before I hung up.

I deleted the voicemail without listening to it.

The sun flooded the room with its bright rays, a citrus glow filtered through the blinds. I closed my eyes and saw the picture of Deirdre I had thrown away. Deirdre in mid-laughter, mouth open, head tilted back and to the left, eyes half-closed. The sun lightening her dark hair. The way she used to be. The way she should have still been.

The Deirdre I used to love.

The Deirdre the old me used to love.

I hid the half-empty bottle of wine behind the bed and made my way down to the beach, crossing the hot sand to rejoin my friends.

***

That evening, after a meal featuring the fish I had caught, we walked to the beach to make a fire.

I had remained relatively quiet most of the afternoon, focusing most of my attention on preparing dinner, to give myself an excuse to be alone with my thoughts. Then I spent some time walking the beach collecting driftwood for the fire, watching as the waves erased my footprints as soon as I left them behind me.

I had decided not to tell my friends about the news. They would have been supportive with their condolences, diluting or polluting my own memories with forced statements of how great Deirdre was, the thick lies served up as padding for my grief. And if I didn't hear it from other people's mouths, the truth was easier to ignore.

We sat around the fire quietly, mesmerized by the pop and lick of the flames illuminating the black beach. The fire idea had been a genius one, allowing me to be alone with my thoughts, though surrounded by friends. The driftwood I had gathered released a pleasant, salty scent, and I thought of the miles each piece had travelled, passively for days or months or years, floating, allowing the sea to dictate its pace and progress.

I contributed little to the conversation, the talk receding periodically into long moments of silence. It was during these bursts of silence that I did most of my thinking. Not only about Deirdre. But about the future. Or the present. About where I was at the moment, physically and mentally, trying to figure out how I felt about it all.

Breaking the tie that bound me to the anchor of my future with my father had gone relatively easily, but with the sudden freedom came the unexpected freedom to choose. But to choose what? The future, no longer figured out for me, was also no longer feared. *"Der Qual der Wahl,"* Stinki had said to me once. The torture of choice.

And the rope that had tethered me to the past, the one that had chafed me for years, the one that had been fraying with the friction of the past six months, had been cut with one painful phone call a few hours earlier.

So what remained? Already my memories of Ankerich were fading like my footsteps on the beach.

Randy finished a beer and tossed the can into the fire.

"What the fuck, man?" Aria yelled at him. "Who's gonna clean that shit up?"

"Simmer down!" Randy yelled back, his voice brutalizing the calm evening. "It'll burn down."

"An aluminum can is not going to burn down in a wimpy-ass fire," she hissed, her face illuminated by the flames.

"Yeah it will," Randy replied. "Put anything in a fire long enough and it'll melt down." He sipped from his freshly opened beer.

We sat in silence, our gazes locked on the fire, mine focused on the can in the embers, slowly blackening and crinkling in the heat.

They're going to have her cremated.

Suddenly it was all too much for me. The silence, the fire, my thoughts. I stood up, making some half-assed attempt at an excuse, something about the sun and jetlag and day-drinking. I was met with a few muttered "goodnights," and I made my way slowly, steadily back to the house, the sand feeling noticeably cold beneath my bare feet.

***

That night I had the dream again. A slightly different variation of the same dream that had haunted me since the previous summer. This time I was underwater, the deep silence threatening. I wasn't moving. Or I was able to move my arms slowly, like treading water though completely submerged, but my feet would not budge. I started to panic and thrash about, terrified that I'd soon have to take a breath to give myself the strength to force my legs to move. I looked down. Through the dark depths of the water I could see that my feet were caught in seaweed, thick and colored a sickly mustard yellow and algae green. I reached down with my hands to try to free myself and saw that the seaweed wasn't seaweed, but long tufts of hair, quickly changing color, darkening by the second. I ripped and pulled at the locks of hair, then felt a hand pulling at my shoulders. I looked up to see a body swimming away, unable to make out the identity. My feet started moving. I looked back down and there was nothing beneath me. No hair. No seaweed. No ocean floor. I swam toward the surface with my last bit of energy, desperately trying to catch up to the figure who had saved me.

I awoke with a start. It took me a few seconds to realize where I was. The sounds of the waves crashing against the shore brought with it reality, and I lay in bed trying to catch my breath.

Then I took off. But not across the dunes separating the house from the ocean. I turned right outside and kept running. I wasn't wearing shoes, and the concrete scraped my feet as I ran. My paper bag lungs strained with the effort and softened with the damp air, the salt rattling around inside me with a raspy wheeze. Faster and faster I ran, my bare feet slapping the asphalt keeping rhythm with my heart pounding in my chest, the words of Tyler and Deirdre running circles in my head, a mantra of *"You left me."* It was late, and the air was cool, the salty breeze coming off the ocean licked my face. I was at the boardwalk and kept running. I sprinted across the boards, and down onto the sand. The beach was empty and loud with the waves. The moon shone bright in the cloudless night sky. I ran toward the ocean, stripping as I went, trying not to slow down. By the time I reached where the water meets the land I was naked. The cold, wet sand felt good against my feet that had just pounded across blocks of concrete and the splintery planks of the boardwalk. The water provided resistance as I ran into the ocean and my speed slowed. Knee-deep, I fell face first into the waves. Underwater, everything was quiet. I stayed under as long as I could hold my breath, listening to the light sounds of the water rushing forward and receding. My hands and feet dug into the hard sand beneath me. I felt the hundreds of tiny clams, they too trying to find a place to hold on to. When I came back up, the loudness of the beach startled me, yet I was calm. I planted my feet in the sand and tried to stay in one position with the restless ocean pushing and pulling me in different directions. I looked up at the sky full of stars, Lyra cutting its way through the blackness.

The funeral would be in a few days.

The semester would start in a few months.

My feet dug deeper into the cold, wet sand, anchoring my body into place. Tears flowed from me in a salty cleansing and blended into the black ink of the ocean surrounding me, which itself bled seamlessly into the infinite sky above. The water pulsed and the stars blinked and I breathed in their rhythm, feeling awash in a warm and blissful release.

Though it is my name that appears on the front cover of this book, none of this would have been possible without the selfless support of so many others.

My sincerest gratitude goes out to Summer and the entire Unsolicited Press crew for believing in this novel and for doing such an excellent job editing. Thank you, also, for being such all-around excellent, big-hearted human beings.

Thank you to Zack Bates and Chris Gottschalk for reading the raw and unedited (and much longer) first draft of this book and for offering constructive criticism and a critical eye.

Thanks also to Scott Marshbank for reading the rough draft and crafting a killer cover design.

To all the musicians who granted me permission to use their lyrics in the book - I am grateful for your generosity and continued inspiration.

Also thanks to my friend Thorsten Nagelschmidt for the countless conversations about writing and music and literature and life, and for asking me way back when if I had ever toyed with the idea of writing. Thanks for planting that seed.

I would also like to thank my family, especially my parents, for being nothing like Jake's family. You have all been so supportive and accepting and understanding my whole life, and I would not be who I am if it weren't for you. I don't say it enough, so I'll put it in writing: thank you and I love you and keep being yourselves.

Finally, I would like to thank my caring and supportive wife, Kate, for believing in me and always encouraging me in all of my far-fetched ideas. Thank you for reading and critiquing my writing, and for listening to me and tolerating me talk about this book for the past 5 years. Thanks, too, for listening to me and tolerating me in general for the past 13 years.

And, if you've made it this far, thank you for making it this far. I hope you've enjoyed the ride.

Danke schön!
-Tim

About the Author

Tim DeMarco earned his bachelor's degree in German from Georgetown University and his master's degree in German Language and Literature from Middlebury College. He has lived, worked, and studied in Tübingen, Dresden, and Mainz. He currently lives in South Jersey where he teaches German at the high school and university level. His translations and original works have been published internationally. "Release Me," is his debut novel.

About the Press

Unsolicited Press is based out of Portland, Oregon and focuses on the works of the unsung and underrepresented. As a womxn-owned, all-volunteer small publisher that doesn't worry about profits as much as championing exceptional literature, we have the privilege of partnering with authors skirting the fringes of the lit world. We've worked with emerging and award-winning authors such as Shann Ray, Amy Shimshon-Santo, Brook Bhagat, Kris Amos, and John W. Bateman.

Learn more at unsolicitedpress.com. Find us on twitter and instagram.